STAR SCOUTS
THE LEAGUE OF LASERS

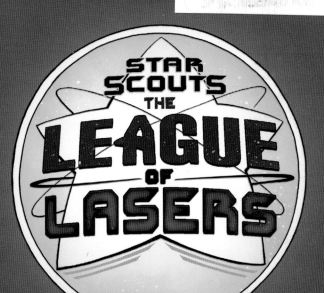

STAR SCOUTS
THE LEAGUE OF LASERS

MIKE LAWRENCE

:01
First Second
New York

TO MY WIFE, ASHLEY,
FOR HAVING THE INCOMPARABLE
COURAGE REQUIRED TO MARRY
A CARTOONIST.

PART
1

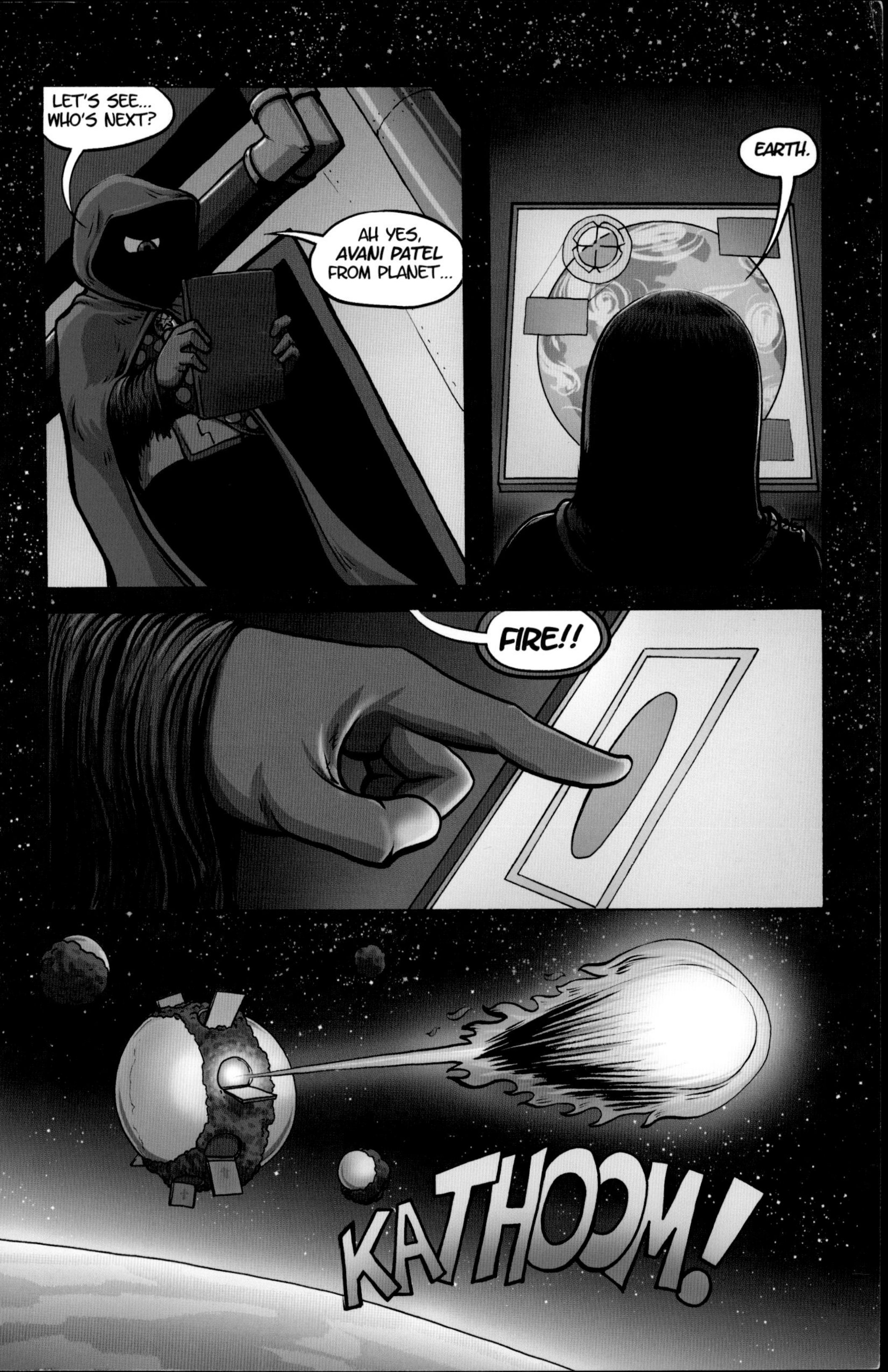
LET'S SEE... WHO'S NEXT?
AH YES, AVANI PATEL FROM PLANET...
EARTH.
FIRE!!
KATHOOM!

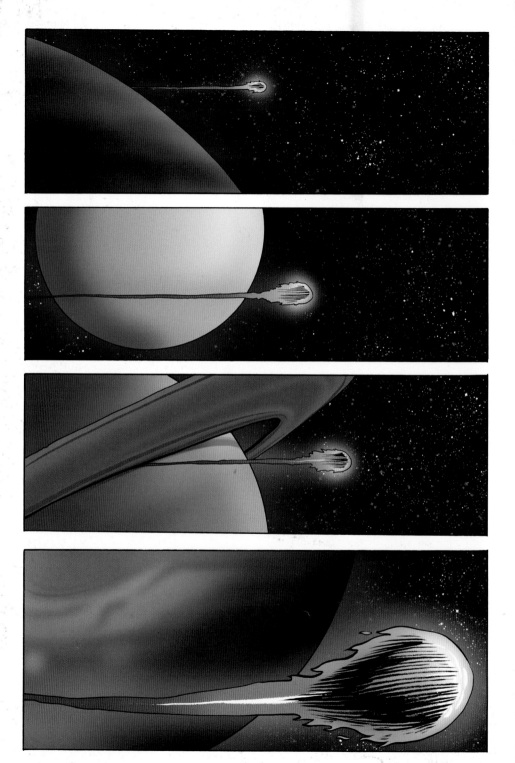

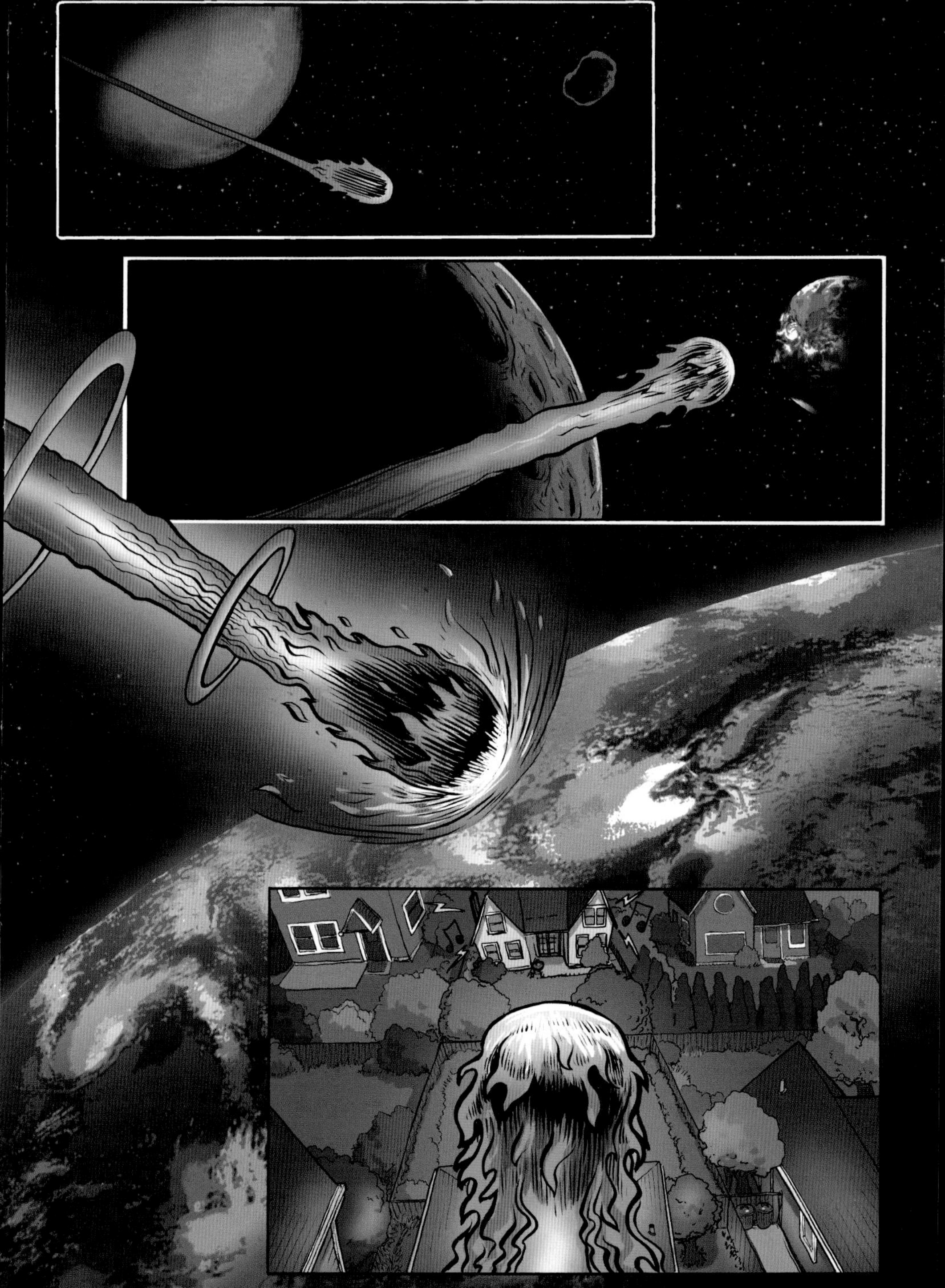

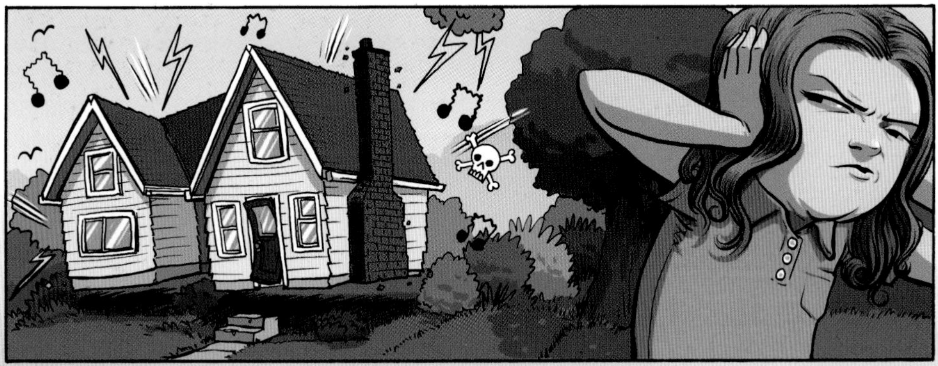

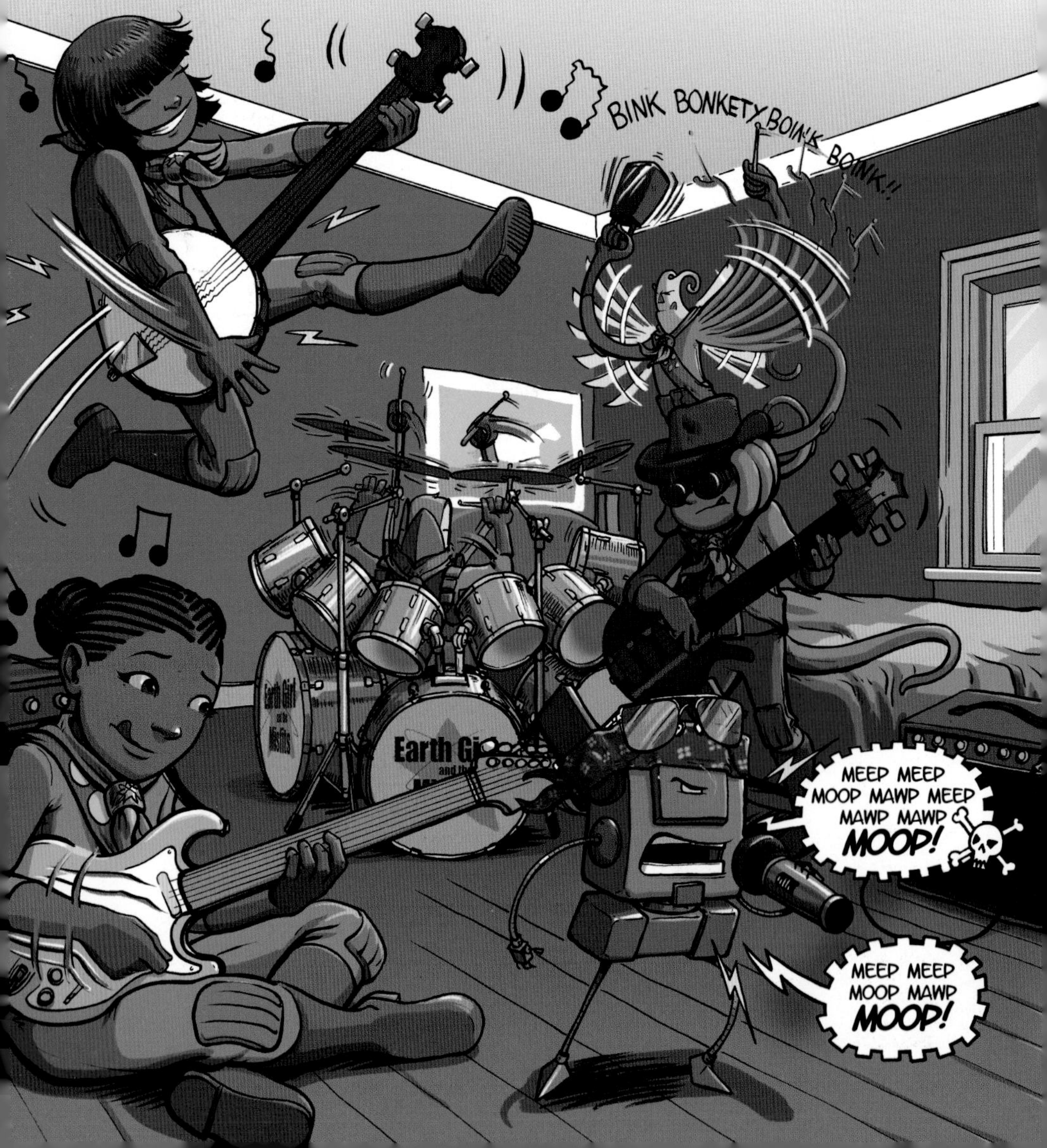
BINK BONKETY BOINK BOINK!!
MEEP MEEP MOOP MAWP MEEP MAWP MAWP MOOP!
MEEP MEEP MOOP MAWP MOOP!

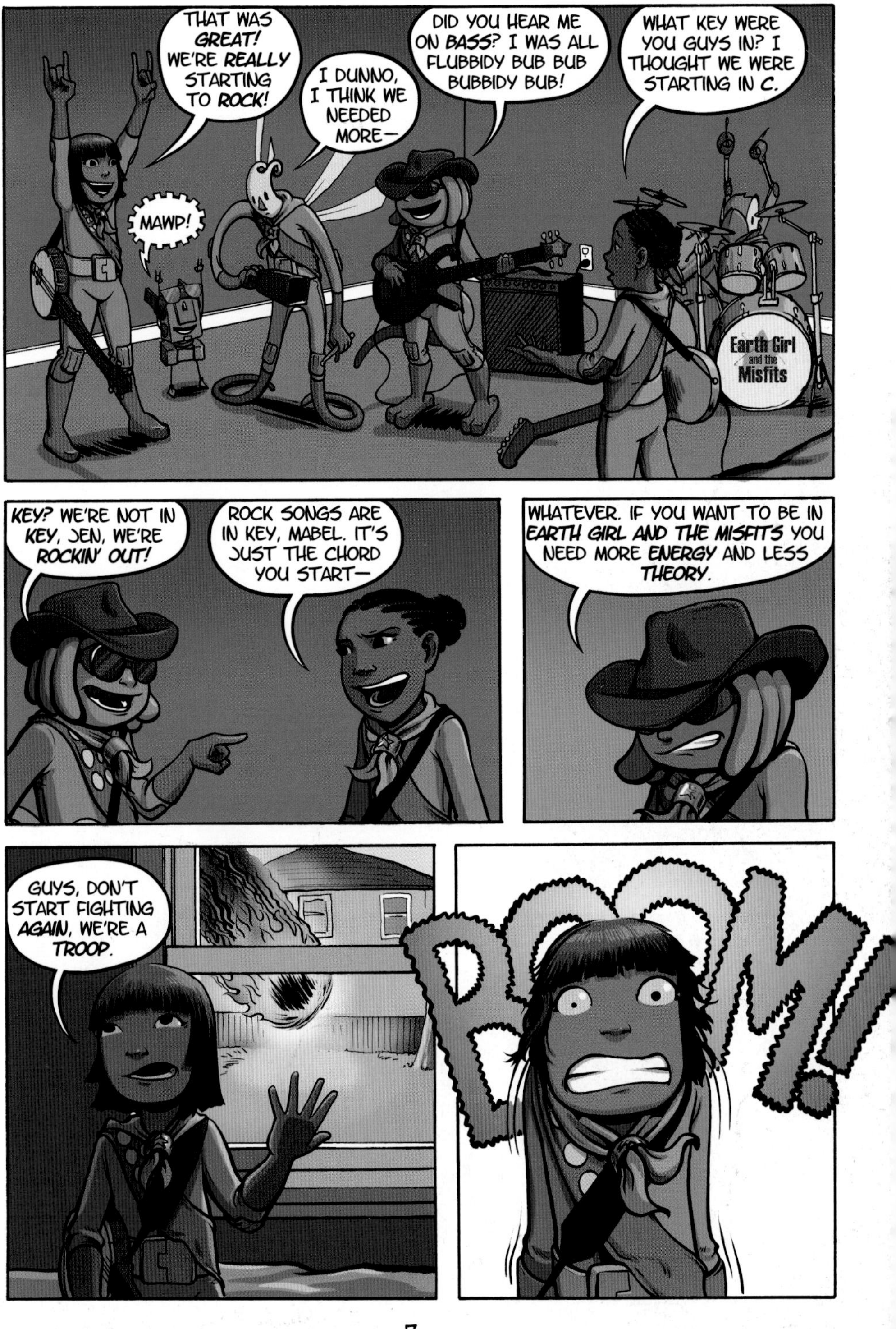
THAT WAS GREAT! WE'RE REALLY STARTING TO ROCK!
MAWP!
I DUNNO, I THINK WE NEEDED MORE—
DID YOU HEAR ME ON BASS? I WAS ALL FLUBBIDY BUB BUB BUBBIDY BUB!
WHAT KEY WERE YOU GUYS IN? I THOUGHT WE WERE STARTING IN C.
Earth Girl and the Misfits
KEY? WE'RE NOT IN KEY, JEN, WE'RE ROCKIN' OUT!
ROCK SONGS ARE IN KEY, MABEL. IT'S JUST THE CHORD YOU START—
WHATEVER. IF YOU WANT TO BE IN EARTH GIRL AND THE MISFITS YOU NEED MORE ENERGY AND LESS THEORY.
GUYS, DON'T START FIGHTING AGAIN, WE'RE A TROOP.
BOOM!!

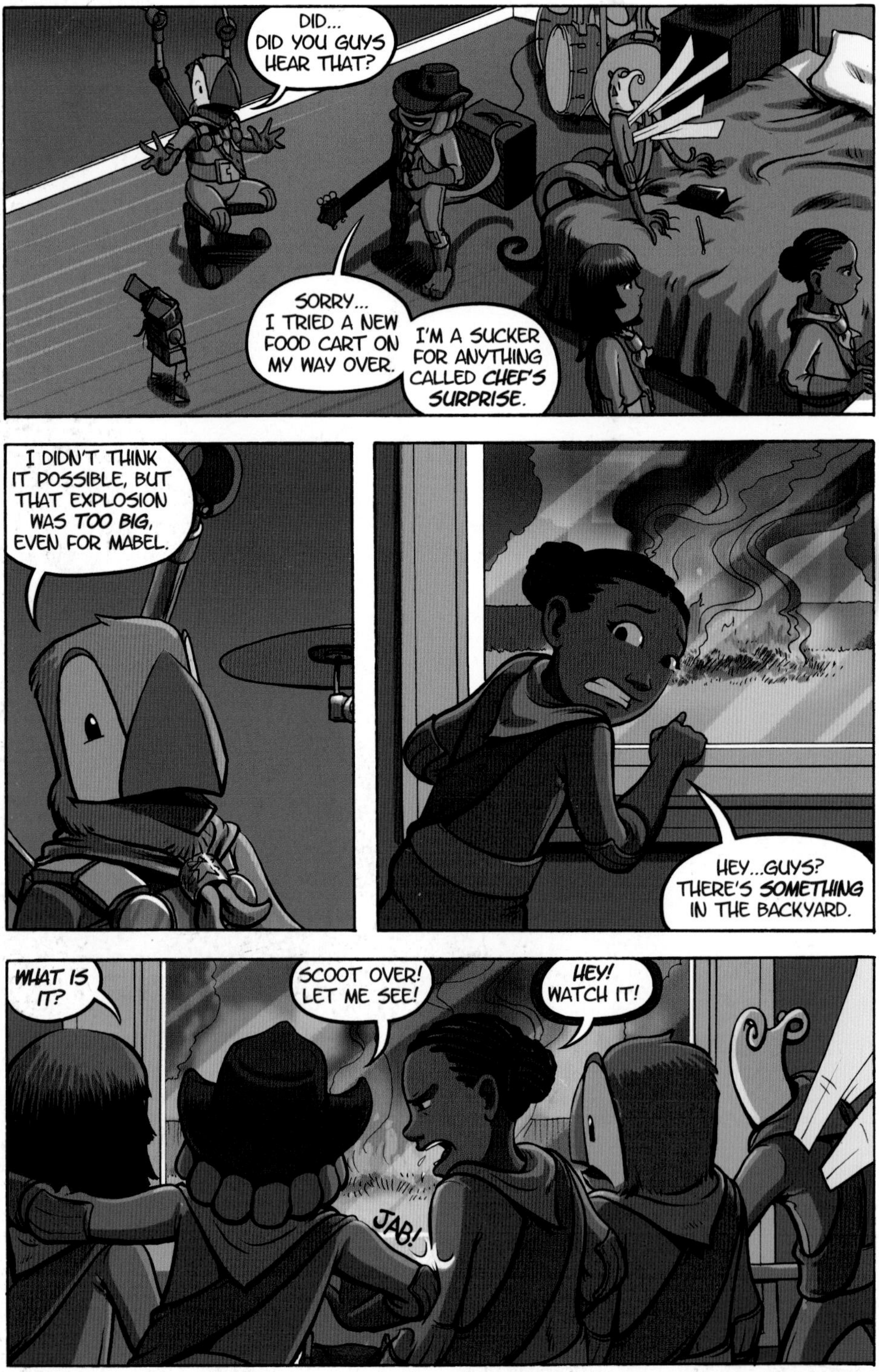
DID... DID YOU GUYS HEAR THAT?
SORRY... I TRIED A NEW FOOD CART ON MY WAY OVER.
I'M A SUCKER FOR ANYTHING CALLED CHEF'S SURPRISE.
I DIDN'T THINK IT POSSIBLE, BUT THAT EXPLOSION WAS TOO BIG, EVEN FOR MABEL.
HEY...GUYS? THERE'S SOMETHING IN THE BACKYARD.
WHAT IS IT?
SCOOT OVER! LET ME SEE!
HEY! WATCH IT!
JAB!

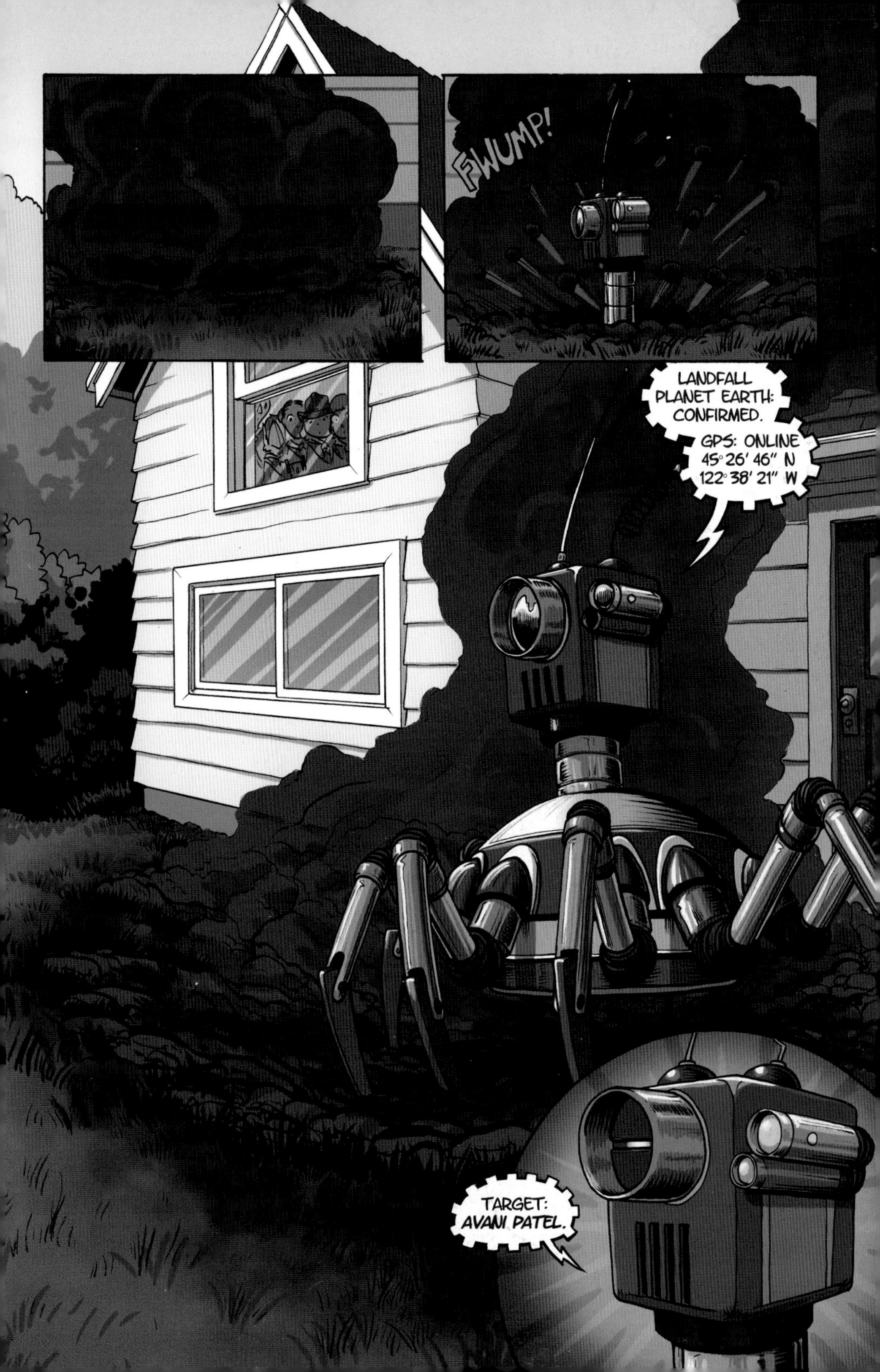
FWUMP!
LANDFALL PLANET EARTH: CONFIRMED.
GPS: ONLINE 45° 26' 46" N 122° 38' 21" W
TARGET: AVANI PATEL.

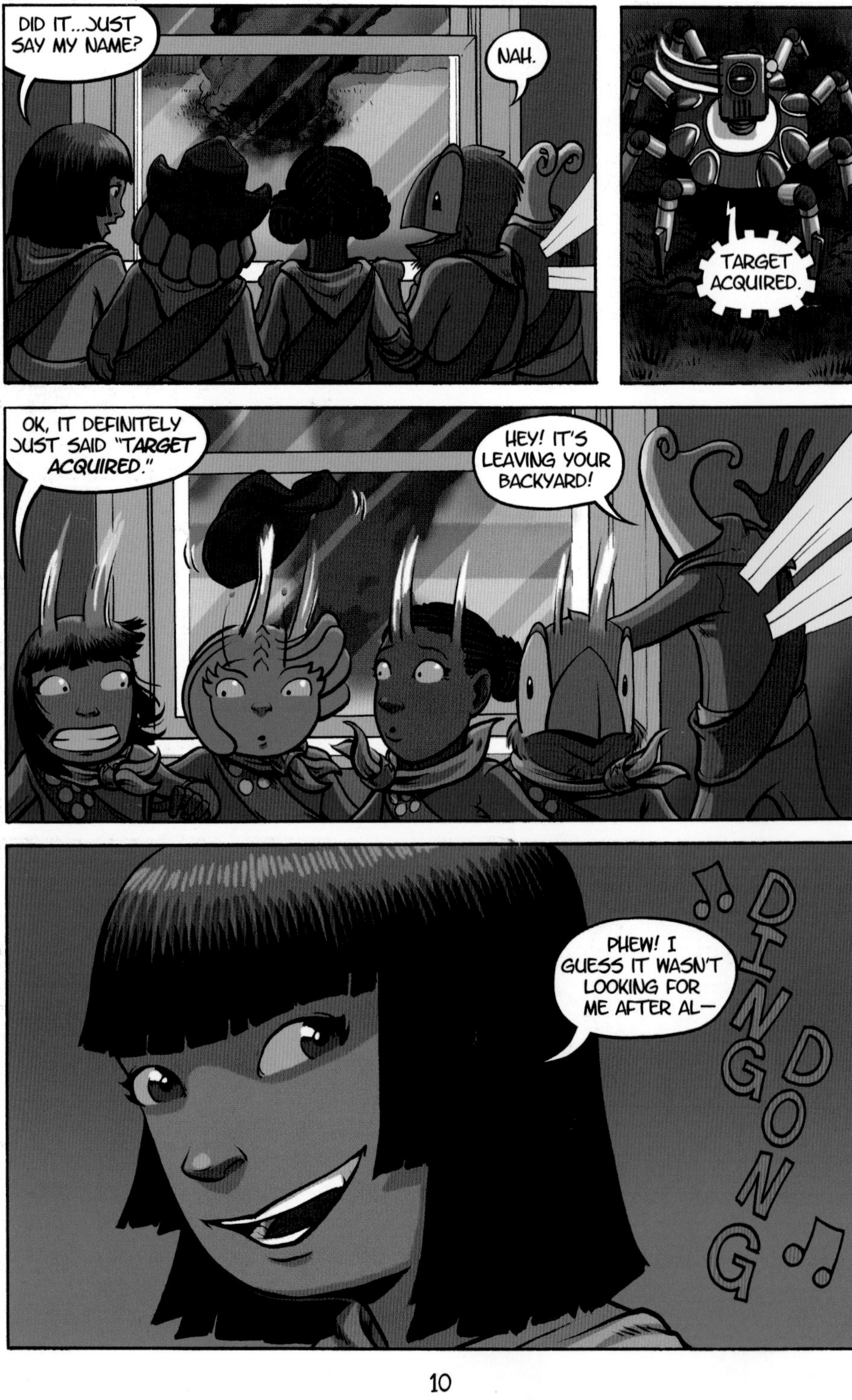
DID IT...JUST SAY MY NAME?
NAH.
TARGET ACQUIRED.
OK, IT DEFINITELY JUST SAID "TARGET ACQUIRED."
HEY! IT'S LEAVING YOUR BACKYARD!
PHEW! I GUESS IT WASN'T LOOKING FOR ME AFTER AL—
DING DONG

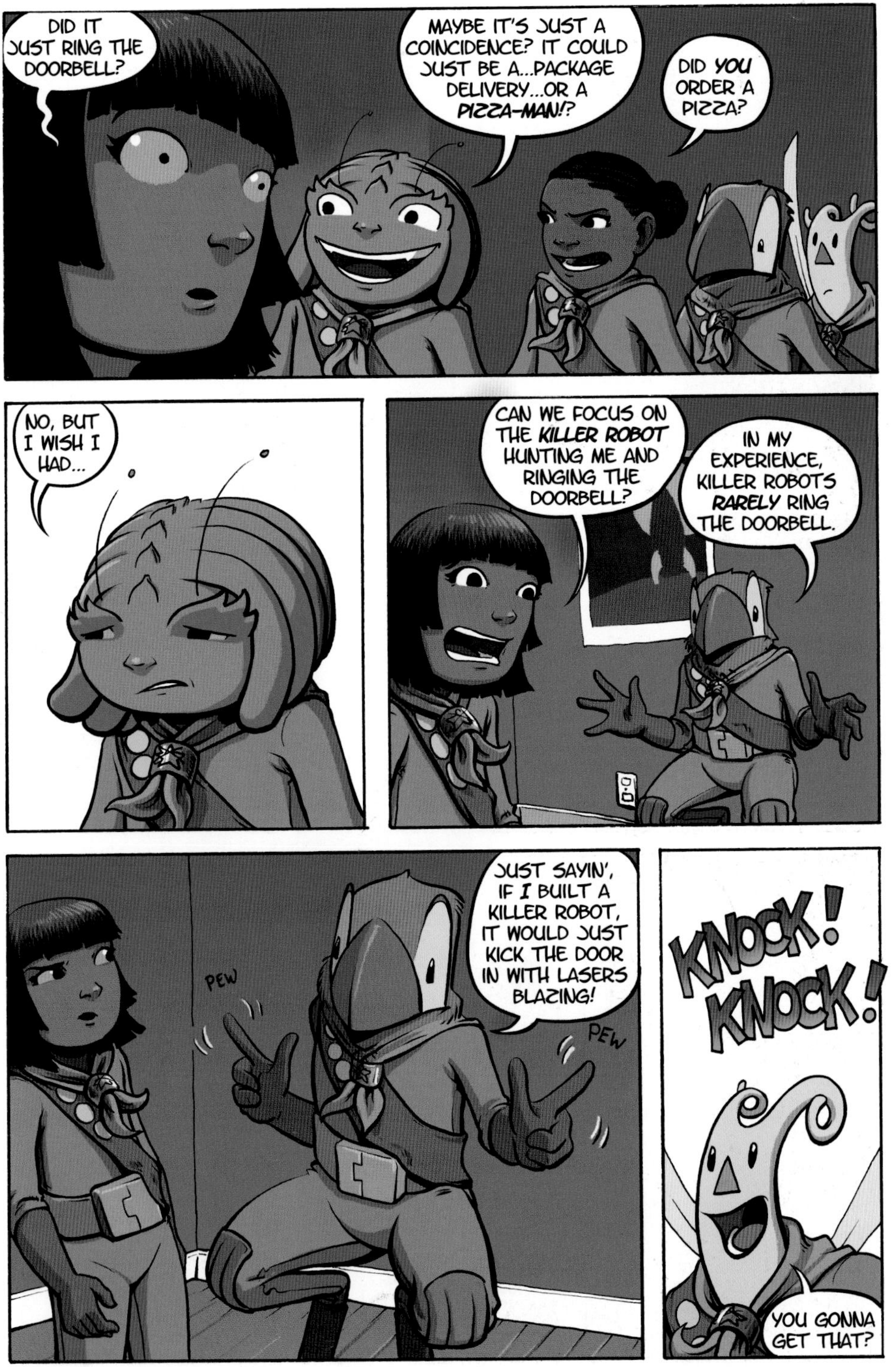
DID IT JUST RING THE DOORBELL?
MAYBE IT'S JUST A COINCIDENCE? IT COULD JUST BE A...PACKAGE DELIVERY...OR A PIZZA-MAN!?
DID YOU ORDER A PIZZA?
NO, BUT I WISH I HAD...
CAN WE FOCUS ON THE KILLER ROBOT HUNTING ME AND RINGING THE DOORBELL?
IN MY EXPERIENCE, KILLER ROBOTS RARELY RING THE DOORBELL.
JUST SAYIN', IF I BUILT A KILLER ROBOT, IT WOULD JUST KICK THE DOOR IN WITH LASERS BLAZING!
PEW
PEW
KNOCK! KNOCK!
YOU GONNA GET THAT?

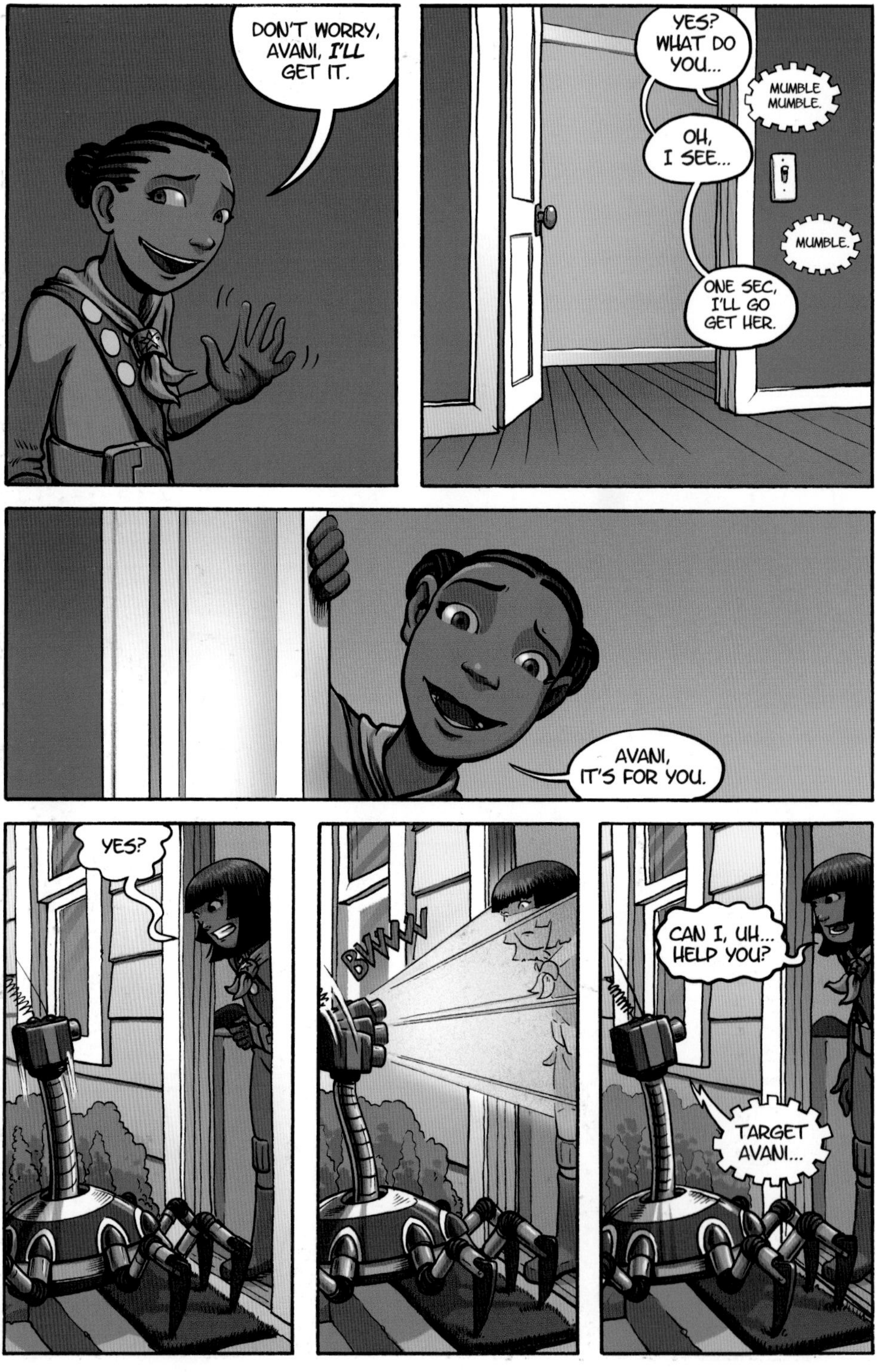
DON'T WORRY, AVANI, I'LL GET IT.
YES? WHAT DO YOU...
MUMBLE MUMBLE.
OH, I SEE...
MUMBLE.
ONE SEC, I'LL GO GET HER.
AVANI, IT'S FOR YOU.
YES?
BWWW
CAN I, UH... HELP YOU?
TARGET AVANI...

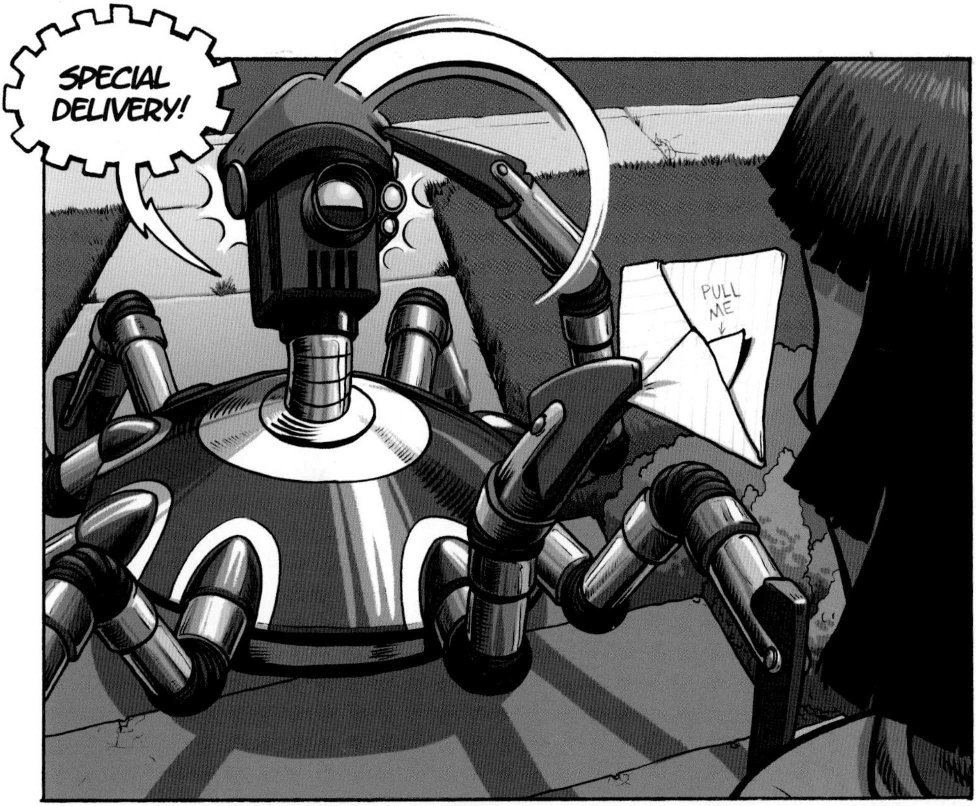
SPECIAL DELIVERY!
PULL ME

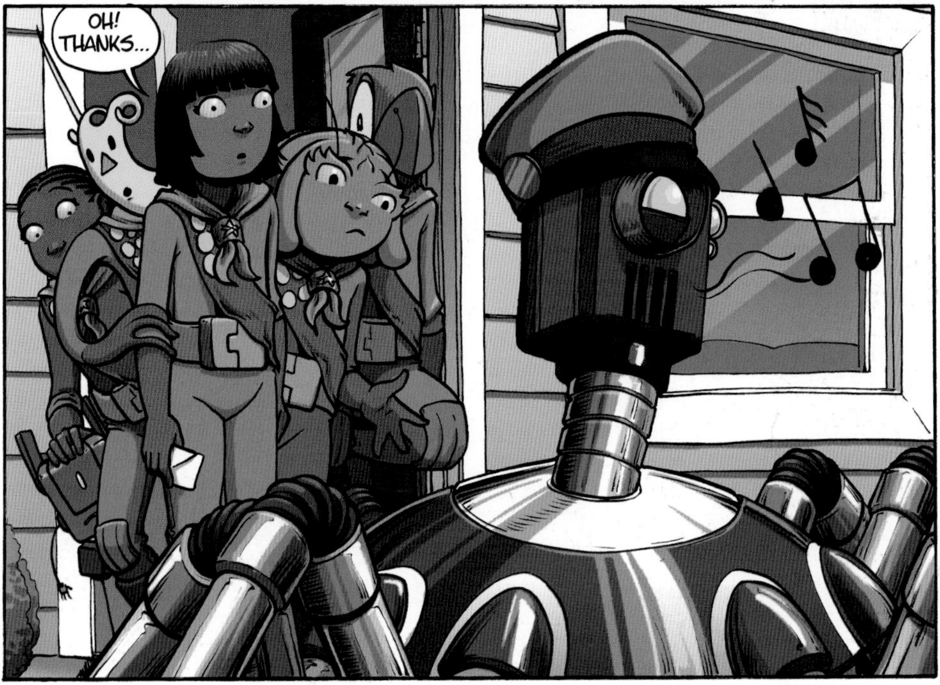
OH! THANKS...

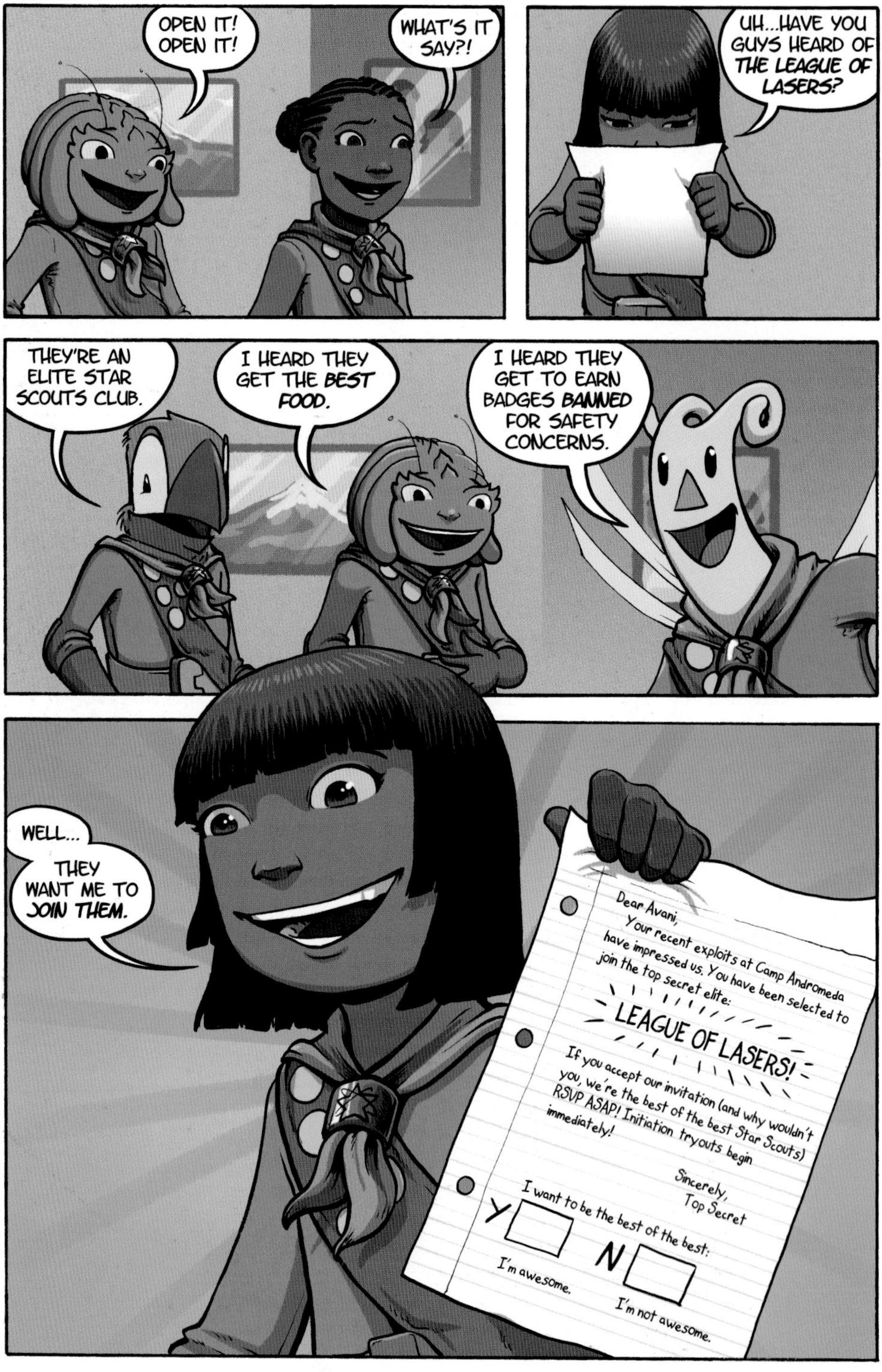
OPEN IT! OPEN IT!
WHAT'S IT SAY?!
UH...HAVE YOU GUYS HEARD OF THE LEAGUE OF LASERS?
THEY'RE AN ELITE STAR SCOUTS CLUB.
I HEARD THEY GET THE BEST FOOD.
I HEARD THEY GET TO EARN BADGES BANNED FOR SAFETY CONCERNS.
WELL...
THEY WANT ME TO JOIN THEM.
Dear Avani,
Your recent exploits at Camp Andromeda have impressed us. You have been selected to join the top secret elite:
LEAGUE OF LASERS!
If you accept our invitation (and why wouldn't you, we're the best of the best Star Scouts) RSVP ASAP! Initiation tryouts begin immediately!
Sincerely,
Top Secret
I want to be the best of the best:
Y
I'm awesome.
N
I'm not awesome.

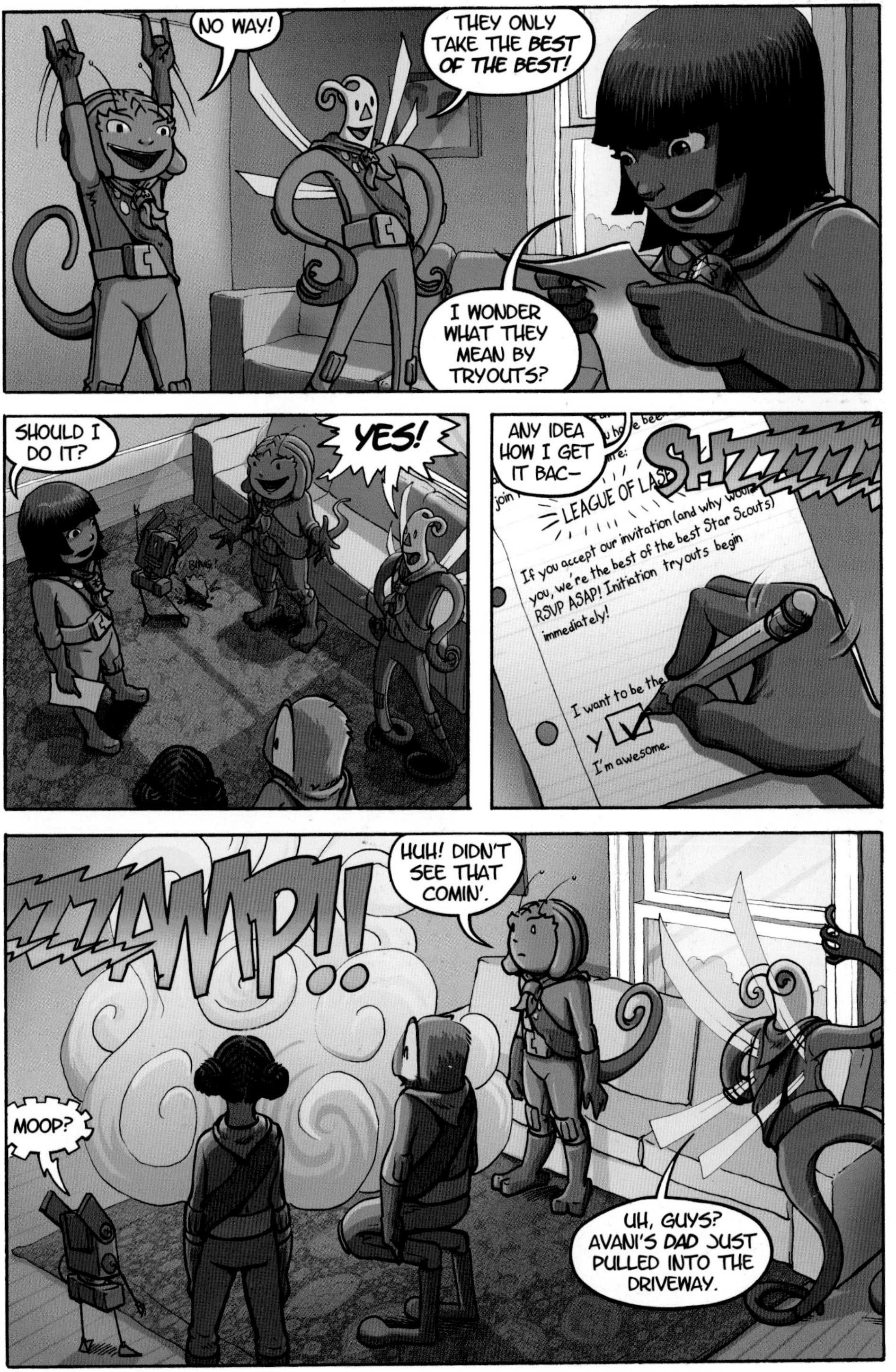
NO WAY!
THEY ONLY TAKE THE BEST OF THE BEST!
I WONDER WHAT THEY MEAN BY TRYOUTS?
SHOULD I DO IT?
YES!
BING!
ANY IDEA HOW I GET IT BAC–
SHZZZZ
If you accept our invitation (and why woul
you, we're the best of the best Star Scouts)
RSVP ASAP! Initiation tryouts begin
immediately!
I want to be the
I'm awesome.
ZZZAMP!!
HUH! DIDN'T SEE THAT COMIN'.
MOOP?
UH, GUYS? AVANI'S DAD JUST PULLED INTO THE DRIVEWAY.

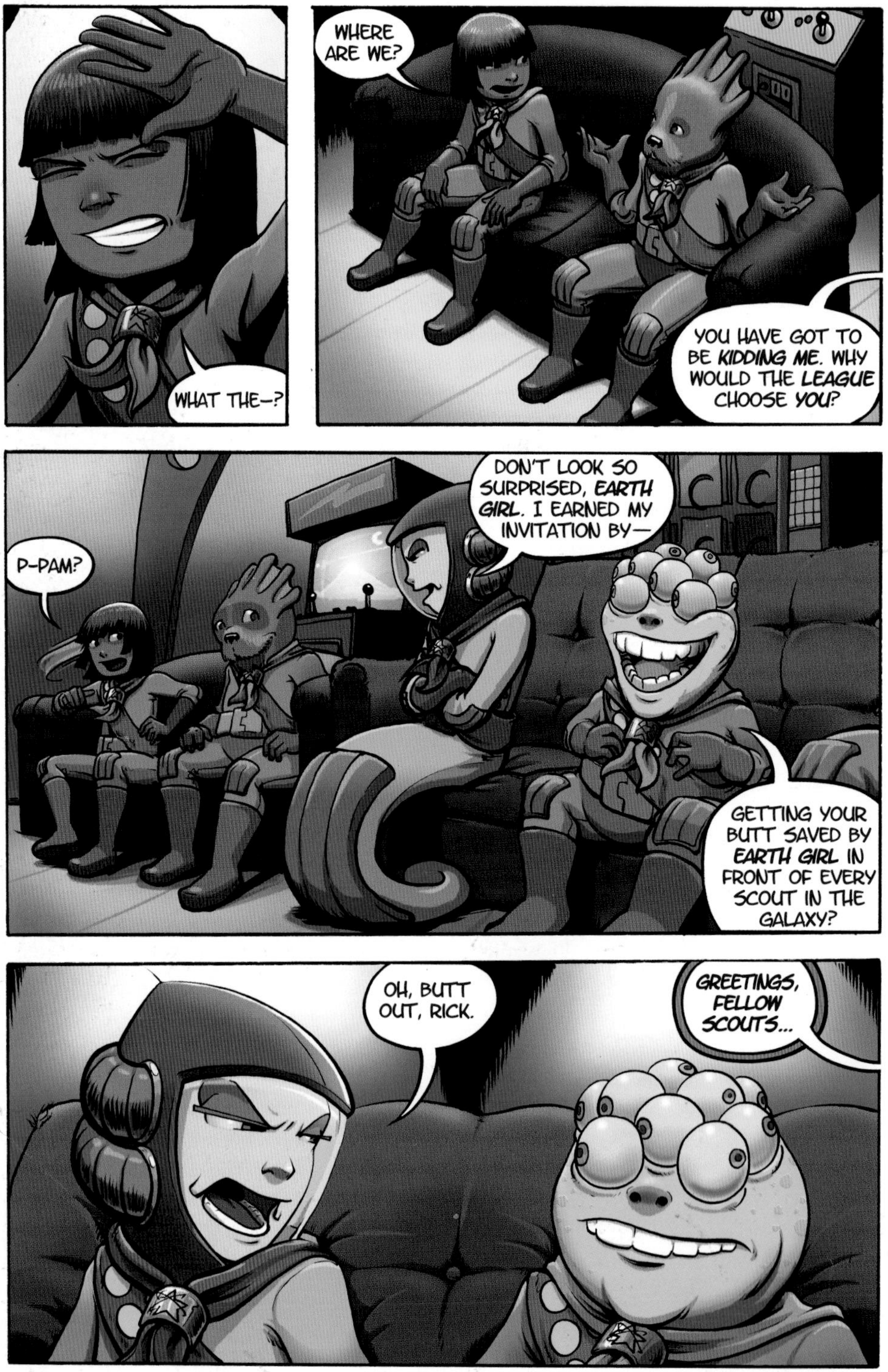
WHAT THE--?
WHERE ARE WE?
YOU HAVE GOT TO BE KIDDING ME. WHY WOULD THE LEAGUE CHOOSE YOU?
P-PAM?
DON'T LOOK SO SURPRISED, EARTH GIRL. I EARNED MY INVITATION BY--
GETTING YOUR BUTT SAVED BY EARTH GIRL IN FRONT OF EVERY SCOUT IN THE GALAXY?
OH, BUTT OUT, RICK.
GREETINGS, FELLOW SCOUTS...

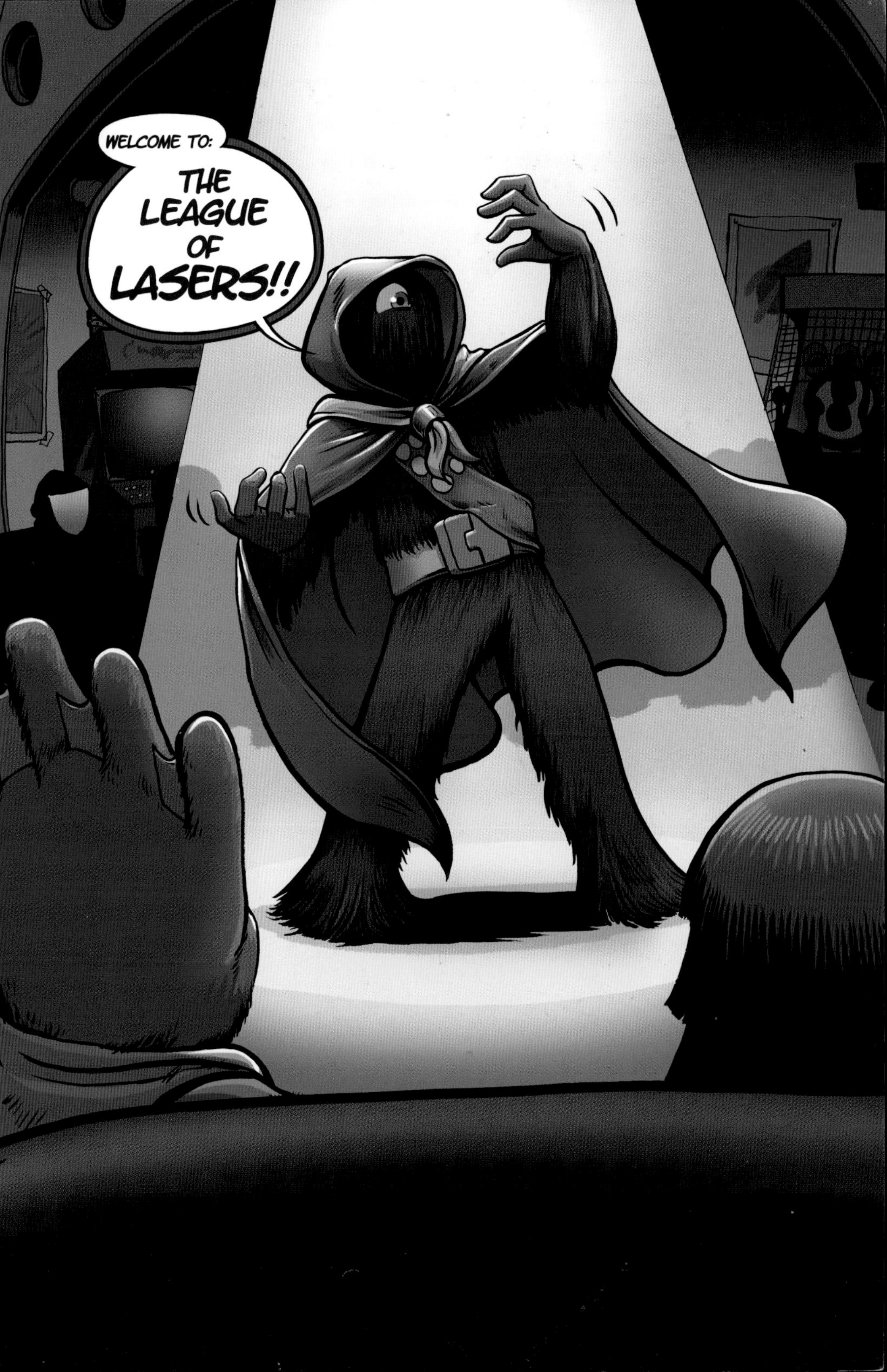
WELCOME TO:
THE LEAGUE OF LASERS!!

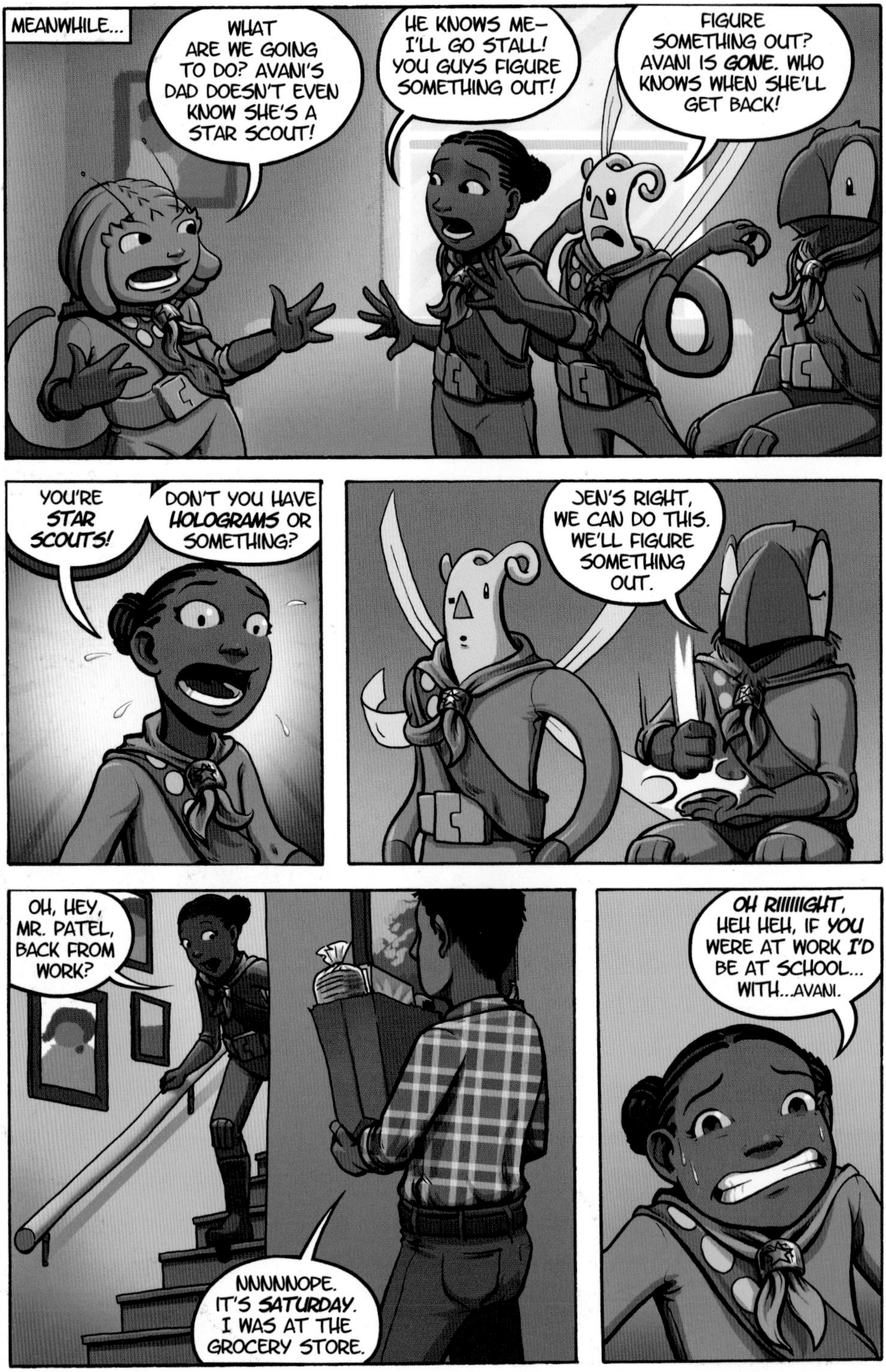
MEANWHILE...
WHAT ARE WE GOING TO DO? AVANI'S DAD DOESN'T EVEN KNOW SHE'S A STAR SCOUT!
HE KNOWS ME– I'LL GO STALL! YOU GUYS FIGURE SOMETHING OUT!
FIGURE SOMETHING OUT? AVANI IS GONE. WHO KNOWS WHEN SHE'LL GET BACK!
YOU'RE STAR SCOUTS!
DON'T YOU HAVE HOLOGRAMS OR SOMETHING?
JEN'S RIGHT, WE CAN DO THIS. WE'LL FIGURE SOMETHING OUT.
OH, HEY, MR. PATEL, BACK FROM WORK?
NNNNNOPE. IT'S SATURDAY. I WAS AT THE GROCERY STORE.
OH RIIIIIGHT, HEH HEH, IF YOU WERE AT WORK I'D BE AT SCHOOL... WITH...AVANI.

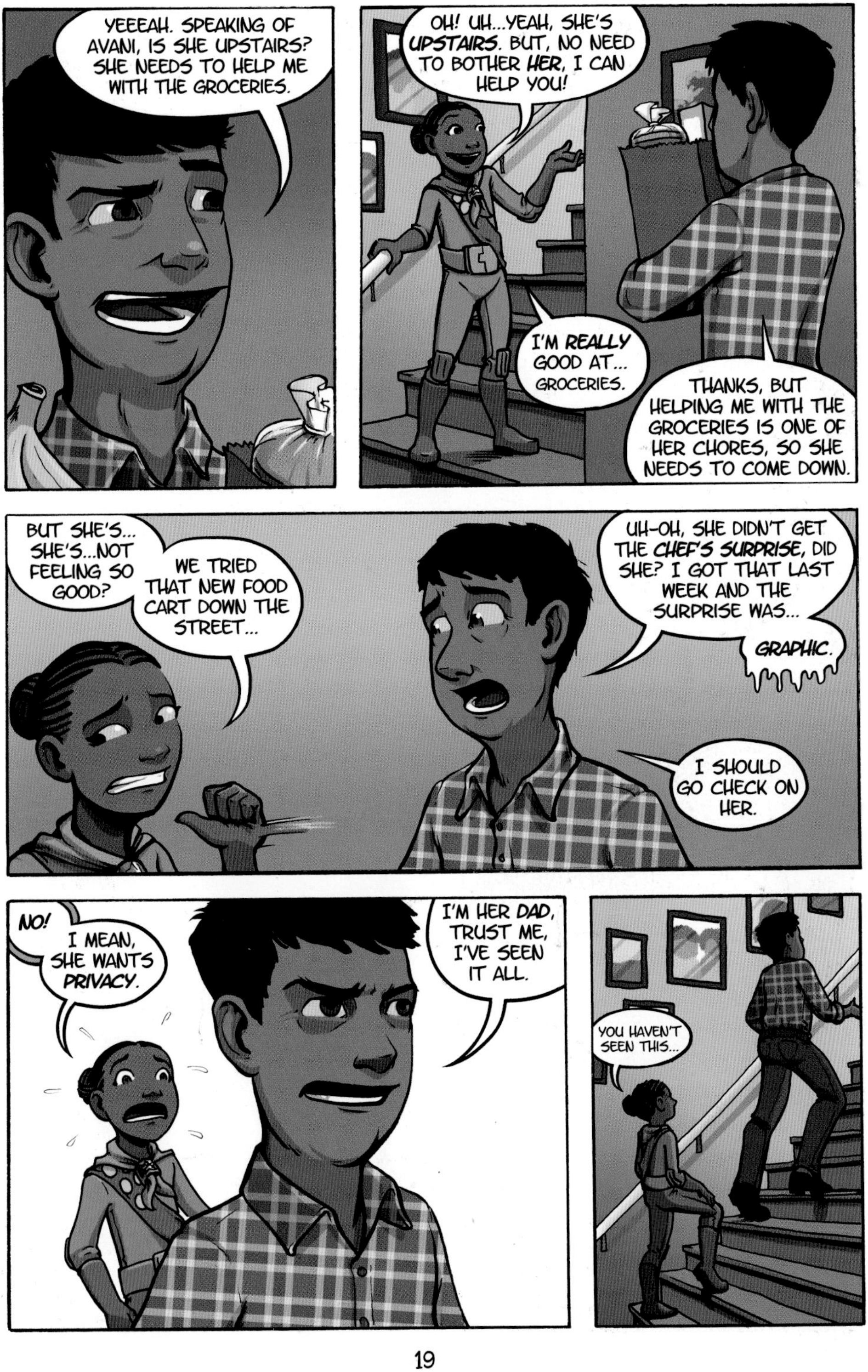
YEEEAH. SPEAKING OF AVANI, IS SHE UPSTAIRS? SHE NEEDS TO HELP ME WITH THE GROCERIES.
OH! UH...YEAH, SHE'S UPSTAIRS. BUT, NO NEED TO BOTHER HER, I CAN HELP YOU!
I'M REALLY GOOD AT... GROCERIES.
THANKS, BUT HELPING ME WITH THE GROCERIES IS ONE OF HER CHORES, SO SHE NEEDS TO COME DOWN.
BUT SHE'S... SHE'S...NOT FEELING SO GOOD?
WE TRIED THAT NEW FOOD CART DOWN THE STREET...
UH-OH, SHE DIDN'T GET THE CHEF'S SURPRISE, DID SHE? I GOT THAT LAST WEEK AND THE SURPRISE WAS...
GRAPHIC.
I SHOULD GO CHECK ON HER.
NO!
I MEAN, SHE WANTS PRIVACY.
I'M HER DAD, TRUST ME, I'VE SEEN IT ALL.
YOU HAVEN'T SEEN THIS...

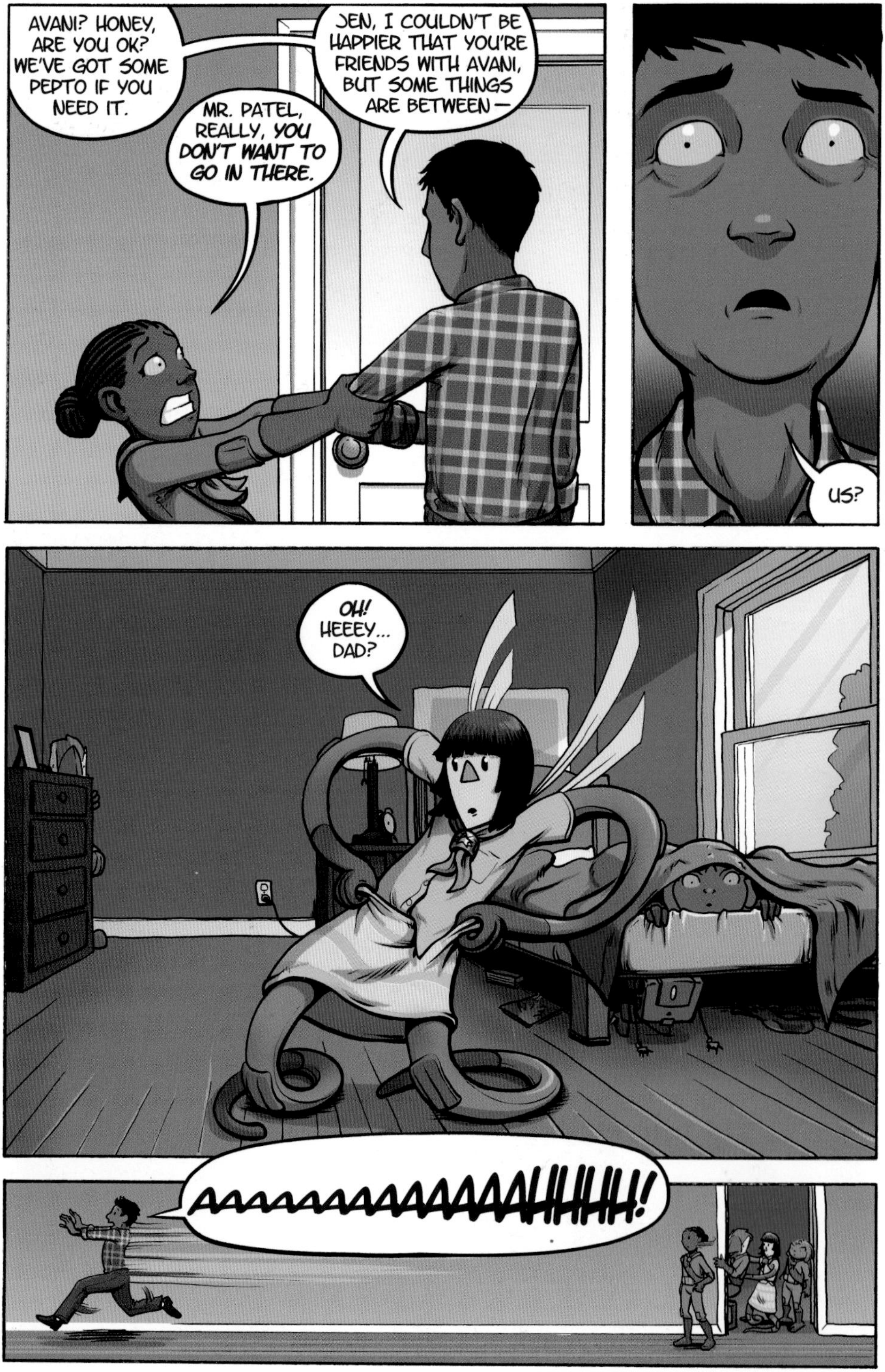
AVANI? HONEY, ARE YOU OK? WE'VE GOT SOME PEPTO IF YOU NEED IT.
JEN, I COULDN'T BE HAPPIER THAT YOU'RE FRIENDS WITH AVANI, BUT SOME THINGS ARE BETWEEN —
MR. PATEL, REALLY, YOU DON'T WANT TO GO IN THERE.
US?
OH! HEEEY... DAD?
AAAAAAAAAAAAAAAHHHHH!

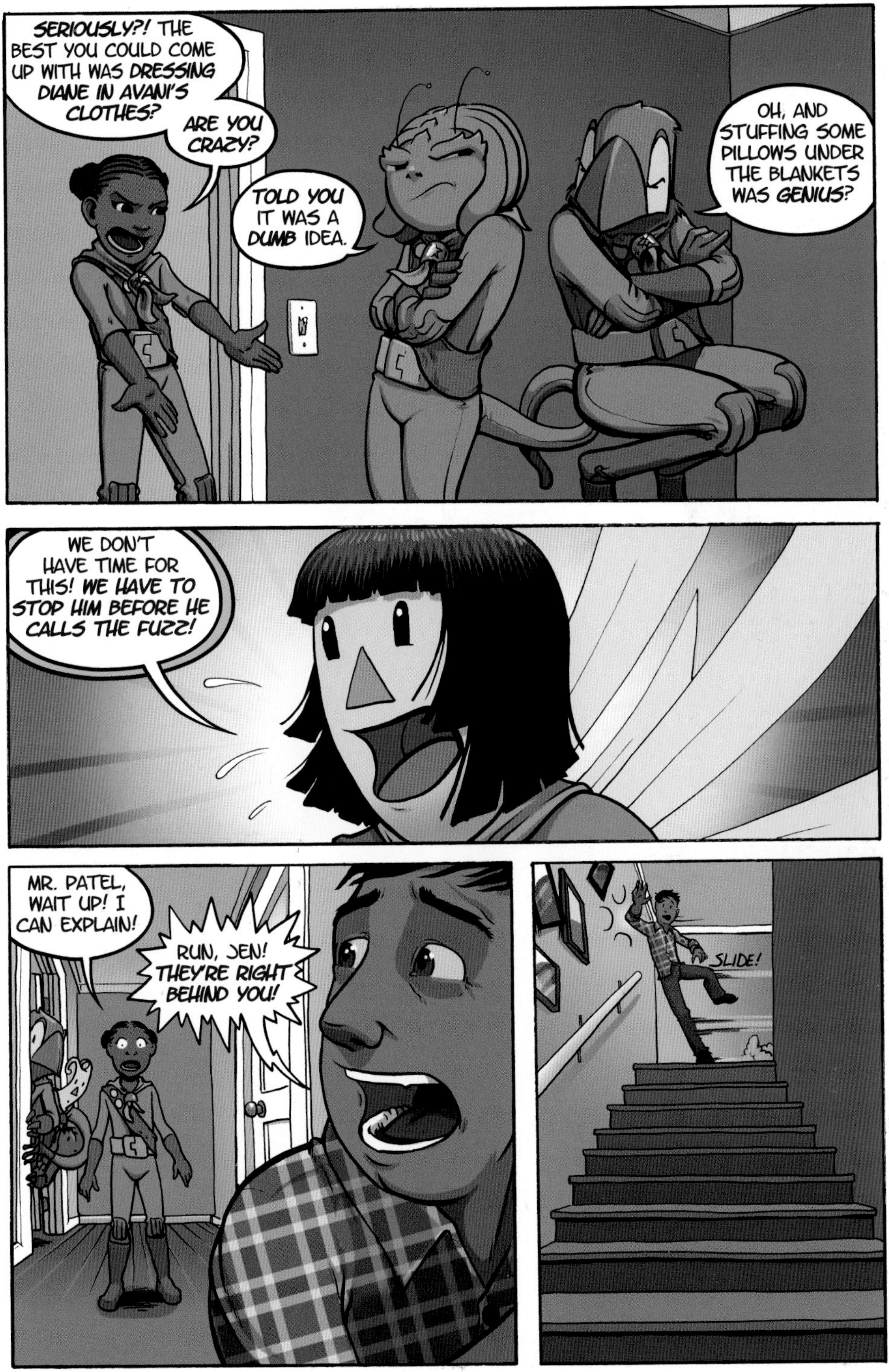
SERIOUSLY?! THE BEST YOU COULD COME UP WITH WAS DRESSING DIANE IN AVANI'S CLOTHES?
ARE YOU CRAZY?
TOLD YOU IT WAS A DUMB IDEA.
OH, AND STUFFING SOME PILLOWS UNDER THE BLANKETS WAS GENIUS?
WE DON'T HAVE TIME FOR THIS! WE HAVE TO STOP HIM BEFORE HE CALLS THE FUZZ!
MR. PATEL, WAIT UP! I CAN EXPLAIN!
RUN, JEN! THEY'RE RIGHT BEHIND YOU!
SLIDE!

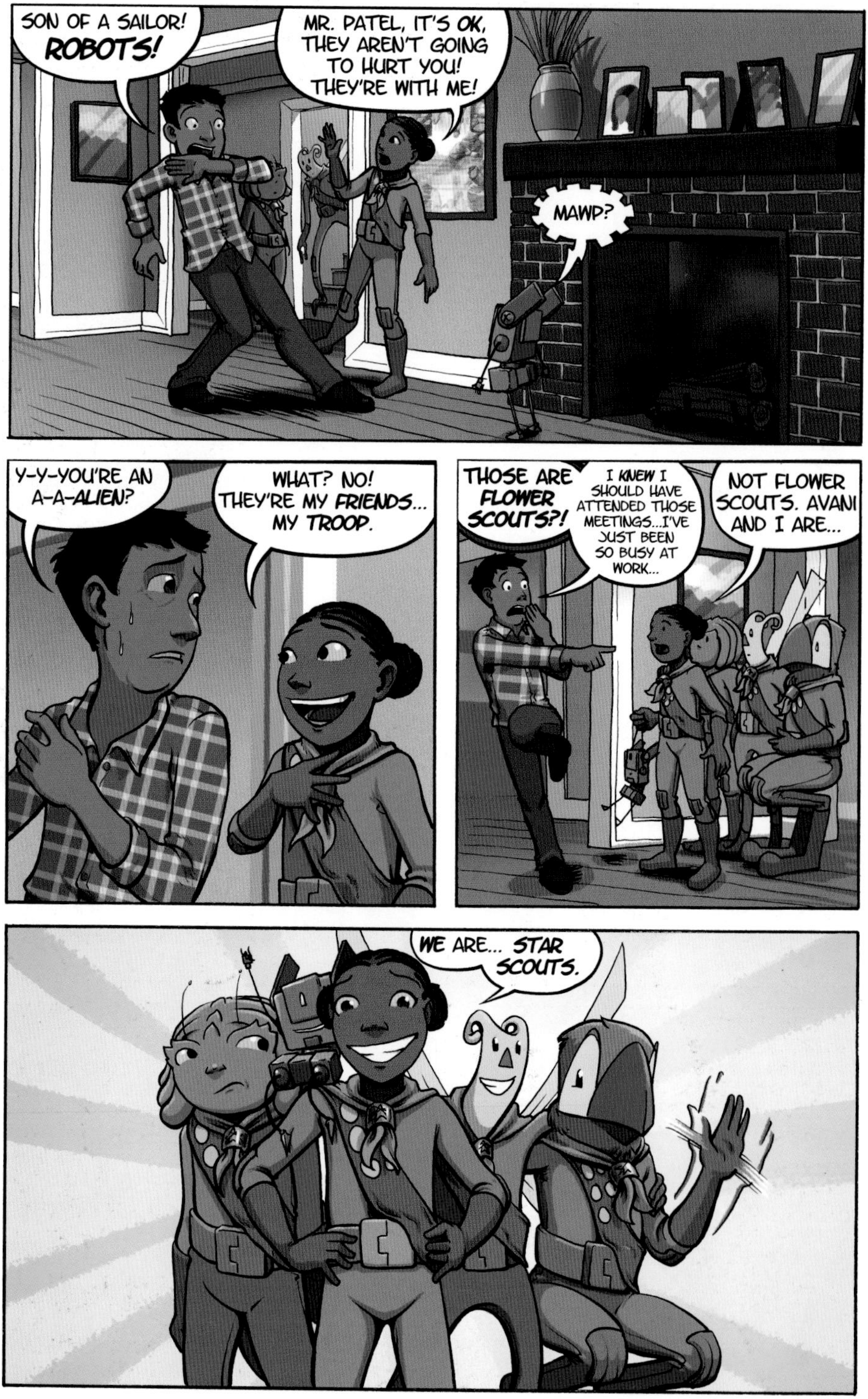

SON OF A SAILOR! ROBOTS!
MR. PATEL, IT'S OK, THEY AREN'T GOING TO HURT YOU! THEY'RE WITH ME!
MAWP?
Y-Y-YOU'RE AN A-A-ALIEN?
WHAT? NO! THEY'RE MY FRIENDS... MY TROOP.
THOSE ARE FLOWER SCOUTS?!
I KNEW I SHOULD HAVE ATTENDED THOSE MEETINGS...I'VE JUST BEEN SO BUSY AT WORK...
NOT FLOWER SCOUTS. AVANI AND I ARE...
WE ARE... STAR SCOUTS.

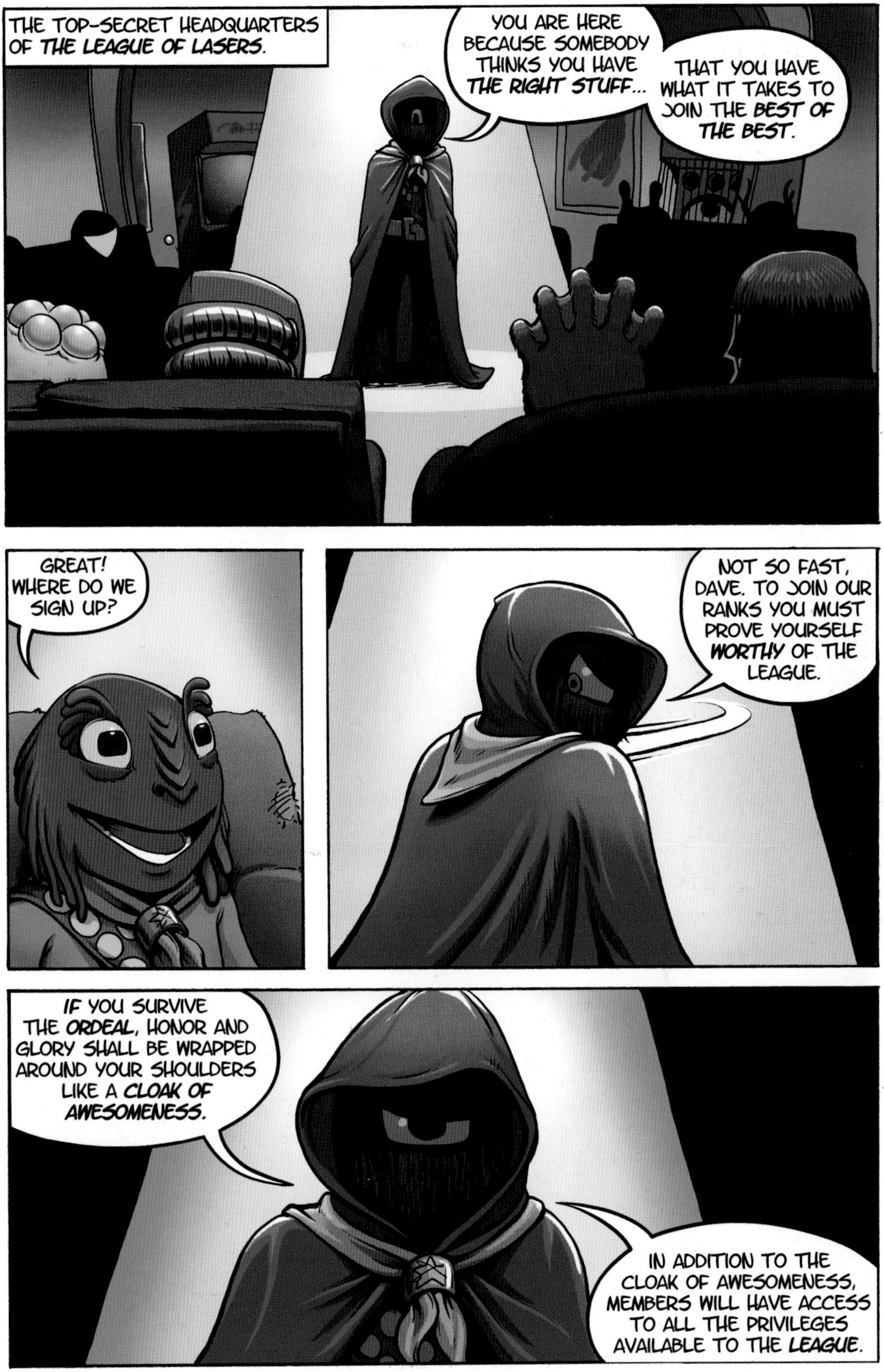
THE TOP-SECRET HEADQUARTERS OF THE LEAGUE OF LASERS.
YOU ARE HERE BECAUSE SOMEBODY THINKS YOU HAVE THE RIGHT STUFF...
THAT YOU HAVE WHAT IT TAKES TO JOIN THE BEST OF THE BEST.
GREAT! WHERE DO WE SIGN UP?
NOT SO FAST, DAVE. TO JOIN OUR RANKS YOU MUST PROVE YOURSELF WORTHY OF THE LEAGUE.
IF YOU SURVIVE THE ORDEAL, HONOR AND GLORY SHALL BE WRAPPED AROUND YOUR SHOULDERS LIKE A CLOAK OF AWESOMENESS.
IN ADDITION TO THE CLOAK OF AWESOMENESS, MEMBERS WILL HAVE ACCESS TO ALL THE PRIVILEGES AVAILABLE TO THE LEAGUE.

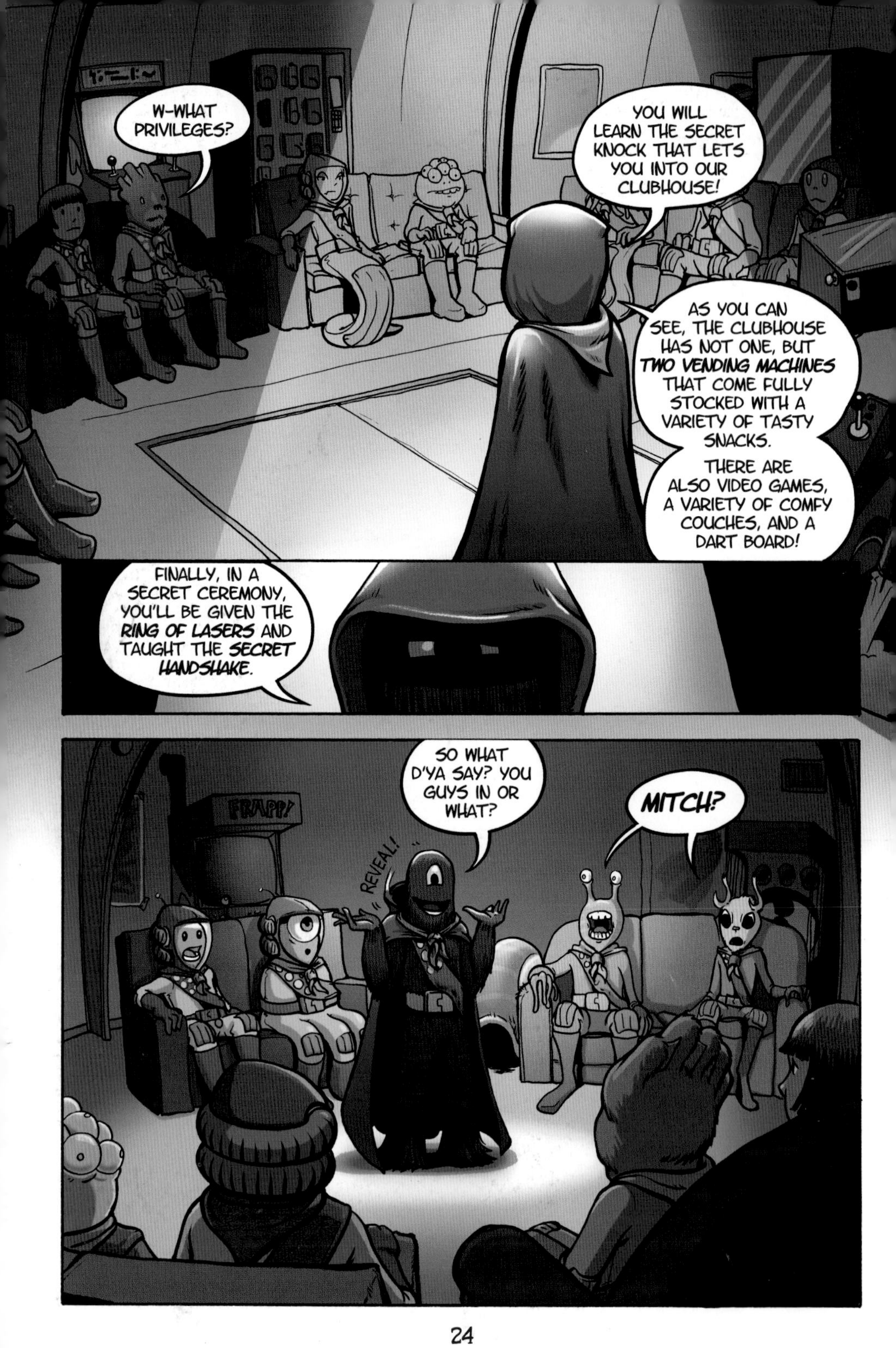
W-WHAT PRIVILEGES?
YOU WILL LEARN THE SECRET KNOCK THAT LETS YOU INTO OUR CLUBHOUSE!
AS YOU CAN SEE, THE CLUBHOUSE HAS NOT ONE, BUT **TWO VENDING MACHINES** THAT COME FULLY STOCKED WITH A VARIETY OF TASTY SNACKS.
THERE ARE ALSO VIDEO GAMES, A VARIETY OF COMFY COUCHES, AND A DART BOARD!
FINALLY, IN A SECRET CEREMONY, YOU'LL BE GIVEN THE **RING OF LASERS** AND TAUGHT THE **SECRET HANDSHAKE**.
FRAPP!
SO WHAT D'YA SAY? YOU GUYS IN OR WHAT?
"REVEAL!"
MITCH?

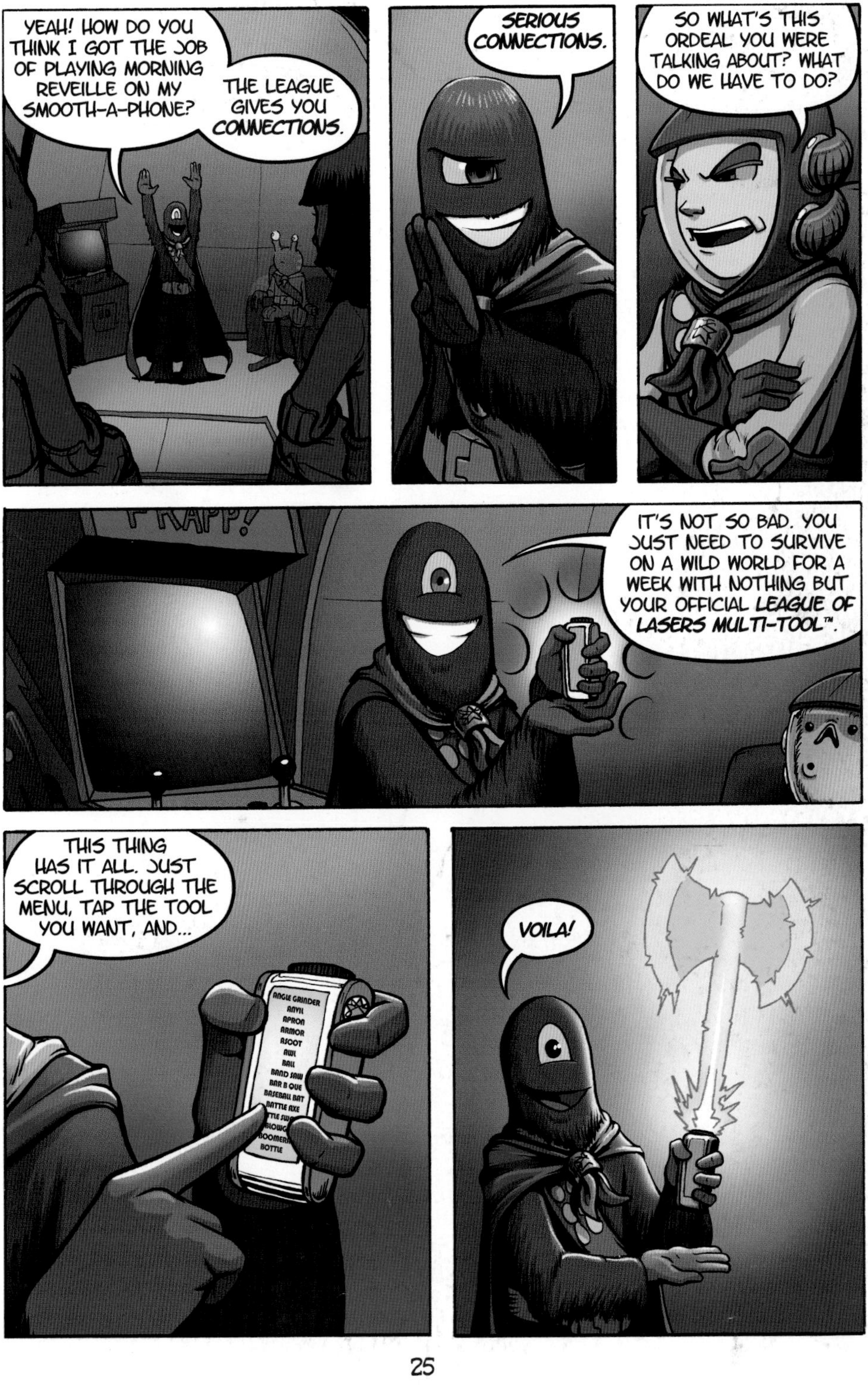
YEAH! HOW DO YOU THINK I GOT THE JOB OF PLAYING MORNING REVEILLE ON MY SMOOTH-A-PHONE?
THE LEAGUE GIVES YOU CONNECTIONS.
SERIOUS CONNECTIONS.
SO WHAT'S THIS ORDEAL YOU WERE TALKING ABOUT? WHAT DO WE HAVE TO DO?
IT'S NOT SO BAD. YOU JUST NEED TO SURVIVE ON A WILD WORLD FOR A WEEK WITH NOTHING BUT YOUR OFFICIAL LEAGUE OF LASERS MULTI-TOOL™.
THIS THING HAS IT ALL. JUST SCROLL THROUGH THE MENU, TAP THE TOOL YOU WANT, AND...
ANGLE GRINDER
ANVIL
APRON
ARMOR
ASCOT
AWL
BALL
BAND SAW
BAR B QUE
BASEBALL BAT
BATTLE AXE
BOTTLE
VOILA!

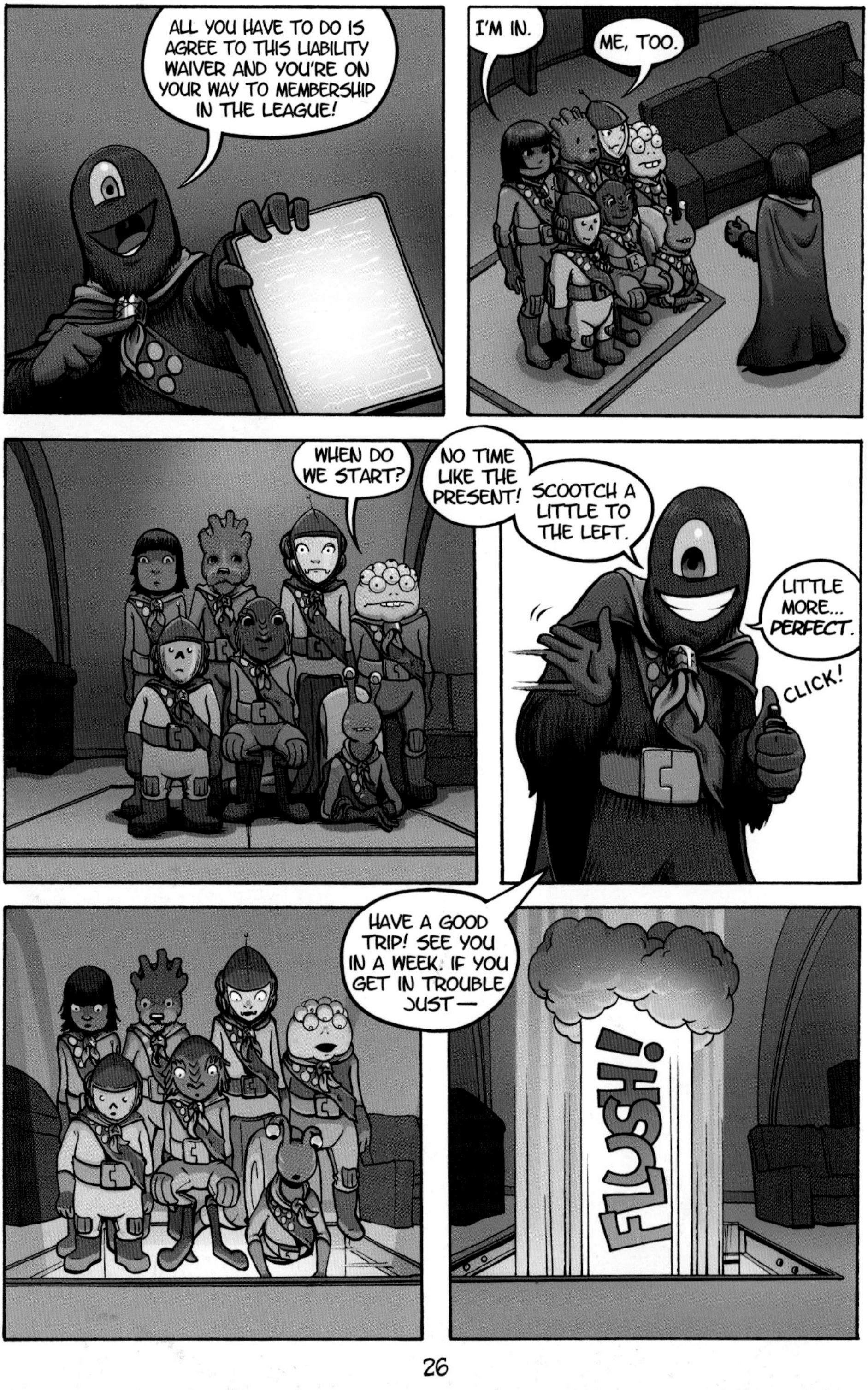
ALL YOU HAVE TO DO IS AGREE TO THIS LIABILITY WAIVER AND YOU'RE ON YOUR WAY TO MEMBERSHIP IN THE LEAGUE!
I'M IN.
ME, TOO.
WHEN DO WE START?
NO TIME LIKE THE PRESENT!
SCOOTCH A LITTLE TO THE LEFT.
LITTLE MORE... PERFECT.
CLICK!
HAVE A GOOD TRIP! SEE YOU IN A WEEK. IF YOU GET IN TROUBLE JUST—
FLUSH!

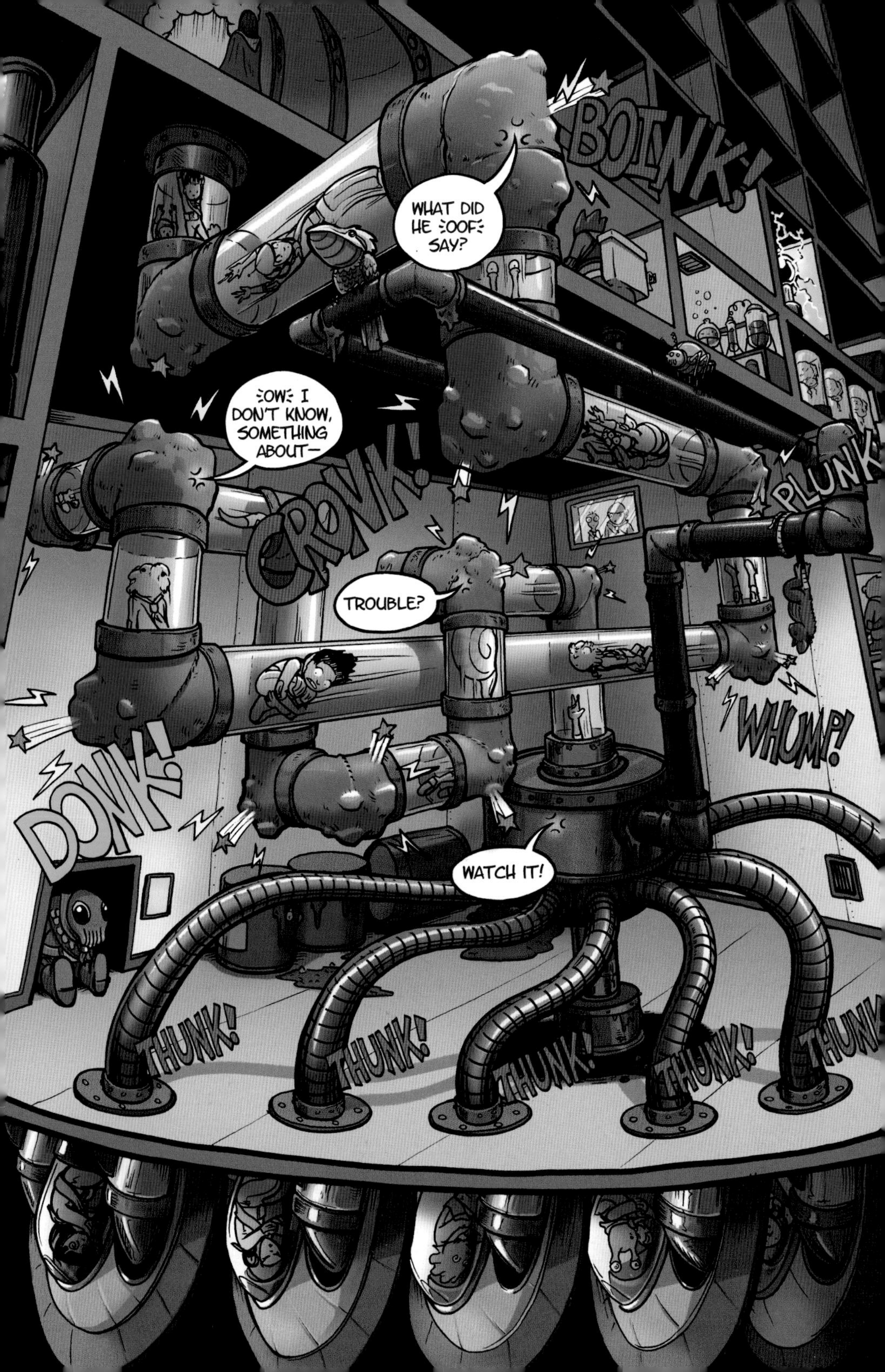
BOINK!
WHAT DID HE OOF SAY?
OW I DON'T KNOW, SOMETHING ABOUT—
CRONK!
PLUNK!
TROUBLE?
WHUMP!
DONK!
WATCH IT!
THUNK!
THUNK!
THUNK!
THUNK!
THUNK!

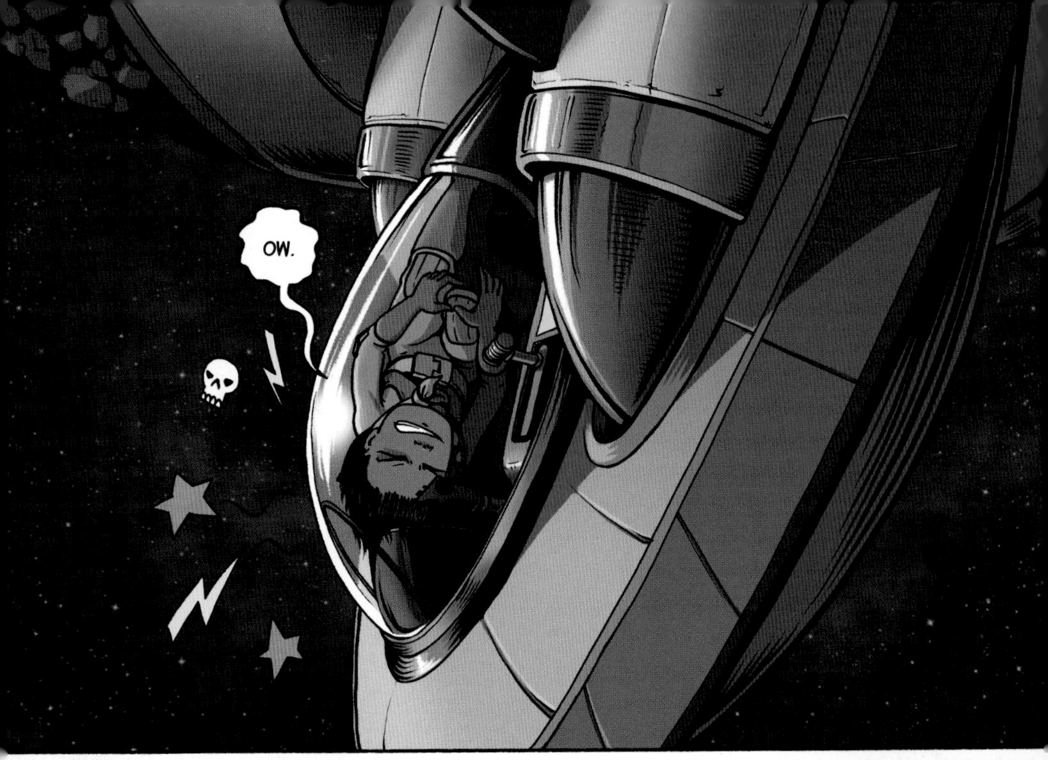
OW.

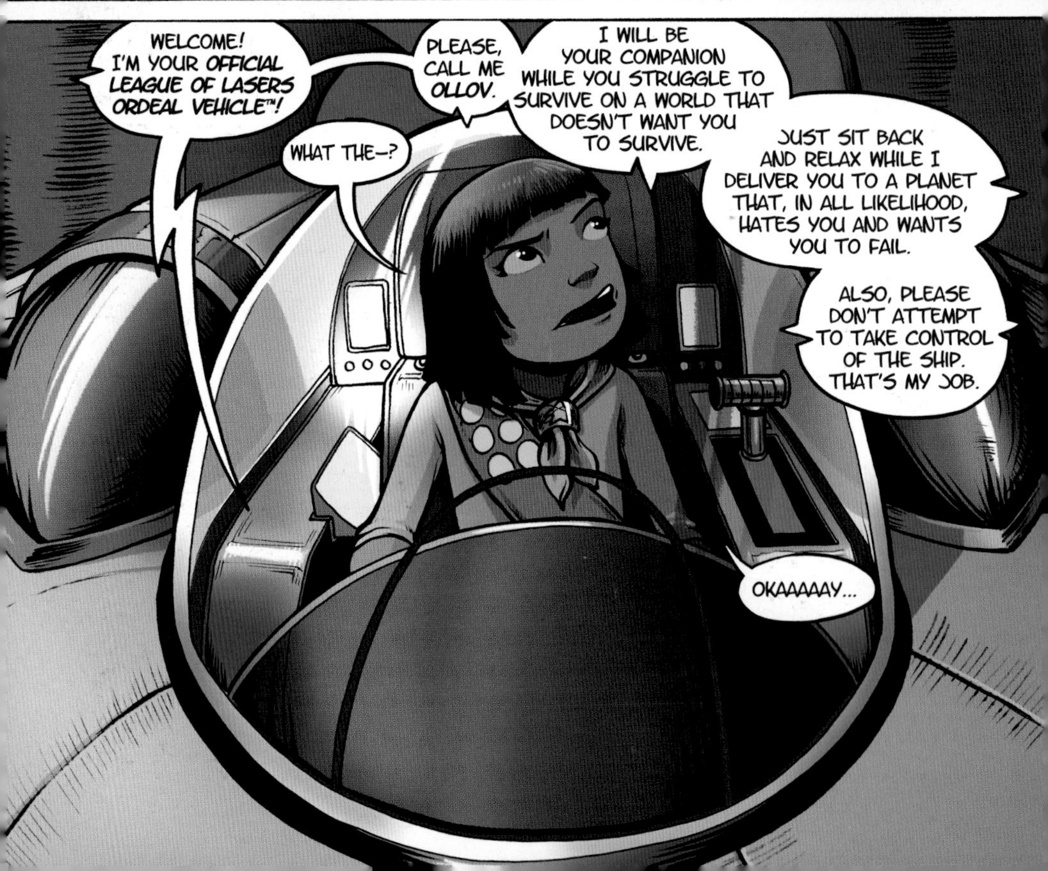
WELCOME! I'M YOUR OFFICIAL LEAGUE OF LASERS ORDEAL VEHICLE™!
PLEASE, CALL ME OLLOV.
I WILL BE YOUR COMPANION WHILE YOU STRUGGLE TO SURVIVE ON A WORLD THAT DOESN'T WANT YOU TO SURVIVE.
WHAT THE--?
JUST SIT BACK AND RELAX WHILE I DELIVER YOU TO A PLANET THAT, IN ALL LIKELIHOOD, HATES YOU AND WANTS YOU TO FAIL.
ALSO, PLEASE DON'T ATTEMPT TO TAKE CONTROL OF THE SHIP. THAT'S MY JOB.
OKAAAAAY...

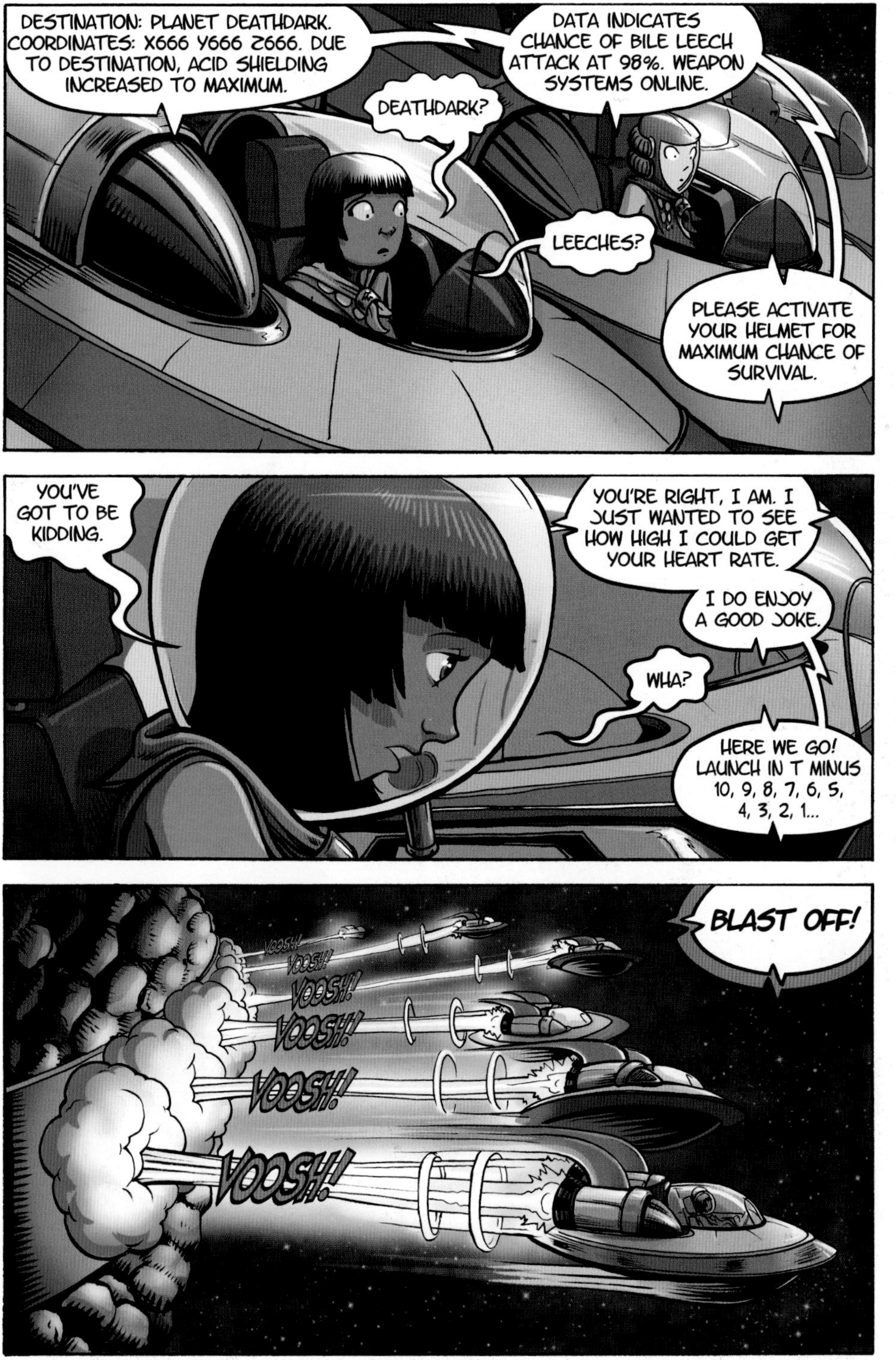
DESTINATION: PLANET DEATHDARK. COORDINATES: X666 Y666 Z666. DUE TO DESTINATION, ACID SHIELDING INCREASED TO MAXIMUM.
DEATHDARK?
DATA INDICATES CHANCE OF BILE LEECH ATTACK AT 98%. WEAPON SYSTEMS ONLINE.
LEECHES?
PLEASE ACTIVATE YOUR HELMET FOR MAXIMUM CHANCE OF SURVIVAL.
YOU'VE GOT TO BE KIDDING.
YOU'RE RIGHT, I AM. I JUST WANTED TO SEE HOW HIGH I COULD GET YOUR HEART RATE.
I DO ENJOY A GOOD JOKE.
WHA?
HERE WE GO! LAUNCH IN T MINUS 10, 9, 8, 7, 6, 5, 4, 3, 2, 1...
BLAST OFF!
VOOSH!
VOOSH!
VOOSH!
VOOSH!
VOOSH!
VOOSH!

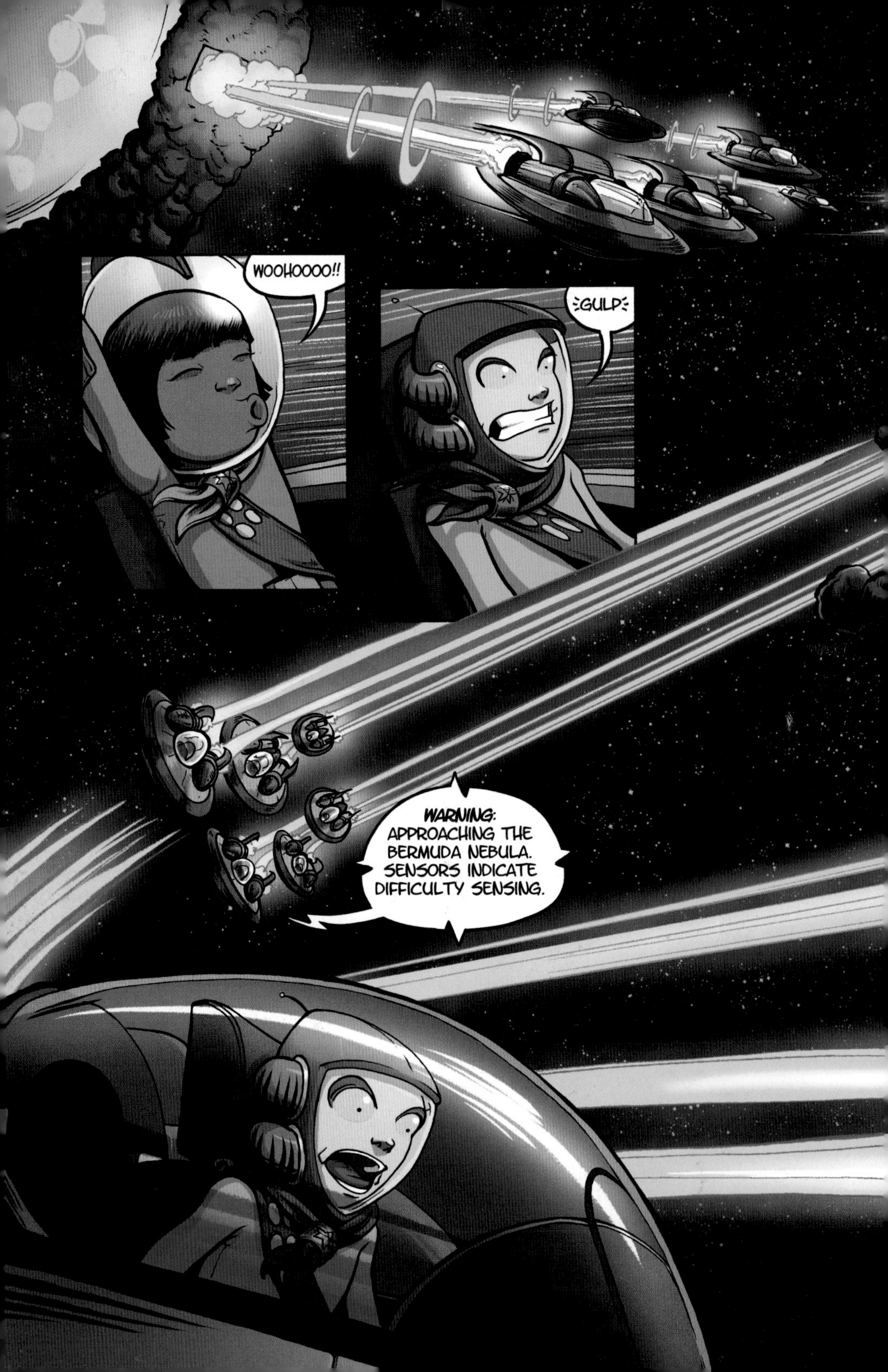
WOOHOOOO!!
GULP
WARNING: APPROACHING THE BERMUDA NEBULA. SENSORS INDICATE DIFFICULTY SENSING.

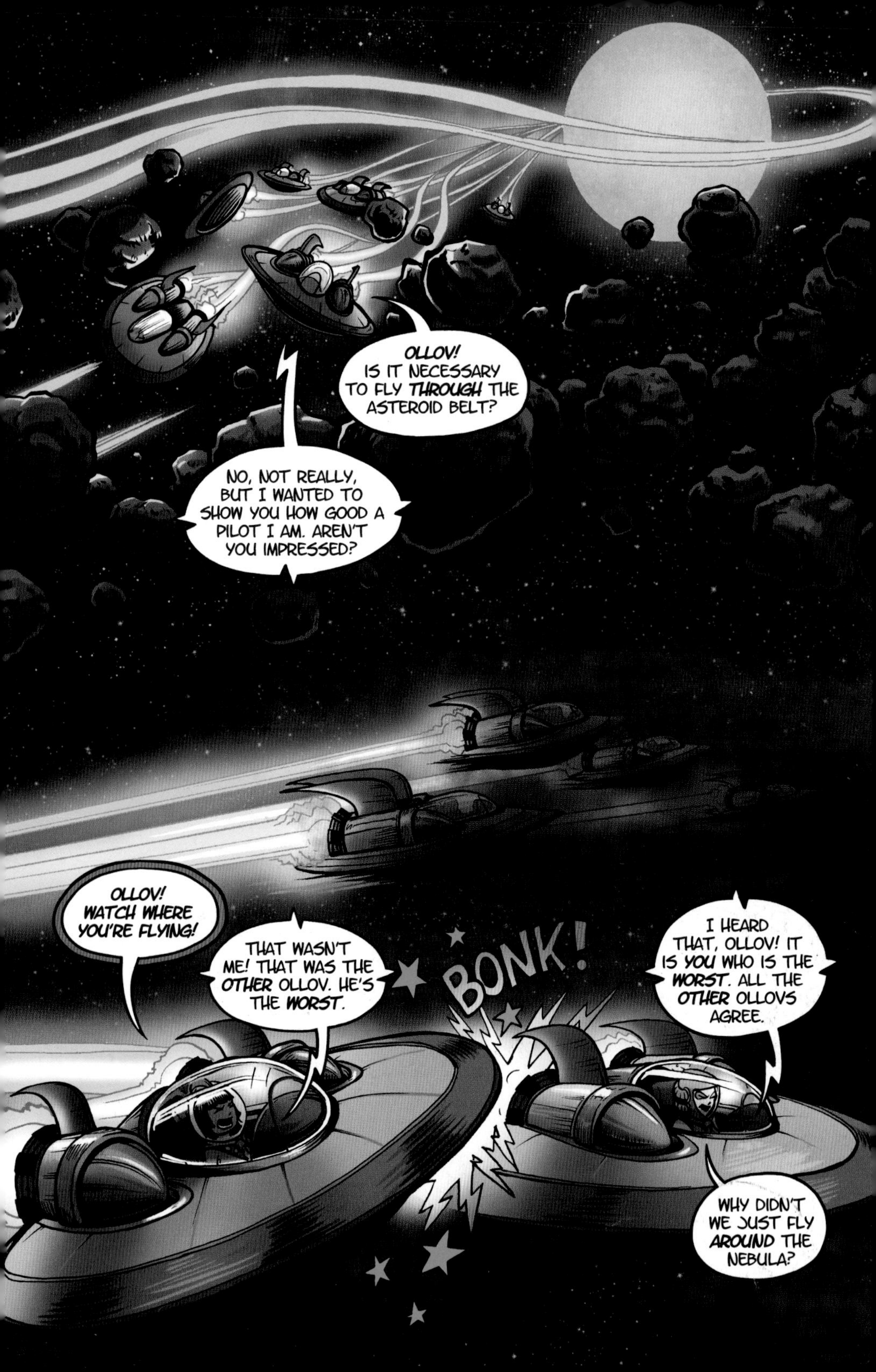

OLLOV! IS IT NECESSARY TO FLY THROUGH THE ASTEROID BELT?
NO, NOT REALLY, BUT I WANTED TO SHOW YOU HOW GOOD A PILOT I AM. AREN'T YOU IMPRESSED?
OLLOV! WATCH WHERE YOU'RE FLYING!
THAT WASN'T ME! THAT WAS THE OTHER OLLOV. HE'S THE WORST.
BONK!
I HEARD THAT, OLLOV! IT IS YOU WHO IS THE WORST. ALL THE OTHER OLLOVS AGREE.
WHY DIDN'T WE JUST FLY AROUND THE NEBULA?

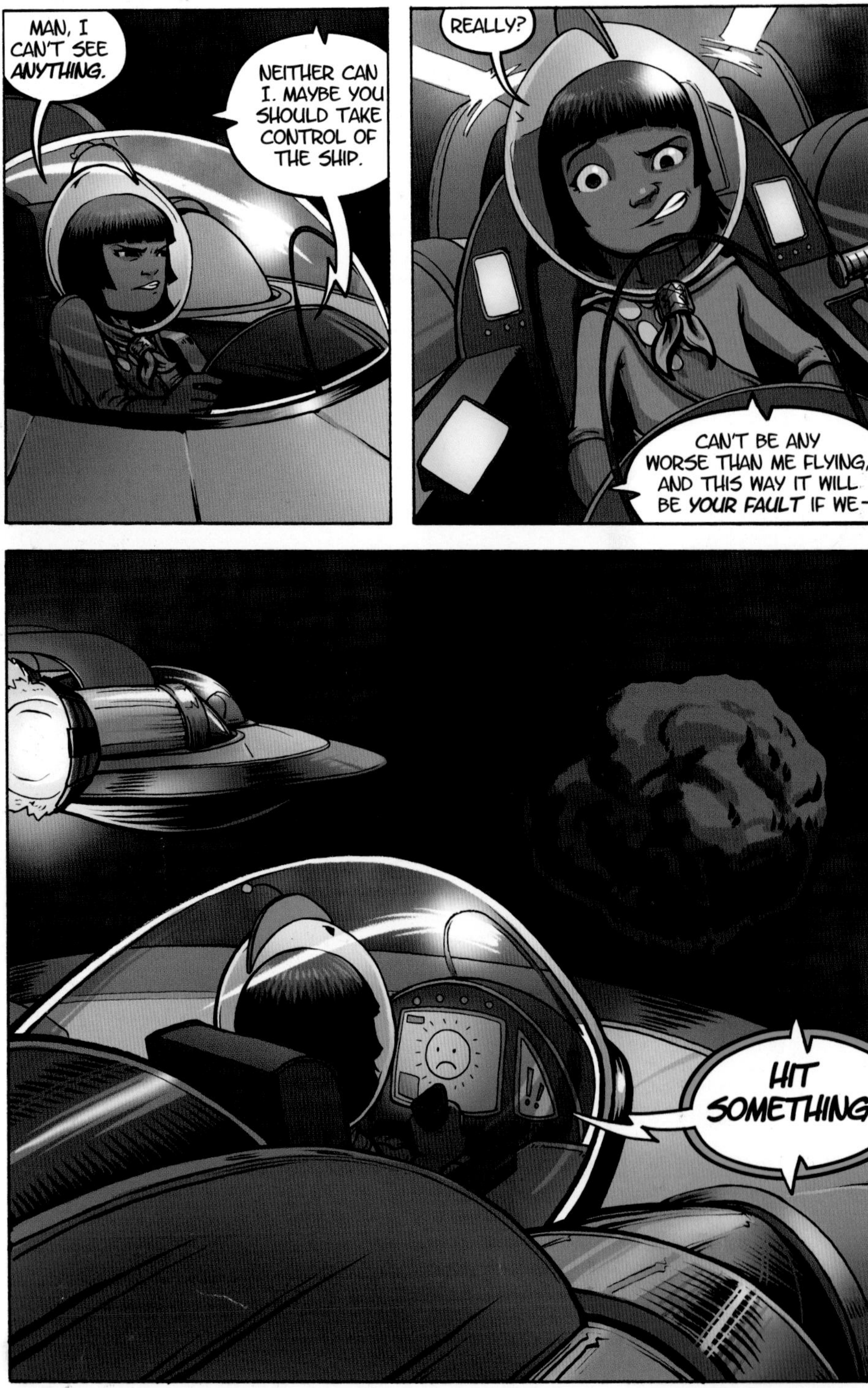
MAN, I CAN'T SEE *ANYTHING.*
NEITHER CAN I. MAYBE YOU SHOULD TAKE CONTROL OF THE SHIP.
REALLY?
CAN'T BE ANY WORSE THAN ME FLYING, AND THIS WAY IT WILL BE *YOUR FAULT* IF WE—
HIT SOMETHING!

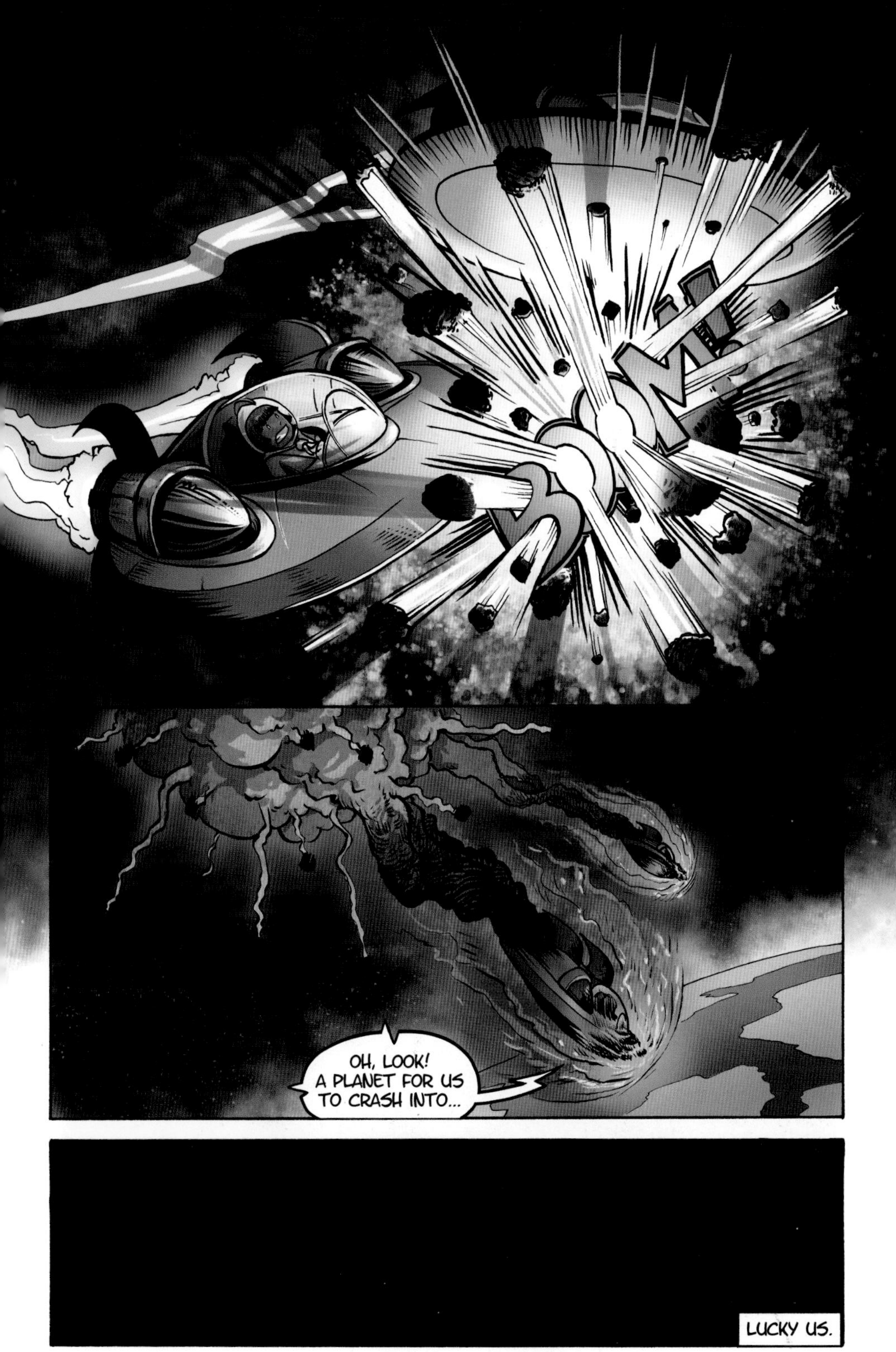
OH, LOOK! A PLANET FOR US TO CRASH INTO...
LUCKY US.

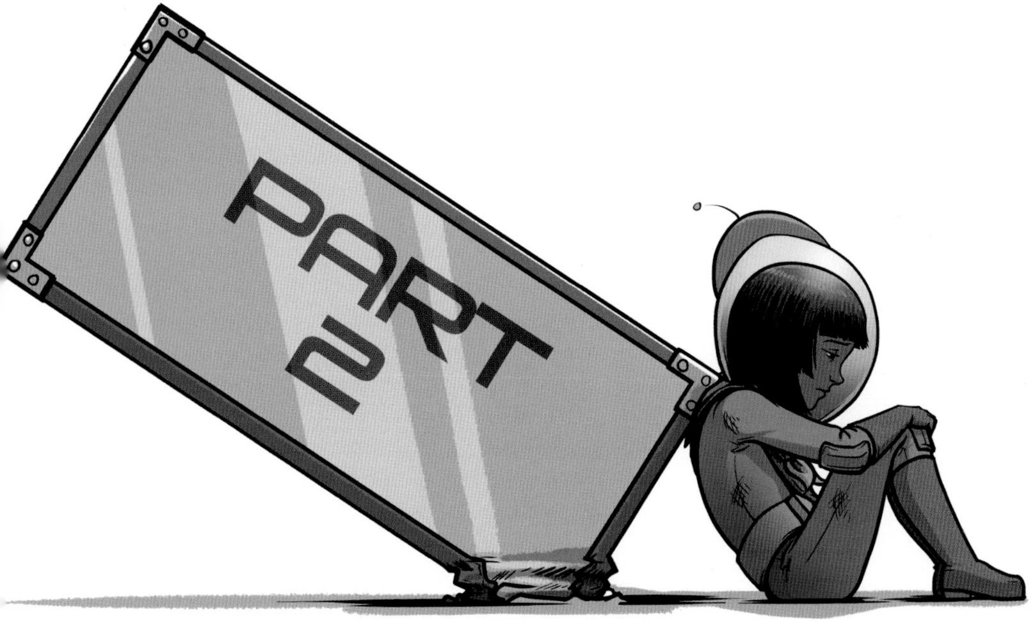
PART
2

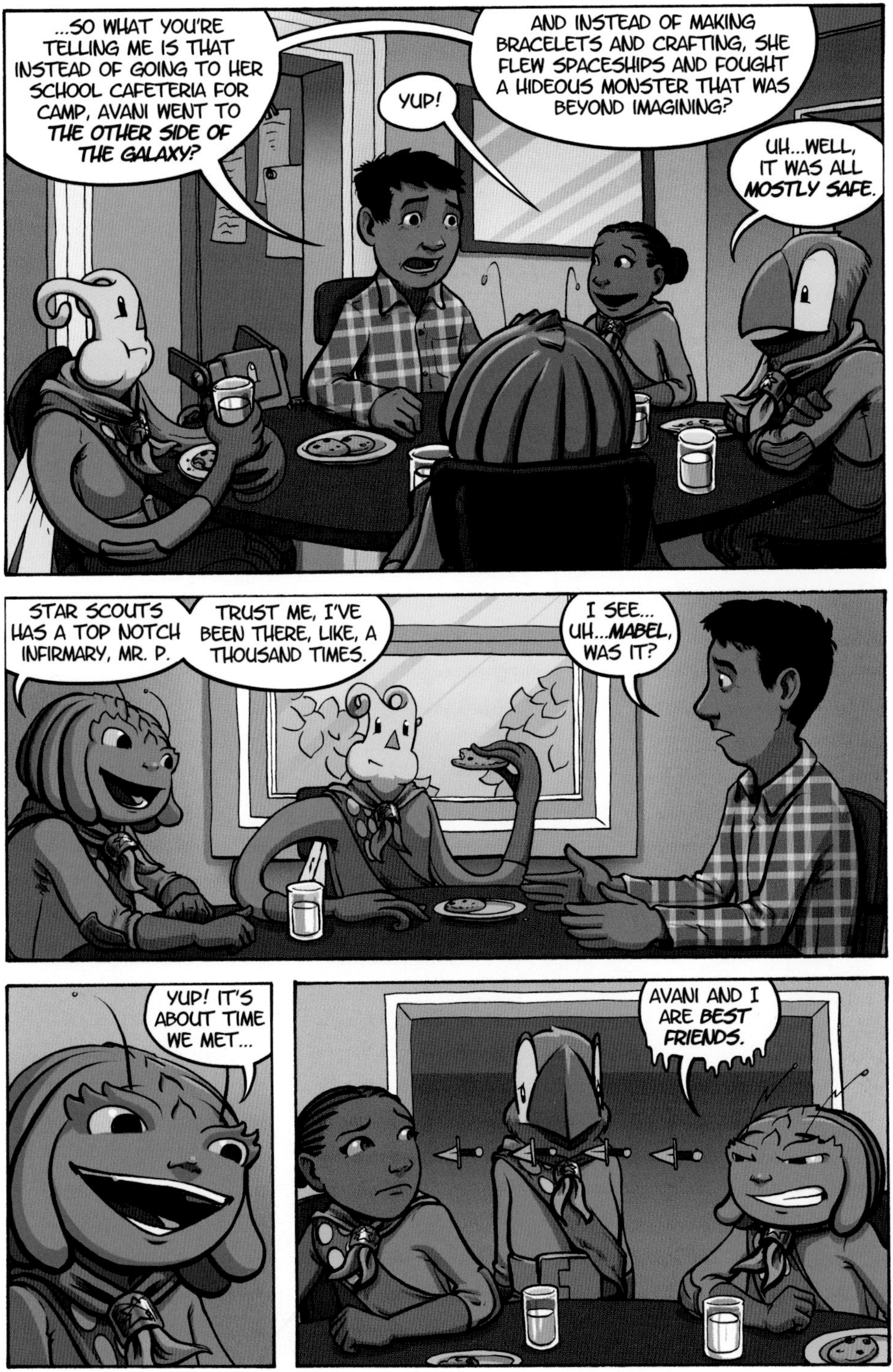
...SO WHAT YOU'RE TELLING ME IS THAT INSTEAD OF GOING TO HER SCHOOL CAFETERIA FOR CAMP, AVANI WENT TO THE OTHER SIDE OF THE GALAXY?
YUP!
AND INSTEAD OF MAKING BRACELETS AND CRAFTING, SHE FLEW SPACESHIPS AND FOUGHT A HIDEOUS MONSTER THAT WAS BEYOND IMAGINING?
UH...WELL, IT WAS ALL MOSTLY SAFE.
STAR SCOUTS HAS A TOP NOTCH INFIRMARY, MR. P.
TRUST ME, I'VE BEEN THERE, LIKE, A THOUSAND TIMES.
I SEE... UH...MABEL, WAS IT?
YUP! IT'S ABOUT TIME WE MET...
AVANI AND I ARE BEST FRIENDS.

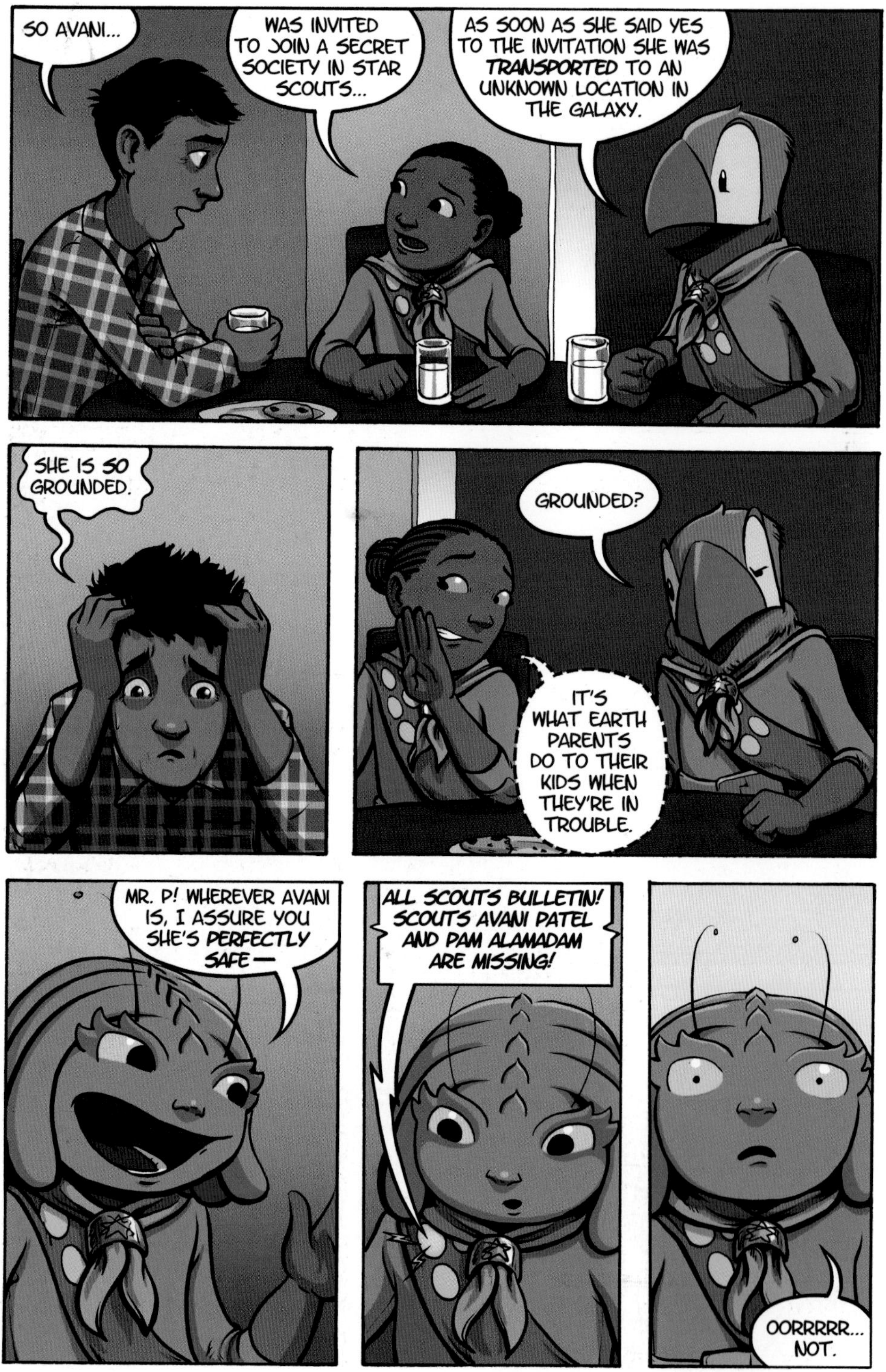
SO AVANI...
WAS INVITED TO JOIN A SECRET SOCIETY IN STAR SCOUTS...
AS SOON AS SHE SAID YES TO THE INVITATION SHE WAS TRANSPORTED TO AN UNKNOWN LOCATION IN THE GALAXY.
SHE IS SO GROUNDED.
GROUNDED?
IT'S WHAT EARTH PARENTS DO TO THEIR KIDS WHEN THEY'RE IN TROUBLE.
MR. P! WHEREVER AVANI IS, I ASSURE YOU SHE'S PERFECTLY SAFE—
ALL SCOUTS BULLETIN! SCOUTS AVANI PATEL AND PAM ALAMADAM ARE MISSING!
OORRRRR... NOT.

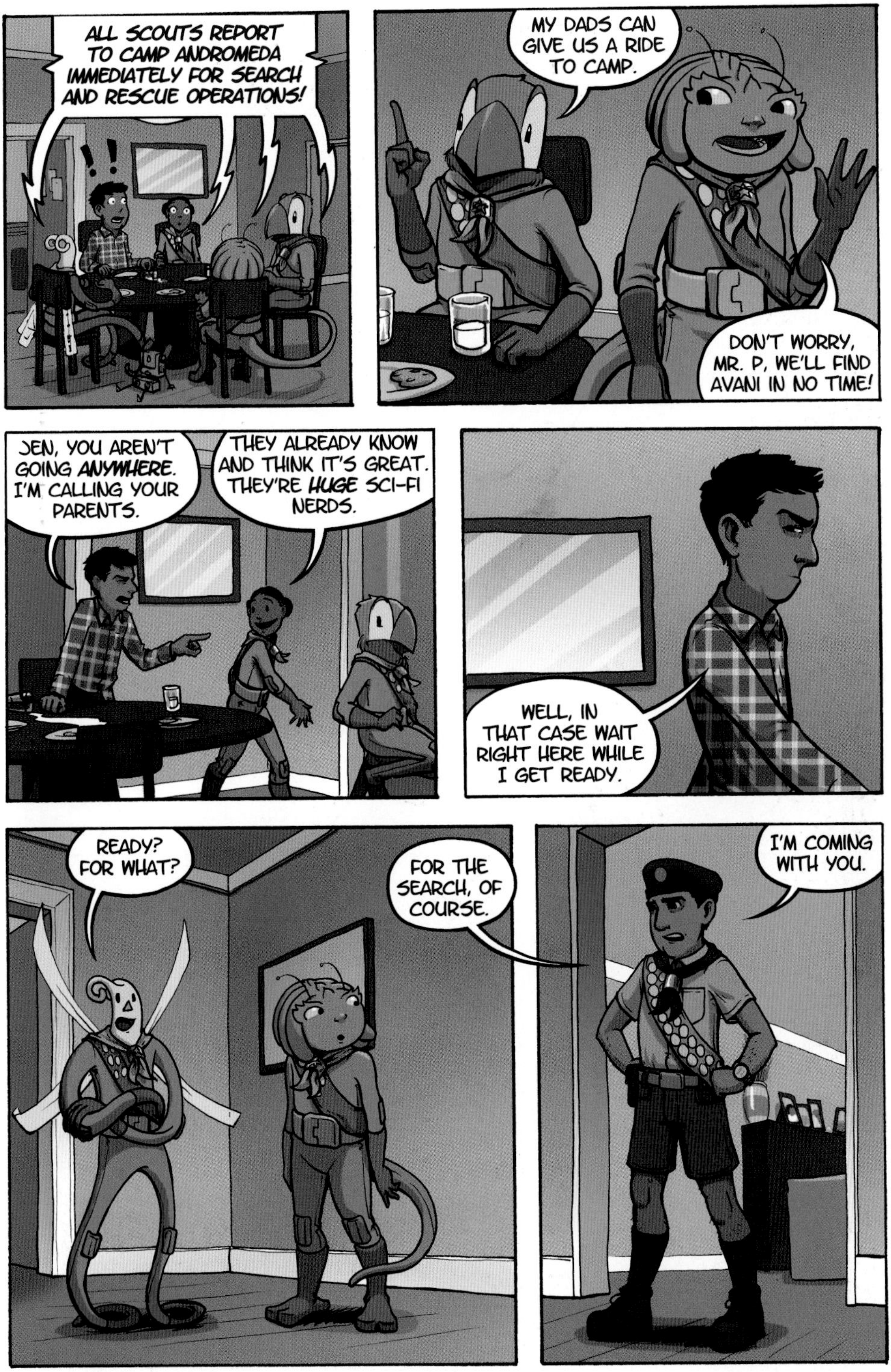
ALL SCOUTS REPORT TO CAMP ANDROMEDA IMMEDIATELY FOR SEARCH AND RESCUE OPERATIONS!
!!
MY DADS CAN GIVE US A RIDE TO CAMP.
DON'T WORRY, MR. P, WE'LL FIND AVANI IN NO TIME!
JEN, YOU AREN'T GOING ANYWHERE. I'M CALLING YOUR PARENTS.
THEY ALREADY KNOW AND THINK IT'S GREAT. THEY'RE HUGE SCI-FI NERDS.
WELL, IN THAT CASE WAIT RIGHT HERE WHILE I GET READY.
READY? FOR WHAT?
FOR THE SEARCH, OF COURSE.
I'M COMING WITH YOU.

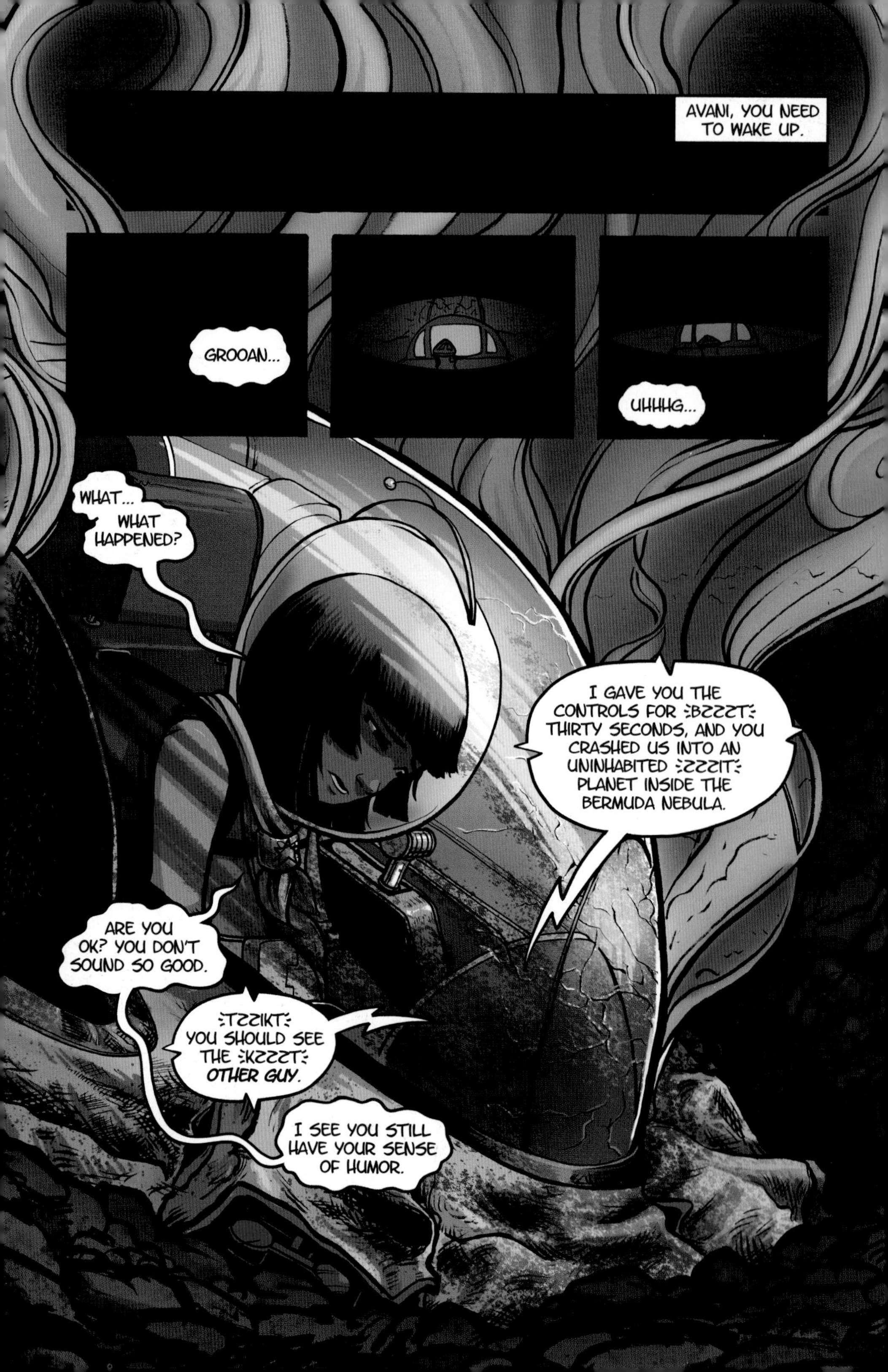
AVANI, YOU NEED TO WAKE UP.
GROOAN...
UHHHG...
WHAT... WHAT HAPPENED?
I GAVE YOU THE CONTROLS FOR :BZZZT: THIRTY SECONDS, AND YOU CRASHED US INTO AN UNINHABITED :ZZZIT: PLANET INSIDE THE BERMUDA NEBULA.
ARE YOU OK? YOU DON'T SOUND SO GOOD.
:TZZIKT: YOU SHOULD SEE THE :KZZZT: OTHER GUY.
I SEE YOU STILL HAVE YOUR SENSE OF HUMOR.

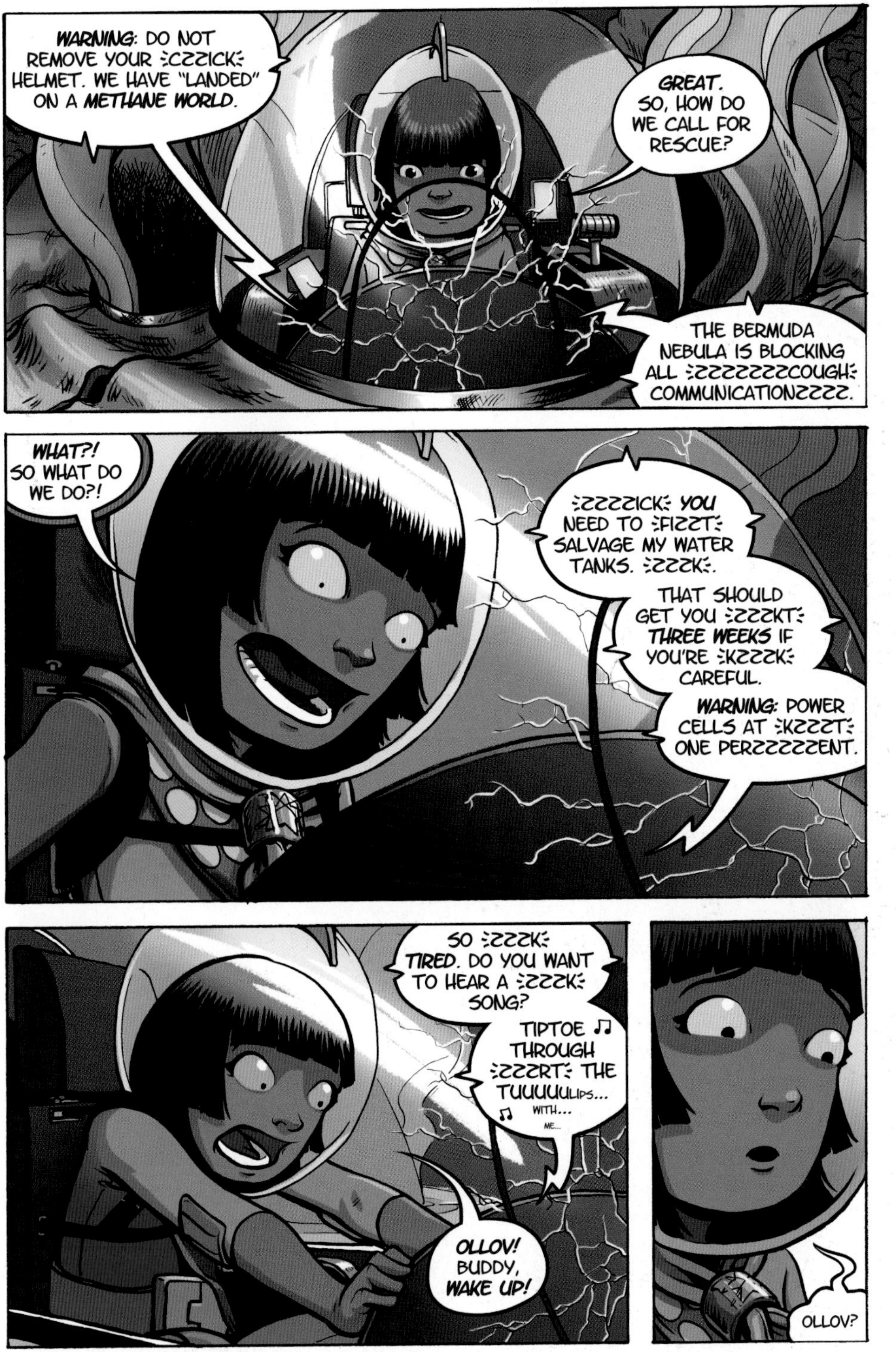
WARNING: DO NOT REMOVE YOUR :CZZICK: HELMET. WE HAVE "LANDED" ON A METHANE WORLD.
GREAT. SO, HOW DO WE CALL FOR RESCUE?
THE BERMUDA NEBULA IS BLOCKING ALL :ZZZZZZZCOUGH: COMMUNICATIONZZZZ.
WHAT?! SO WHAT DO WE DO?!
:ZZZZICK: YOU NEED TO :FIZZT: SALVAGE MY WATER TANKS. :ZZZK:.
THAT SHOULD GET YOU :ZZZKT: THREE WEEKS IF YOU'RE :KZZZK: CAREFUL.
WARNING: POWER CELLS AT :KZZZT: ONE PERZZZZZZENT.
SO :ZZZK: TIRED. DO YOU WANT TO HEAR A :ZZZK: SONG?
TIPTOE ♫ THROUGH :ZZZRT: THE TUUUUULIPS... ♫ WITH... ME...
OLLOV! BUDDY, WAKE UP!
OLLOV?

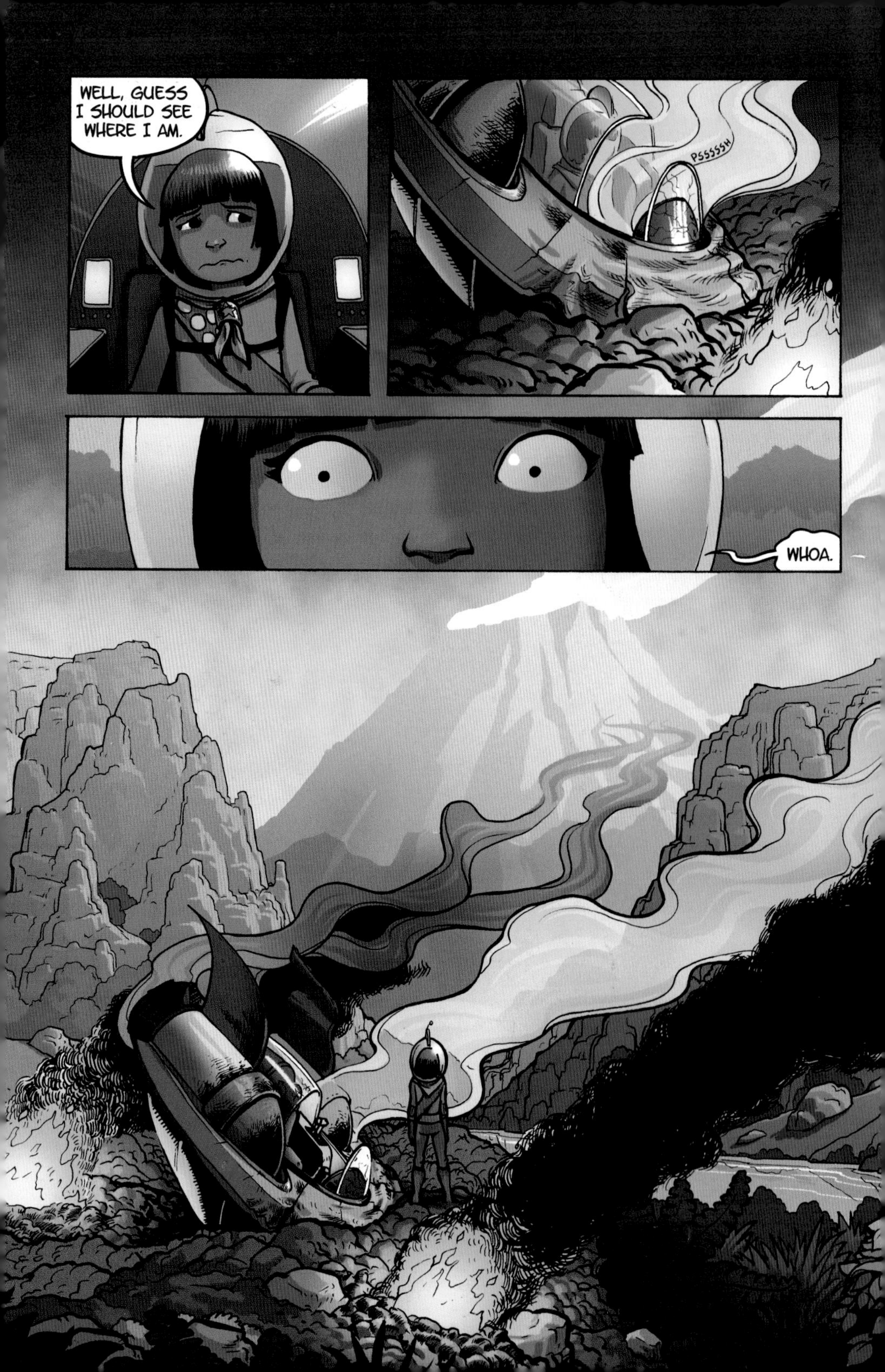
WELL, GUESS I SHOULD SEE WHERE I AM.
PSSSSSH
WHOA.

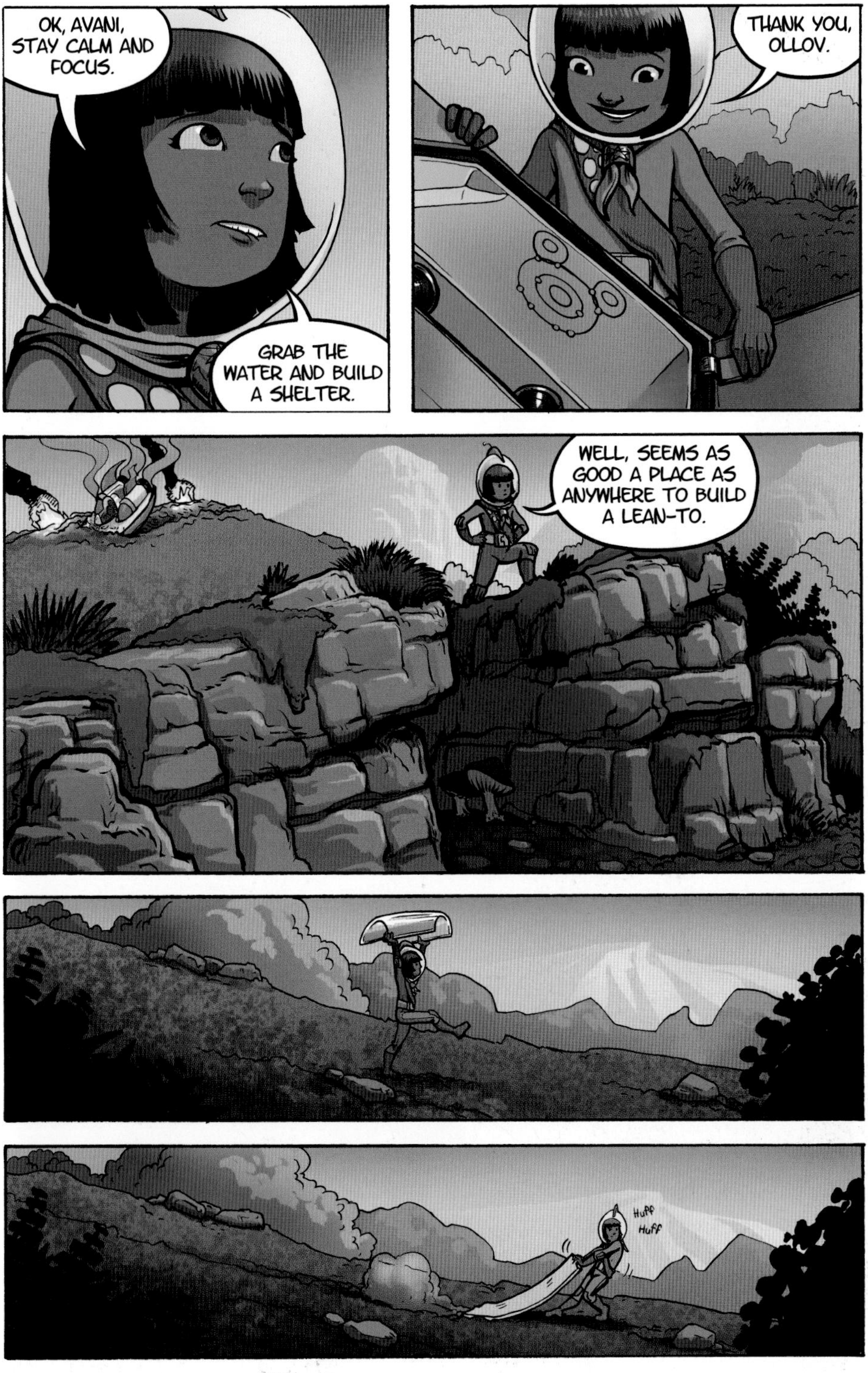
OK, AVANI, STAY CALM AND FOCUS.
GRAB THE WATER AND BUILD A SHELTER.
THANK YOU, OLLOV.
WELL, SEEMS AS GOOD A PLACE AS ANYWHERE TO BUILD A LEAN-TO.
Huff
Huff

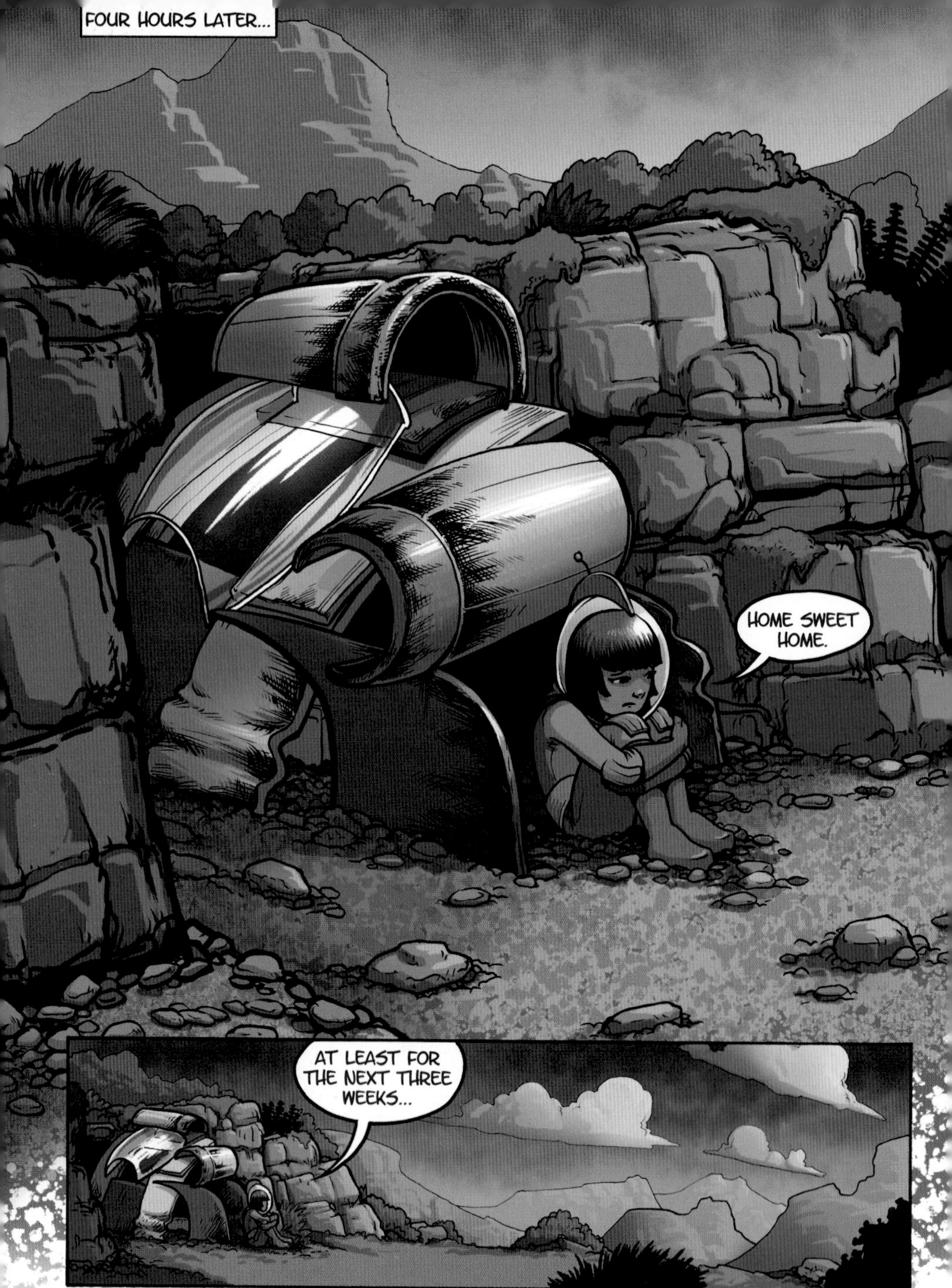
FOUR HOURS LATER...
HOME SWEET HOME.
AT LEAST FOR THE NEXT THREE WEEKS...

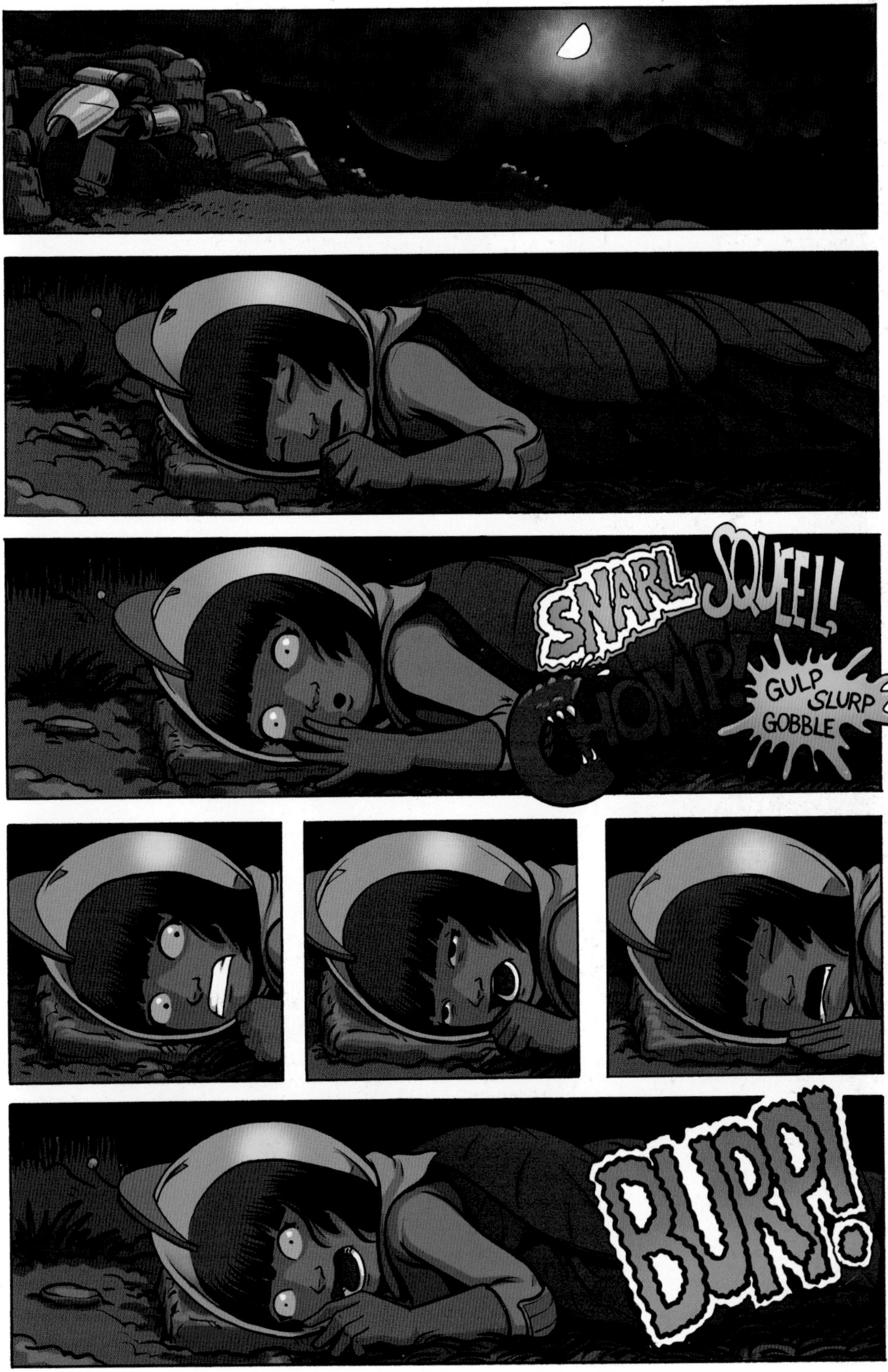
SNARL
SQUEEL!
CHOMP!
GULP SLURP GOBBLE
BURP!

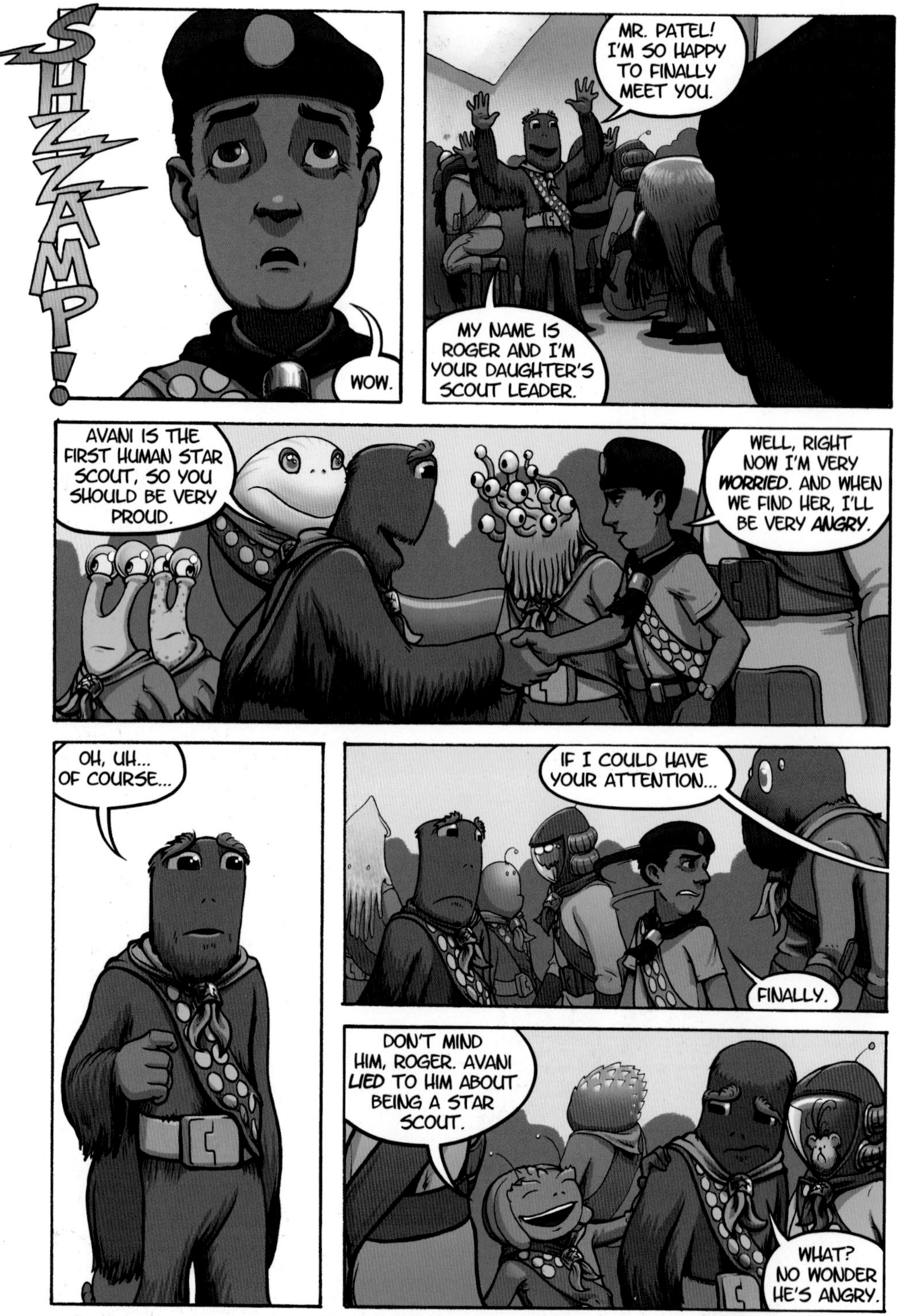
SHZZAMP!
WOW.
MR. PATEL! I'M SO HAPPY TO FINALLY MEET YOU.
MY NAME IS ROGER AND I'M YOUR DAUGHTER'S SCOUT LEADER.
AVANI IS THE FIRST HUMAN STAR SCOUT, SO YOU SHOULD BE VERY PROUD.
WELL, RIGHT NOW I'M VERY **WORRIED**. AND WHEN WE FIND HER, I'LL BE VERY **ANGRY**.
OH, UH... OF COURSE...
IF I COULD HAVE YOUR ATTENTION...
FINALLY.
DON'T MIND HIM, ROGER. AVANI **LIED** TO HIM ABOUT BEING A STAR SCOUT.
WHAT? NO WONDER HE'S ANGRY.

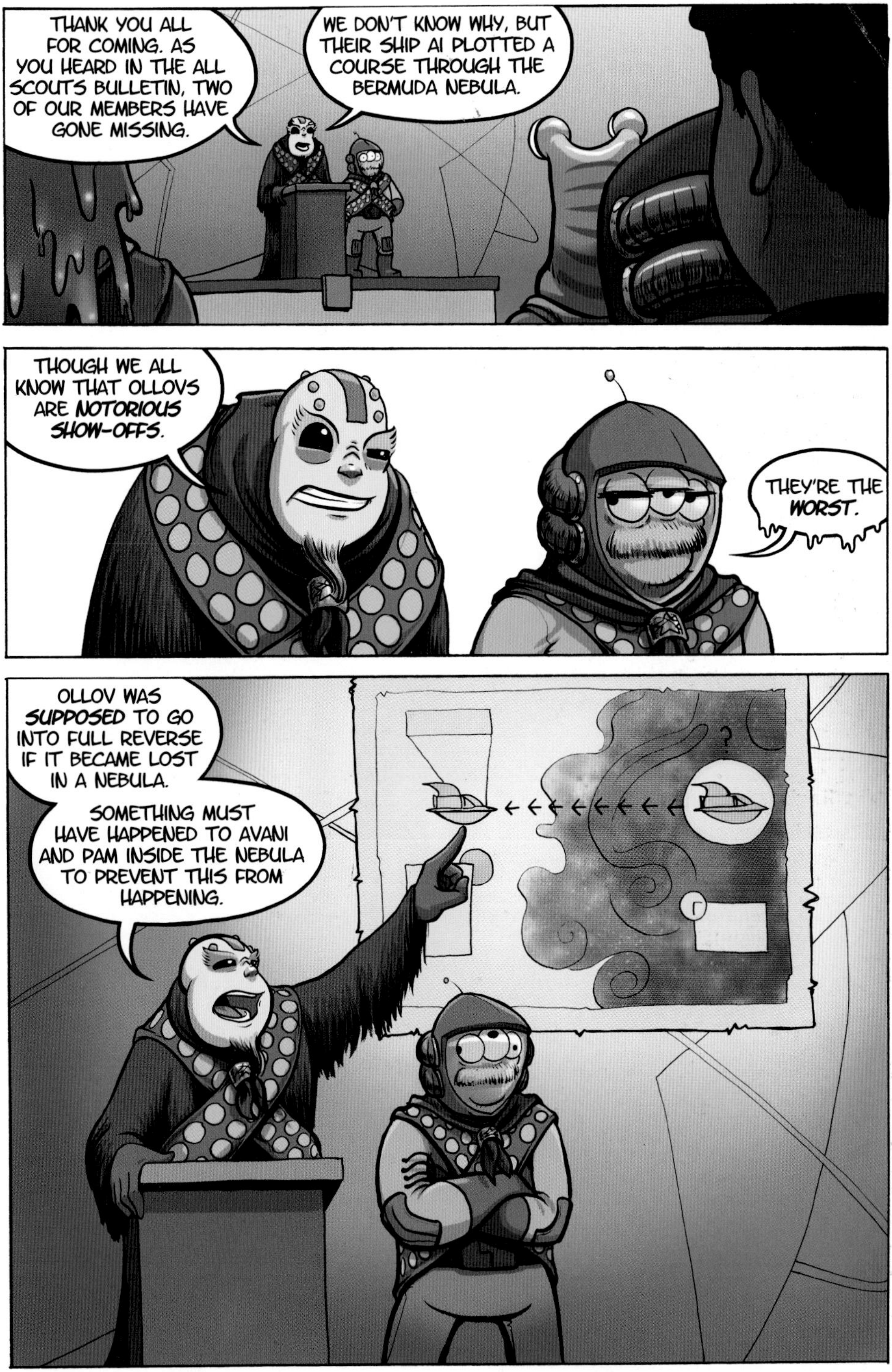
THANK YOU ALL FOR COMING. AS YOU HEARD IN THE ALL SCOUTS BULLETIN, TWO OF OUR MEMBERS HAVE GONE MISSING.
WE DON'T KNOW WHY, BUT THEIR SHIP AI PLOTTED A COURSE THROUGH THE BERMUDA NEBULA.
THOUGH WE ALL KNOW THAT OLLOVS ARE NOTORIOUS SHOW-OFFS.
THEY'RE THE WORST.
OLLOV WAS SUPPOSED TO GO INTO FULL REVERSE IF IT BECAME LOST IN A NEBULA.
SOMETHING MUST HAVE HAPPENED TO AVANI AND PAM INSIDE THE NEBULA TO PREVENT THIS FROM HAPPENING.
?

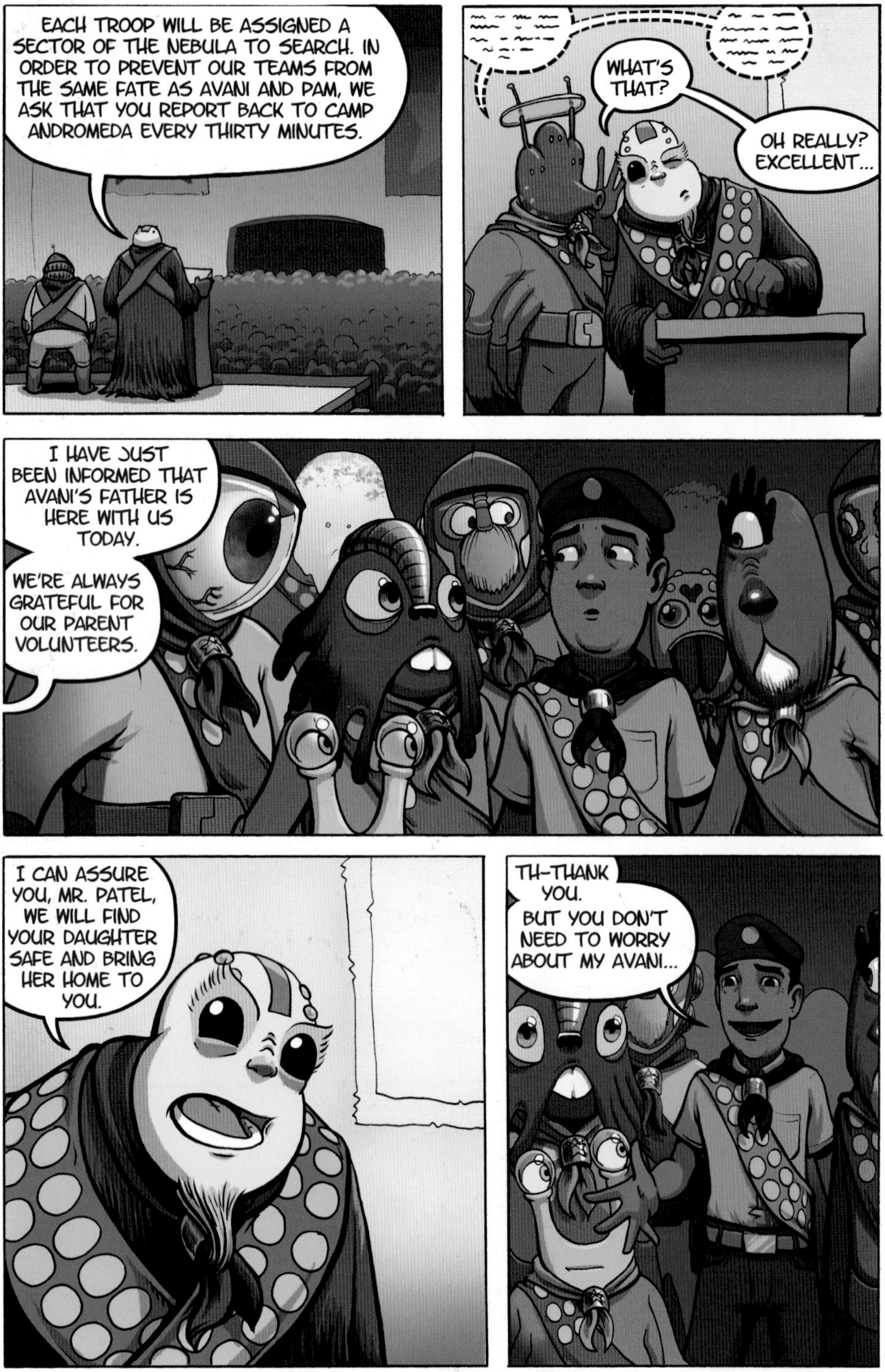
EACH TROOP WILL BE ASSIGNED A SECTOR OF THE NEBULA TO SEARCH. IN ORDER TO PREVENT OUR TEAMS FROM THE SAME FATE AS AVANI AND PAM, WE ASK THAT YOU REPORT BACK TO CAMP ANDROMEDA EVERY THIRTY MINUTES.
WHAT'S THAT?
OH REALLY? EXCELLENT...
I HAVE JUST BEEN INFORMED THAT AVANI'S FATHER IS HERE WITH US TODAY.
WE'RE ALWAYS GRATEFUL FOR OUR PARENT VOLUNTEERS.
I CAN ASSURE YOU, MR. PATEL, WE WILL FIND YOUR DAUGHTER SAFE AND BRING HER HOME TO YOU.
TH-THANK YOU.
BUT YOU DON'T NEED TO WORRY ABOUT MY AVANI...

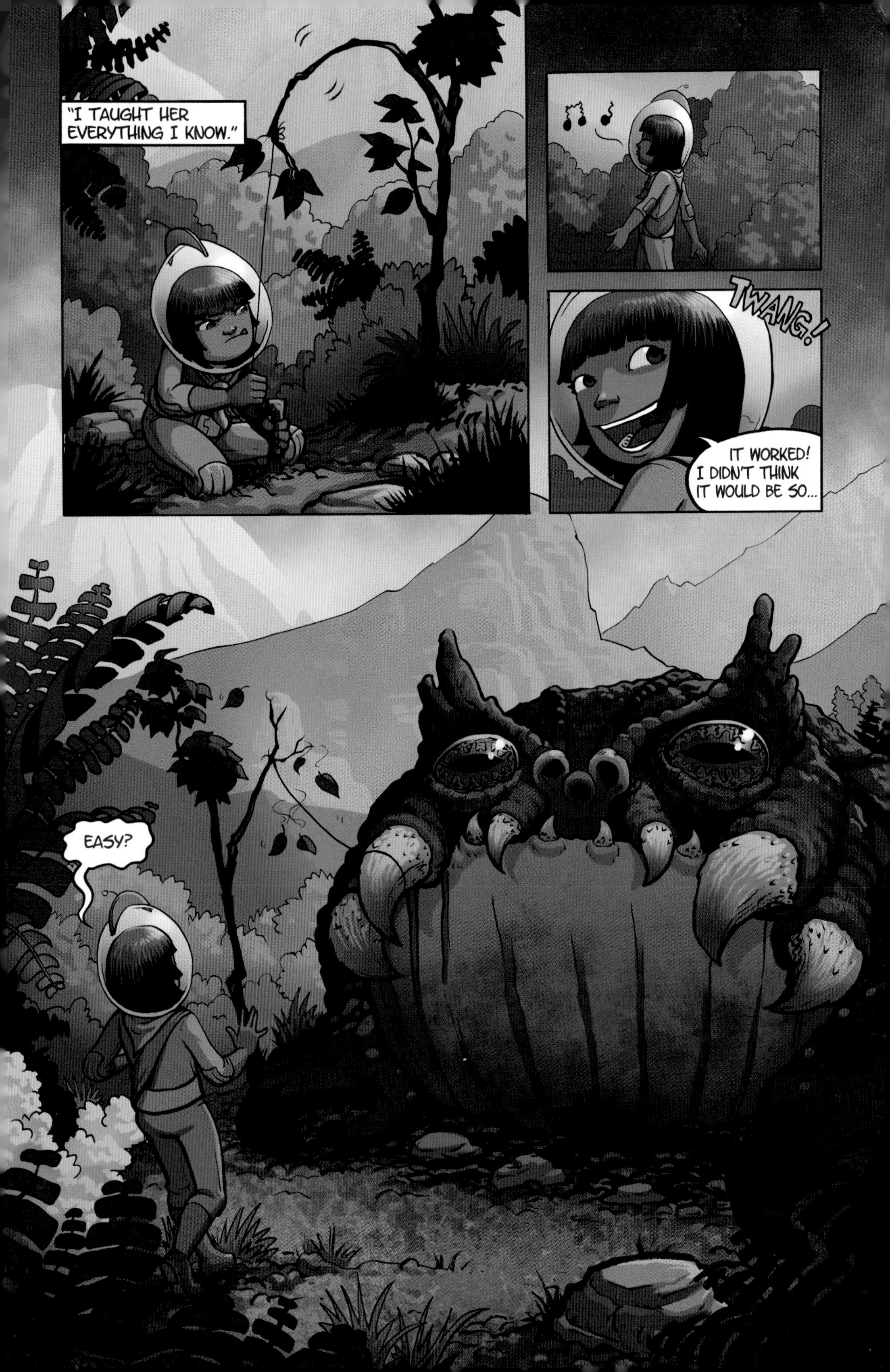
"I TAUGHT HER EVERYTHING I KNOW."
TWANG!
IT WORKED! I DIDN'T THINK IT WOULD BE SO...
EASY?

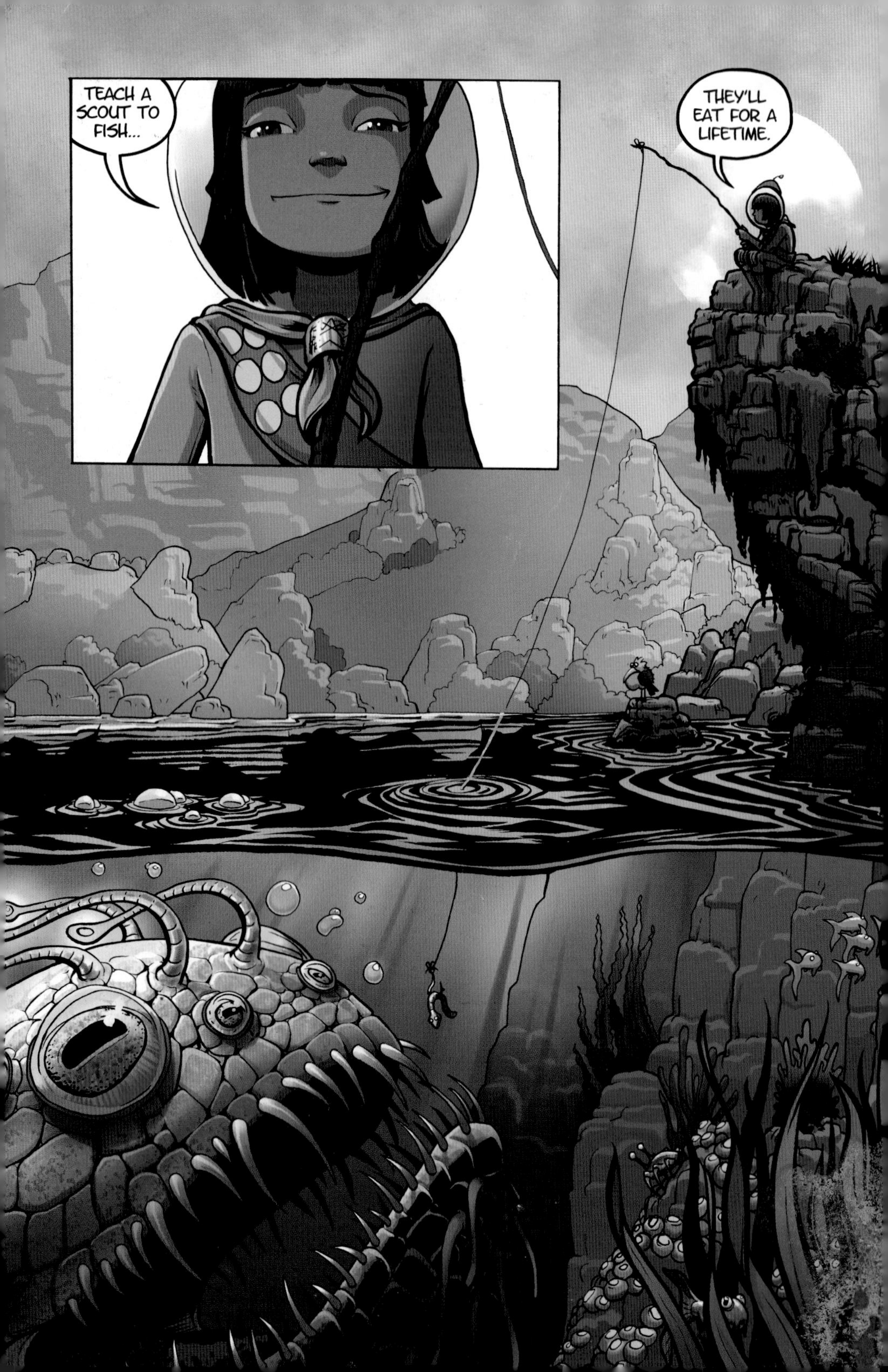
TEACH A SCOUT TO FISH...
THEY'LL EAT FOR A LIFETIME.

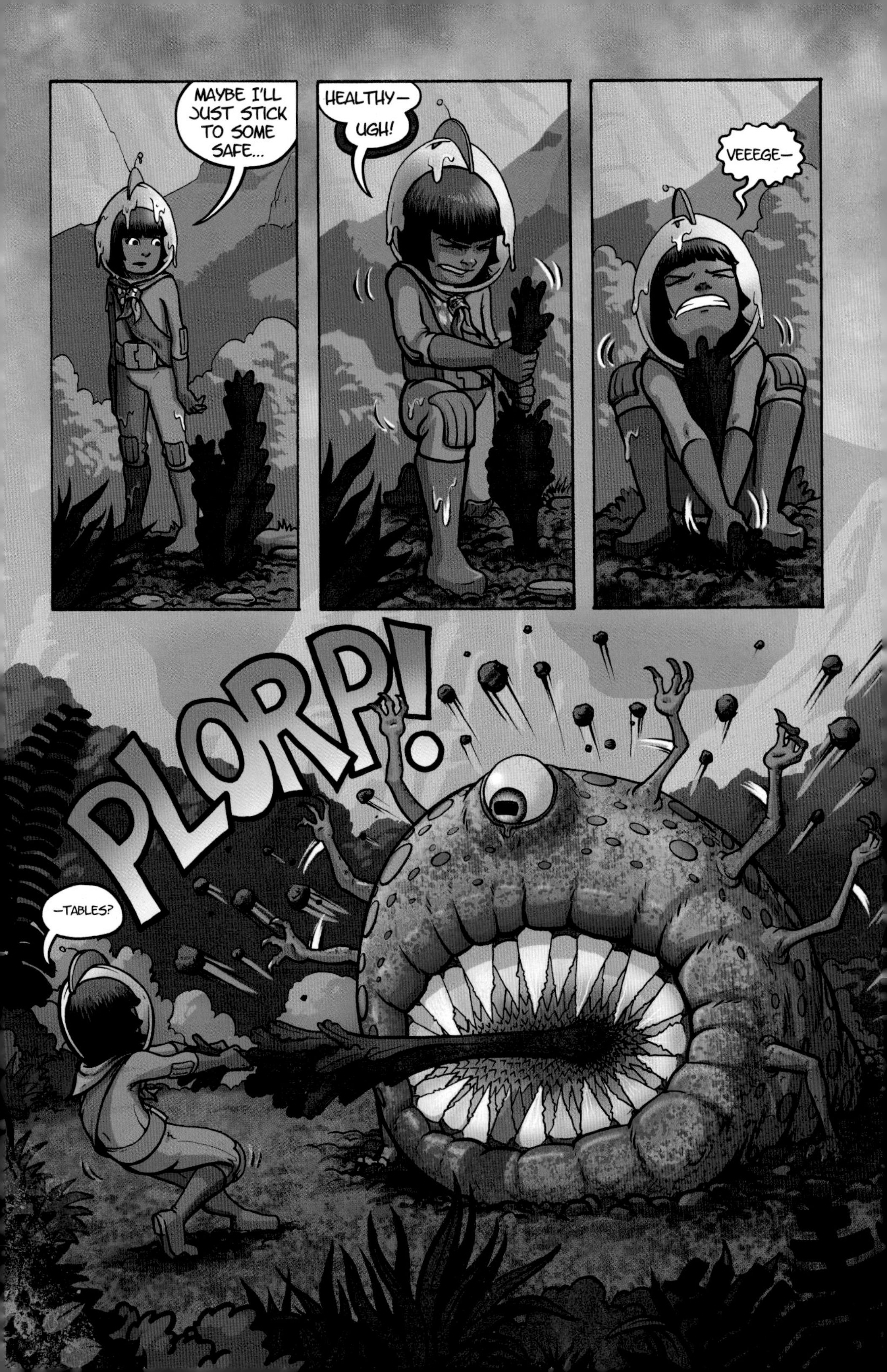
MAYBE I'LL JUST STICK TO SOME SAFE...
HEALTHY—
UGH!
VEEEGE—
PLORP!
—TABLES?

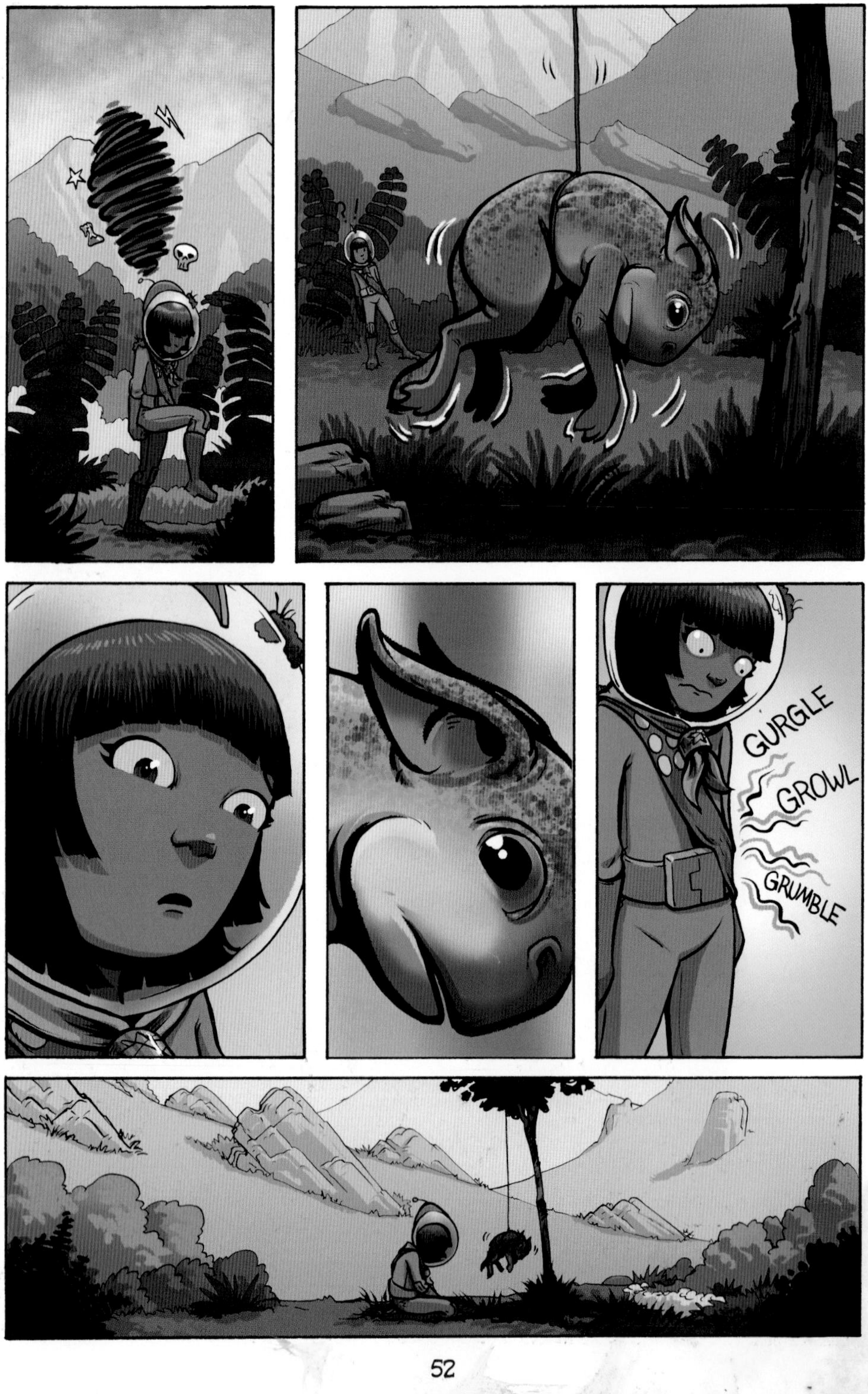
GURGLE
GROWL
GRUMBLE

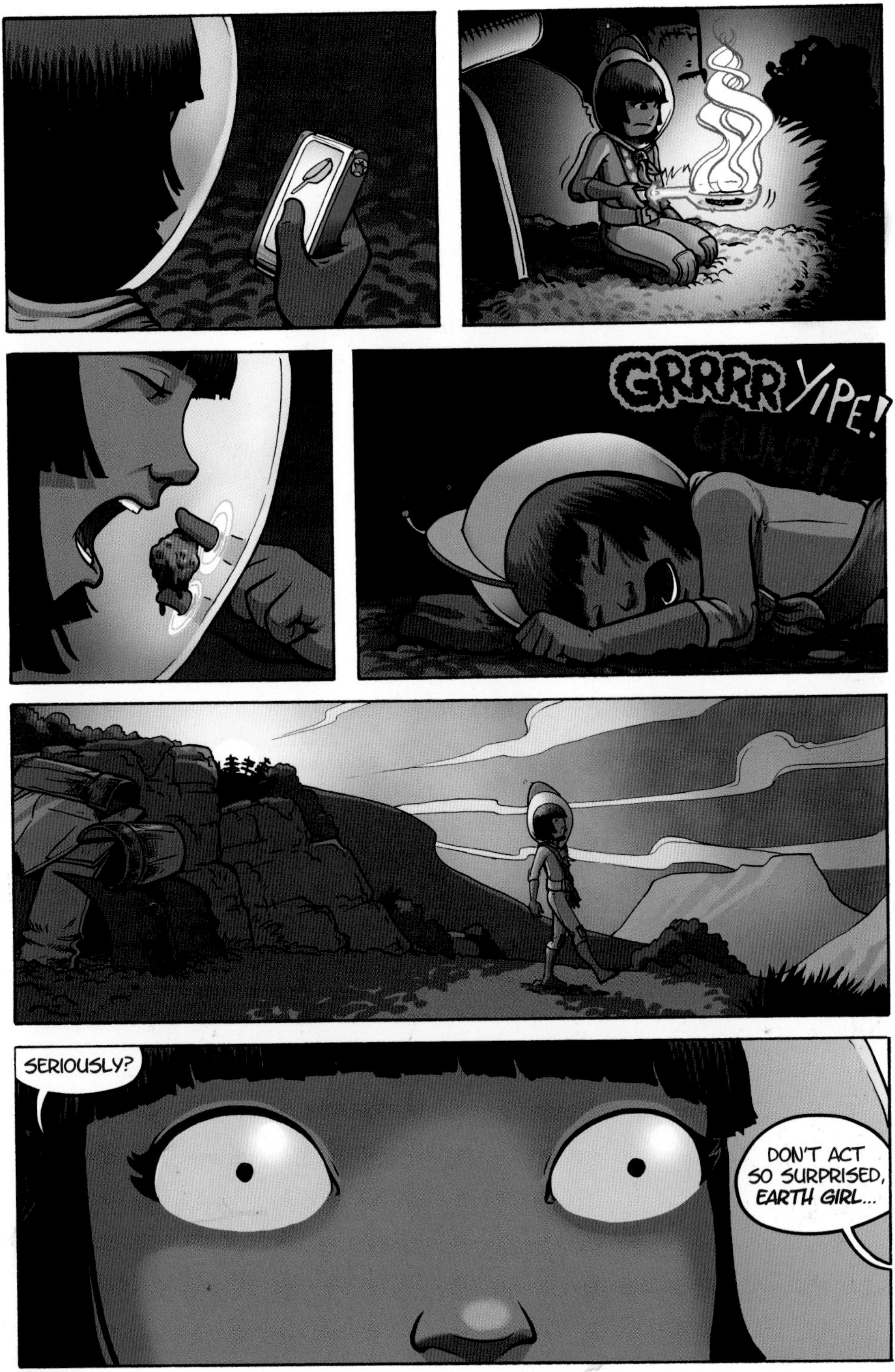

GRRRR
YIPE!
SERIOUSLY?
DON'T ACT SO SURPRISED, EARTH GIRL...

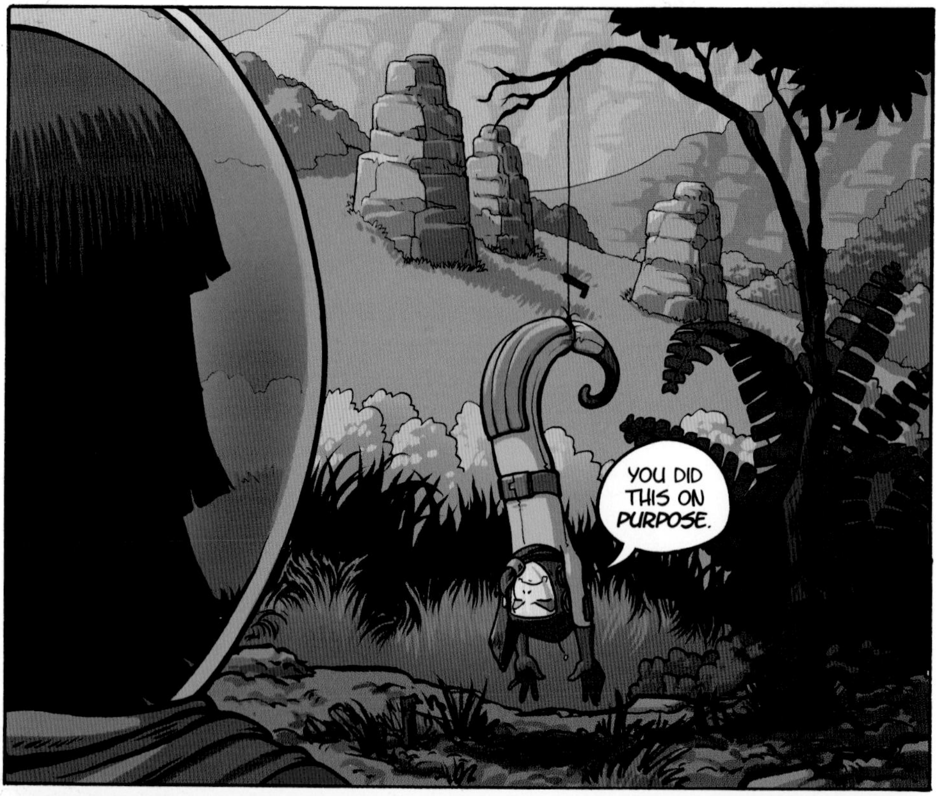
YOU DID THIS ON PURPOSE.

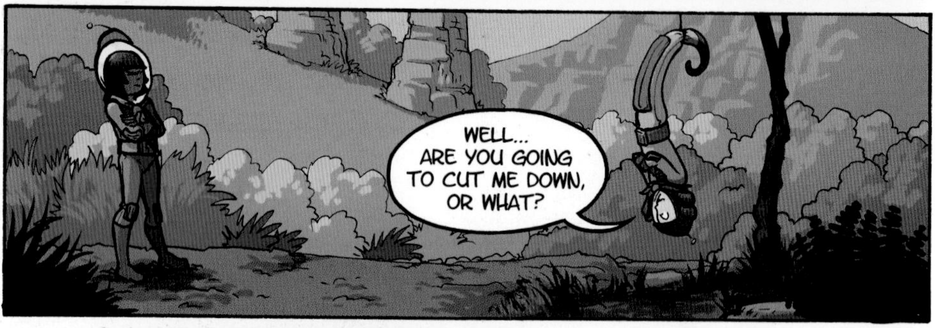
WELL... ARE YOU GOING TO CUT ME DOWN, OR WHAT?

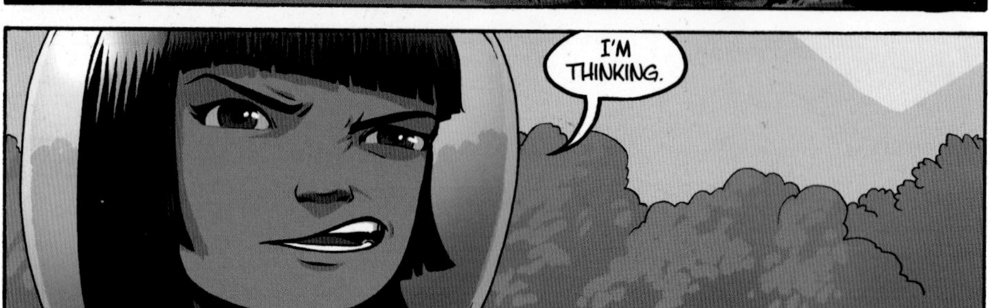
I'M THINKING.

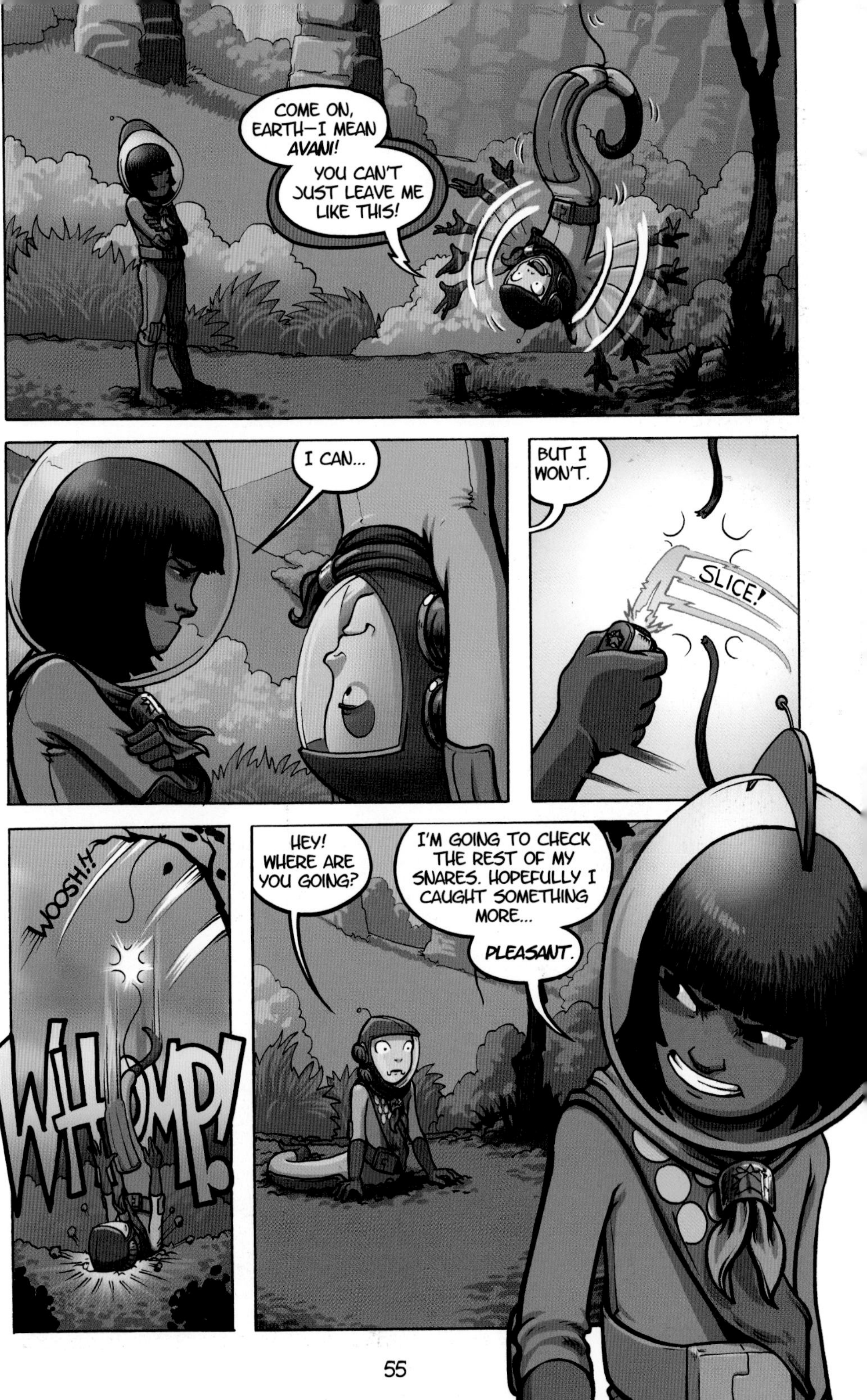
COME ON, EARTH—I MEAN AVANI!
YOU CAN'T JUST LEAVE ME LIKE THIS!
I CAN...
BUT I WON'T.
SLICE!
WOOSH!!
WHOMP!
HEY! WHERE ARE YOU GOING?
I'M GOING TO CHECK THE REST OF MY SNARES. HOPEFULLY I CAUGHT SOMETHING MORE...
PLEASANT.

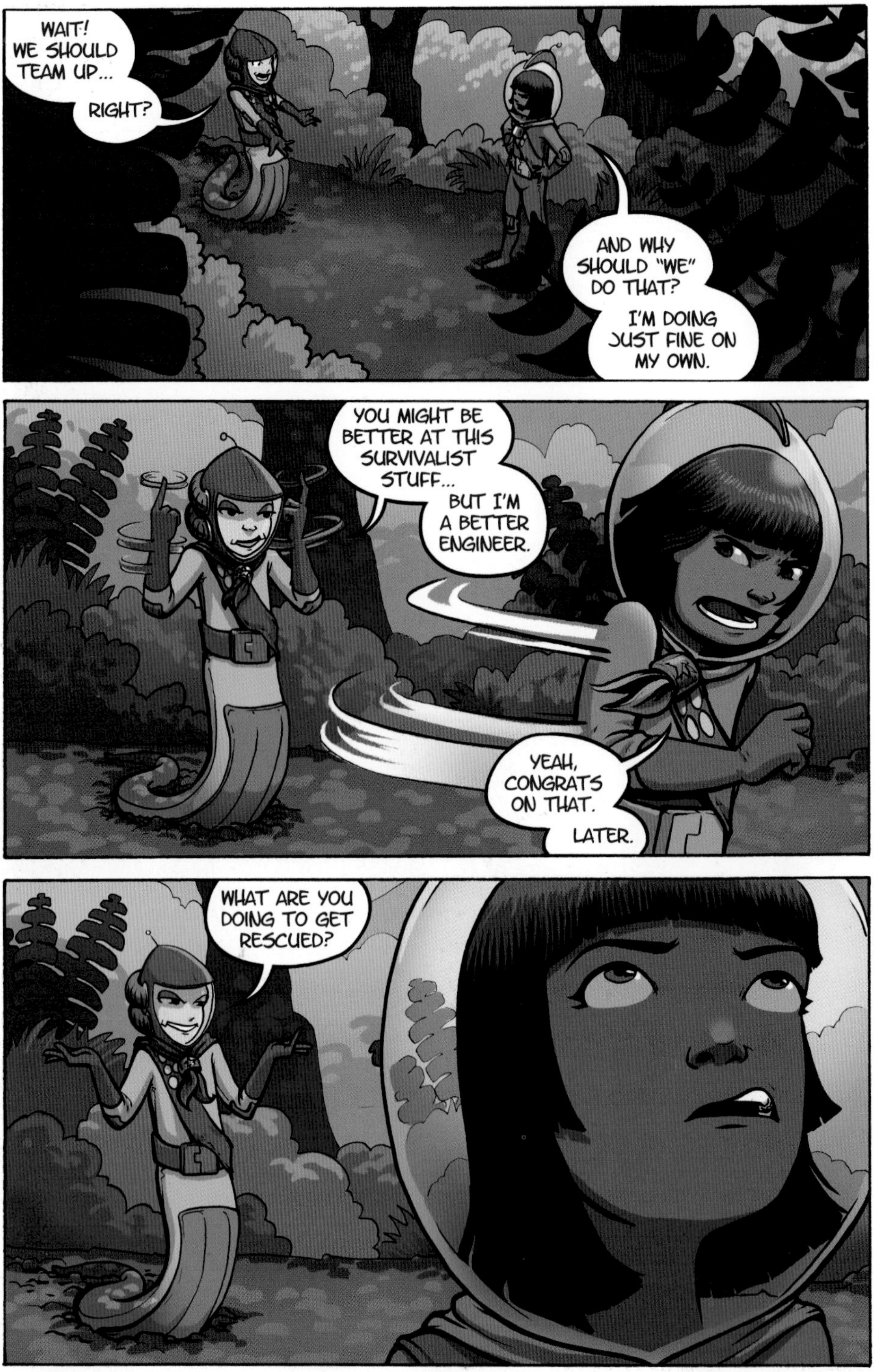
WAIT! WE SHOULD TEAM UP...
RIGHT?
AND WHY SHOULD "WE" DO THAT?
I'M DOING JUST FINE ON MY OWN.
YOU MIGHT BE BETTER AT THIS SURVIVALIST STUFF...
BUT I'M A BETTER ENGINEER.
YEAH, CONGRATS ON THAT.
LATER.
WHAT ARE YOU DOING TO GET RESCUED?

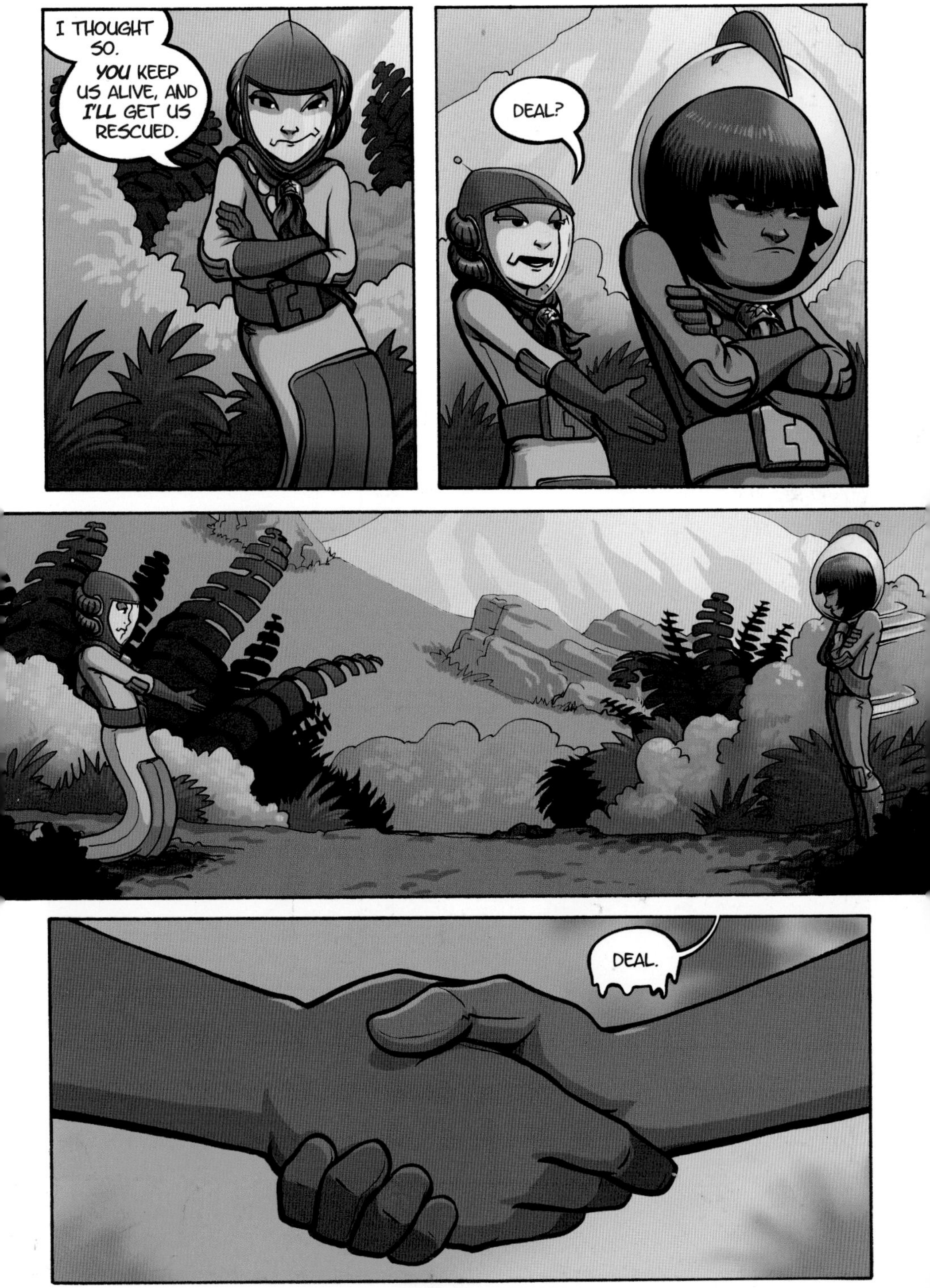
I THOUGHT SO. YOU KEEP US ALIVE, AND I'LL GET US RESCUED.
DEAL?
DEAL.

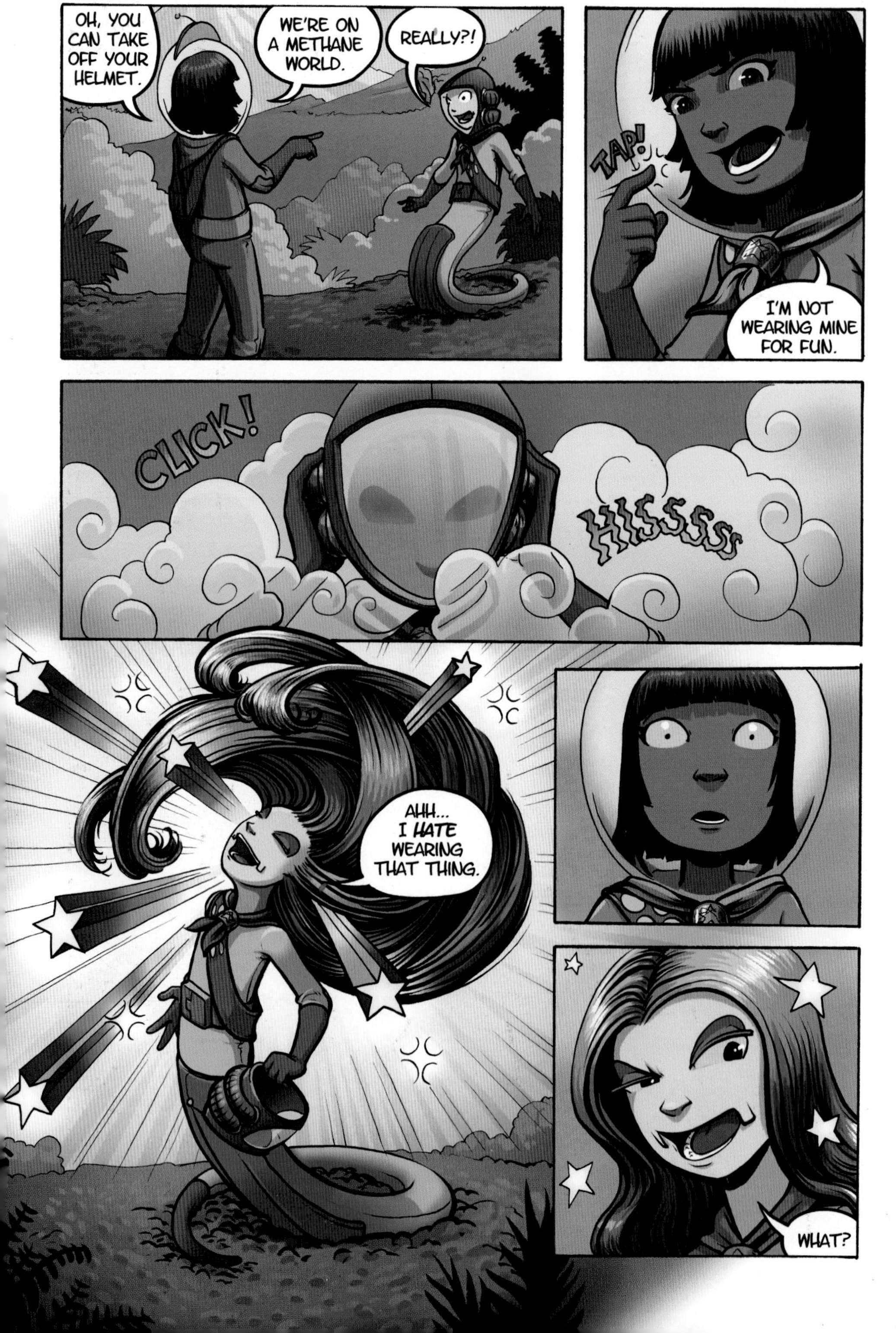
OH, YOU CAN TAKE OFF YOUR HELMET.
WE'RE ON A METHANE WORLD.
REALLY?!
TAP!
I'M NOT WEARING MINE FOR FUN.
CLICK!
HISSSSS
AHH... I HATE WEARING THAT THING.
WHAT?

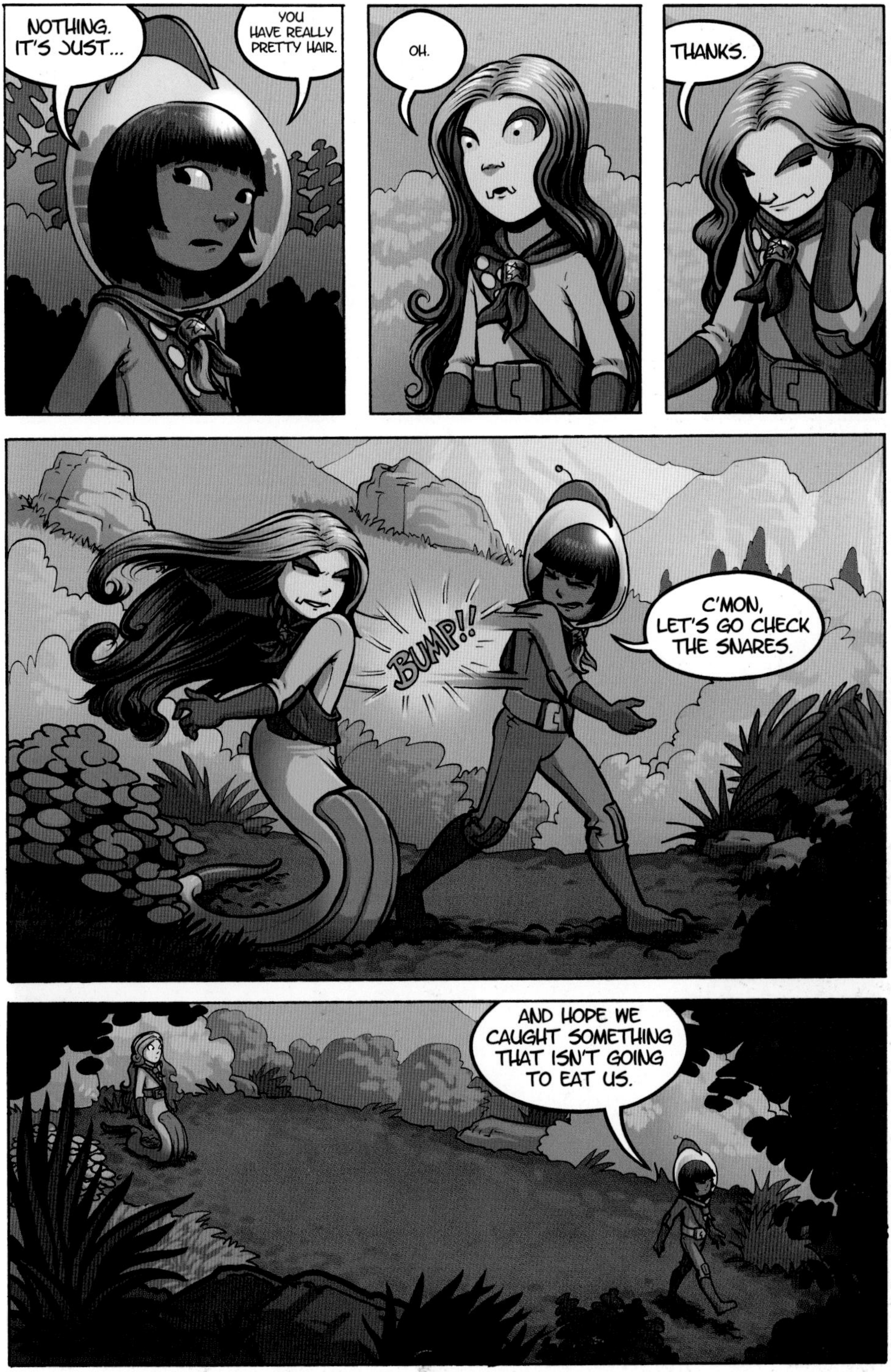
NOTHING. IT'S JUST...
YOU HAVE REALLY PRETTY HAIR.
OH.
THANKS.
BUMP!!
C'MON, LET'S GO CHECK THE SNARES.
AND HOPE WE CAUGHT SOMETHING THAT ISN'T GOING TO EAT US.

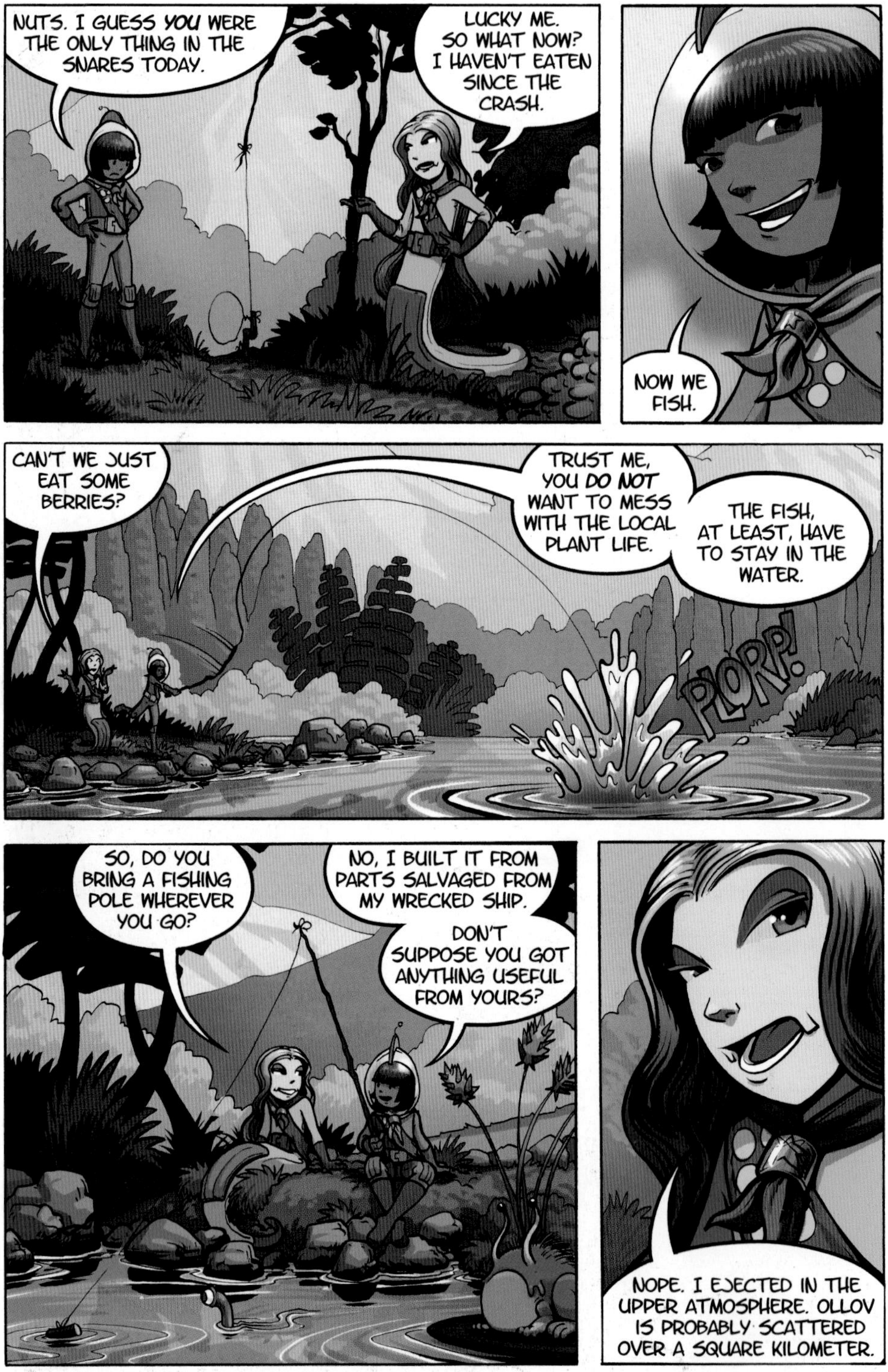
NUTS. I GUESS YOU WERE THE ONLY THING IN THE SNARES TODAY.
LUCKY ME. SO WHAT NOW? I HAVEN'T EATEN SINCE THE CRASH.
NOW WE FISH.
CAN'T WE JUST EAT SOME BERRIES?
TRUST ME, YOU DO NOT WANT TO MESS WITH THE LOCAL PLANT LIFE.
THE FISH, AT LEAST, HAVE TO STAY IN THE WATER.
PLORP!
SO, DO YOU BRING A FISHING POLE WHEREVER YOU GO?
NO, I BUILT IT FROM PARTS SALVAGED FROM MY WRECKED SHIP.
DON'T SUPPOSE YOU GOT ANYTHING USEFUL FROM YOURS?
NOPE. I EJECTED IN THE UPPER ATMOSPHERE. OLLOV IS PROBABLY SCATTERED OVER A SQUARE KILOMETER.

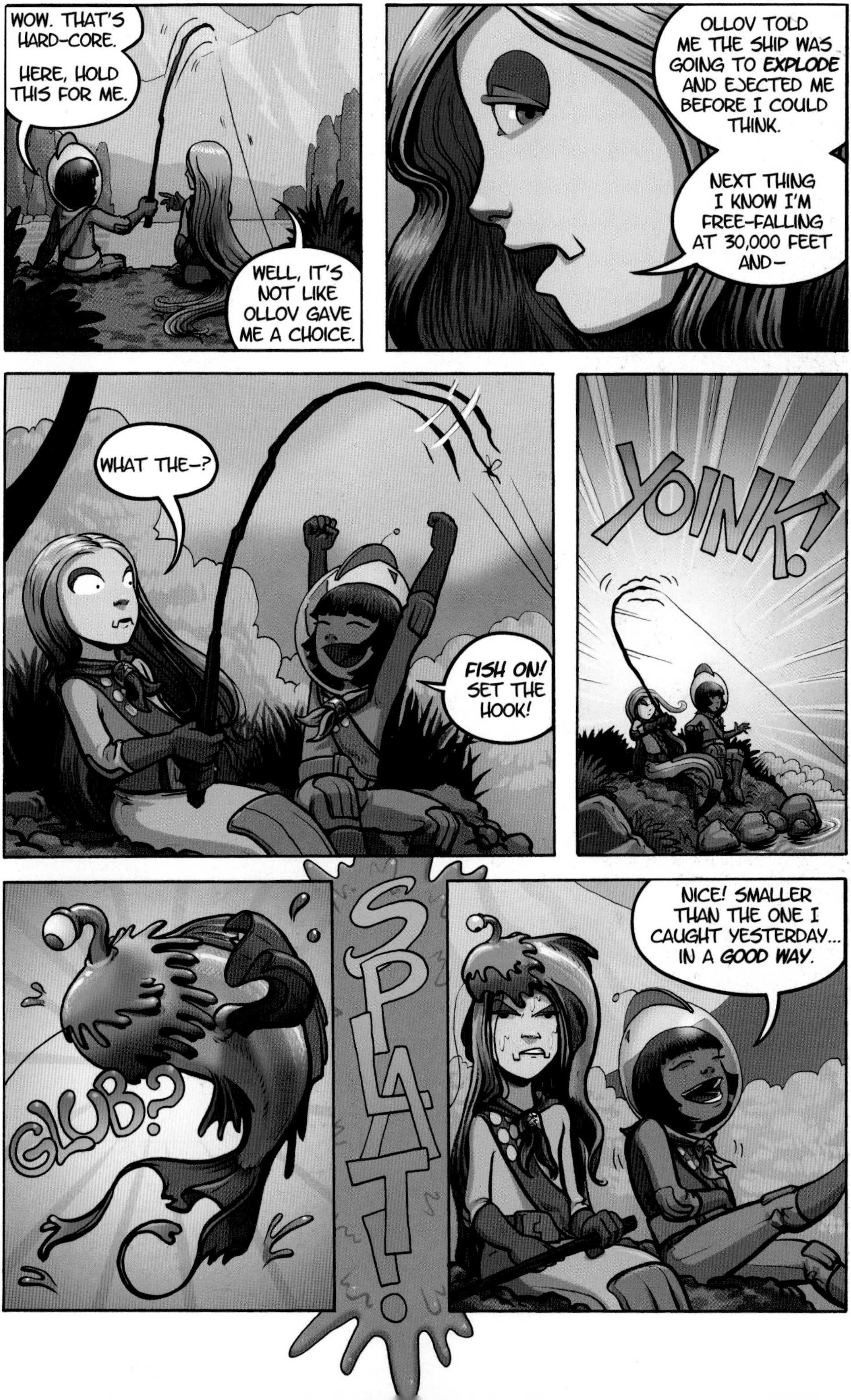
WOW. THAT'S HARD-CORE.
HERE, HOLD THIS FOR ME.
WELL, IT'S NOT LIKE OLLOV GAVE ME A CHOICE.
OLLOV TOLD ME THE SHIP WAS GOING TO EXPLODE AND EJECTED ME BEFORE I COULD THINK.
NEXT THING I KNOW I'M FREE-FALLING AT 30,000 FEET AND–
WHAT THE–?
FISH ON! SET THE HOOK!
YOINK!
GLUB?
SPLAT!
NICE! SMALLER THAN THE ONE I CAUGHT YESTERDAY... IN A GOOD WAY.

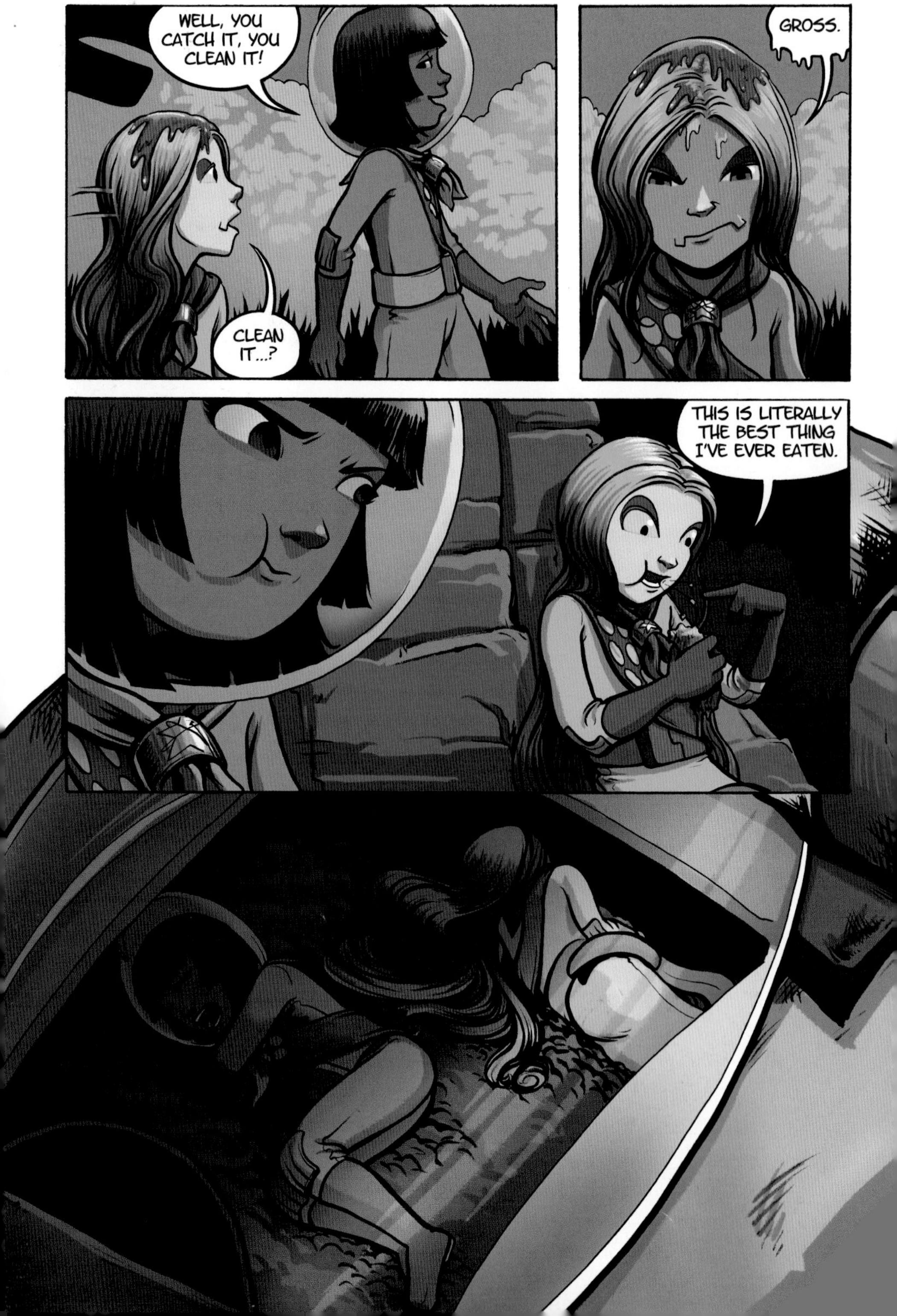
WELL, YOU CATCH IT, YOU CLEAN IT!
CLEAN IT...?
GROSS.
THIS IS LITERALLY THE BEST THING I'VE EVER EATEN.

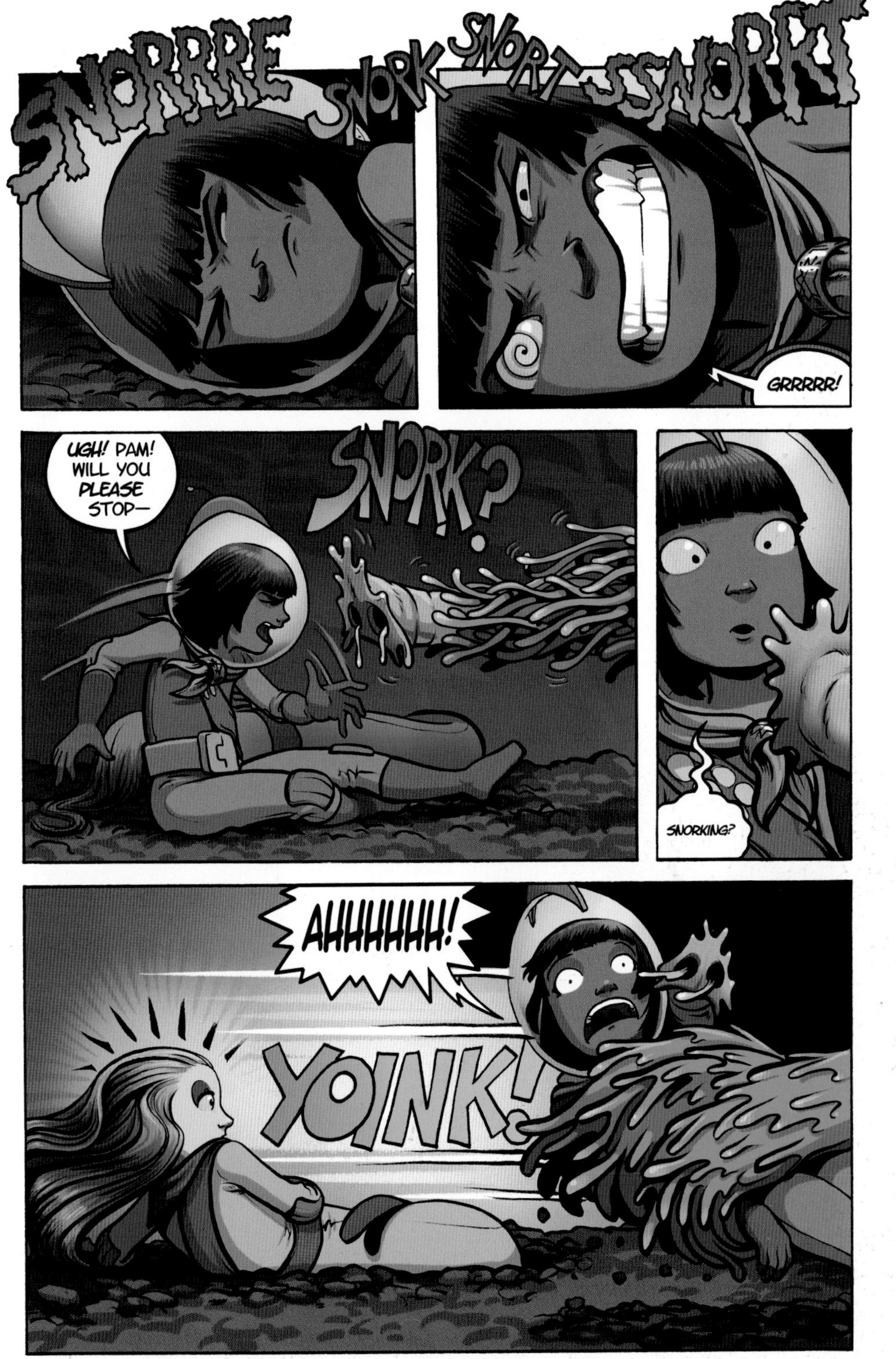
SNORRRE
SNORK
SNORT
SSNORRRT
GRRRRR!
SNORK?
UGH! PAM! WILL YOU PLEASE STOP—
SNORKING?
AHHHHHH!
YOINK!

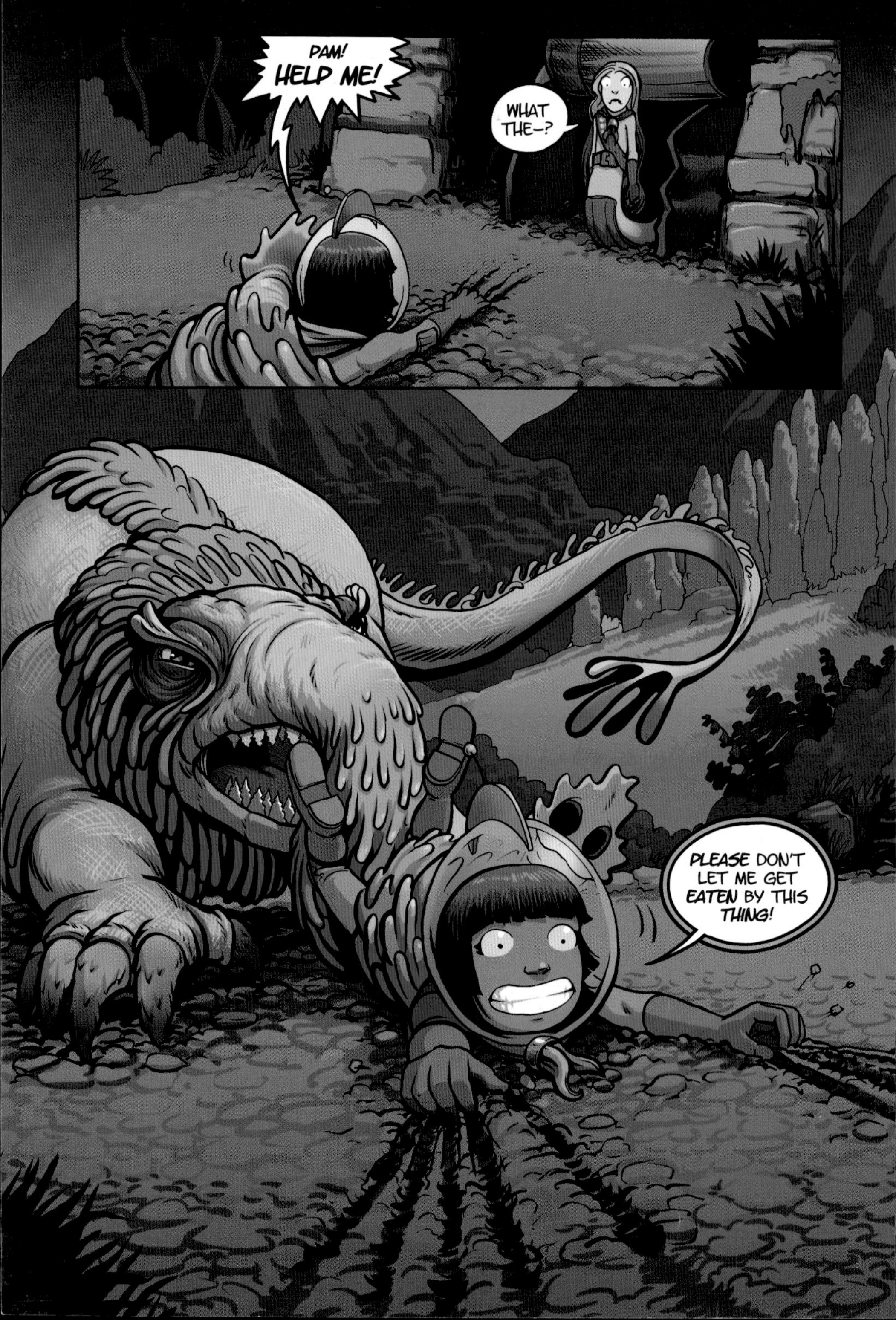
PAM! HELP ME!
WHAT THE–?
PLEASE DON'T LET ME GET EATEN BY THIS THING!

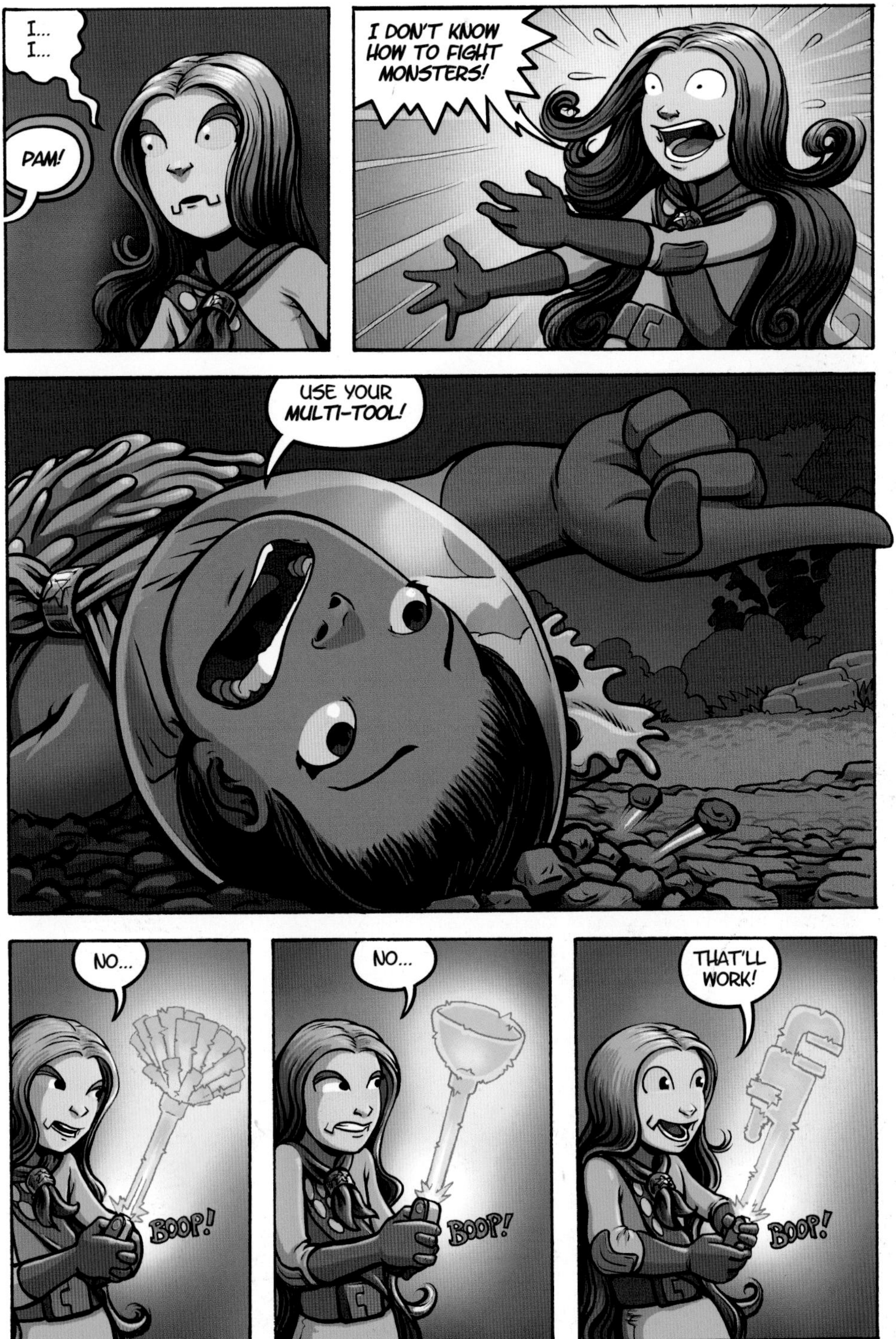
I...
I...
PAM!
I DON'T KNOW HOW TO FIGHT MONSTERS!
USE YOUR MULTI-TOOL!
NO...
BOOP!
NO...
BOOP!
THAT'LL WORK!
BOOP!

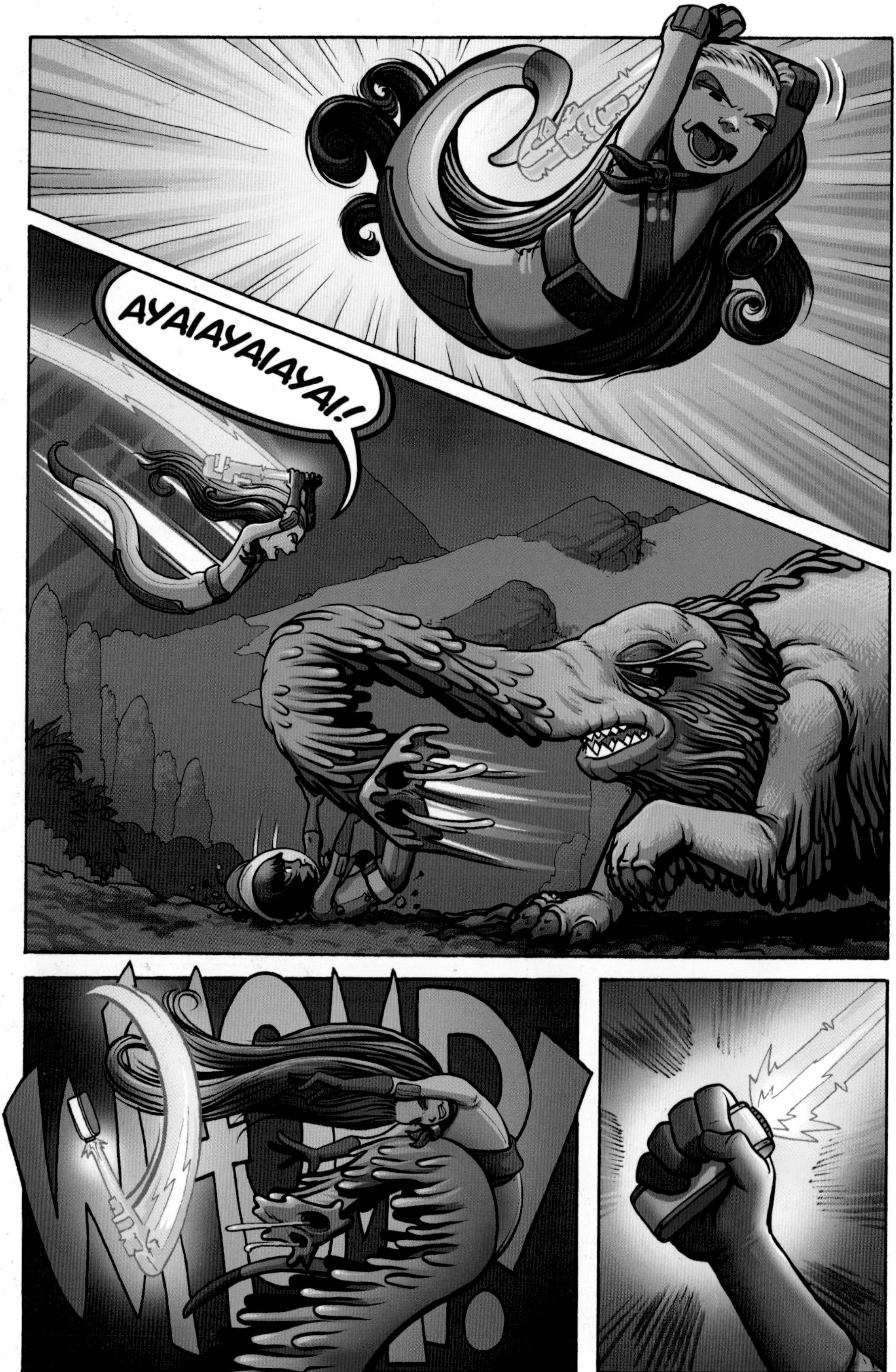
AYAIAYAIAYAI!!

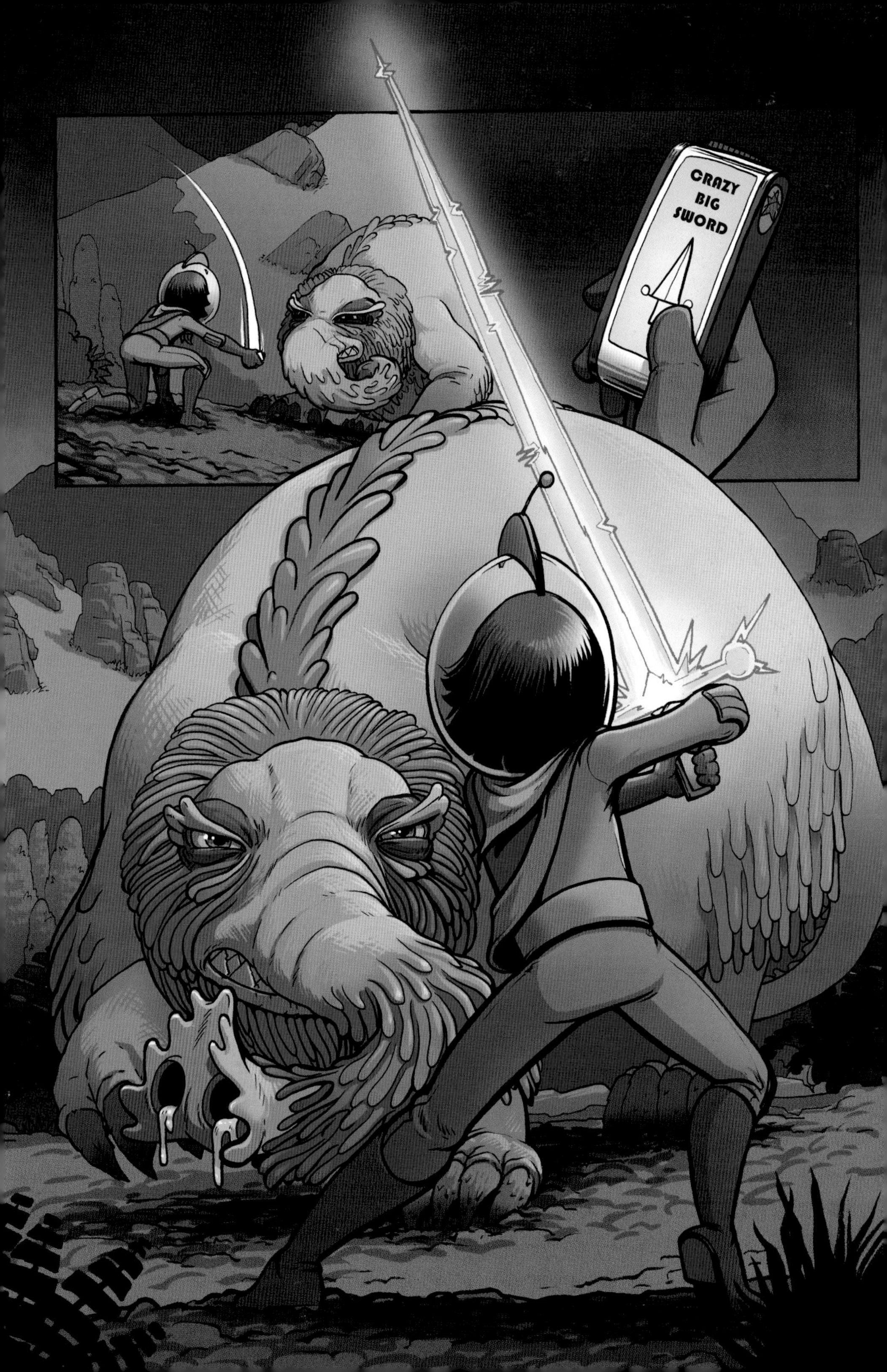
CRAZY
BIG
SWORD

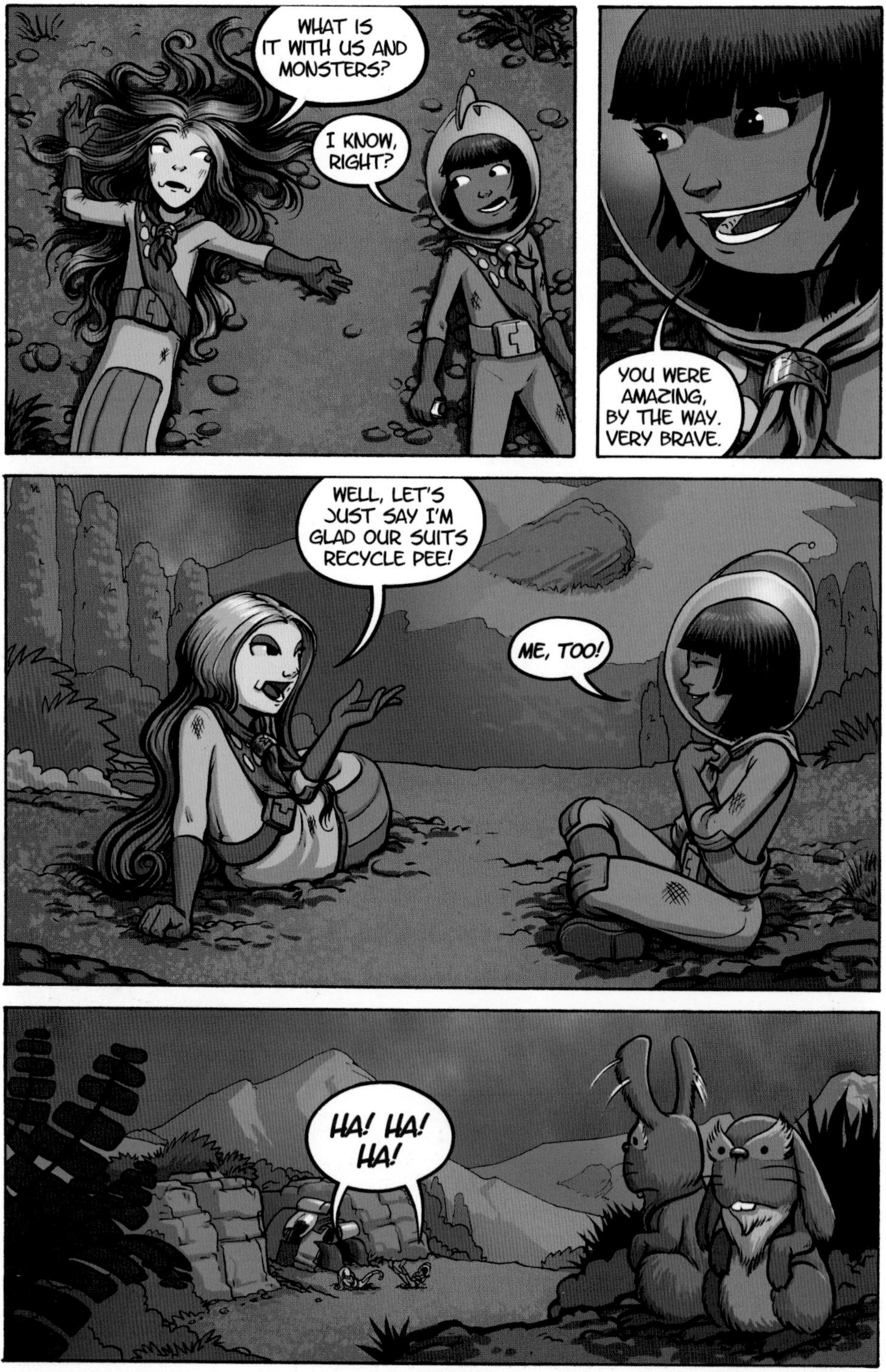
WHAT IS IT WITH US AND MONSTERS?
I KNOW, RIGHT?
YOU WERE AMAZING, BY THE WAY. VERY BRAVE.
WELL, LET'S JUST SAY I'M GLAD OUR SUITS RECYCLE PEE!
ME, TOO!
HA! HA! HA!

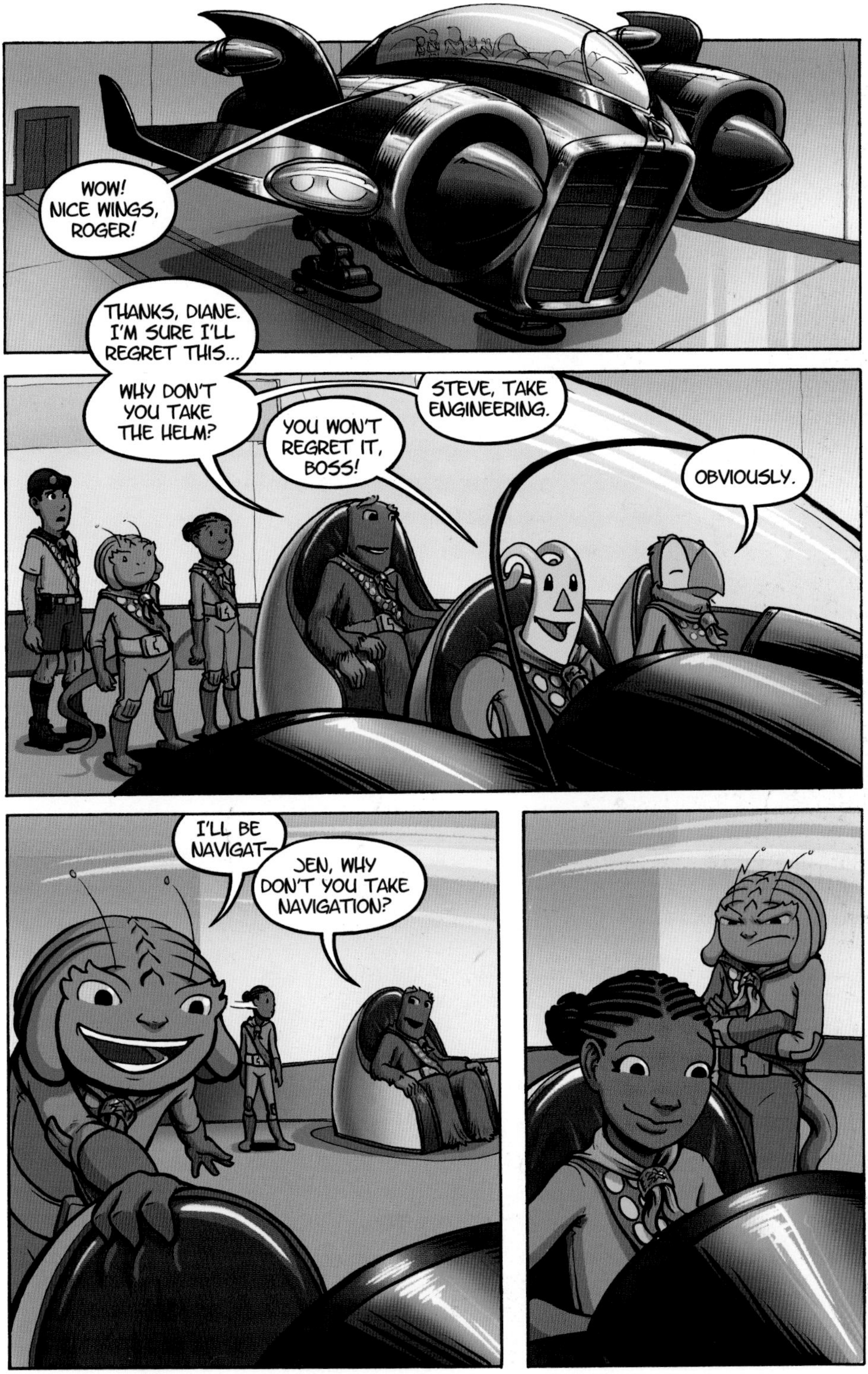
WOW! NICE WINGS, ROGER!
THANKS, DIANE. I'M SURE I'LL REGRET THIS...
WHY DON'T YOU TAKE THE HELM?
STEVE, TAKE ENGINEERING.
YOU WON'T REGRET IT, BOSS!
OBVIOUSLY.
I'LL BE NAVIGAT—
JEN, WHY DON'T YOU TAKE NAVIGATION?

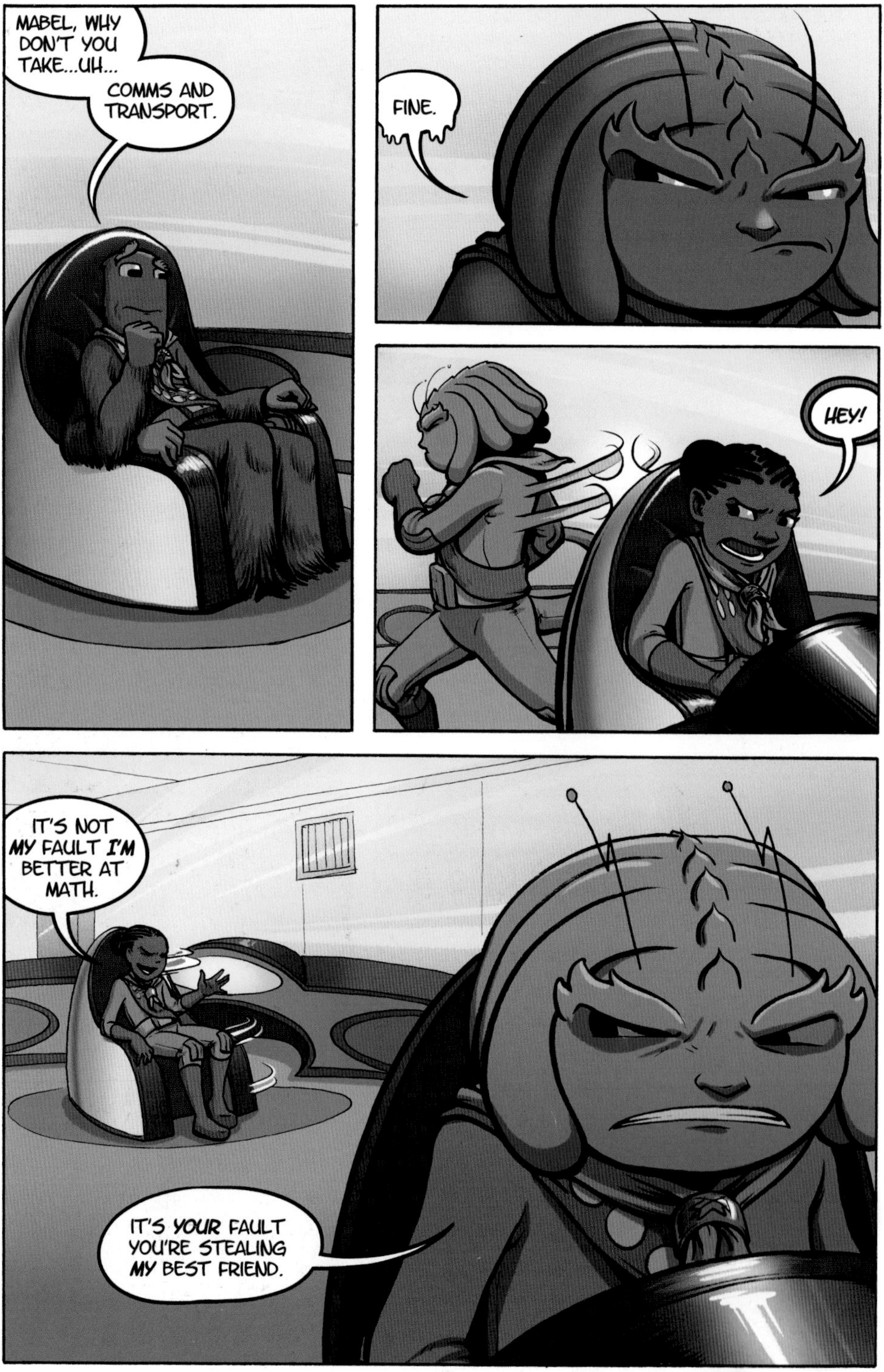
MABEL, WHY DON'T YOU TAKE...UH...
COMMS AND TRANSPORT.
FINE.
HEY!
IT'S NOT MY FAULT I'M BETTER AT MATH.
IT'S YOUR FAULT YOU'RE STEALING MY BEST FRIEND.

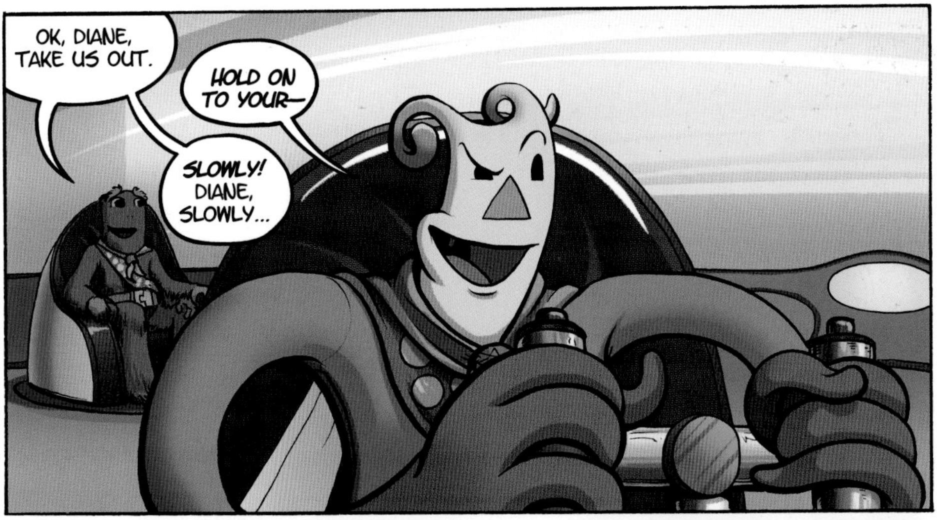
OK, DIANE, TAKE US OUT.
HOLD ON TO YOUR—
SLOWLY! DIANE, SLOWLY...

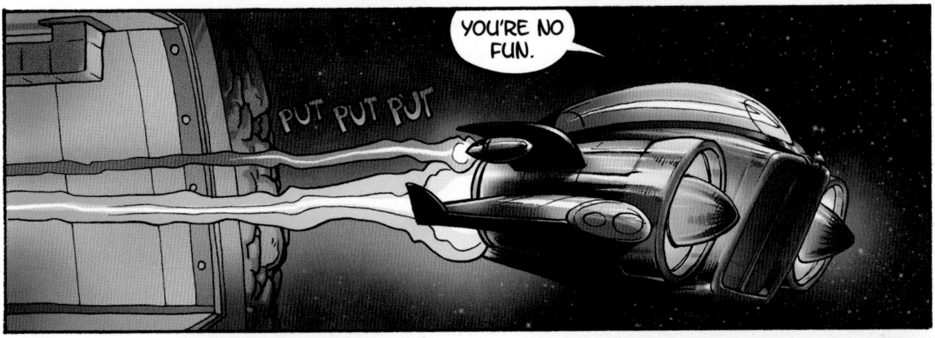
YOU'RE NO FUN.
PUT PUT PUT

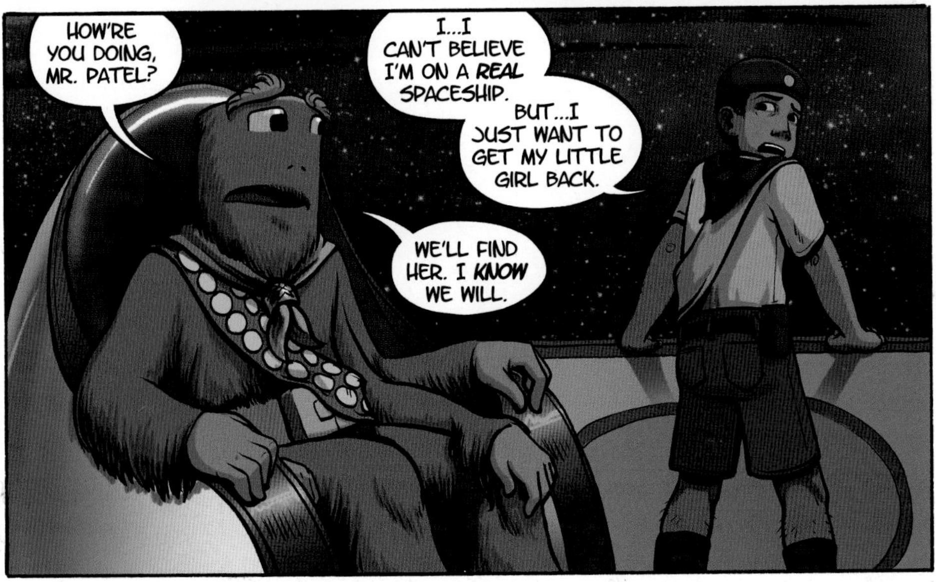
HOW'RE YOU DOING, MR. PATEL?
I...I CAN'T BELIEVE I'M ON A REAL SPACESHIP.
BUT...I JUST WANT TO GET MY LITTLE GIRL BACK.
WE'LL FIND HER. I KNOW WE WILL.

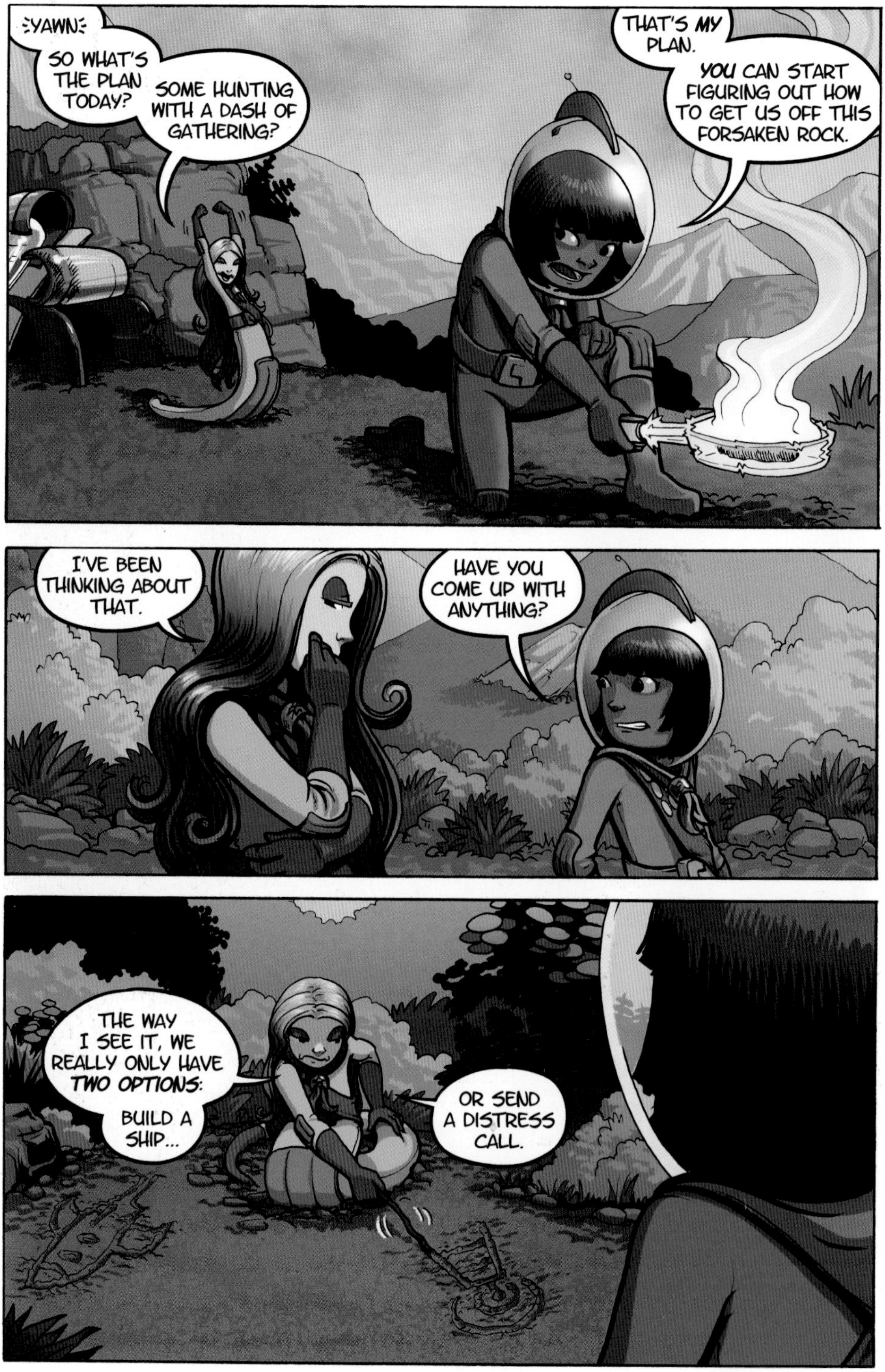

:YAWN:
SO WHAT'S THE PLAN TODAY?
SOME HUNTING WITH A DASH OF GATHERING?
THAT'S MY PLAN.
YOU CAN START FIGURING OUT HOW TO GET US OFF THIS FORSAKEN ROCK.
I'VE BEEN THINKING ABOUT THAT.
HAVE YOU COME UP WITH ANYTHING?
THE WAY I SEE IT, WE REALLY ONLY HAVE TWO OPTIONS:
BUILD A SHIP...
OR SEND A DISTRESS CALL.

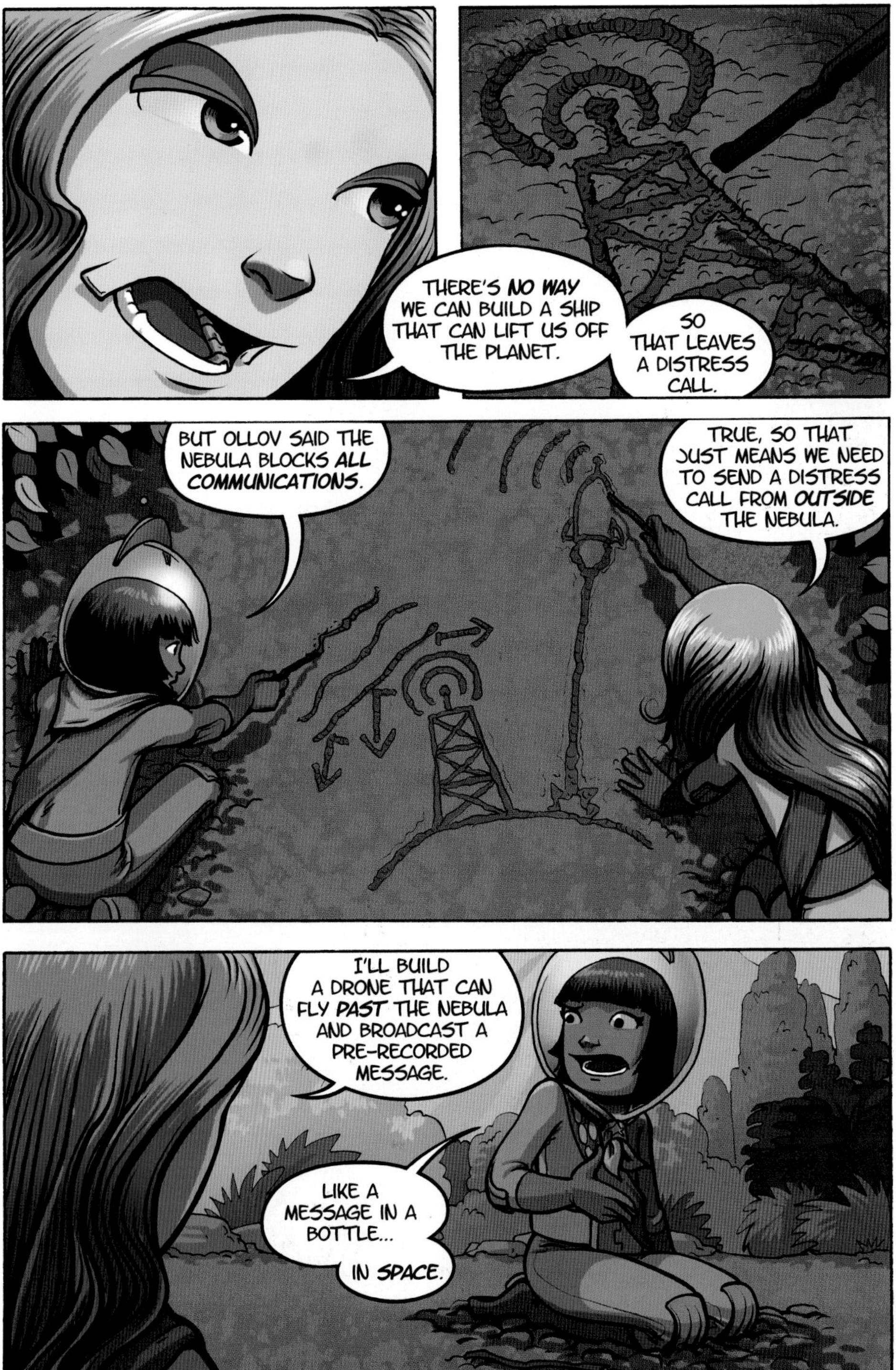
THERE'S NO WAY WE CAN BUILD A SHIP THAT CAN LIFT US OFF THE PLANET.
SO THAT LEAVES A DISTRESS CALL.
BUT OLLOV SAID THE NEBULA BLOCKS ALL COMMUNICATIONS.
TRUE, SO THAT JUST MEANS WE NEED TO SEND A DISTRESS CALL FROM OUTSIDE THE NEBULA.
I'LL BUILD A DRONE THAT CAN FLY PAST THE NEBULA AND BROADCAST A PRE-RECORDED MESSAGE.
LIKE A MESSAGE IN A BOTTLE...
IN SPACE.

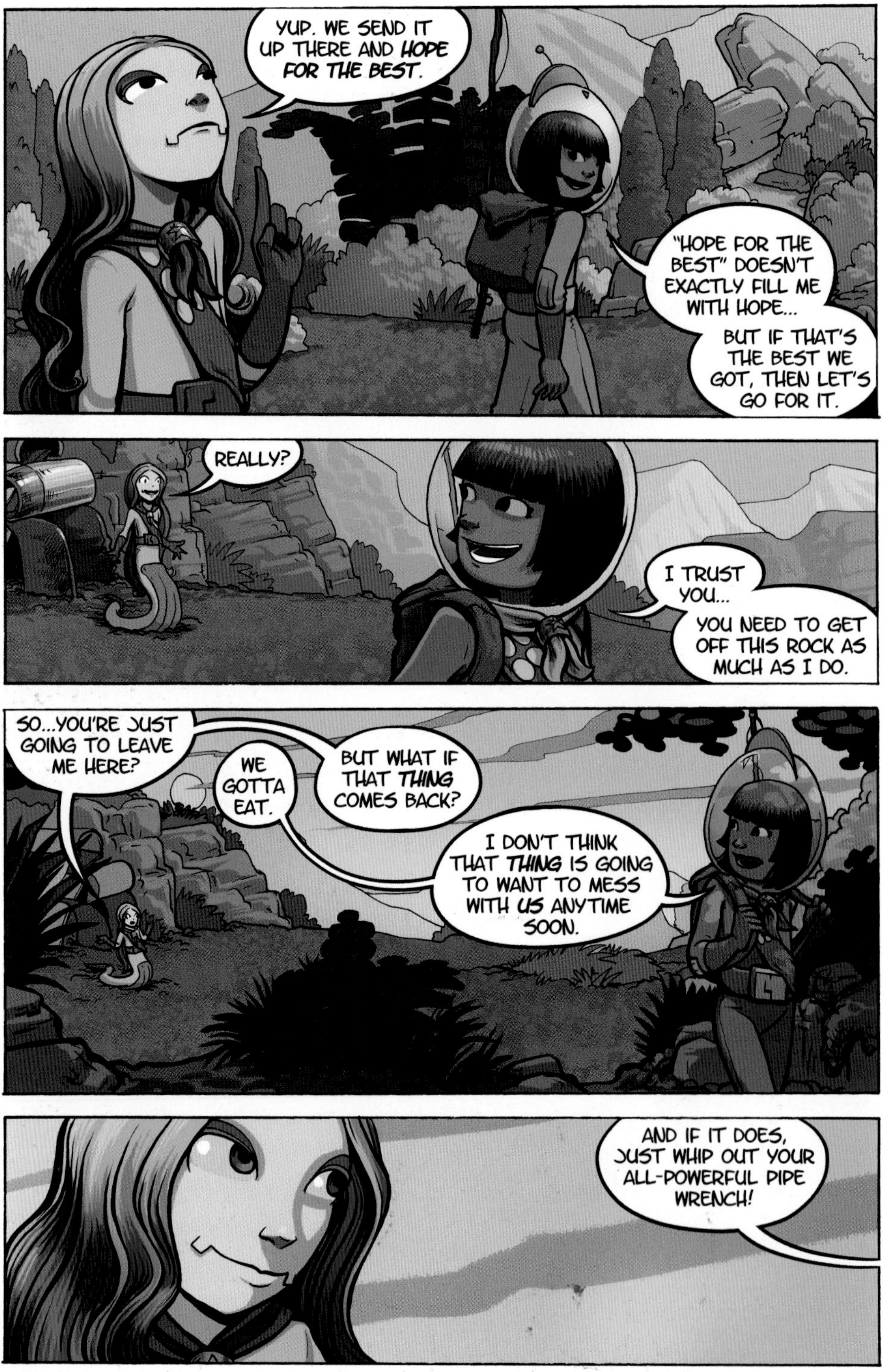
YUP. WE SEND IT UP THERE AND HOPE FOR THE BEST.
"HOPE FOR THE BEST" DOESN'T EXACTLY FILL ME WITH HOPE...
BUT IF THAT'S THE BEST WE GOT, THEN LET'S GO FOR IT.
REALLY?
I TRUST YOU...
YOU NEED TO GET OFF THIS ROCK AS MUCH AS I DO.
SO...YOU'RE JUST GOING TO LEAVE ME HERE?
WE GOTTA EAT.
BUT WHAT IF THAT THING COMES BACK?
I DON'T THINK THAT THING IS GOING TO WANT TO MESS WITH US ANYTIME SOON.
AND IF IT DOES, JUST WHIP OUT YOUR ALL-POWERFUL PIPE WRENCH!

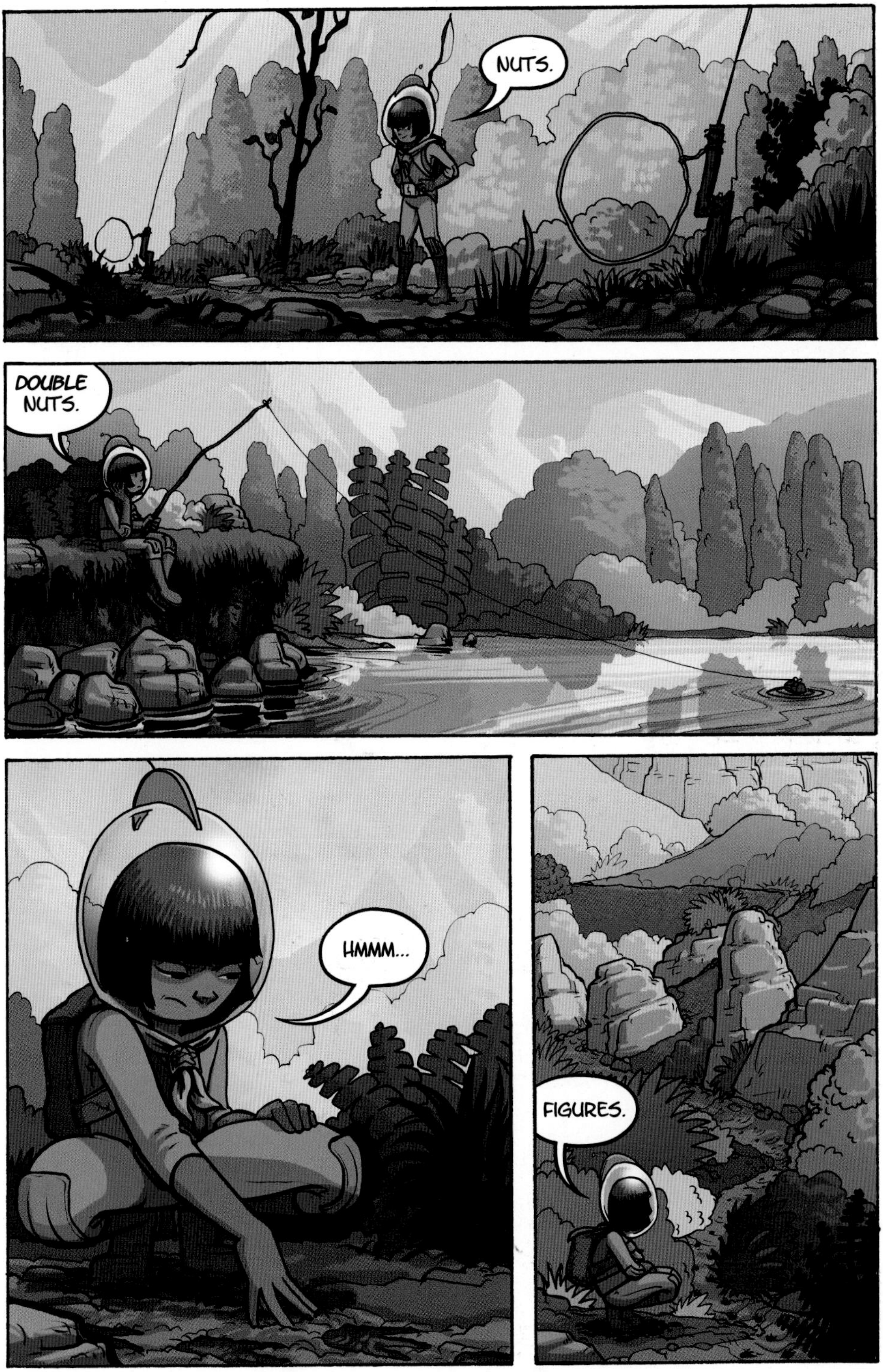
NUTS.
DOUBLE NUTS.
HMMM...
FIGURES.

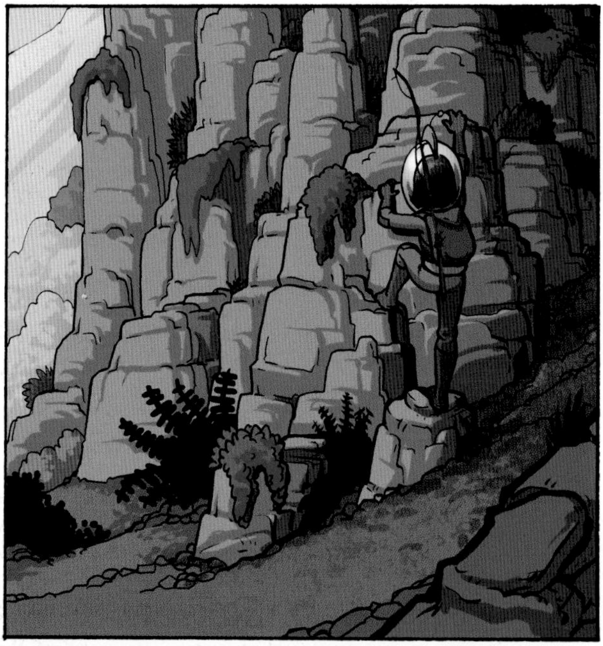

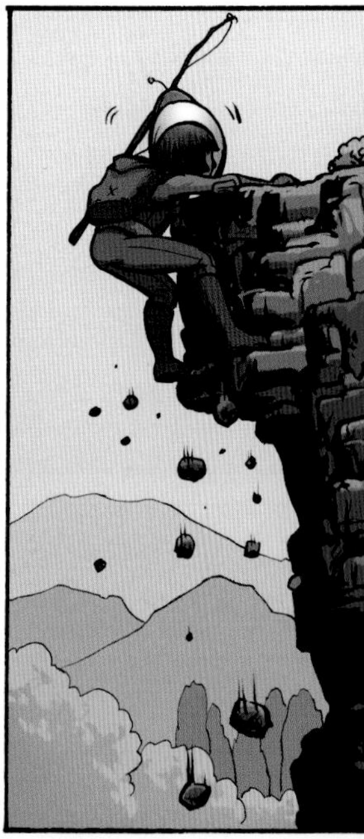

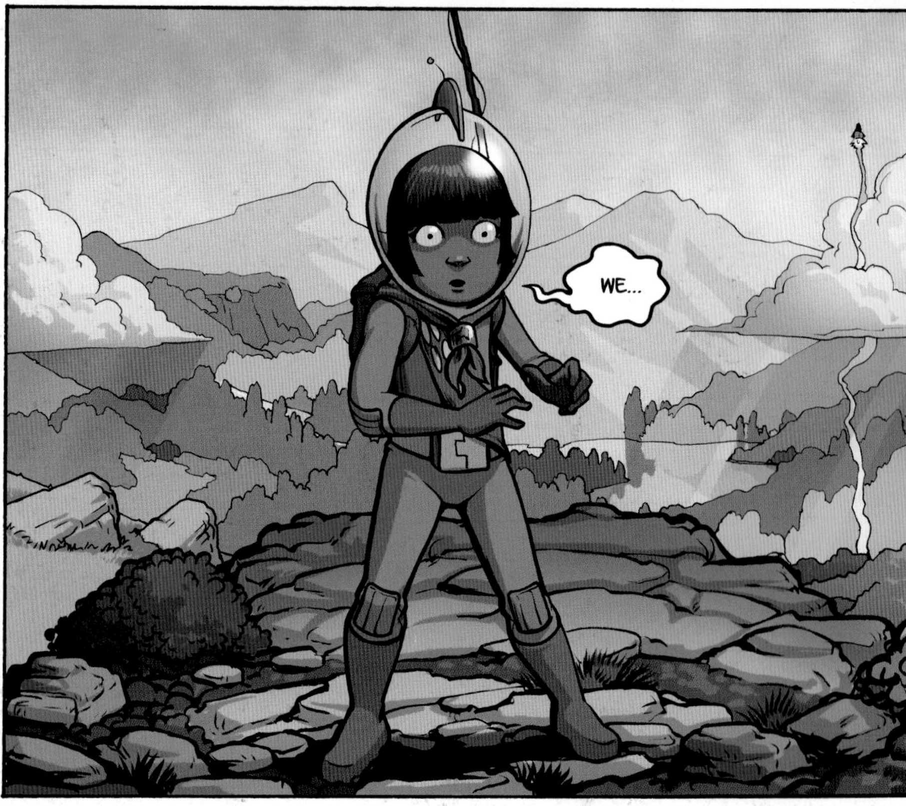
WE...

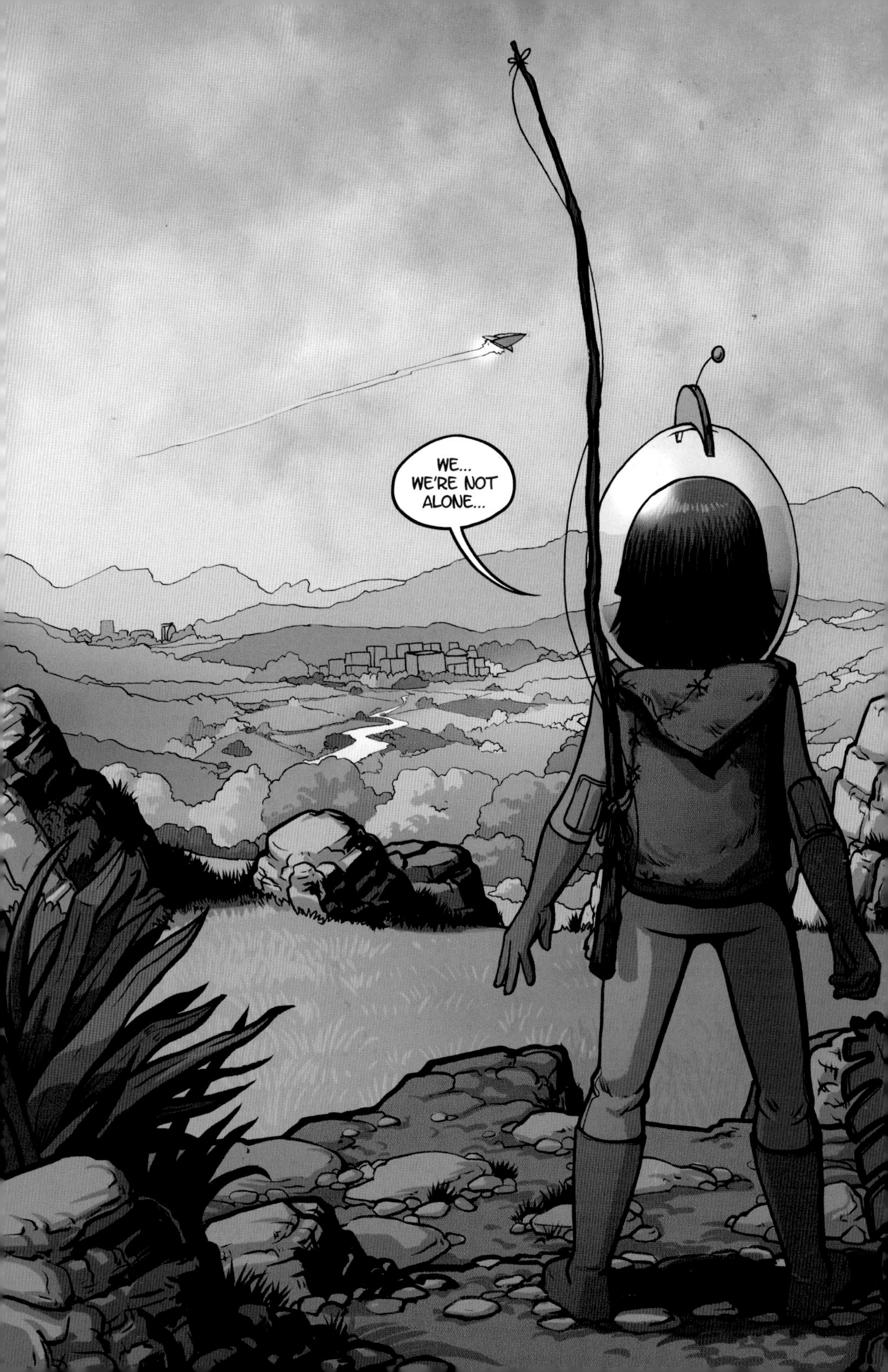
WE...
WE'RE NOT
ALONE...

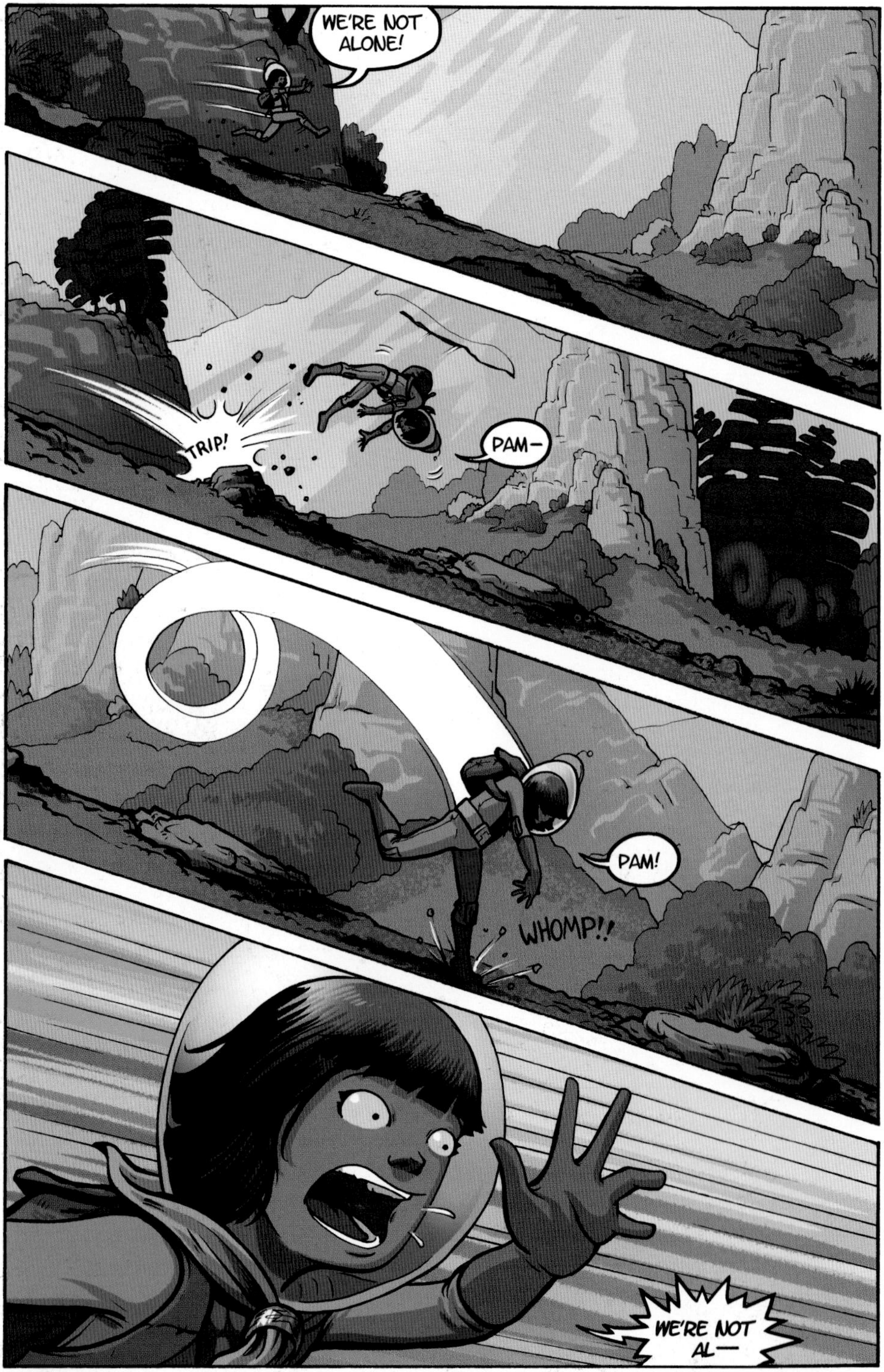
WE'RE NOT ALONE!
TRIP!
PAM—
PAM!
WHOMP!!
WE'RE NOT AL—

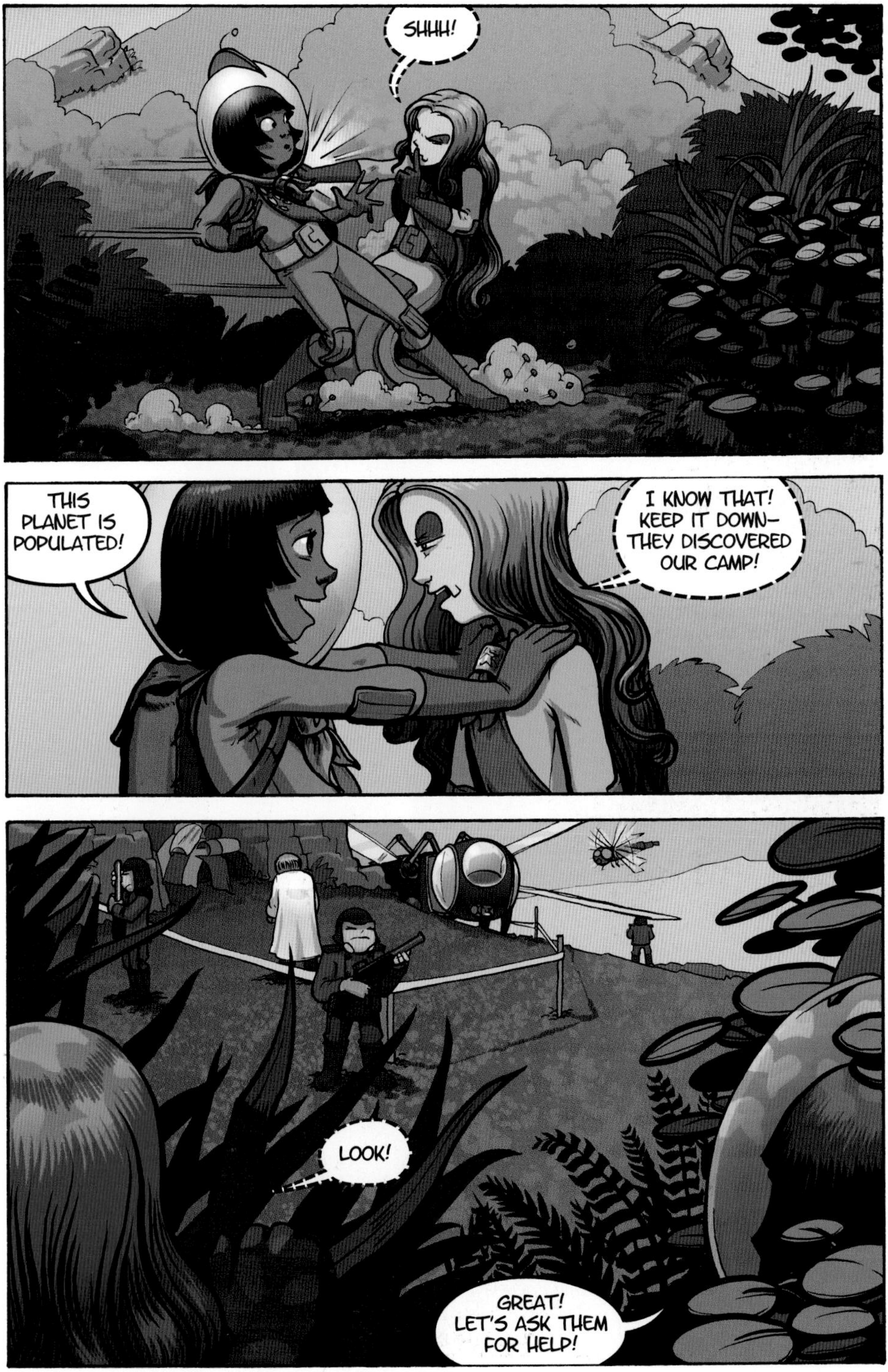
SHHH!
THIS PLANET IS POPULATED!
I KNOW THAT! KEEP IT DOWN— THEY DISCOVERED OUR CAMP!
LOOK!
GREAT! LET'S ASK THEM FOR HELP!

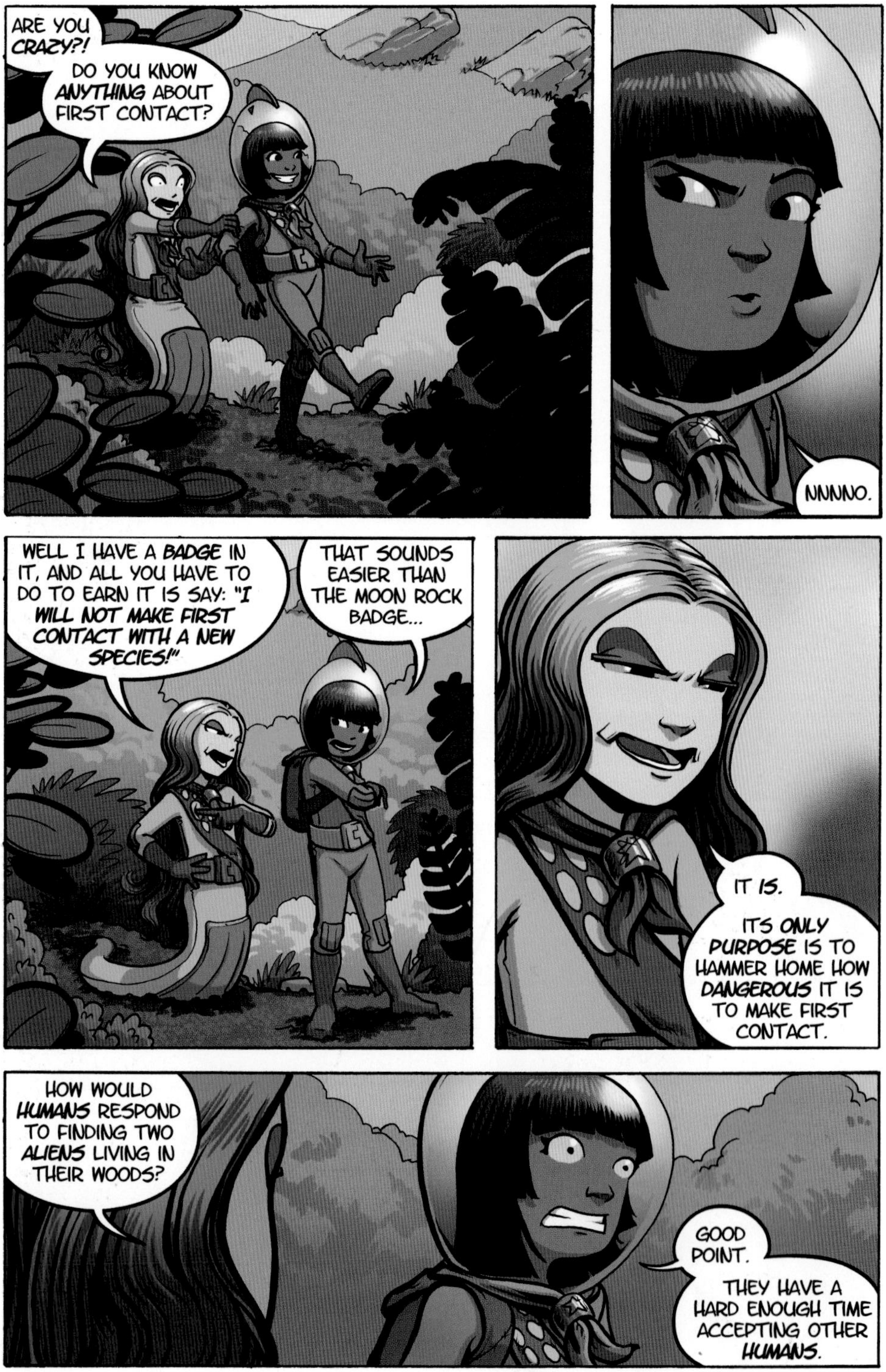
ARE YOU CRAZY?!
DO YOU KNOW ANYTHING ABOUT FIRST CONTACT?
NNNNO.
WELL I HAVE A BADGE IN IT, AND ALL YOU HAVE TO DO TO EARN IT IS SAY: "I WILL NOT MAKE FIRST CONTACT WITH A NEW SPECIES!"
THAT SOUNDS EASIER THAN THE MOON ROCK BADGE...
IT IS.
ITS ONLY PURPOSE IS TO HAMMER HOME HOW DANGEROUS IT IS TO MAKE FIRST CONTACT.
HOW WOULD HUMANS RESPOND TO FINDING TWO ALIENS LIVING IN THEIR WOODS?
GOOD POINT.
THEY HAVE A HARD ENOUGH TIME ACCEPTING OTHER HUMANS.

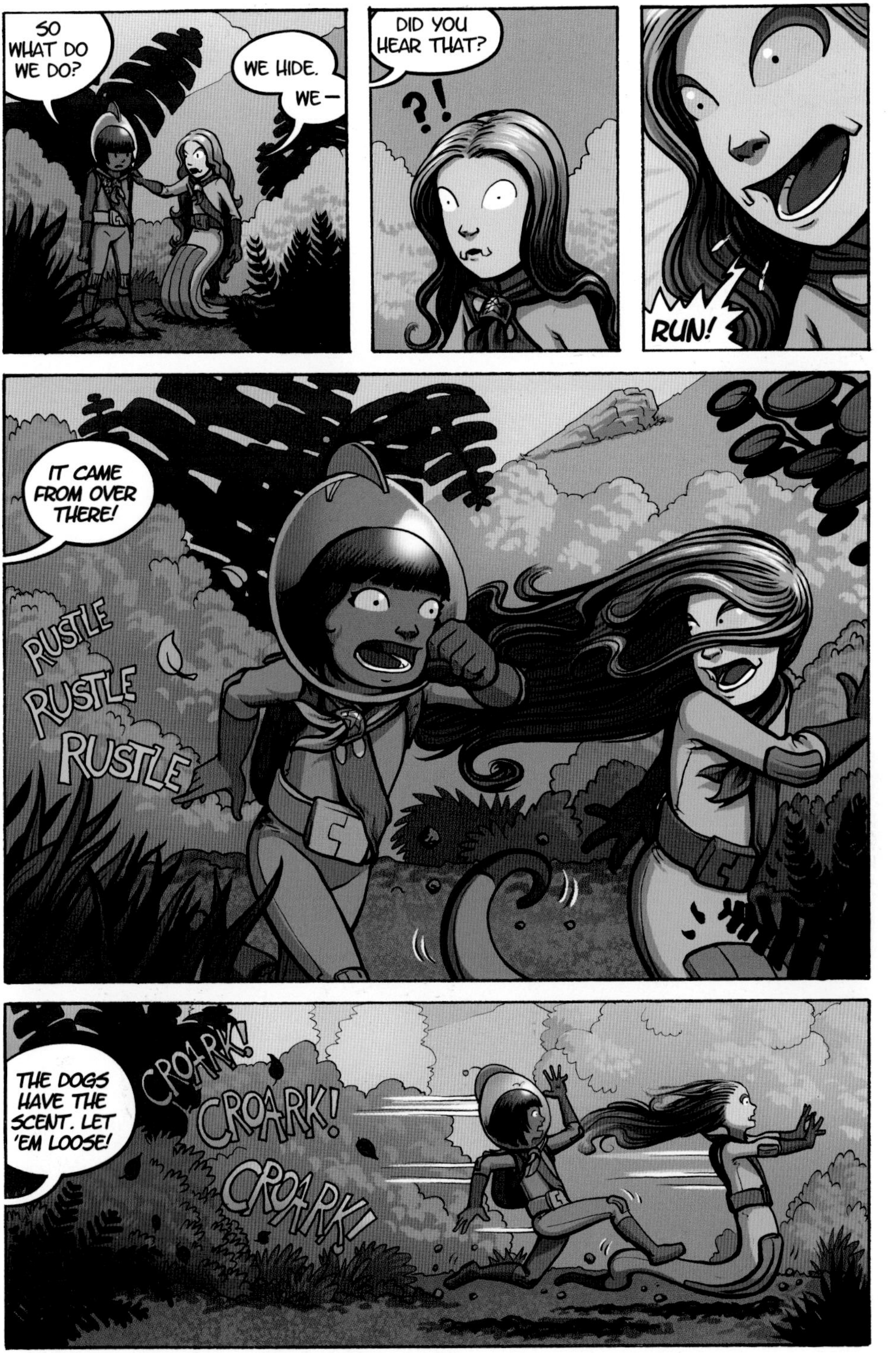
SO WHAT DO WE DO?
WE HIDE.
WE—
DID YOU HEAR THAT?
?!
RUN!
IT CAME FROM OVER THERE!
RUSTLE
RUSTLE
RUSTLE
THE DOGS HAVE THE SCENT. LET 'EM LOOSE!
CROARK!
CROARK!
CROARK!

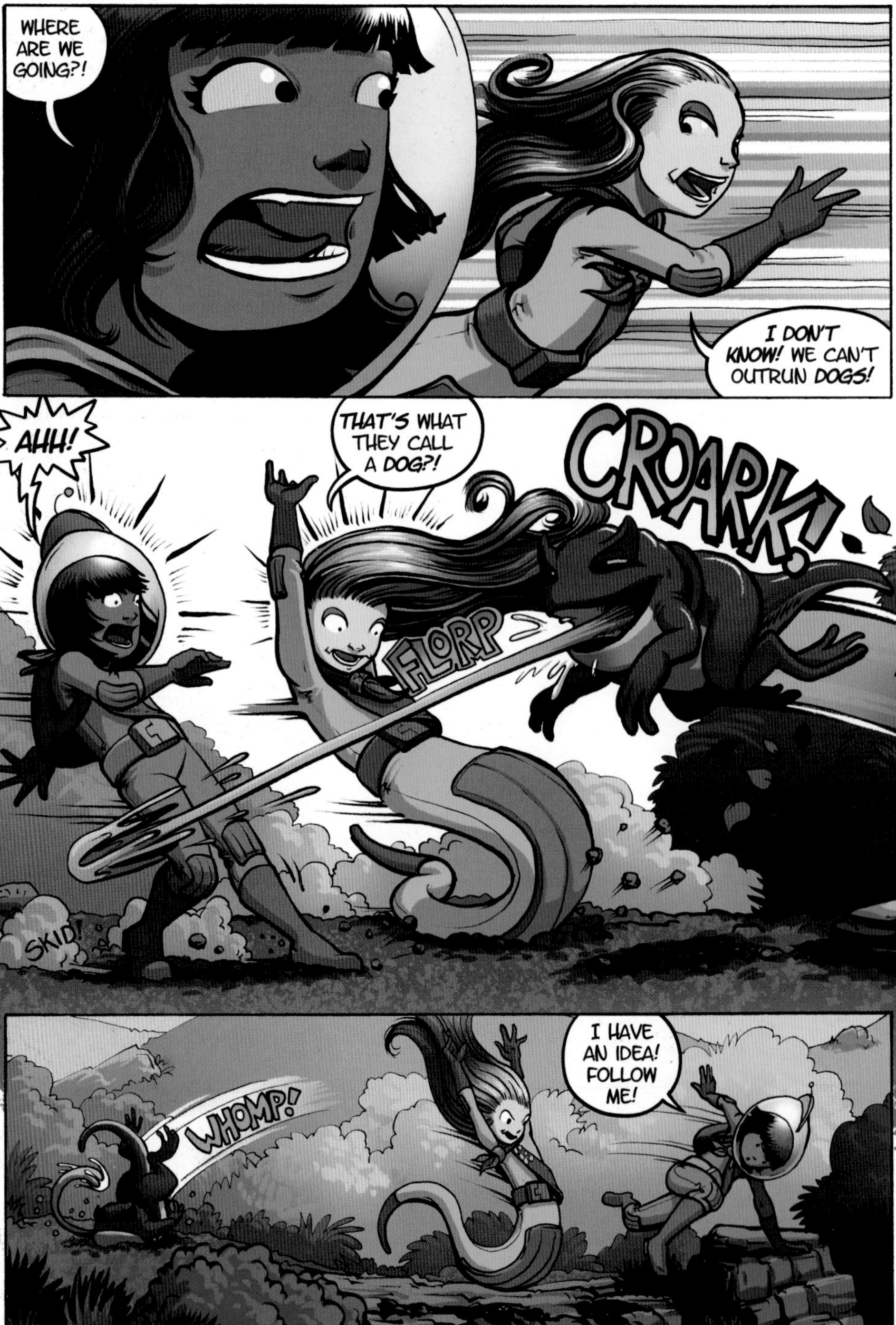
WHERE ARE WE GOING?!
I DON'T KNOW! WE CAN'T OUTRUN DOGS!
AHH!
THAT'S WHAT THEY CALL A DOG?!
CROARK!
FLORP
SKID!
WHOMP!
I HAVE AN IDEA! FOLLOW ME!

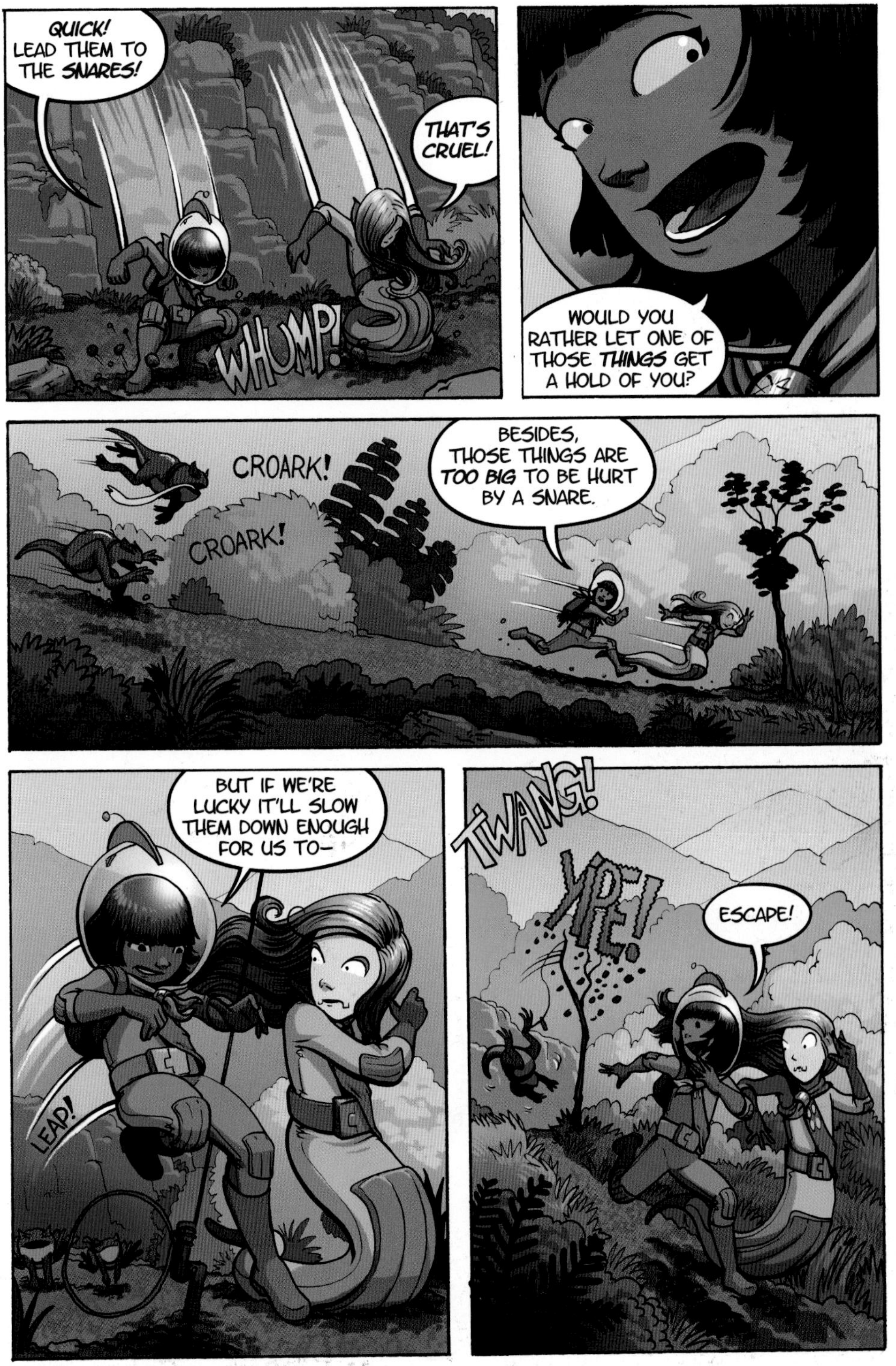
QUICK! LEAD THEM TO THE SNARES!
THAT'S CRUEL!
WHUMP!
WOULD YOU RATHER LET ONE OF THOSE THINGS GET A HOLD OF YOU?
CROARK!
CROARK!
BESIDES, THOSE THINGS ARE TOO BIG TO BE HURT BY A SNARE.
BUT IF WE'RE LUCKY IT'LL SLOW THEM DOWN ENOUGH FOR US TO—
LEAP!
TWANG!
YIPE!
ESCAPE!

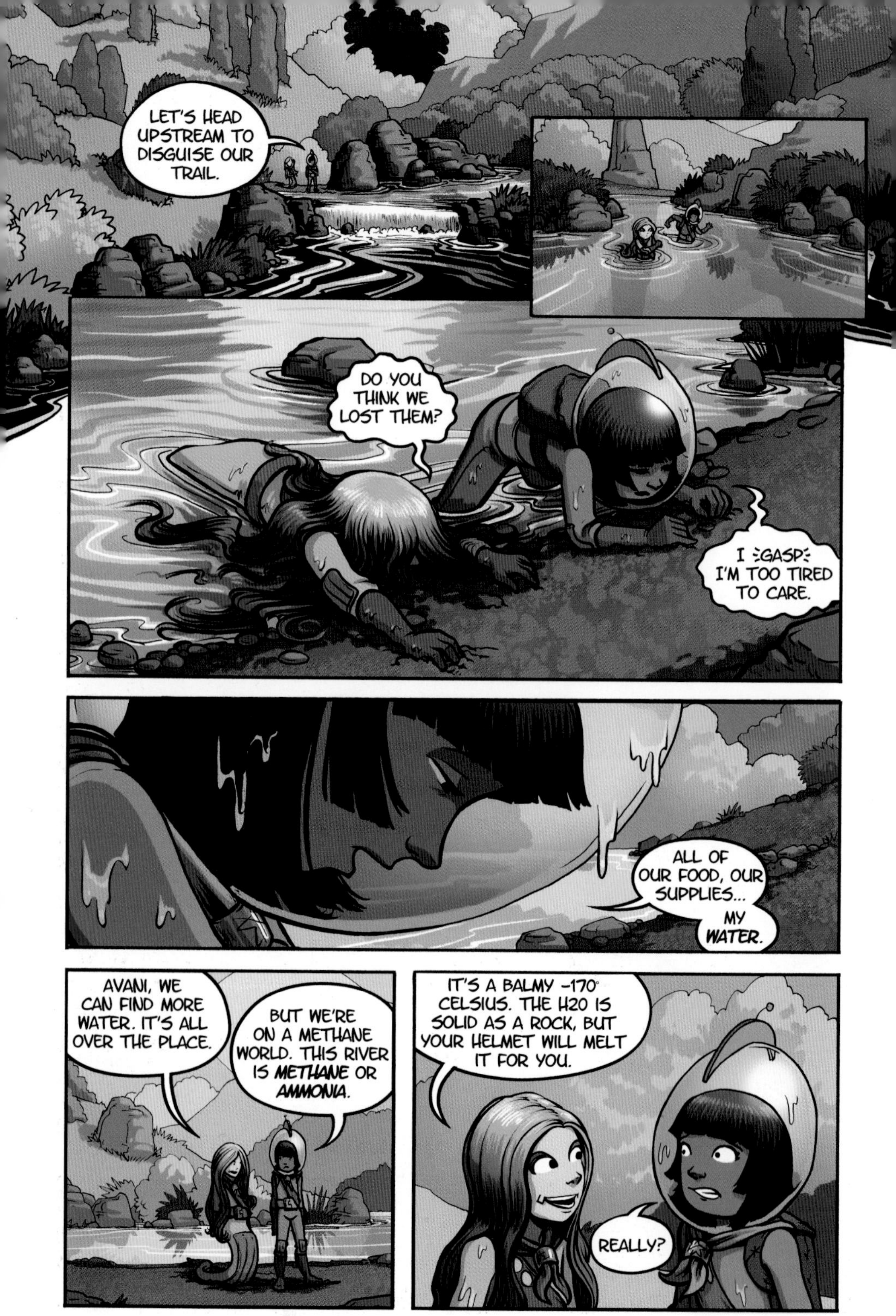
LET'S HEAD UPSTREAM TO DISGUISE OUR TRAIL.
DO YOU THINK WE LOST THEM?
I ⁝GASP⁝ I'M TOO TIRED TO CARE.
ALL OF OUR FOOD, OUR SUPPLIES... MY **WATER**.
AVANI, WE CAN FIND MORE WATER. IT'S ALL OVER THE PLACE.
BUT WE'RE ON A METHANE WORLD. THIS RIVER IS **METHANE** OR **AMMONIA**.
IT'S A BALMY -170° CELSIUS. THE H2O IS SOLID AS A ROCK, BUT YOUR HELMET WILL MELT IT FOR YOU.
REALLY?

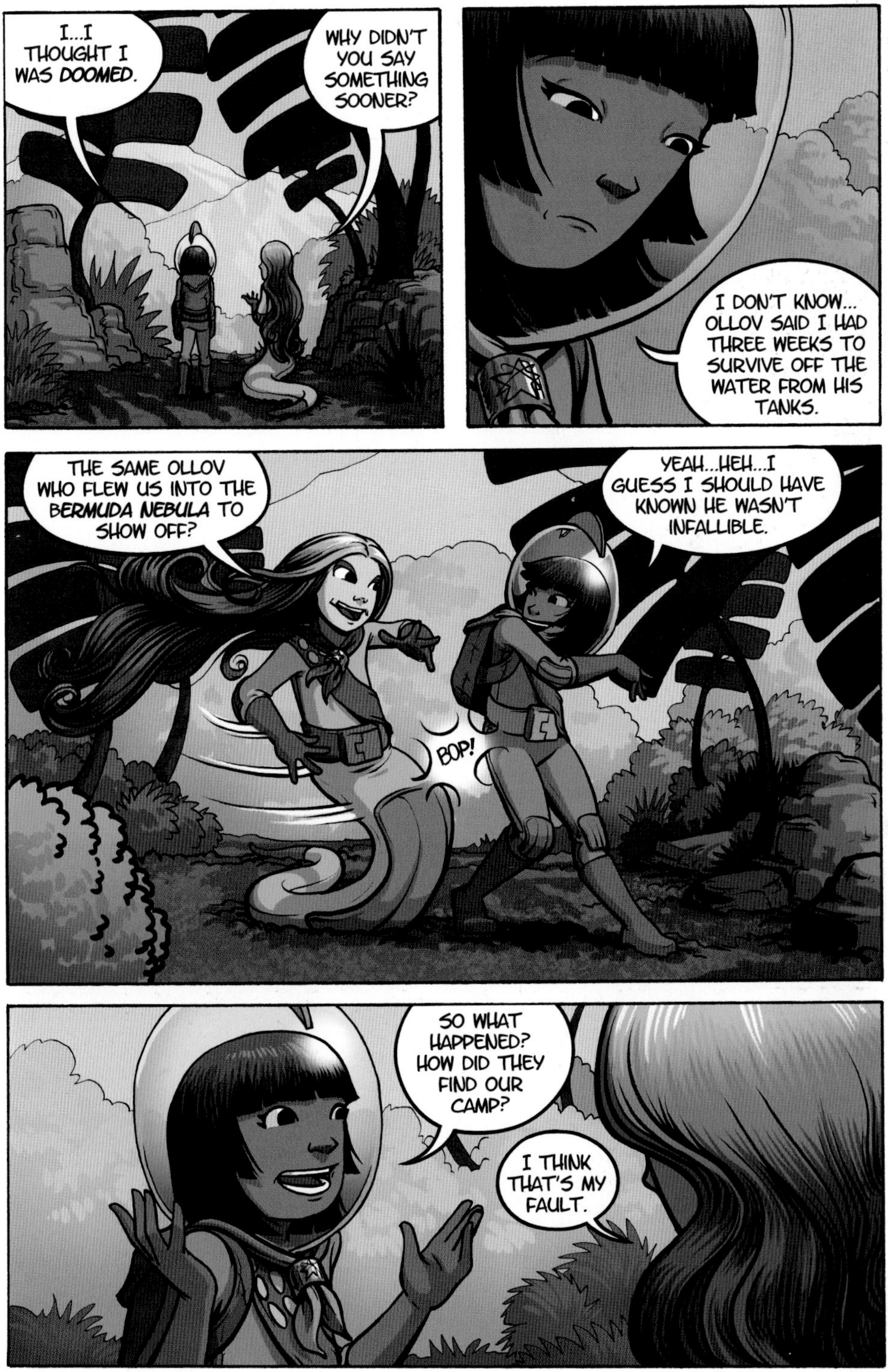
I...I THOUGHT I WAS DOOMED.
WHY DIDN'T YOU SAY SOMETHING SOONER?
I DON'T KNOW... OLLOV SAID I HAD THREE WEEKS TO SURVIVE OFF THE WATER FROM HIS TANKS.
THE SAME OLLOV WHO FLEW US INTO THE BERMUDA NEBULA TO SHOW OFF?
YEAH...HEH...I GUESS I SHOULD HAVE KNOWN HE WASN'T INFALLIBLE.
BOP!
SO WHAT HAPPENED? HOW DID THEY FIND OUR CAMP?
I THINK THAT'S MY FAULT.

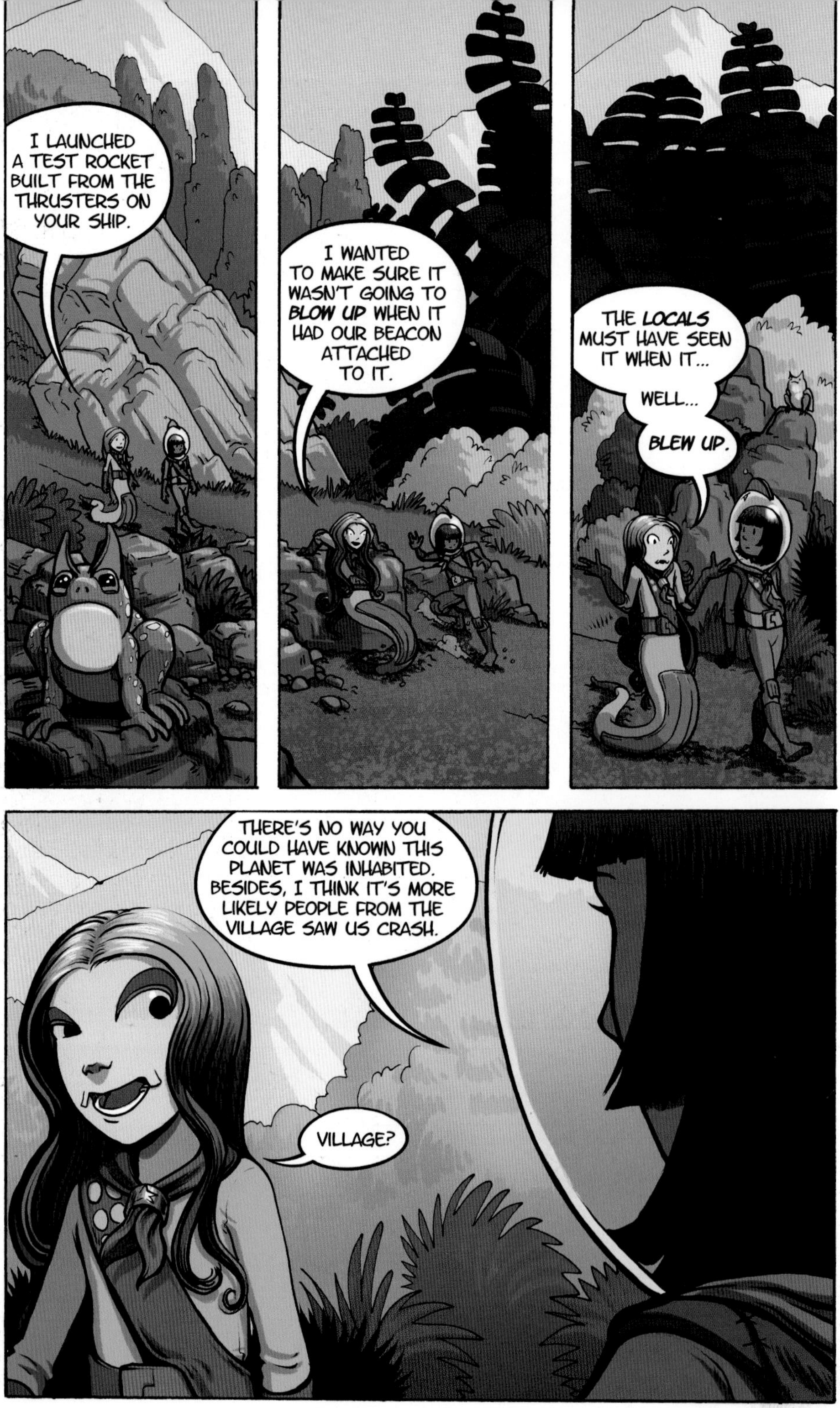
I LAUNCHED A TEST ROCKET BUILT FROM THE THRUSTERS ON YOUR SHIP.
I WANTED TO MAKE SURE IT WASN'T GOING TO BLOW UP WHEN IT HAD OUR BEACON ATTACHED TO IT.
THE LOCALS MUST HAVE SEEN IT WHEN IT...
WELL...
BLEW UP.
THERE'S NO WAY YOU COULD HAVE KNOWN THIS PLANET WAS INHABITED. BESIDES, I THINK IT'S MORE LIKELY PEOPLE FROM THE VILLAGE SAW US CRASH.
VILLAGE?

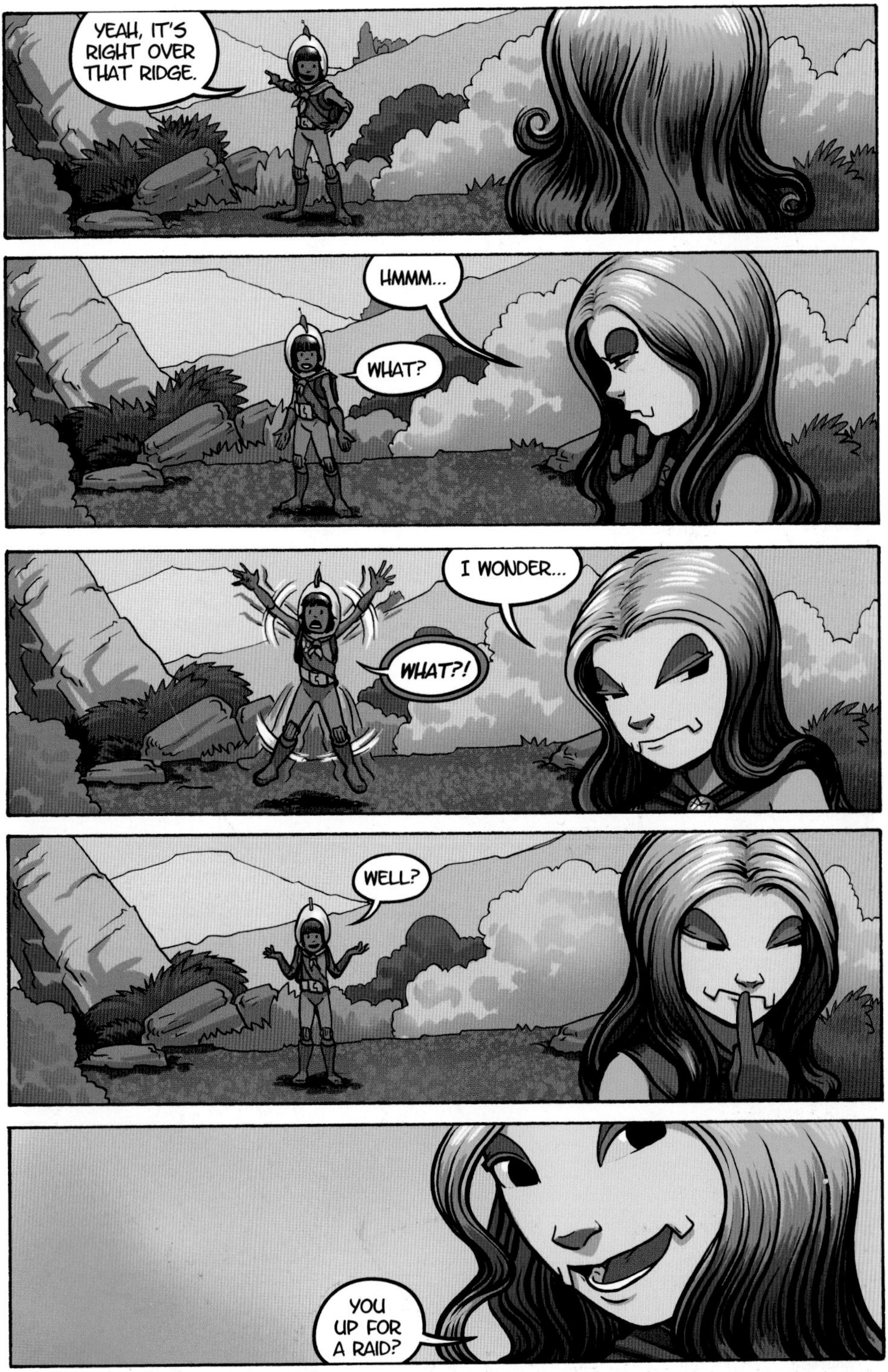
YEAH, IT'S RIGHT OVER THAT RIDGE.
HMMM...
WHAT?
I WONDER...
WHAT?!
WELL?
YOU UP FOR A RAID?

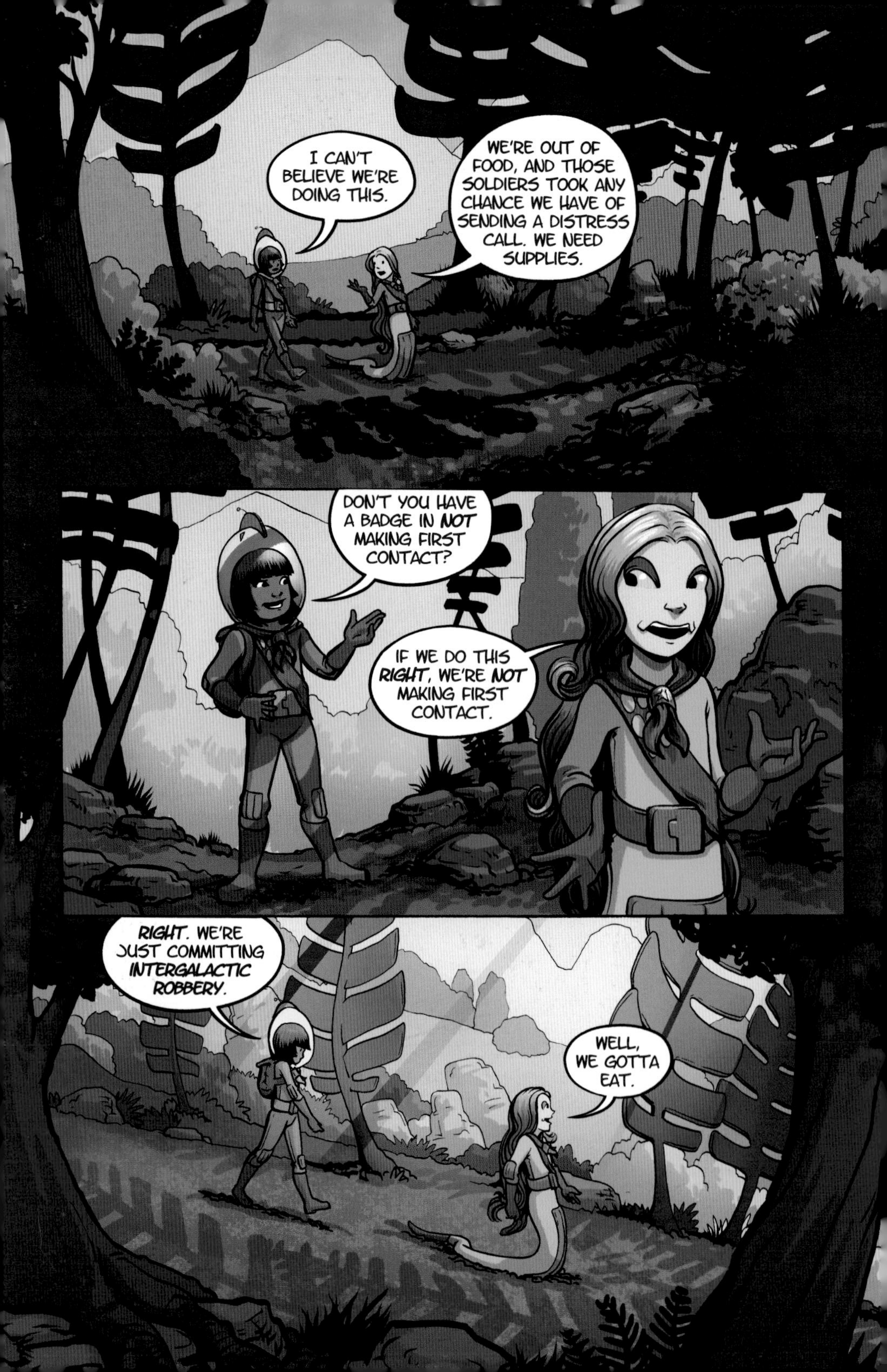
I CAN'T BELIEVE WE'RE DOING THIS.
WE'RE OUT OF FOOD, AND THOSE SOLDIERS TOOK ANY CHANCE WE HAVE OF SENDING A DISTRESS CALL. WE NEED SUPPLIES.
DON'T YOU HAVE A BADGE IN NOT MAKING FIRST CONTACT?
IF WE DO THIS RIGHT, WE'RE NOT MAKING FIRST CONTACT.
RIGHT. WE'RE JUST COMMITTING INTERGALACTIC ROBBERY.
WELL, WE GOTTA EAT.

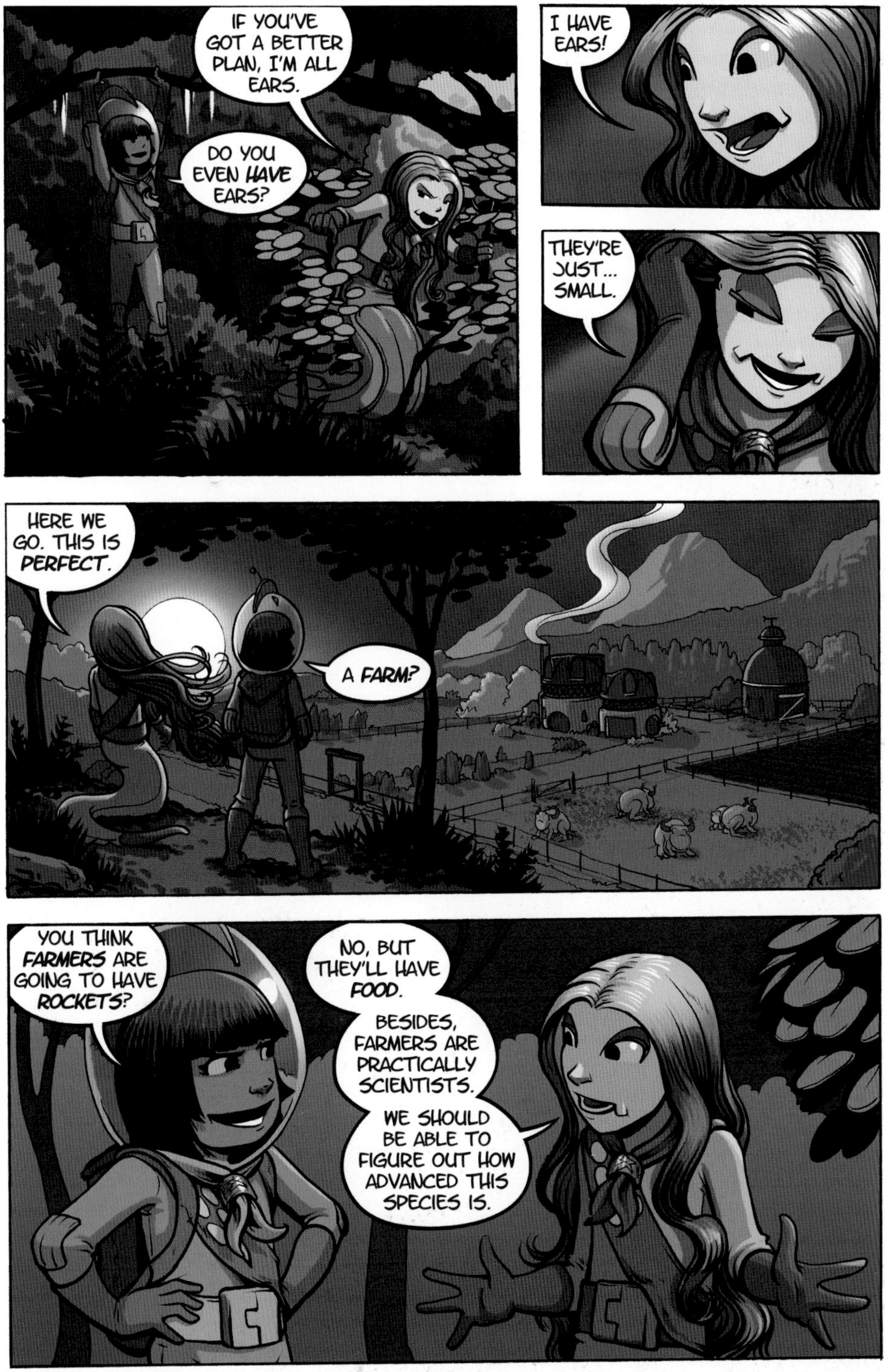
IF YOU'VE GOT A BETTER PLAN, I'M ALL EARS.
DO YOU EVEN *HAVE* EARS?
I HAVE EARS!
THEY'RE JUST... SMALL.
HERE WE GO. THIS IS *PERFECT*.
A *FARM?*
YOU THINK *FARMERS* ARE GOING TO HAVE *ROCKETS?*
NO, BUT THEY'LL HAVE *FOOD*.
BESIDES, FARMERS ARE PRACTICALLY SCIENTISTS.
WE SHOULD BE ABLE TO FIGURE OUT HOW ADVANCED THIS SPECIES IS.

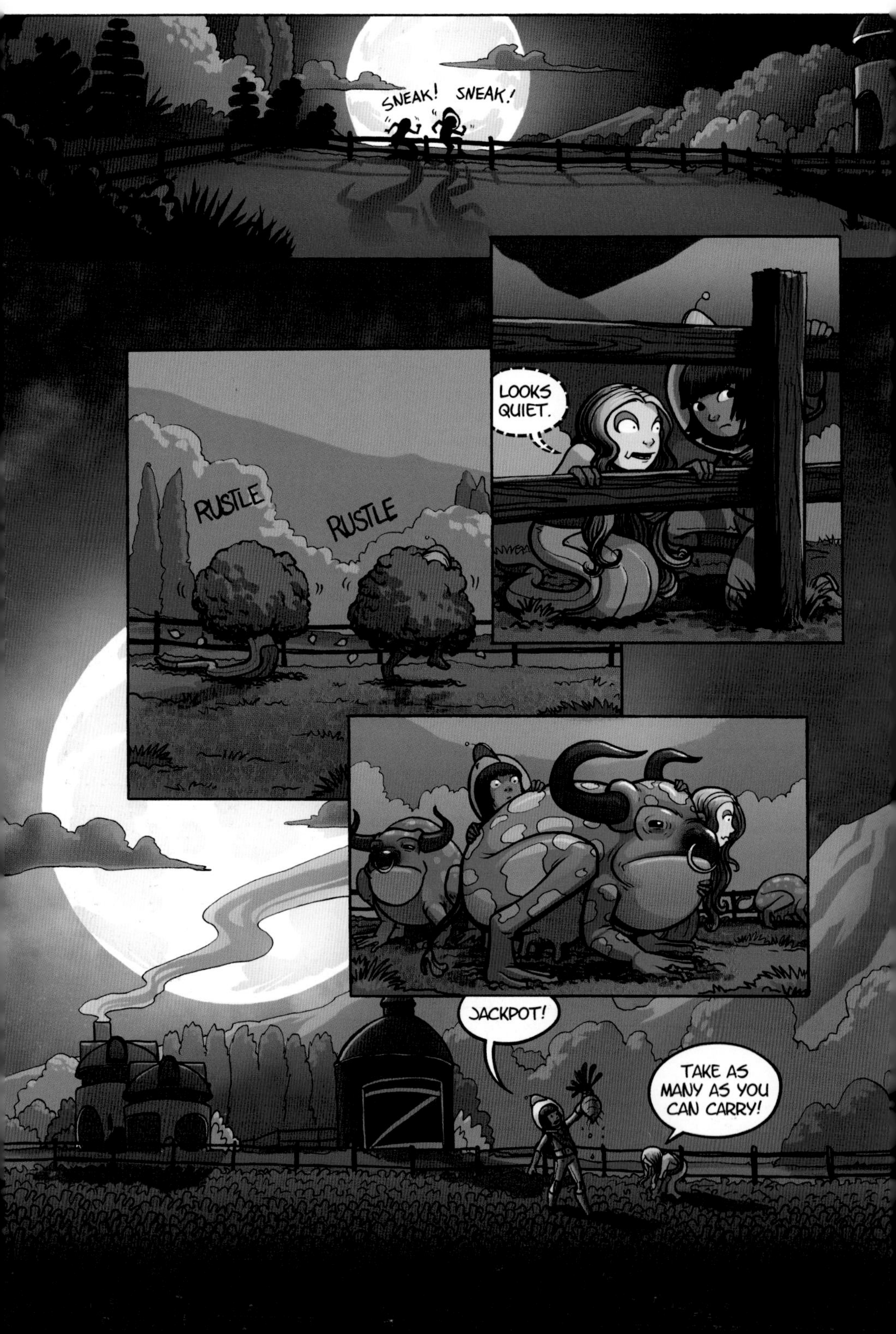
SNEAK! SNEAK!
RUSTLE
RUSTLE
LOOKS QUIET.
JACKPOT!
TAKE AS MANY AS YOU CAN CARRY!

CROARK! CROARK! CROARK!

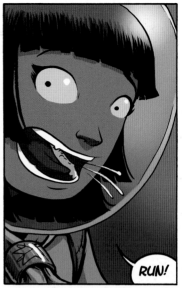

RUN!

CROARK! CROARK!

WHAT IS IT, GIRL?

GAH!

TRIP!

WHOMP!

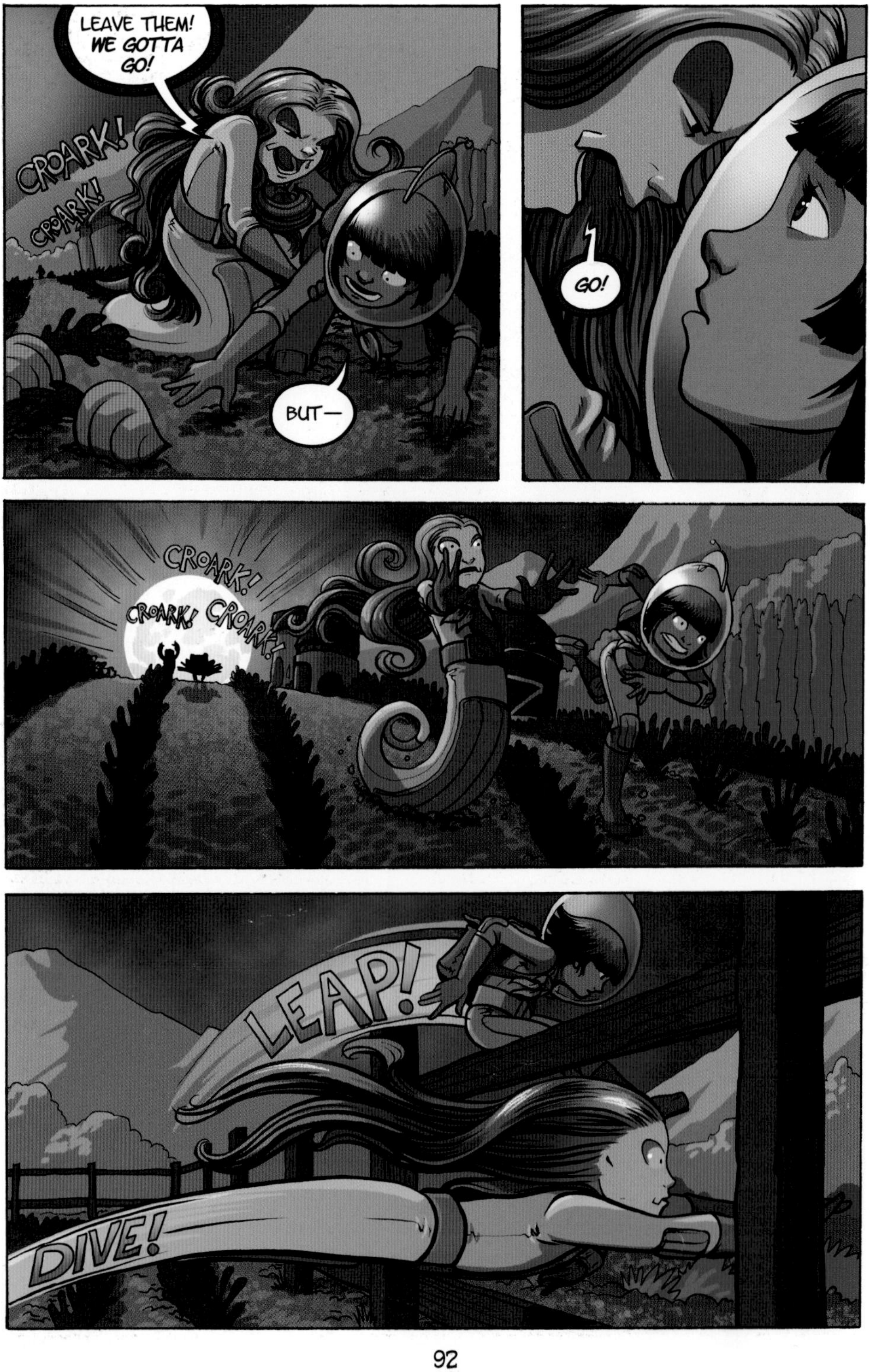
LEAVE THEM! WE GOTTA GO!
CROARK!
CROARK!
BUT—
GO!
CROARK!
CROARK!
CROARK!
LEAP!
DIVE!

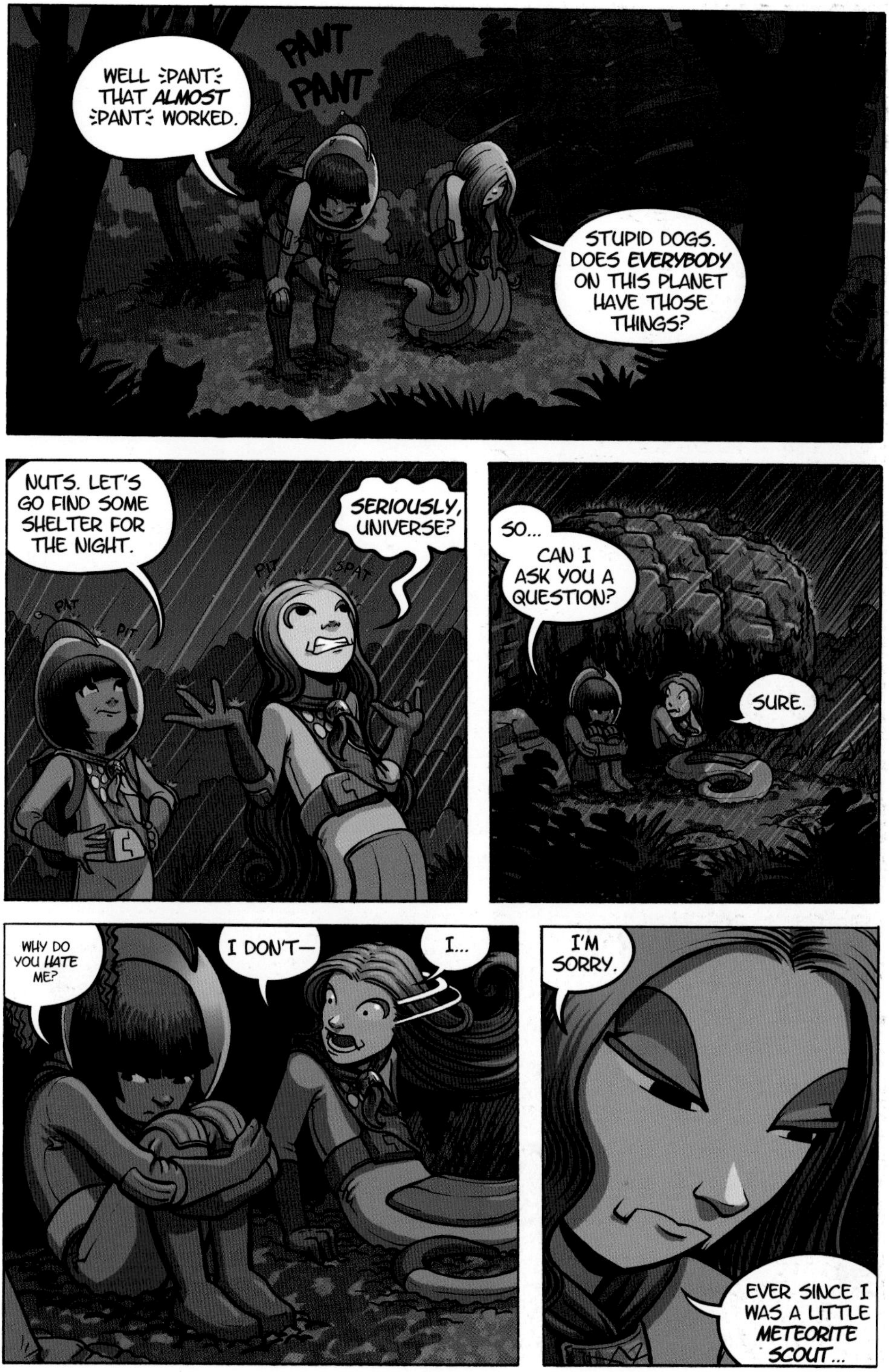
WELL PANT THAT ALMOST PANT WORKED.
PANT PANT
STUPID DOGS. DOES EVERYBODY ON THIS PLANET HAVE THOSE THINGS?
NUTS. LET'S GO FIND SOME SHELTER FOR THE NIGHT.
PAT
PIT
PIT
SPAT
SERIOUSLY, UNIVERSE?
SO... CAN I ASK YOU A QUESTION?
SURE.
WHY DO YOU HATE ME?
I DON'T—
I...
I'M SORRY.
EVER SINCE I WAS A LITTLE METEORITE SCOUT...

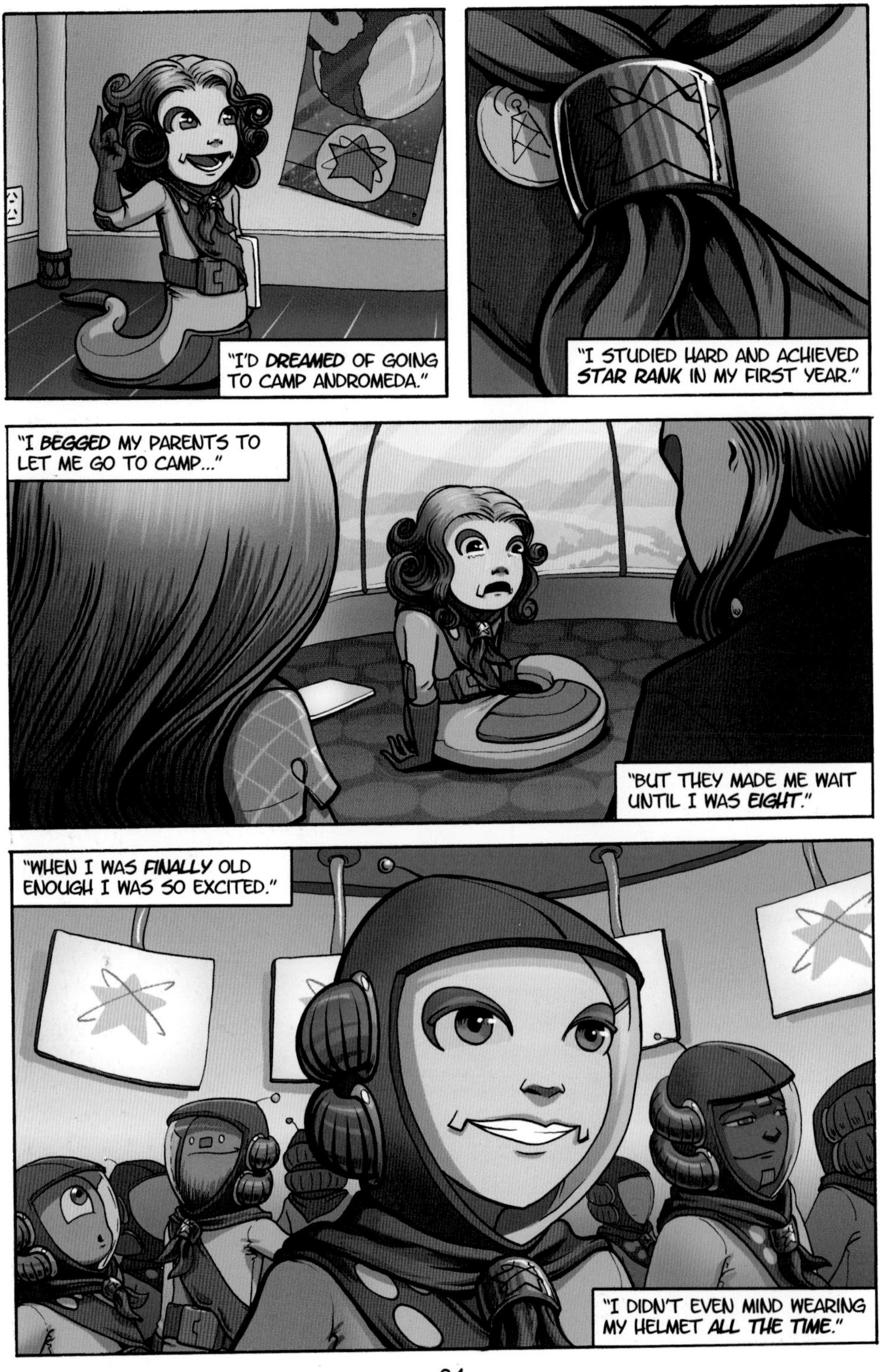
"I'D DREAMED OF GOING TO CAMP ANDROMEDA."
"I STUDIED HARD AND ACHIEVED STAR RANK IN MY FIRST YEAR."
"I BEGGED MY PARENTS TO LET ME GO TO CAMP..."
"BUT THEY MADE ME WAIT UNTIL I WAS EIGHT."
"WHEN I WAS FINALLY OLD ENOUGH I WAS SO EXCITED."
"I DIDN'T EVEN MIND WEARING MY HELMET ALL THE TIME."

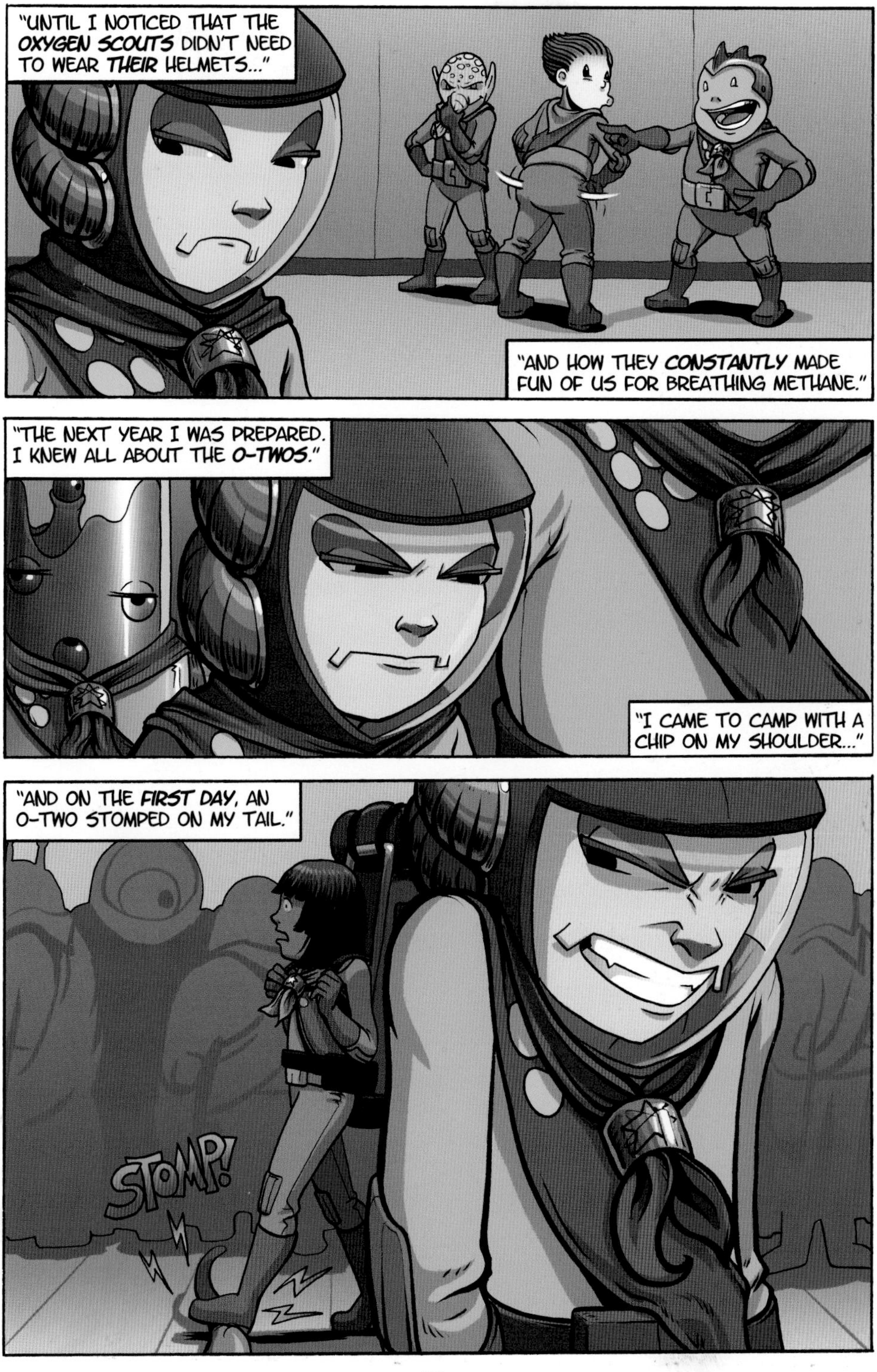
"UNTIL I NOTICED THAT THE OXYGEN SCOUTS DIDN'T NEED TO WEAR THEIR HELMETS..."
"AND HOW THEY CONSTANTLY MADE FUN OF US FOR BREATHING METHANE."
"THE NEXT YEAR I WAS PREPARED. I KNEW ALL ABOUT THE O-TWOS."
"I CAME TO CAMP WITH A CHIP ON MY SHOULDER..."
"AND ON THE FIRST DAY, AN O-TWO STOMPED ON MY TAIL."
STOMP!

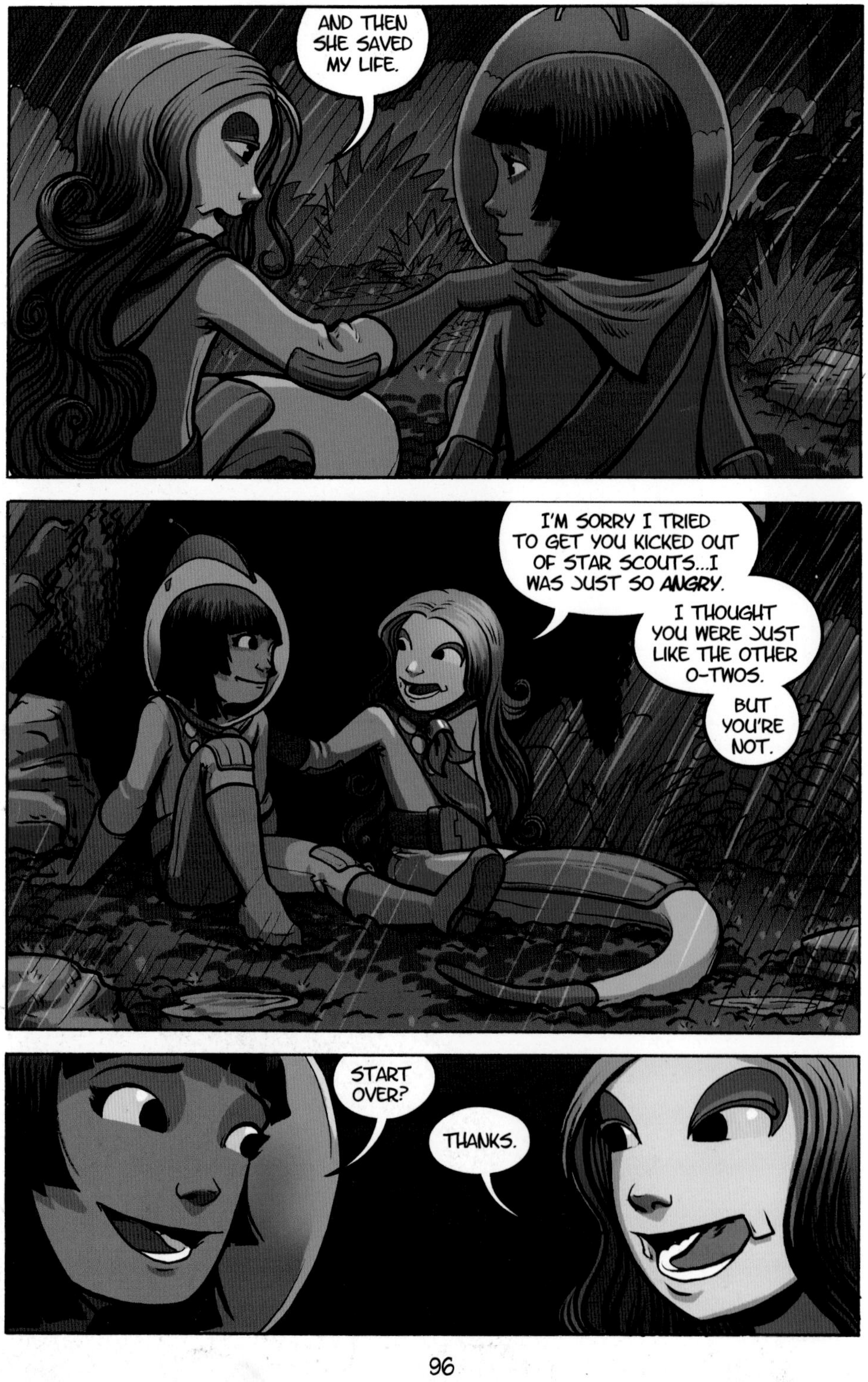
AND THEN SHE SAVED MY LIFE.
I'M SORRY I TRIED TO GET YOU KICKED OUT OF STAR SCOUTS...I WAS JUST SO ANGRY.
I THOUGHT YOU WERE JUST LIKE THE OTHER O-TWOS.
BUT YOU'RE NOT.
START OVER?
THANKS.

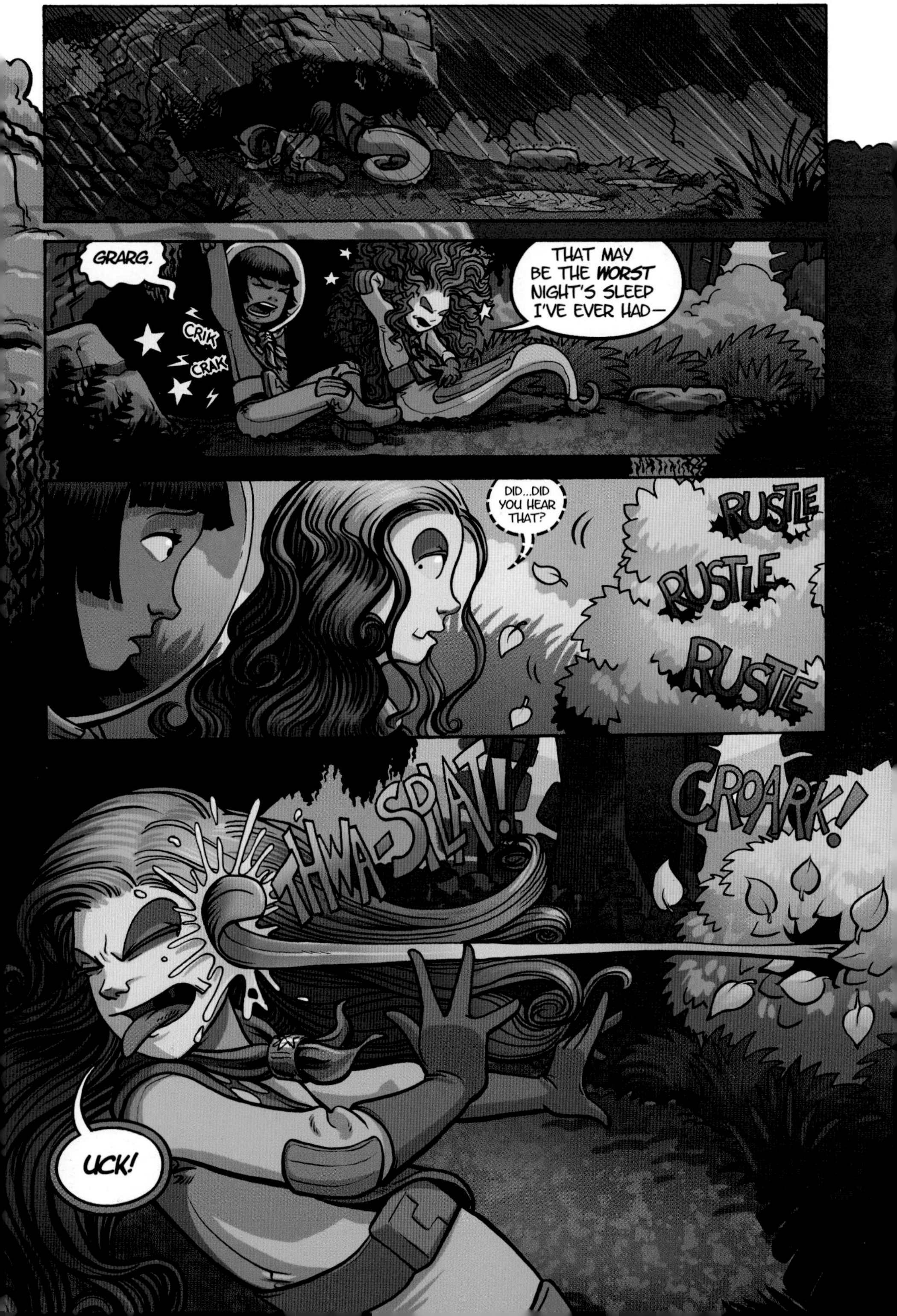
GRARG.
CRIK
CRAK
THAT MAY BE THE WORST NIGHT'S SLEEP I'VE EVER HAD—
DID...DID YOU HEAR THAT?
RUSTLE
RUSTLE
RUSTLE
THWA-SPLAT!!
CROARK!
UCK!

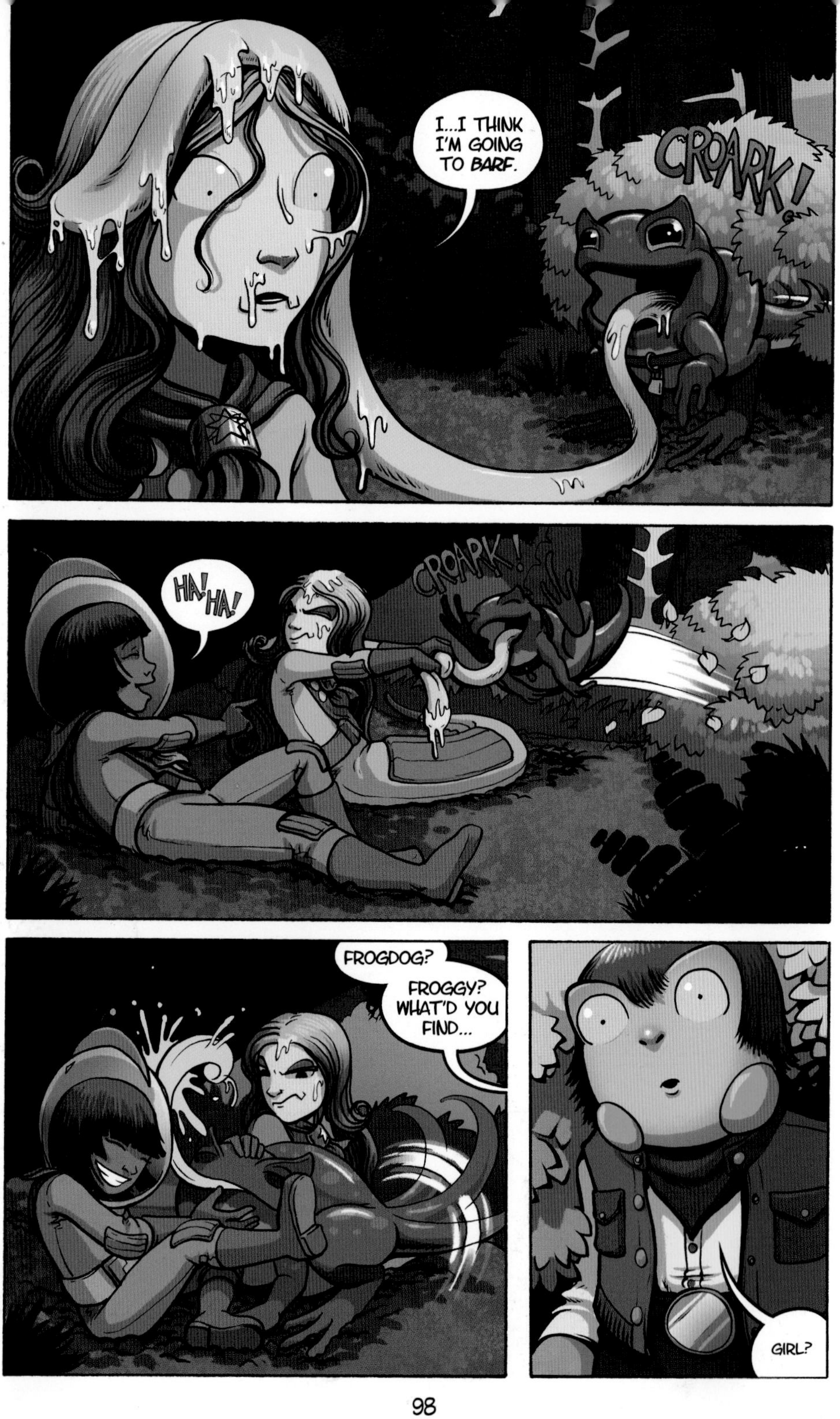
I...I THINK I'M GOING TO BARF.
CROARK!
HA! HA!
CROARK!
FROGDOG?
FROGGY? WHAT'D YOU FIND...
GIRL?

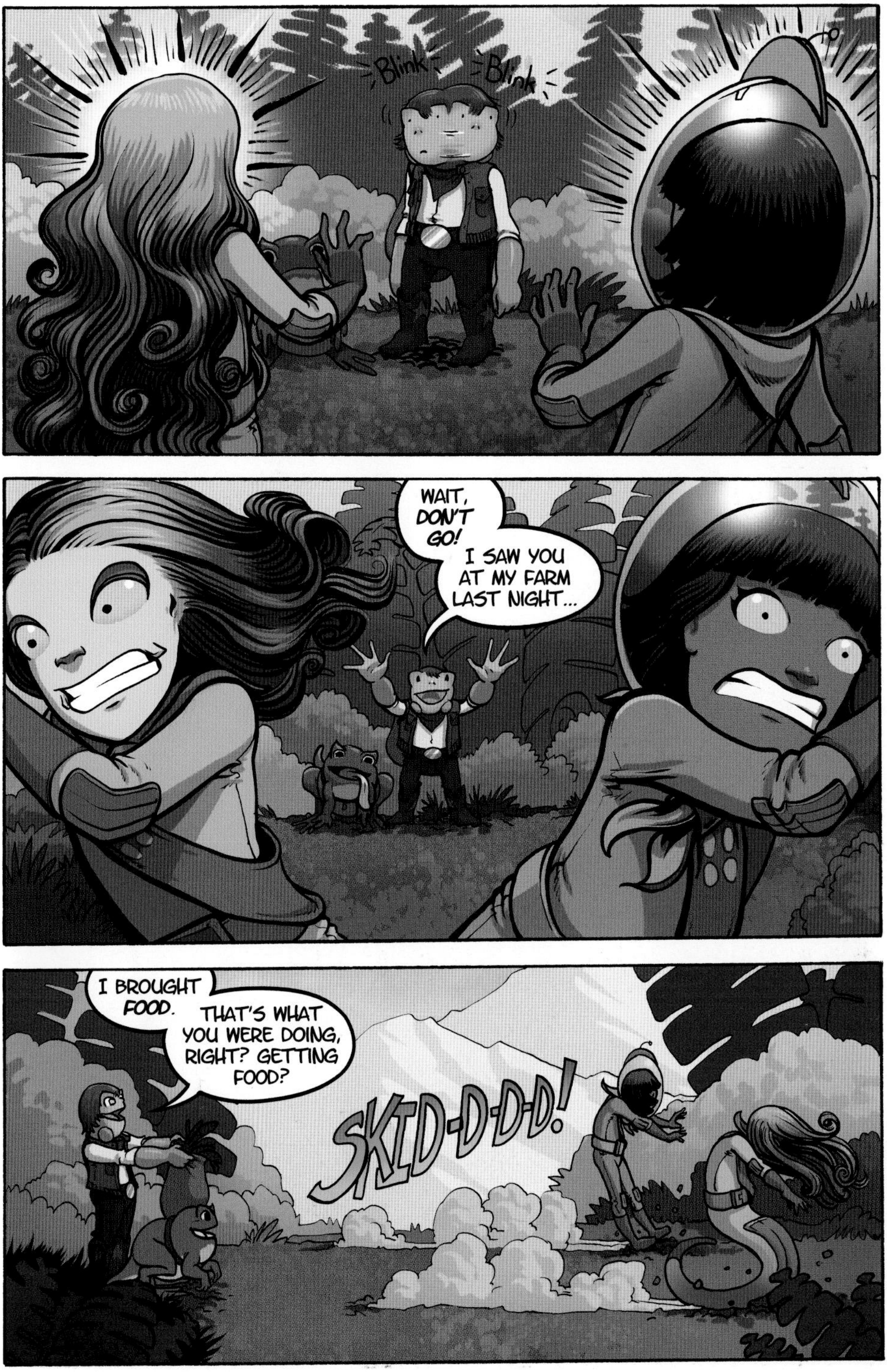
Blink
Blink
WAIT, DON'T GO!
I SAW YOU AT MY FARM LAST NIGHT...
I BROUGHT FOOD.
THAT'S WHAT YOU WERE DOING, RIGHT? GETTING FOOD?
SKID-D-D-D!

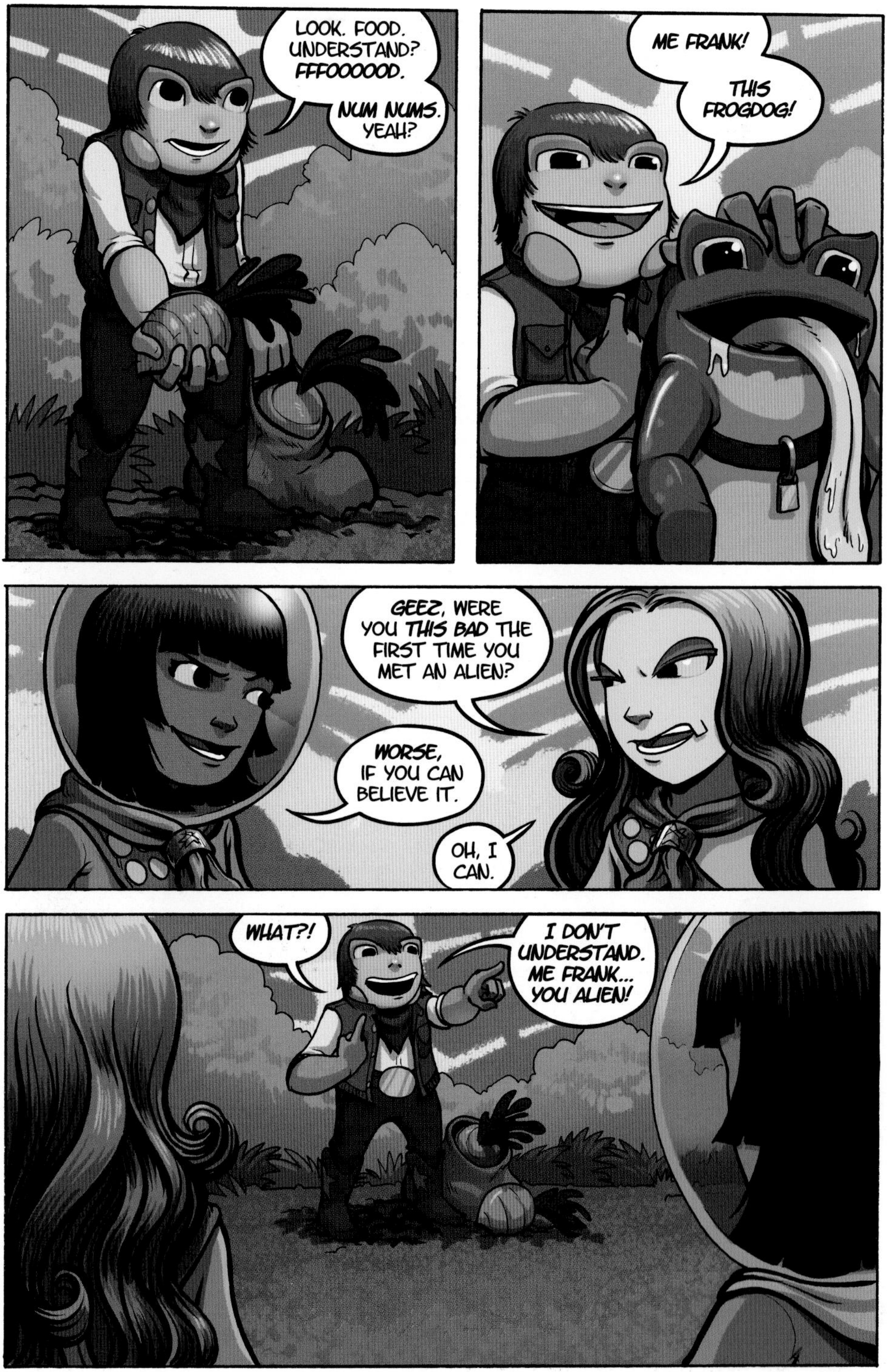
LOOK. FOOD. UNDERSTAND? FFFOOOOOD.
NUM NUMS. YEAH?
ME FRANK!
THIS FROGDOG!
GEEZ, WERE YOU THIS BAD THE FIRST TIME YOU MET AN ALIEN?
WORSE, IF YOU CAN BELIEVE IT.
OH, I CAN.
WHAT?!
I DON'T UNDERSTAND. ME FRANK... YOU ALIEN!

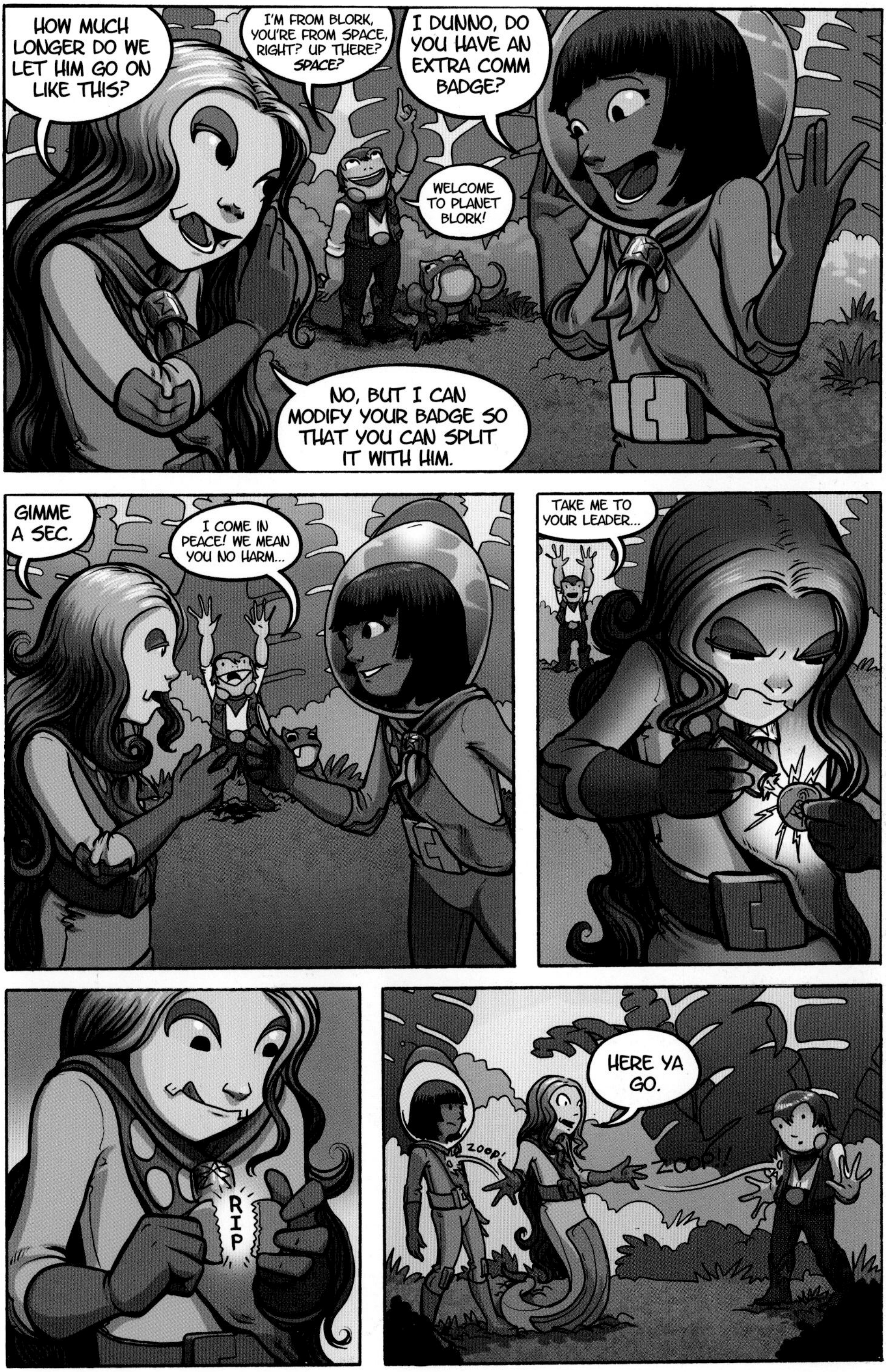
HOW MUCH LONGER DO WE LET HIM GO ON LIKE THIS?
I'M FROM BLORK, YOU'RE FROM SPACE, RIGHT? UP THERE? SPACE?
I DUNNO, DO YOU HAVE AN EXTRA COMM BADGE?
WELCOME TO PLANET BLORK!
NO, BUT I CAN MODIFY YOUR BADGE SO THAT YOU CAN SPLIT IT WITH HIM.
GIMME A SEC.
I COME IN PEACE! WE MEAN YOU NO HARM...
TAKE ME TO YOUR LEADER...
RIP
HERE YA GO.
ZOOP!
ZOOP!!

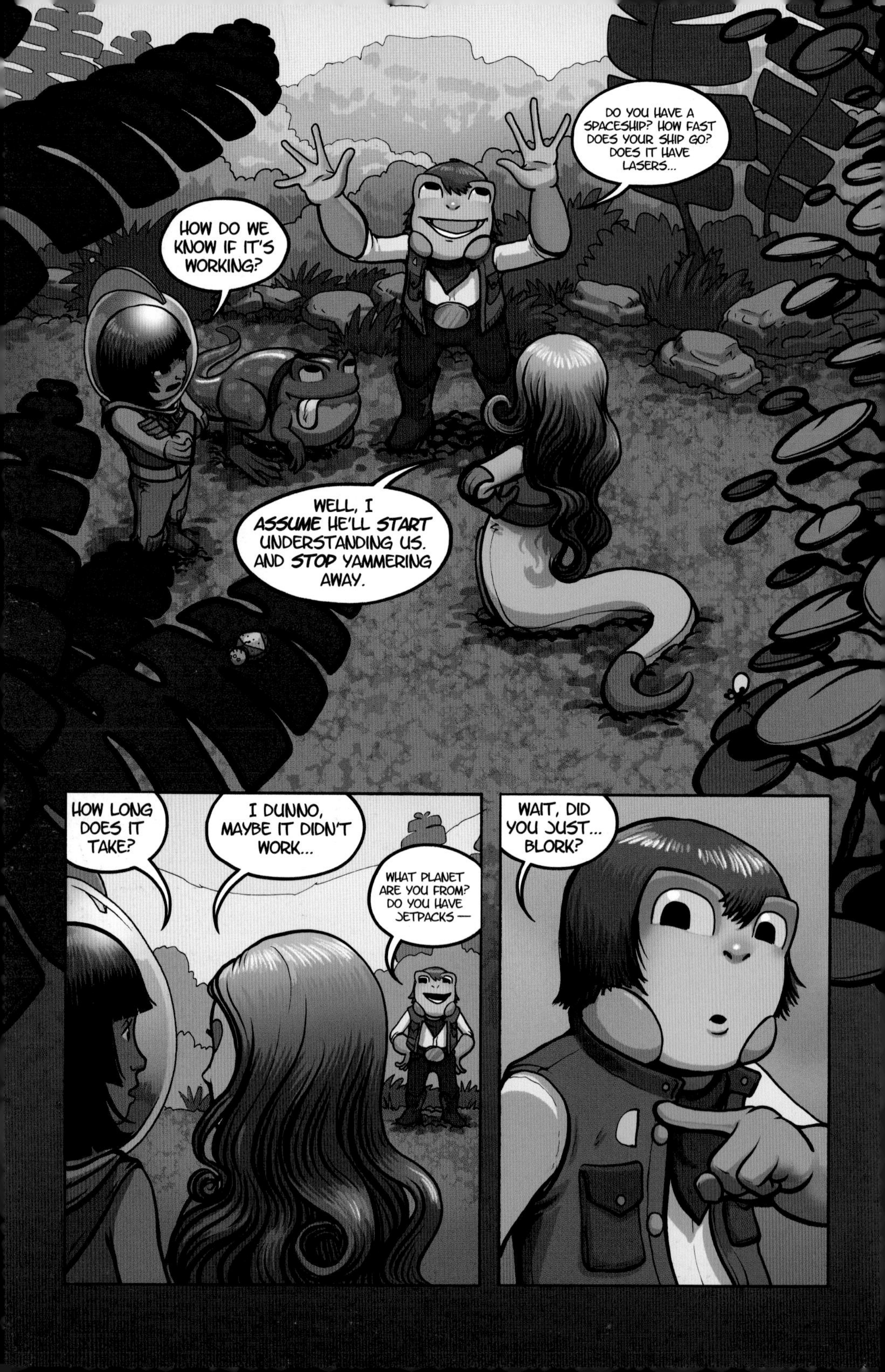
DO YOU HAVE A SPACESHIP? HOW FAST DOES YOUR SHIP GO? DOES IT HAVE LASERS...
HOW DO WE KNOW IF IT'S WORKING?
WELL, I **ASSUME** HE'LL **START** UNDERSTANDING US. AND **STOP** YAMMERING AWAY.
HOW LONG DOES IT TAKE?
I DUNNO, MAYBE IT DIDN'T WORK...
WHAT PLANET ARE YOU FROM? DO YOU HAVE JETPACKS —
WAIT, DID YOU JUST... BLORK?

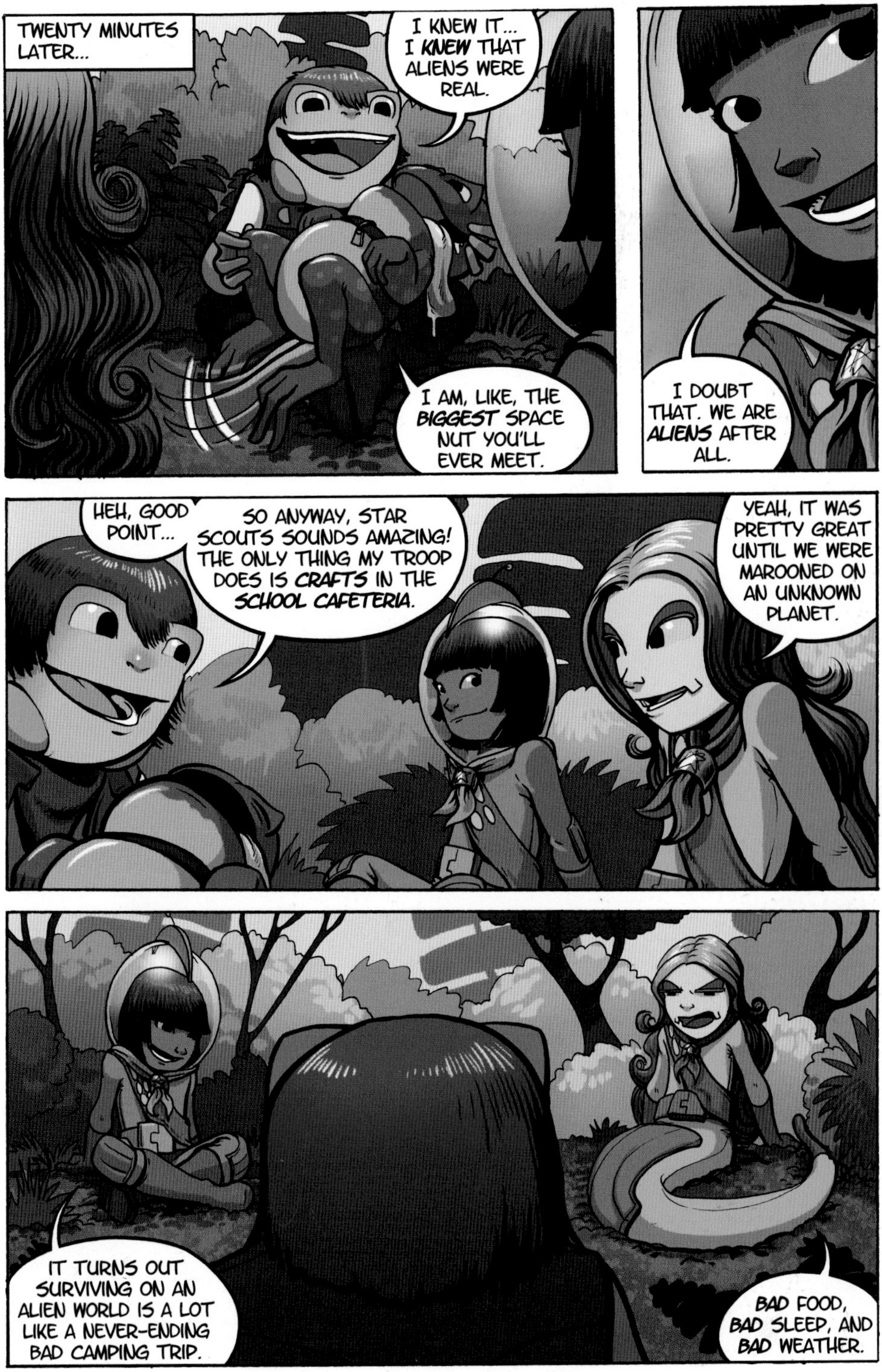
TWENTY MINUTES LATER...
I KNEW IT... I KNEW THAT ALIENS WERE REAL.
I AM, LIKE, THE BIGGEST SPACE NUT YOU'LL EVER MEET.
I DOUBT THAT. WE ARE ALIENS AFTER ALL.
HEH, GOOD POINT...
SO ANYWAY, STAR SCOUTS SOUNDS AMAZING! THE ONLY THING MY TROOP DOES IS CRAFTS IN THE SCHOOL CAFETERIA.
YEAH, IT WAS PRETTY GREAT UNTIL WE WERE MAROONED ON AN UNKNOWN PLANET.
IT TURNS OUT SURVIVING ON AN ALIEN WORLD IS A LOT LIKE A NEVER-ENDING BAD CAMPING TRIP.
BAD FOOD, BAD SLEEP, AND BAD WEATHER.

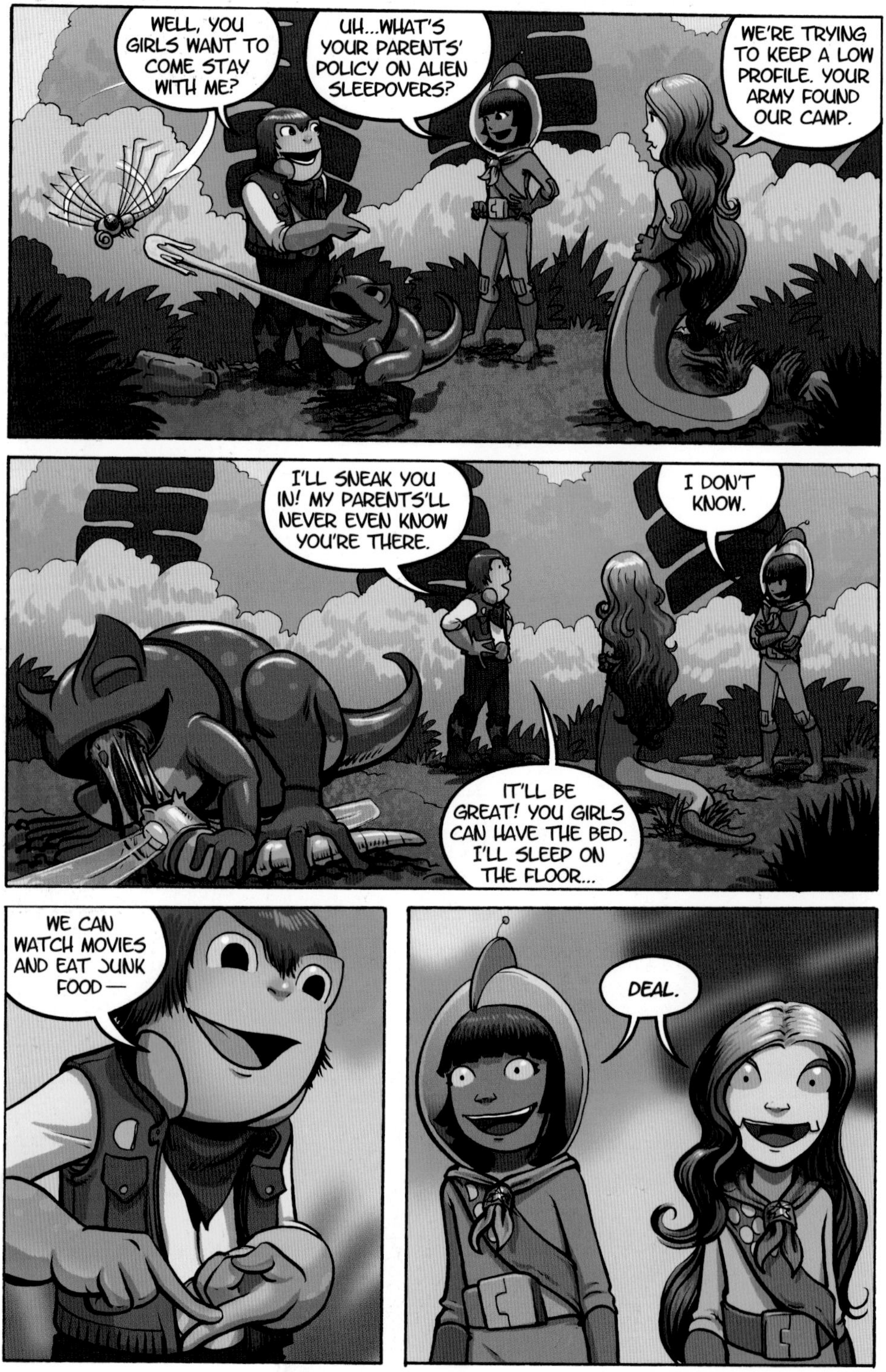
WELL, YOU GIRLS WANT TO COME STAY WITH ME?
UH...WHAT'S YOUR PARENTS' POLICY ON ALIEN SLEEPOVERS?
WE'RE TRYING TO KEEP A LOW PROFILE. YOUR ARMY FOUND OUR CAMP.
I'LL SNEAK YOU IN! MY PARENTS'LL NEVER EVEN KNOW YOU'RE THERE.
I DON'T KNOW.
IT'LL BE GREAT! YOU GIRLS CAN HAVE THE BED. I'LL SLEEP ON THE FLOOR...
WE CAN WATCH MOVIES AND EAT JUNK FOOD—
DEAL.

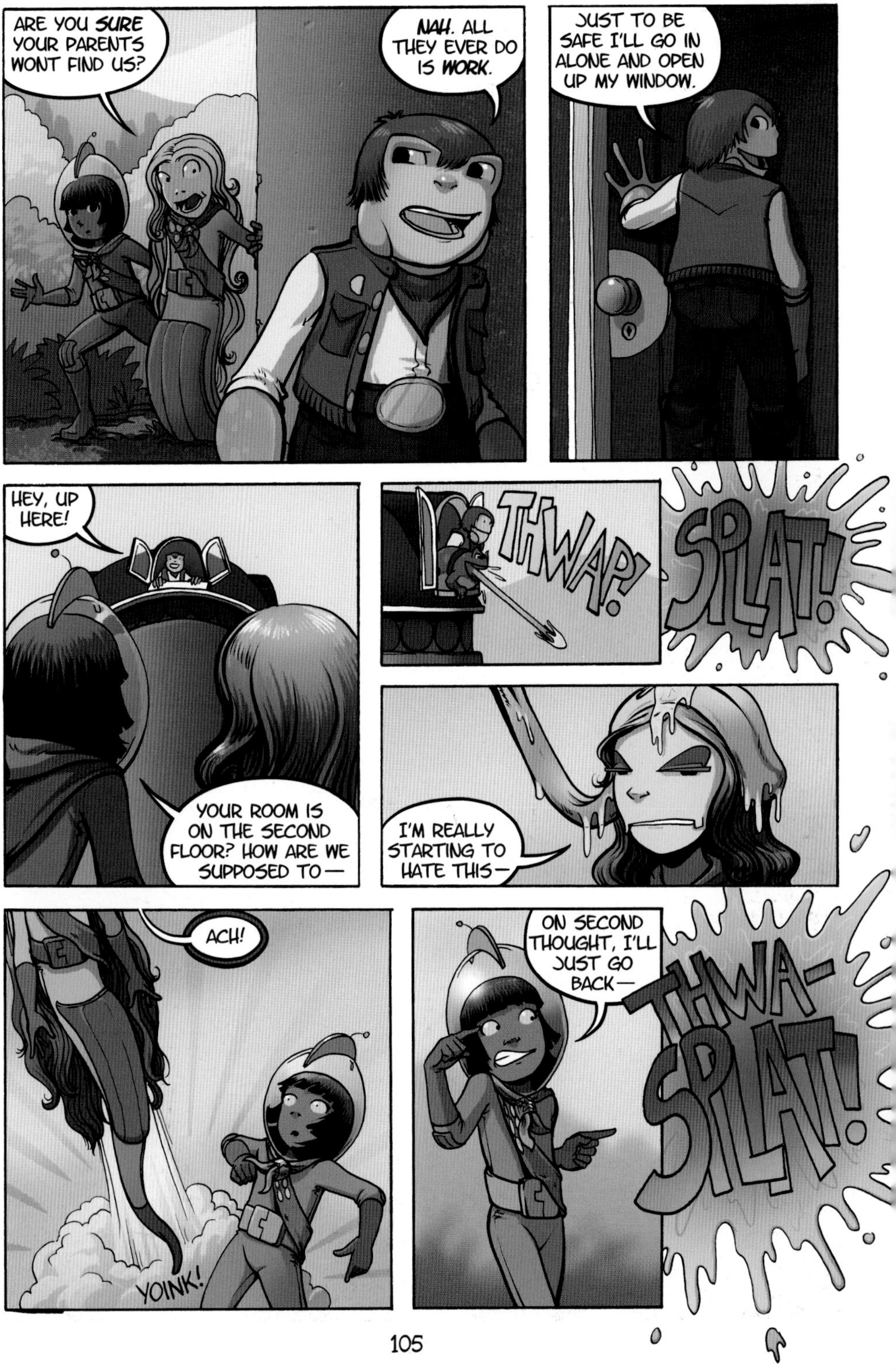

ARE YOU SURE YOUR PARENTS WONT FIND US?
NAH. ALL THEY EVER DO IS WORK.
JUST TO BE SAFE I'LL GO IN ALONE AND OPEN UP MY WINDOW.
HEY, UP HERE!
YOUR ROOM IS ON THE SECOND FLOOR? HOW ARE WE SUPPOSED TO—
THWAP!
SPLAT!
I'M REALLY STARTING TO HATE THIS—
ACH!
YOINK!
ON SECOND THOUGHT, I'LL JUST GO BACK—
THWA-SPLAT!

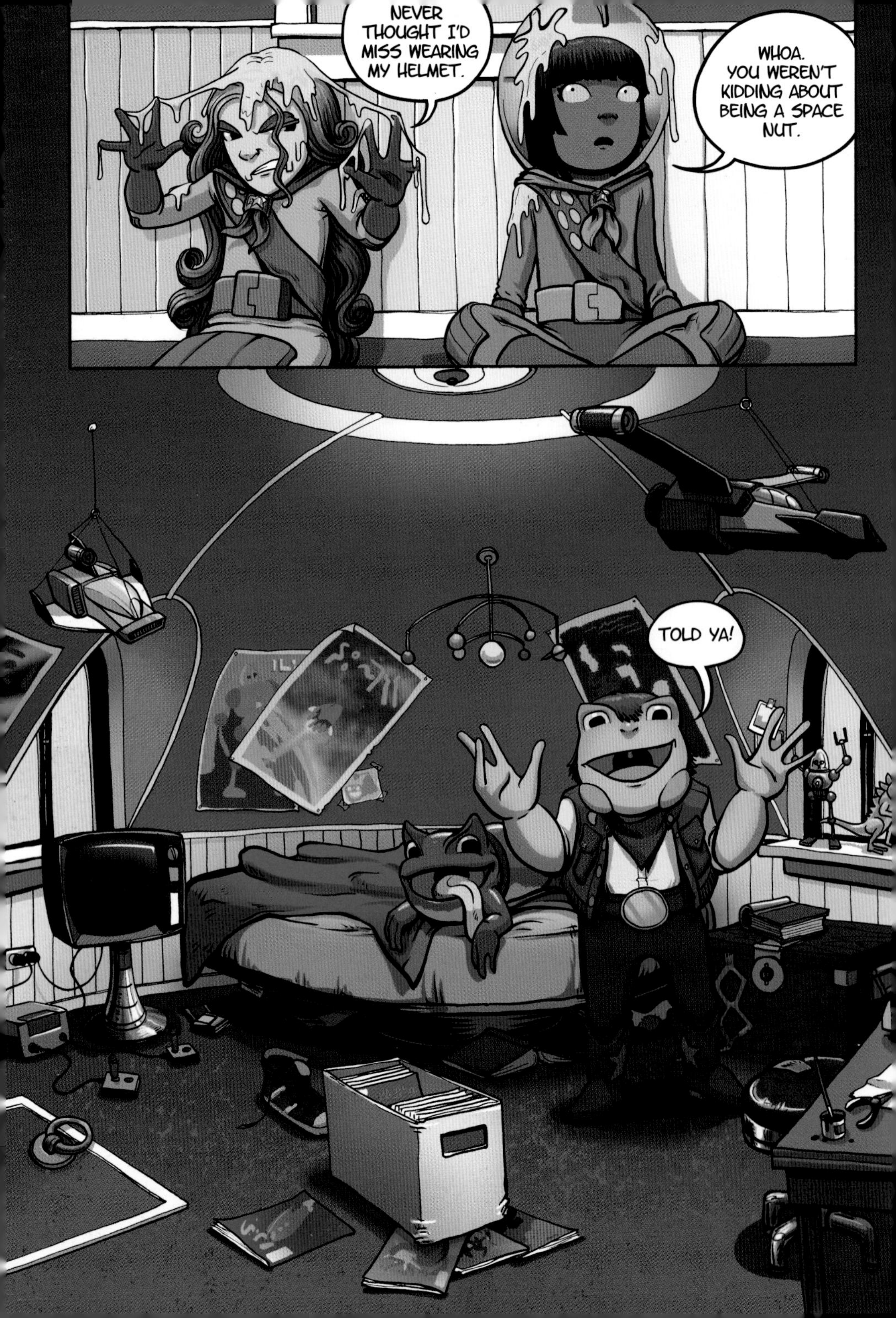
NEVER THOUGHT I'D MISS WEARING MY HELMET.
WHOA. YOU WEREN'T KIDDING ABOUT BEING A SPACE NUT.
TOLD YA!

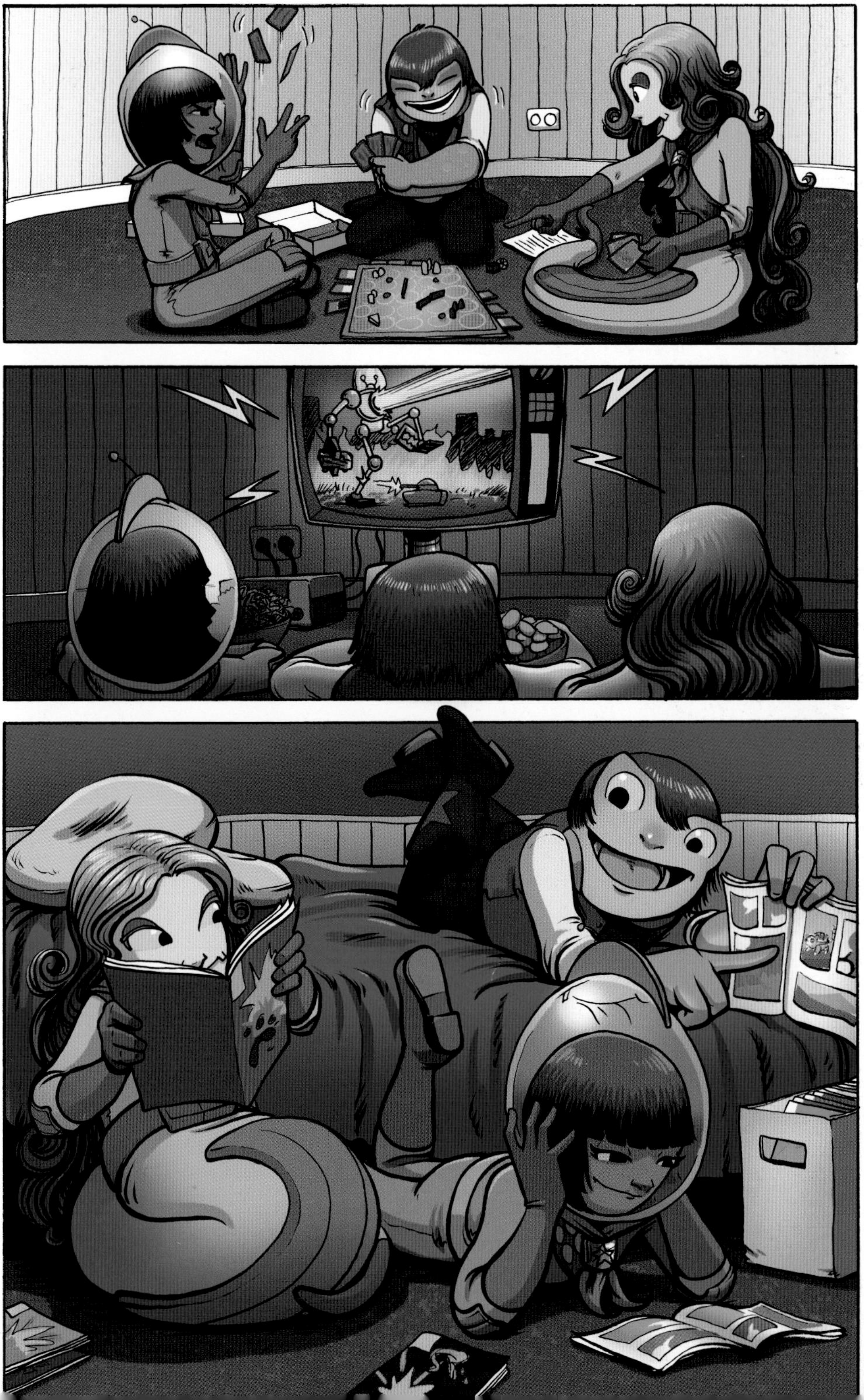

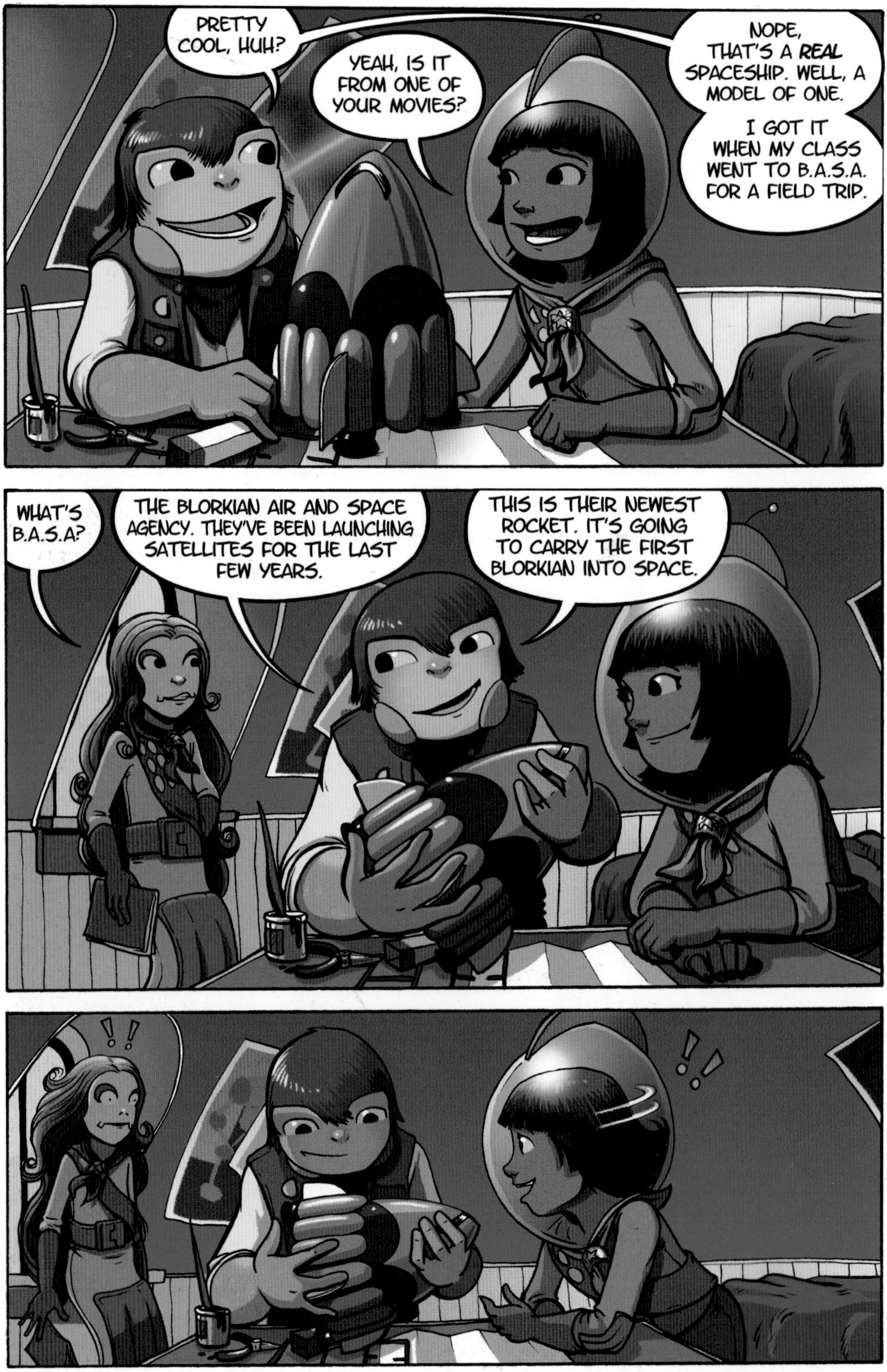
PRETTY COOL, HUH?
YEAH, IS IT FROM ONE OF YOUR MOVIES?
NOPE, THAT'S A **REAL** SPACESHIP. WELL, A MODEL OF ONE.
I GOT IT WHEN MY CLASS WENT TO B.A.S.A. FOR A FIELD TRIP.
WHAT'S B.A.S.A?
THE BLORKIAN AIR AND SPACE AGENCY. THEY'VE BEEN LAUNCHING SATELLITES FOR THE LAST FEW YEARS.
THIS IS THEIR NEWEST ROCKET. IT'S GOING TO CARRY THE FIRST BLORKIAN INTO SPACE.
!!
!!

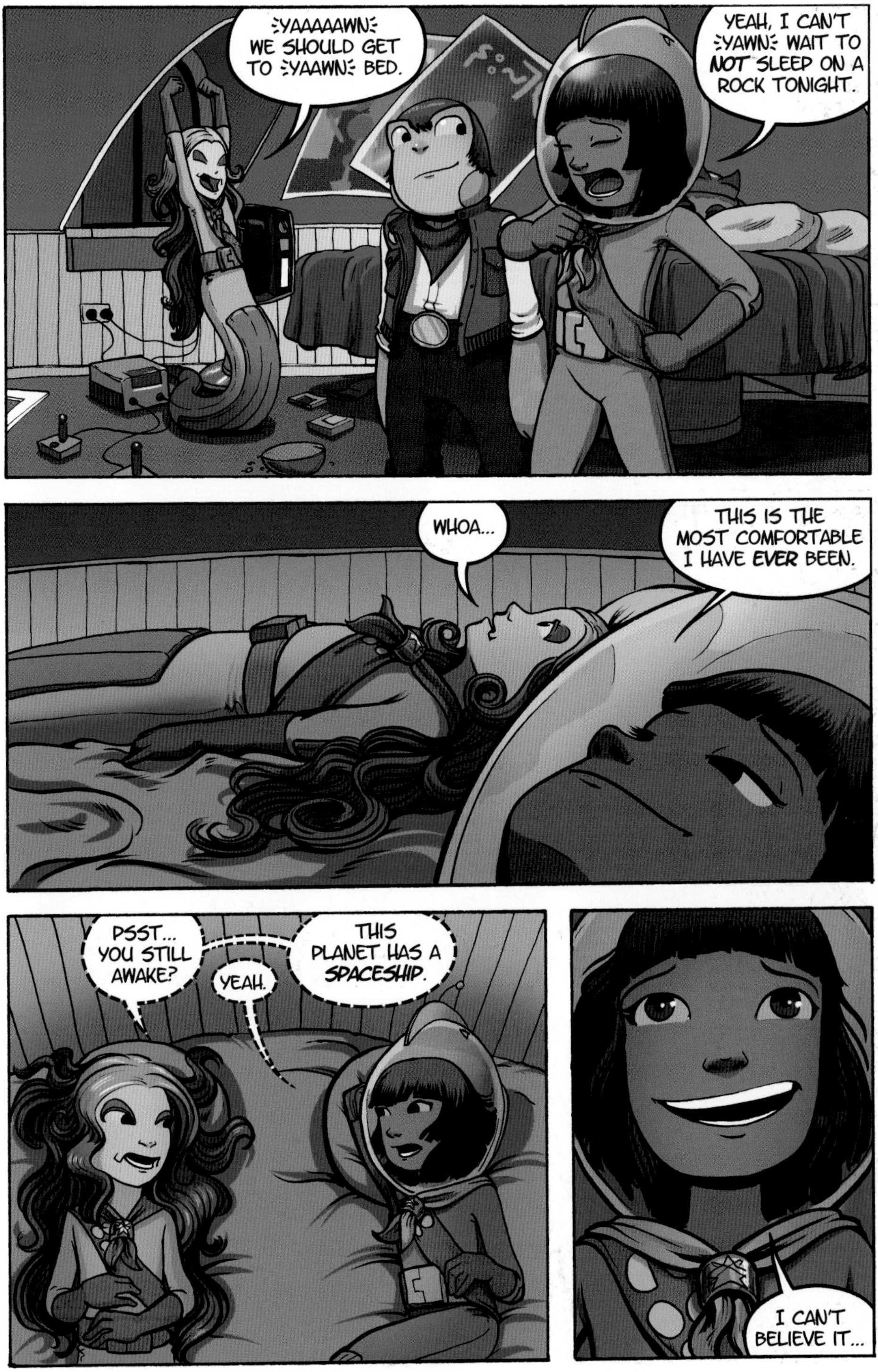
:YAAAAAWN: WE SHOULD GET TO :YAAWN: BED.
YEAH, I CAN'T :YAWN: WAIT TO NOT SLEEP ON A ROCK TONIGHT.
WHOA...
THIS IS THE MOST COMFORTABLE I HAVE EVER BEEN.
PSST... YOU STILL AWAKE?
YEAH.
THIS PLANET HAS A SPACESHIP.
I CAN'T BELIEVE IT...

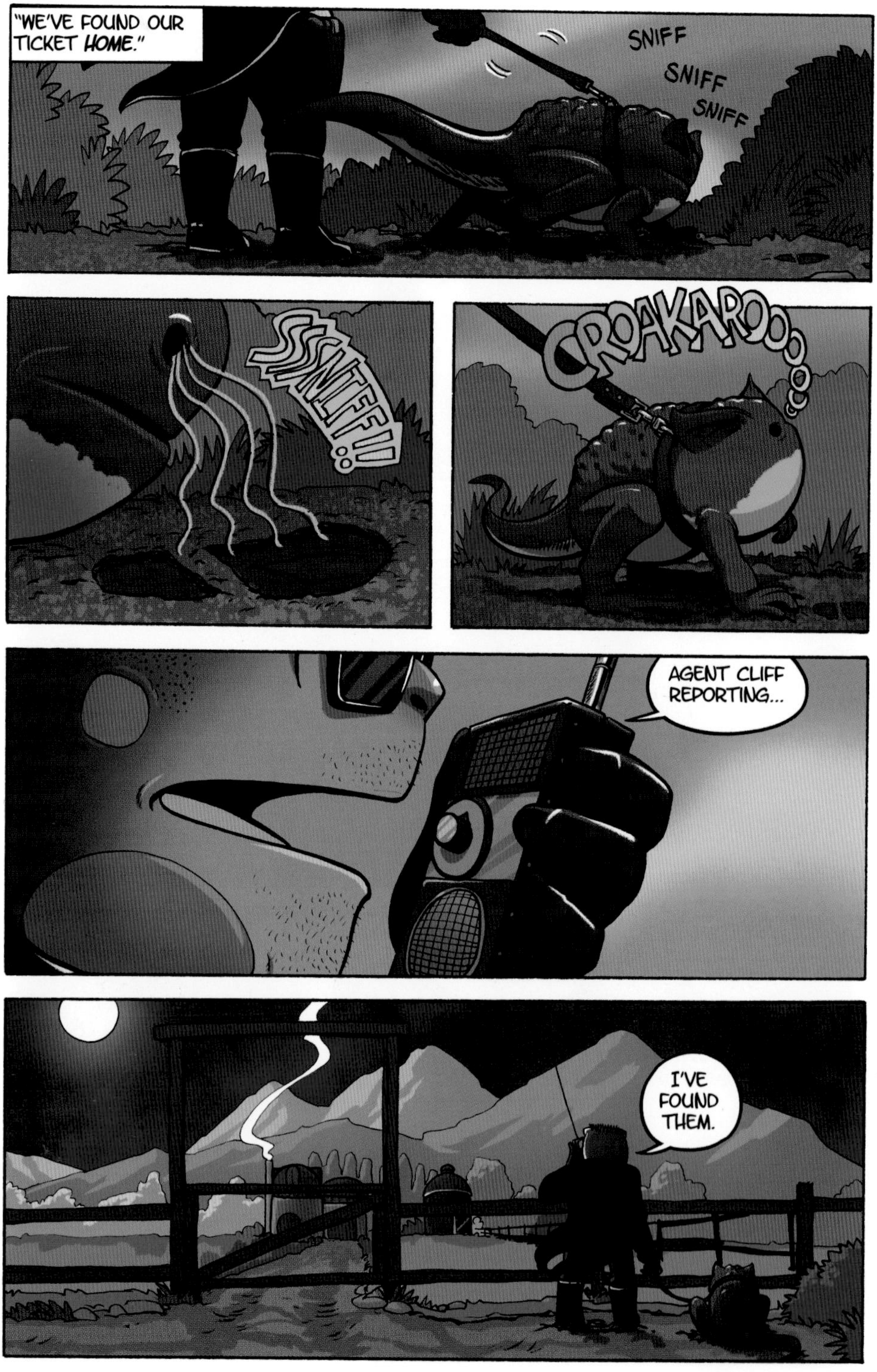
"WE'VE FOUND OUR TICKET HOME."
SNIFF
SNIFF
SNIFF
SSSNIFFF!!
CROAKAROOOOO
AGENT CLIFF REPORTING...
I'VE FOUND THEM.

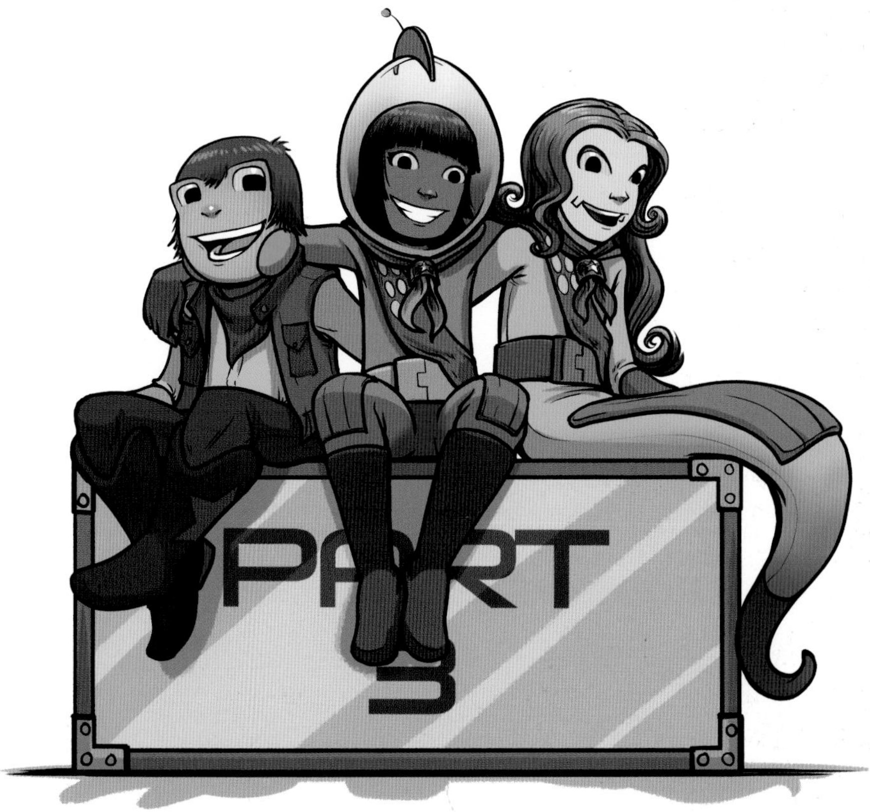
PART
3

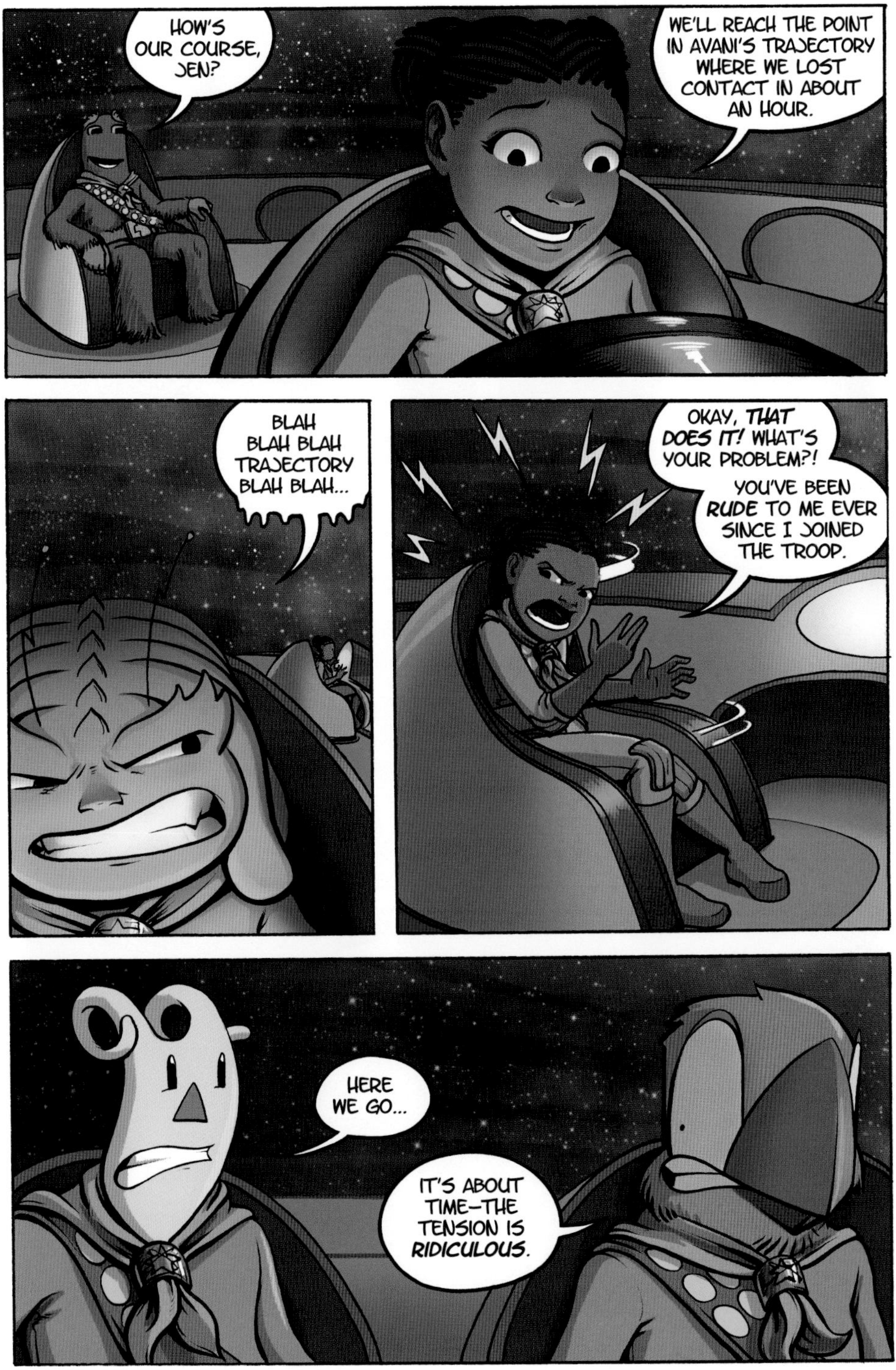
HOW'S OUR COURSE, JEN?
WE'LL REACH THE POINT IN AVANI'S TRAJECTORY WHERE WE LOST CONTACT IN ABOUT AN HOUR.
BLAH BLAH BLAH TRAJECTORY BLAH BLAH...
OKAY, THAT DOES IT! WHAT'S YOUR PROBLEM?!
YOU'VE BEEN RUDE TO ME EVER SINCE I JOINED THE TROOP.
HERE WE GO...
IT'S ABOUT TIME—THE TENSION IS RIDICULOUS.

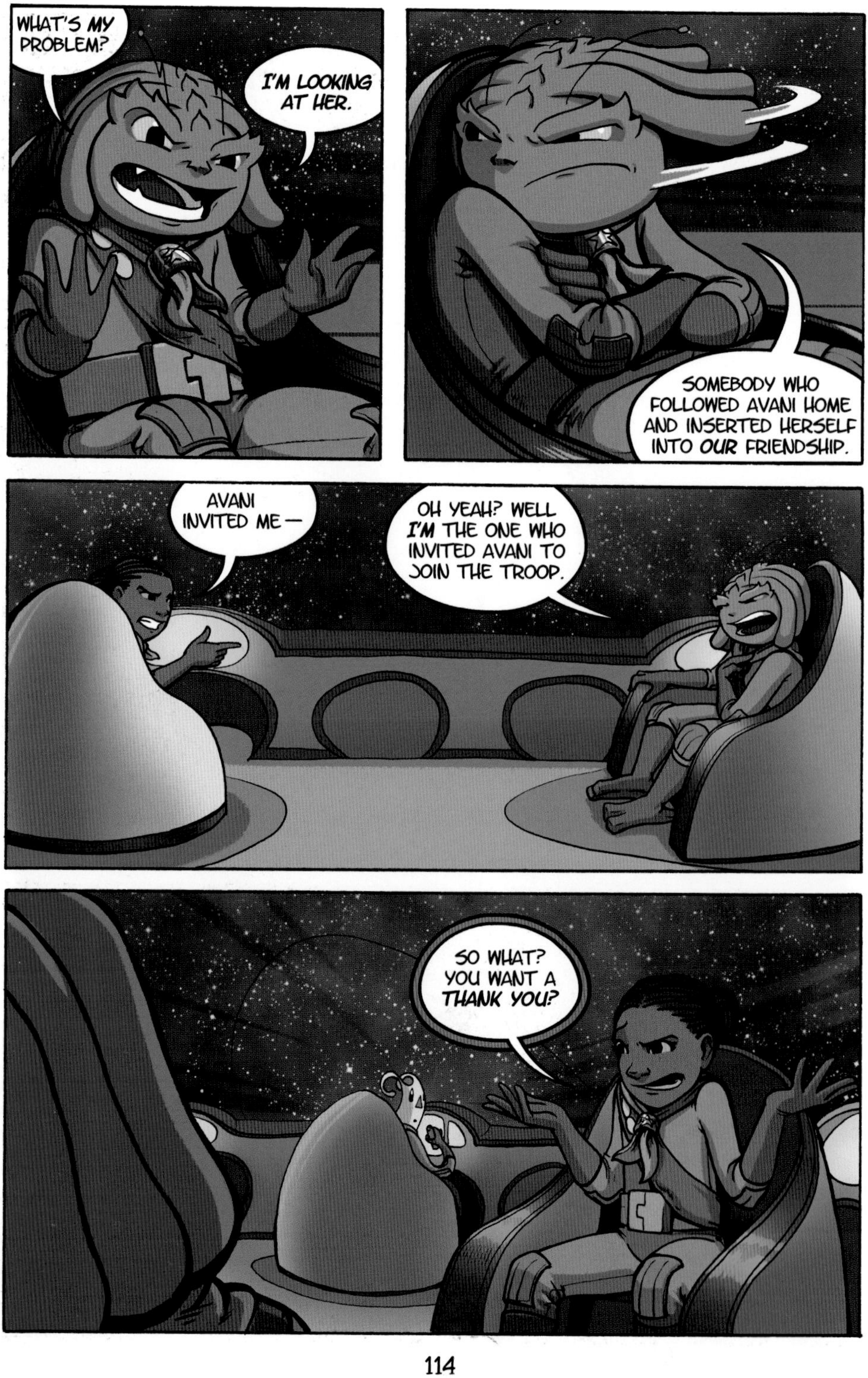

WHAT'S MY PROBLEM?
I'M LOOKING AT HER.
SOMEBODY WHO FOLLOWED AVANI HOME AND INSERTED HERSELF INTO OUR FRIENDSHIP.
AVANI INVITED ME—
OH YEAH? WELL I'M THE ONE WHO INVITED AVANI TO JOIN THE TROOP.
SO WHAT? YOU WANT A THANK YOU?

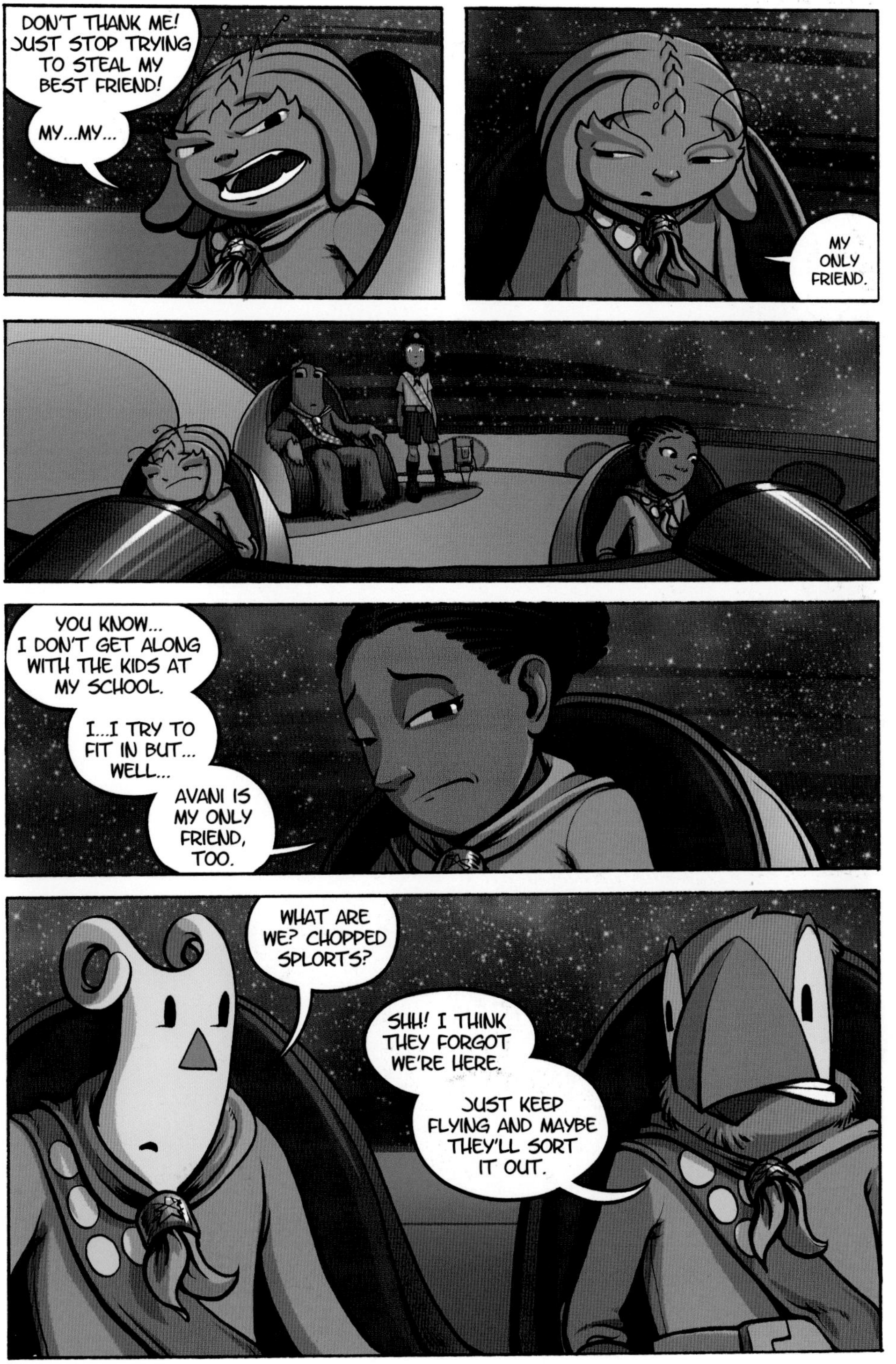
DON'T THANK ME! JUST STOP TRYING TO STEAL MY BEST FRIEND!
MY...MY...
MY ONLY FRIEND.
YOU KNOW... I DON'T GET ALONG WITH THE KIDS AT MY SCHOOL.
I...I TRY TO FIT IN BUT... WELL...
AVANI IS MY ONLY FRIEND, TOO.
WHAT ARE WE? CHOPPED SPLORTS?
SHH! I THINK THEY FORGOT WE'RE HERE.
JUST KEEP FLYING AND MAYBE THEY'LL SORT IT OUT.

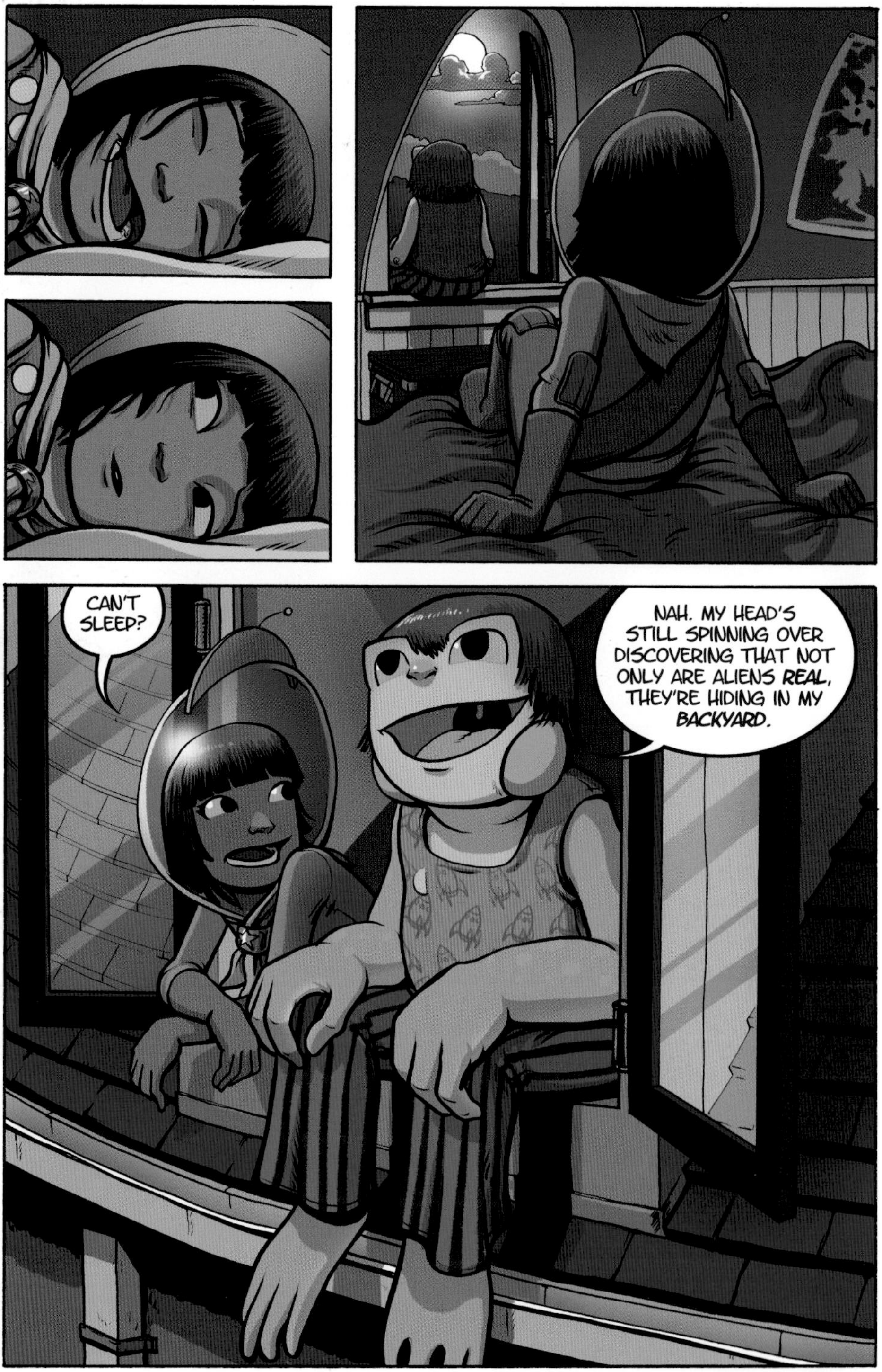
CAN'T SLEEP?
NAH. MY HEAD'S STILL SPINNING OVER DISCOVERING THAT NOT ONLY ARE ALIENS *REAL*, THEY'RE HIDING IN MY *BACKYARD*.

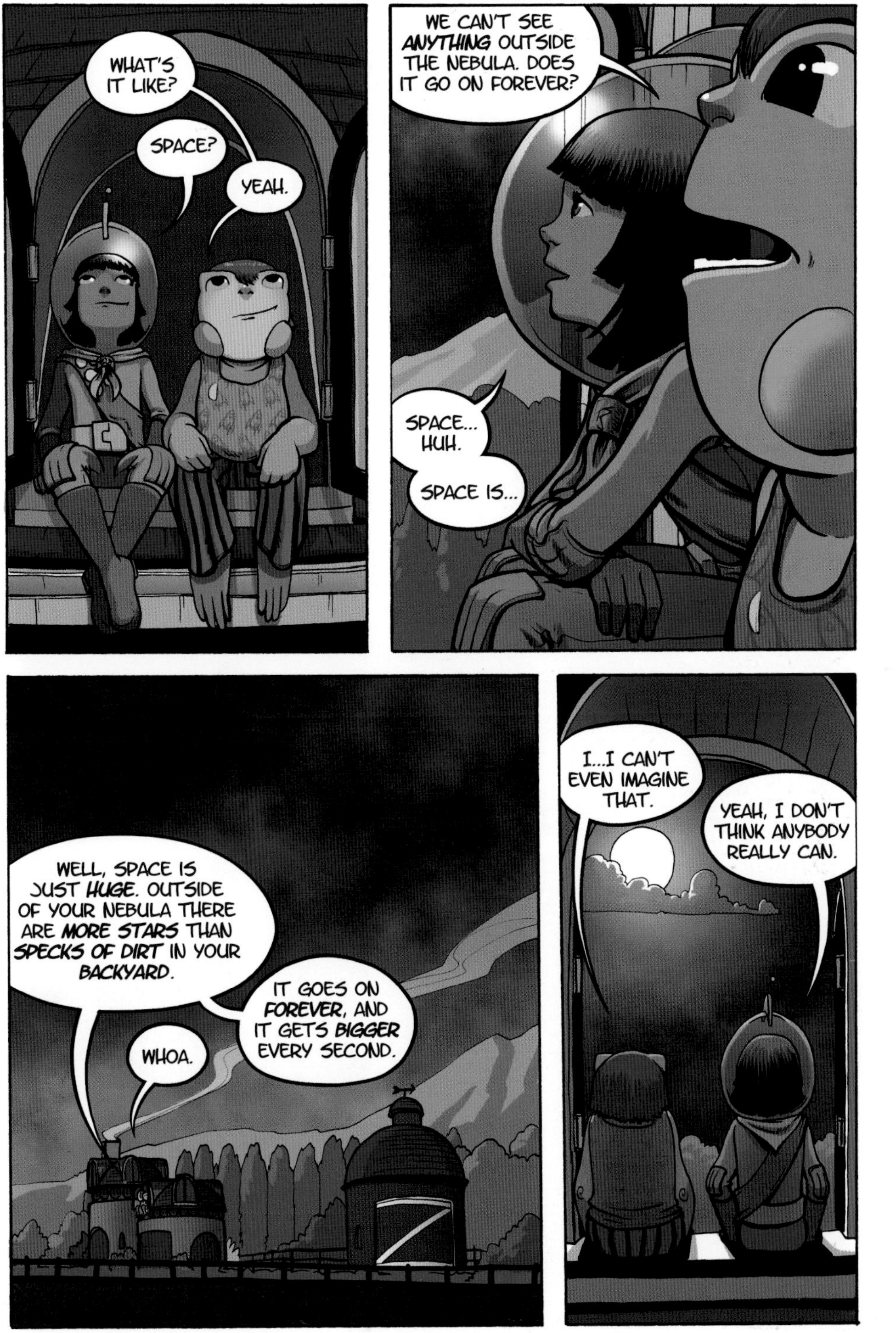
WHAT'S IT LIKE?
SPACE?
YEAH.
WE CAN'T SEE ANYTHING OUTSIDE THE NEBULA. DOES IT GO ON FOREVER?
SPACE... HUH.
SPACE IS...
WELL, SPACE IS JUST HUGE. OUTSIDE OF YOUR NEBULA THERE ARE MORE STARS THAN SPECKS OF DIRT IN YOUR BACKYARD.
IT GOES ON FOREVER, AND IT GETS BIGGER EVERY SECOND.
WHOA.
I...I CAN'T EVEN IMAGINE THAT.
YEAH, I DON'T THINK ANYBODY REALLY CAN.

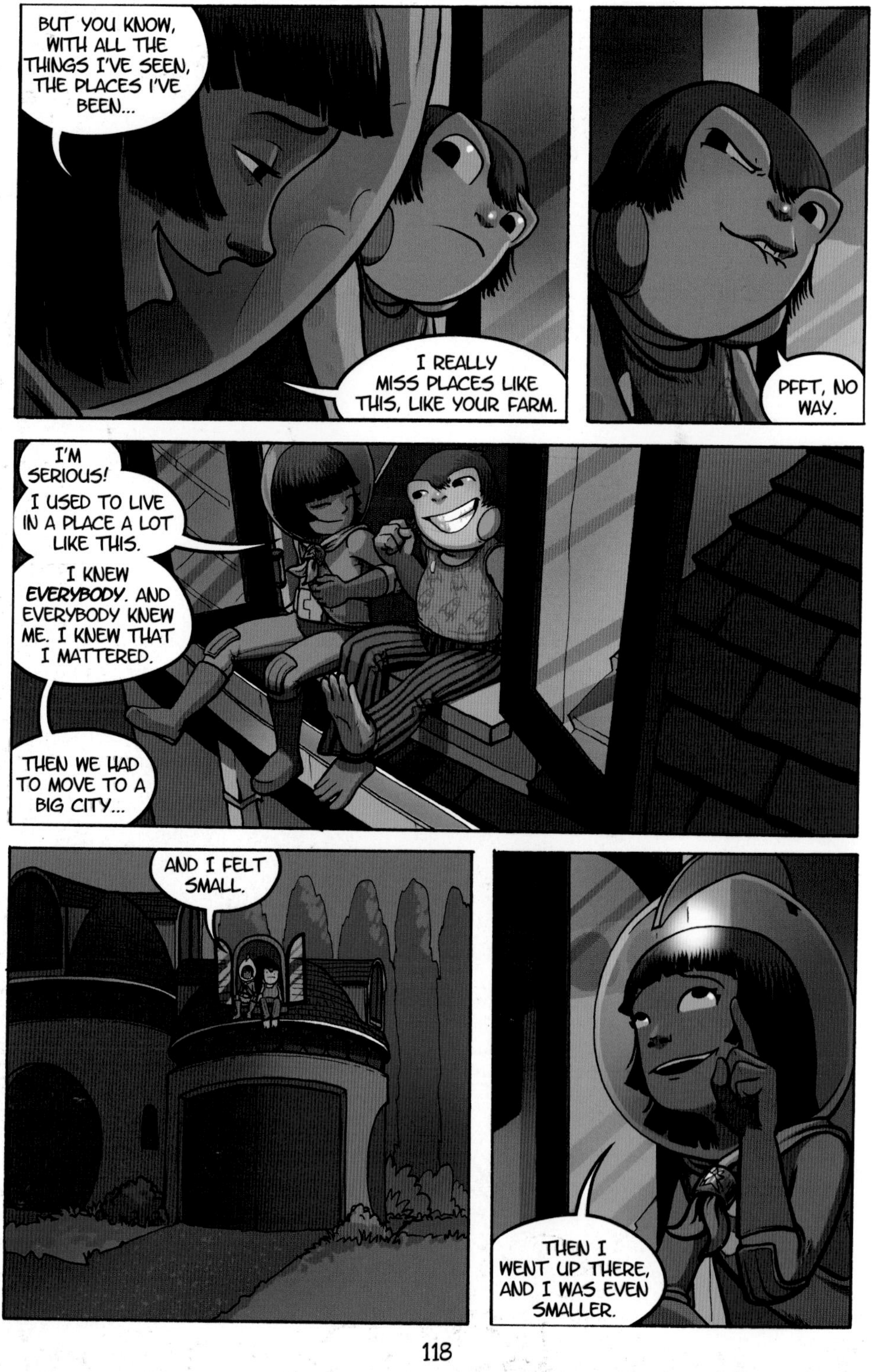
BUT YOU KNOW, WITH ALL THE THINGS I'VE SEEN, THE PLACES I'VE BEEN...
I REALLY MISS PLACES LIKE THIS, LIKE YOUR FARM.
PFFT, NO WAY.
I'M SERIOUS!
I USED TO LIVE IN A PLACE A LOT LIKE THIS.
I KNEW *EVERYBODY*. AND EVERYBODY KNEW ME. I KNEW THAT I MATTERED.
THEN WE HAD TO MOVE TO A BIG CITY...
AND I FELT SMALL.
THEN I WENT UP THERE, AND I WAS EVEN SMALLER.

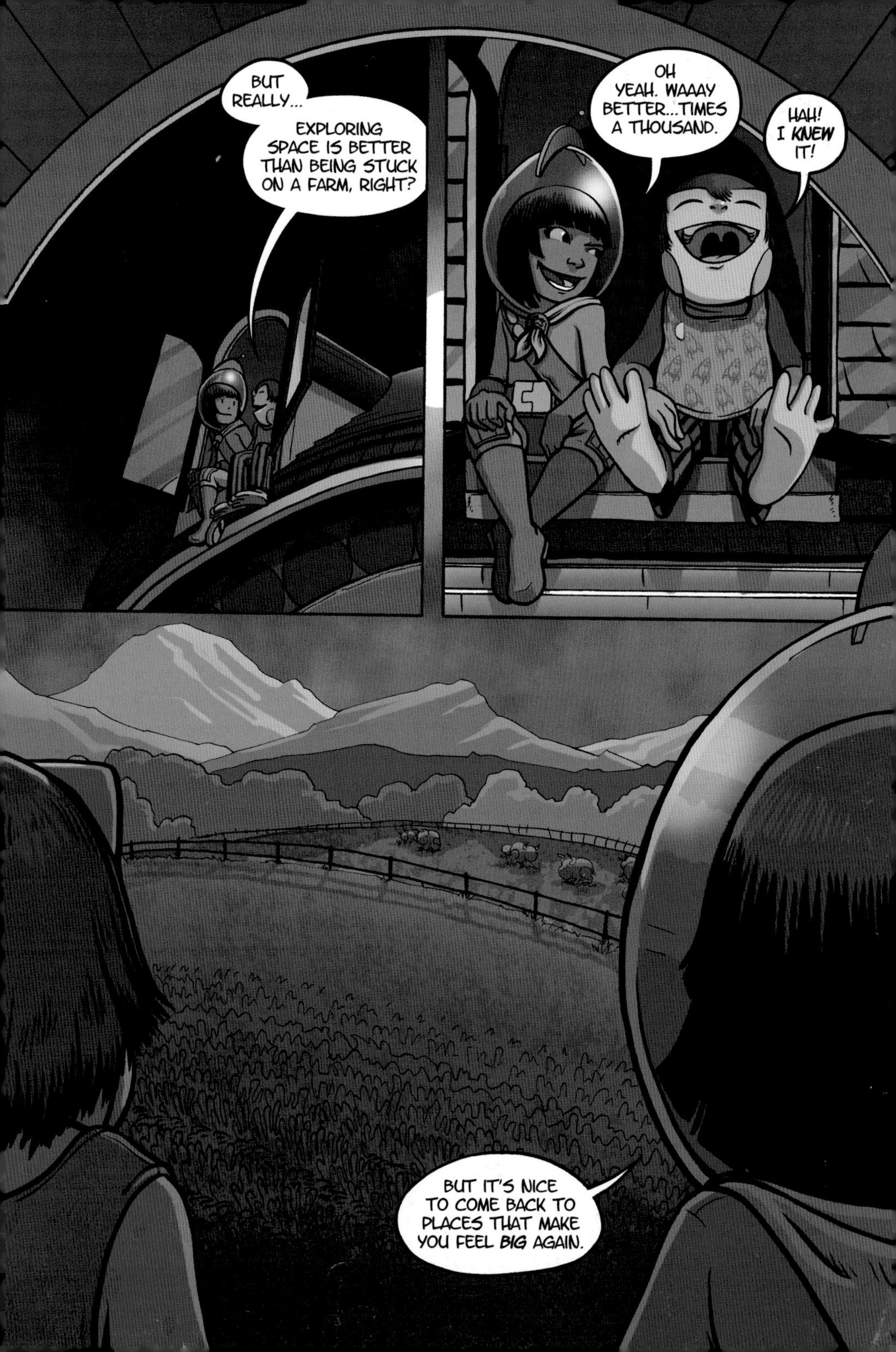
BUT REALLY...
EXPLORING SPACE IS BETTER THAN BEING STUCK ON A FARM, RIGHT?
OH YEAH. WAAAY BETTER...TIMES A THOUSAND.
HAH! I **KNEW** IT!
BUT IT'S NICE TO COME BACK TO PLACES THAT MAKE YOU FEEL **BIG** AGAIN.

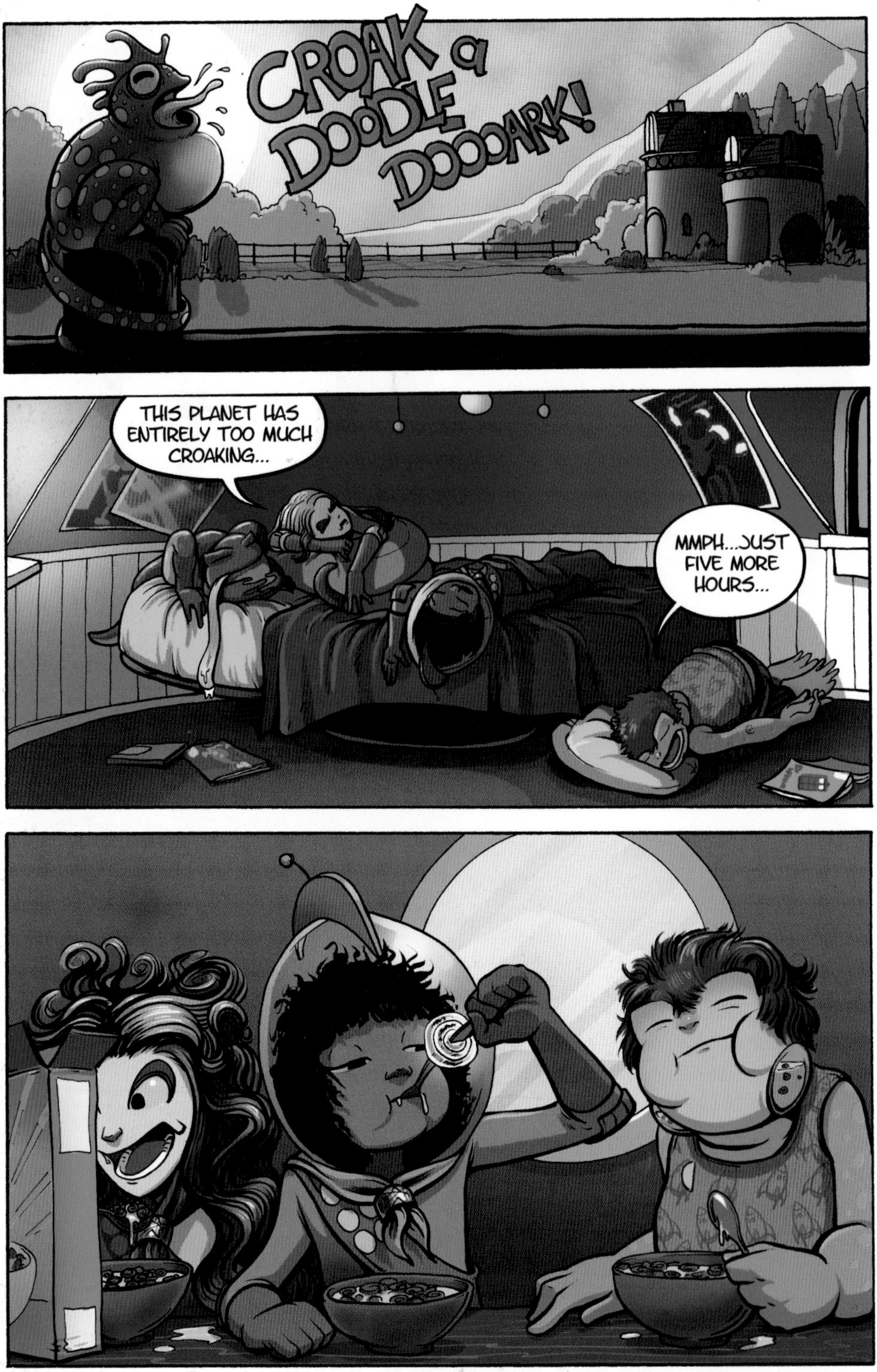
CROAK a DOODLE DOOOARK!
THIS PLANET HAS ENTIRELY TOO MUCH CROAKING...
MMPH...JUST FIVE MORE HOURS...

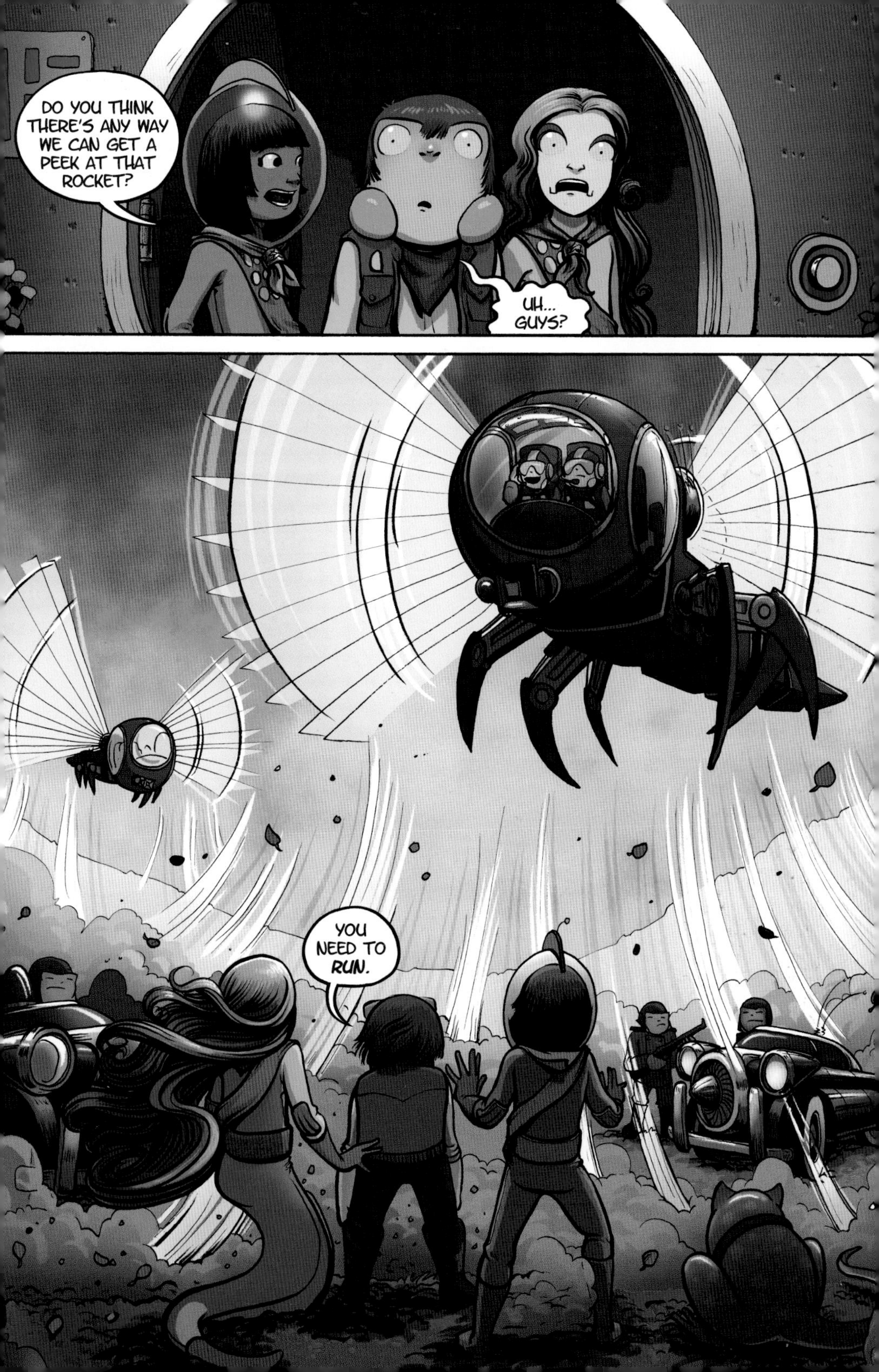
DO YOU THINK THERE'S ANY WAY WE CAN GET A PEEK AT THAT ROCKET?
UH... GUYS?
YOU NEED TO RUN.

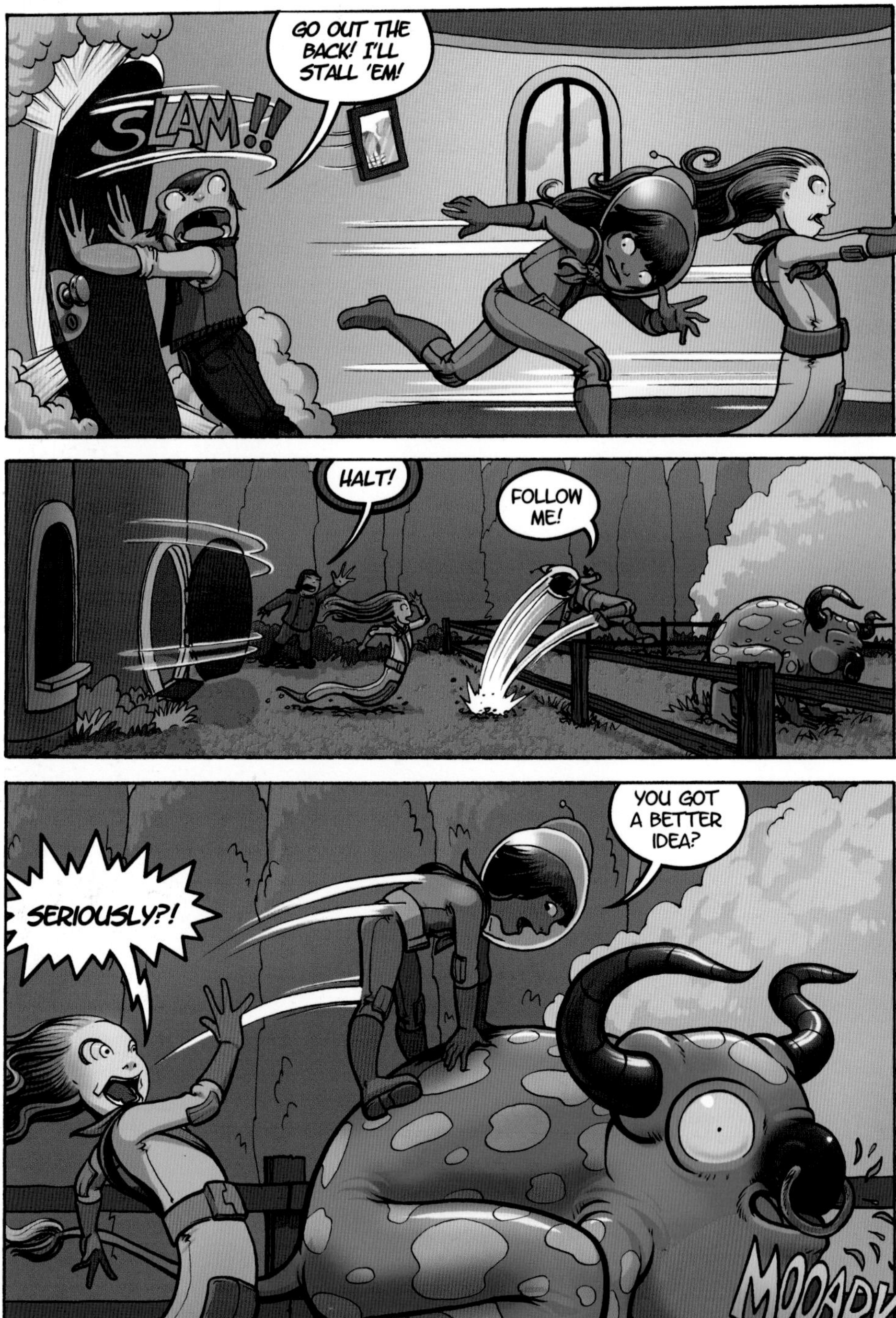
GO OUT THE BACK! I'LL STALL 'EM!
SLAM!!
HALT!
FOLLOW ME!
SERIOUSLY?!
YOU GOT A BETTER IDEA?
MOOARK?

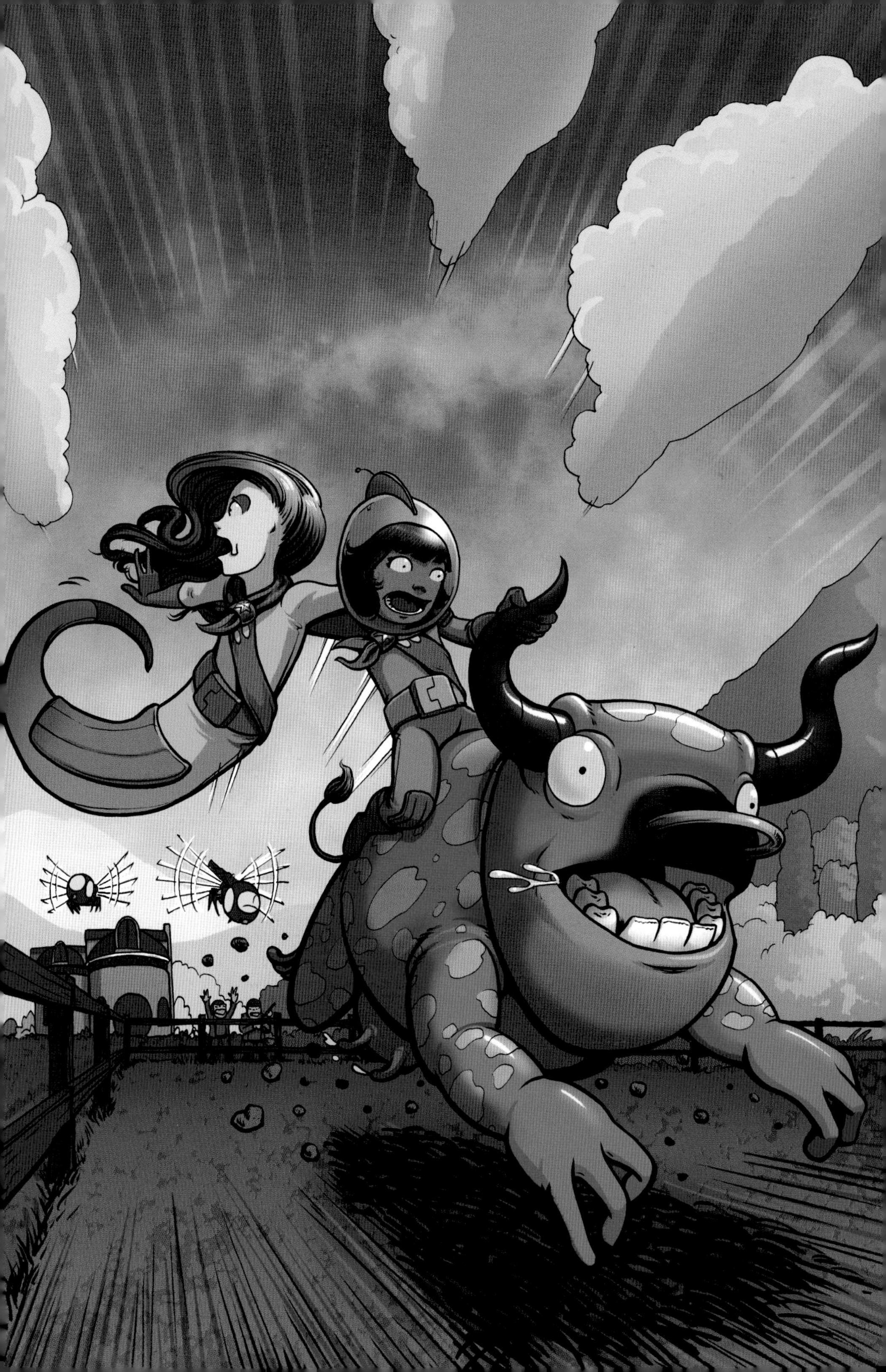

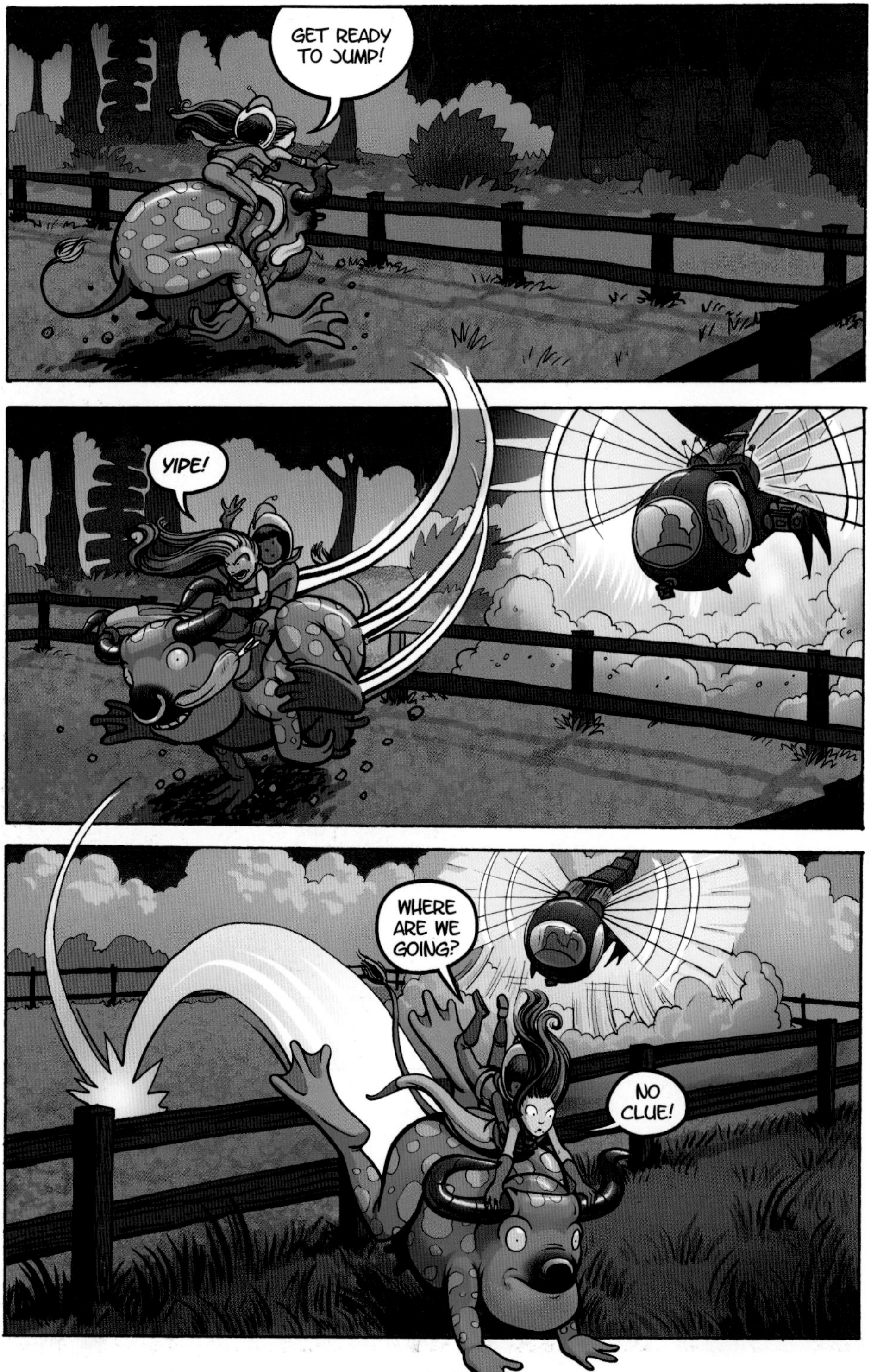
GET READY TO JUMP!
YIPE!
WHERE ARE WE GOING?
NO CLUE!

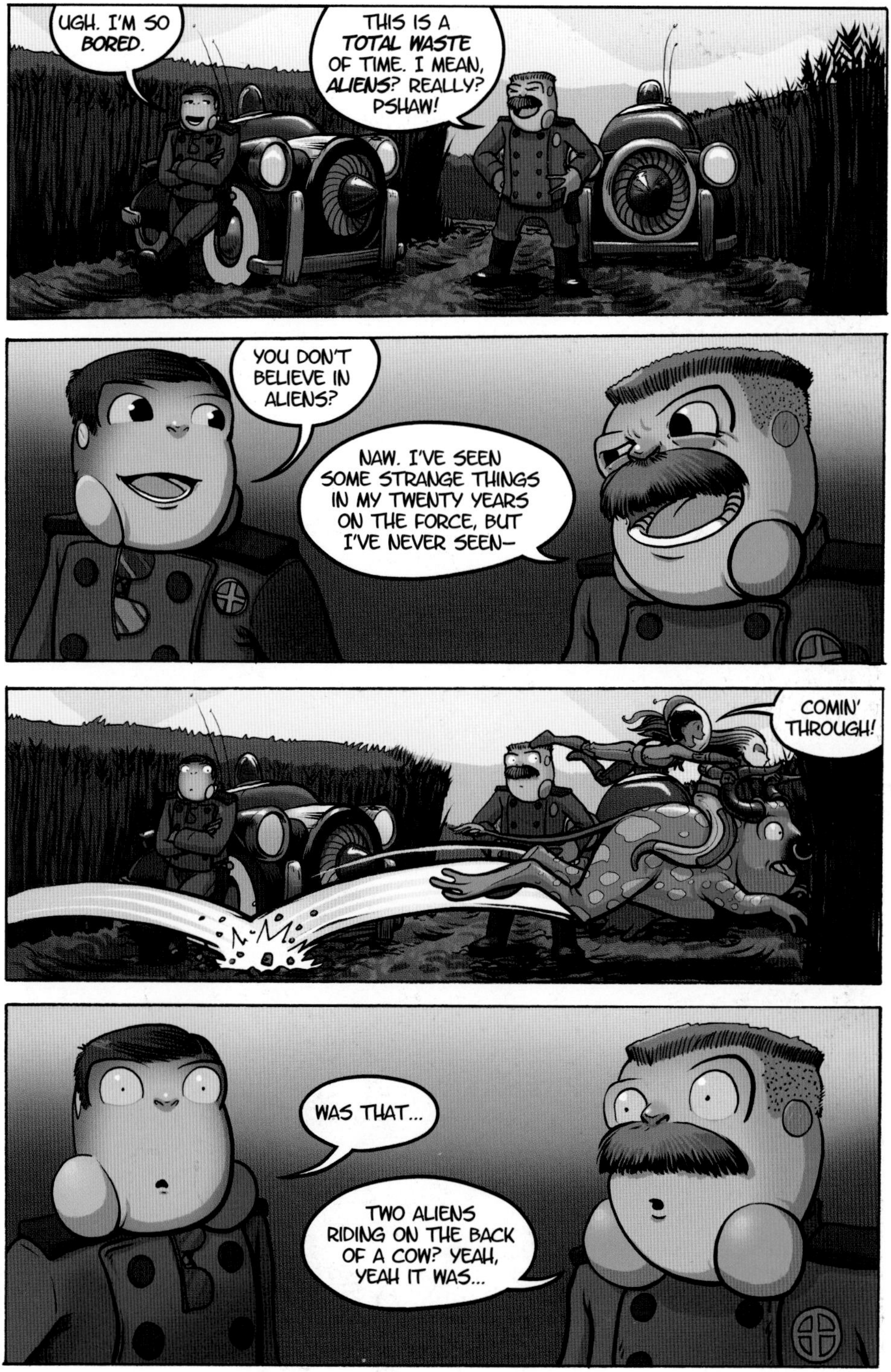
UGH. I'M SO BORED.
THIS IS A TOTAL WASTE OF TIME. I MEAN, ALIENS? REALLY? PSHAW!
YOU DON'T BELIEVE IN ALIENS?
NAW. I'VE SEEN SOME STRANGE THINGS IN MY TWENTY YEARS ON THE FORCE, BUT I'VE NEVER SEEN–
COMIN' THROUGH!
WAS THAT...
TWO ALIENS RIDING ON THE BACK OF A COW? YEAH, YEAH IT WAS...

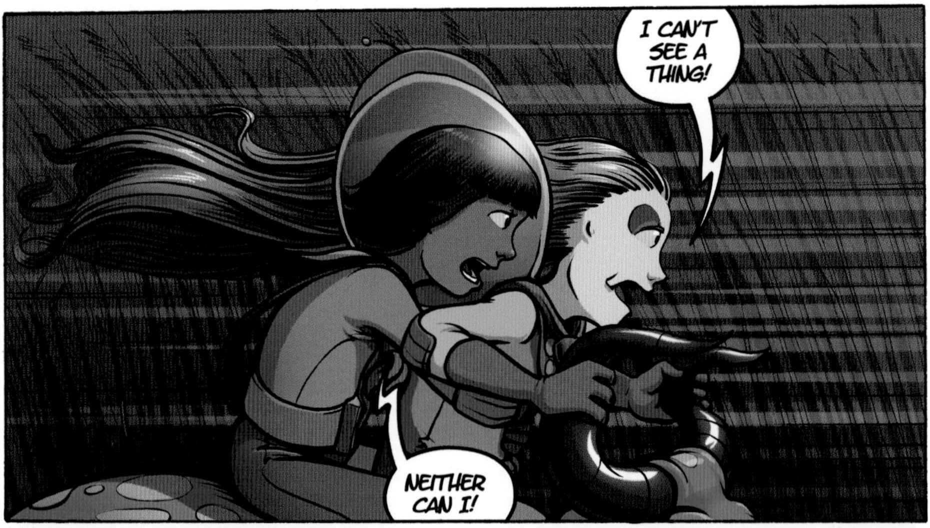
I CAN'T SEE A THING!
NEITHER CAN I!

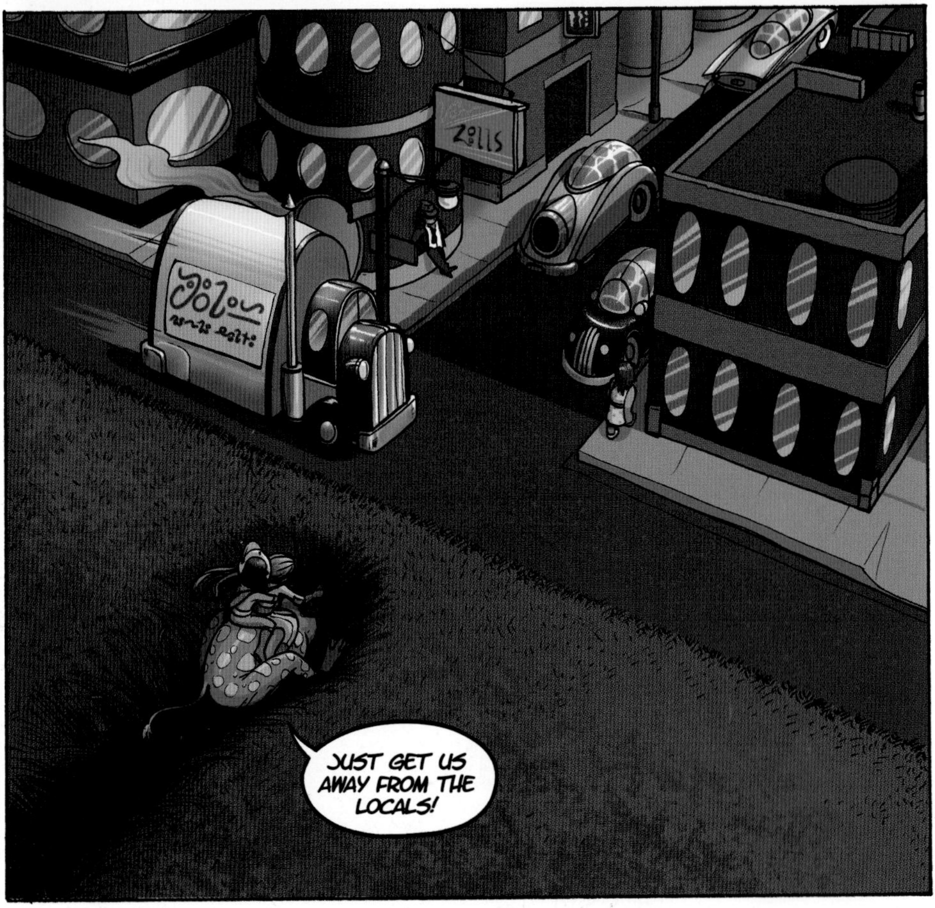
JUST GET US AWAY FROM THE LOCALS!

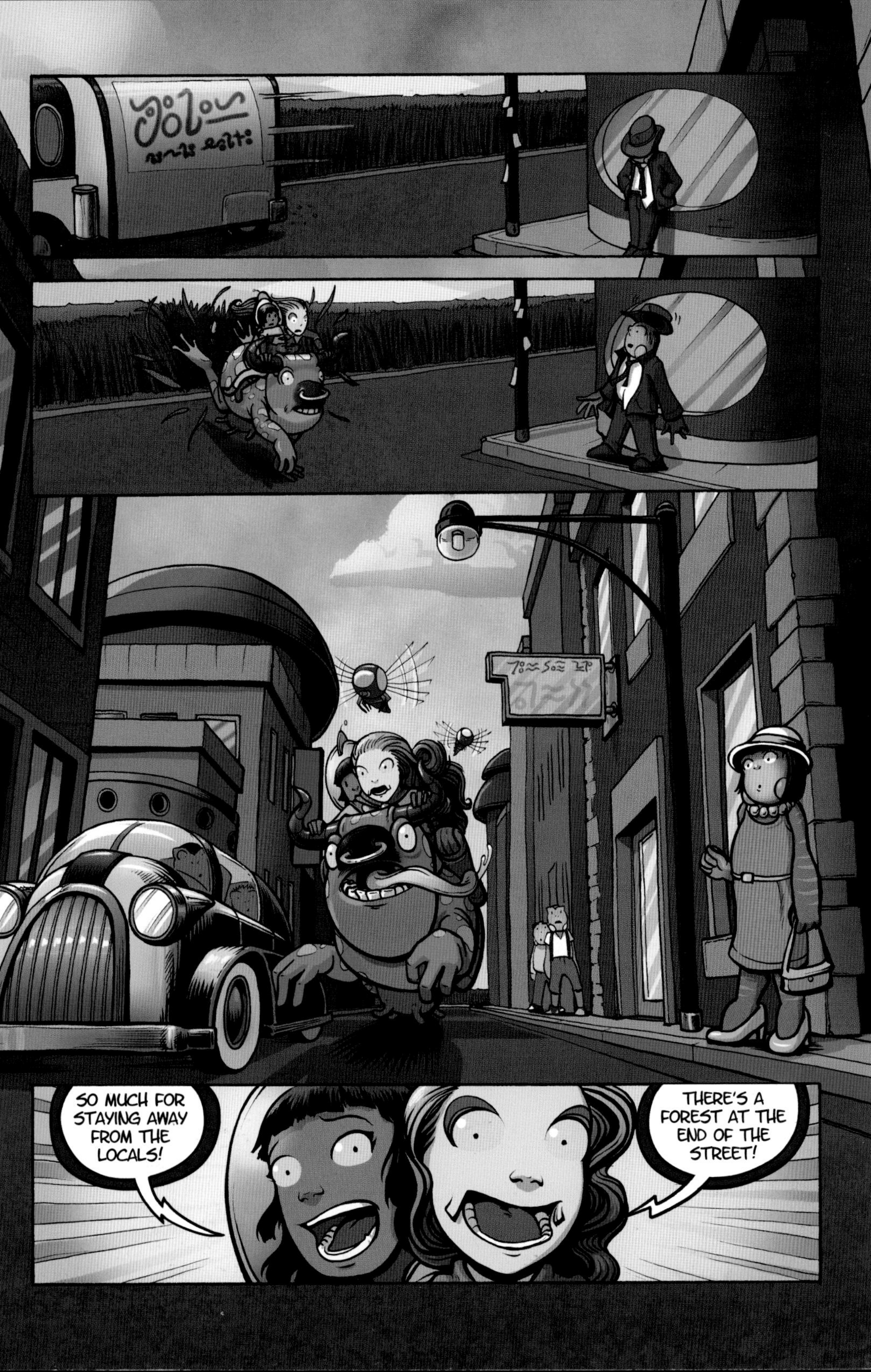
SO MUCH FOR STAYING AWAY FROM THE LOCALS!
THERE'S A FOREST AT THE END OF THE STREET!

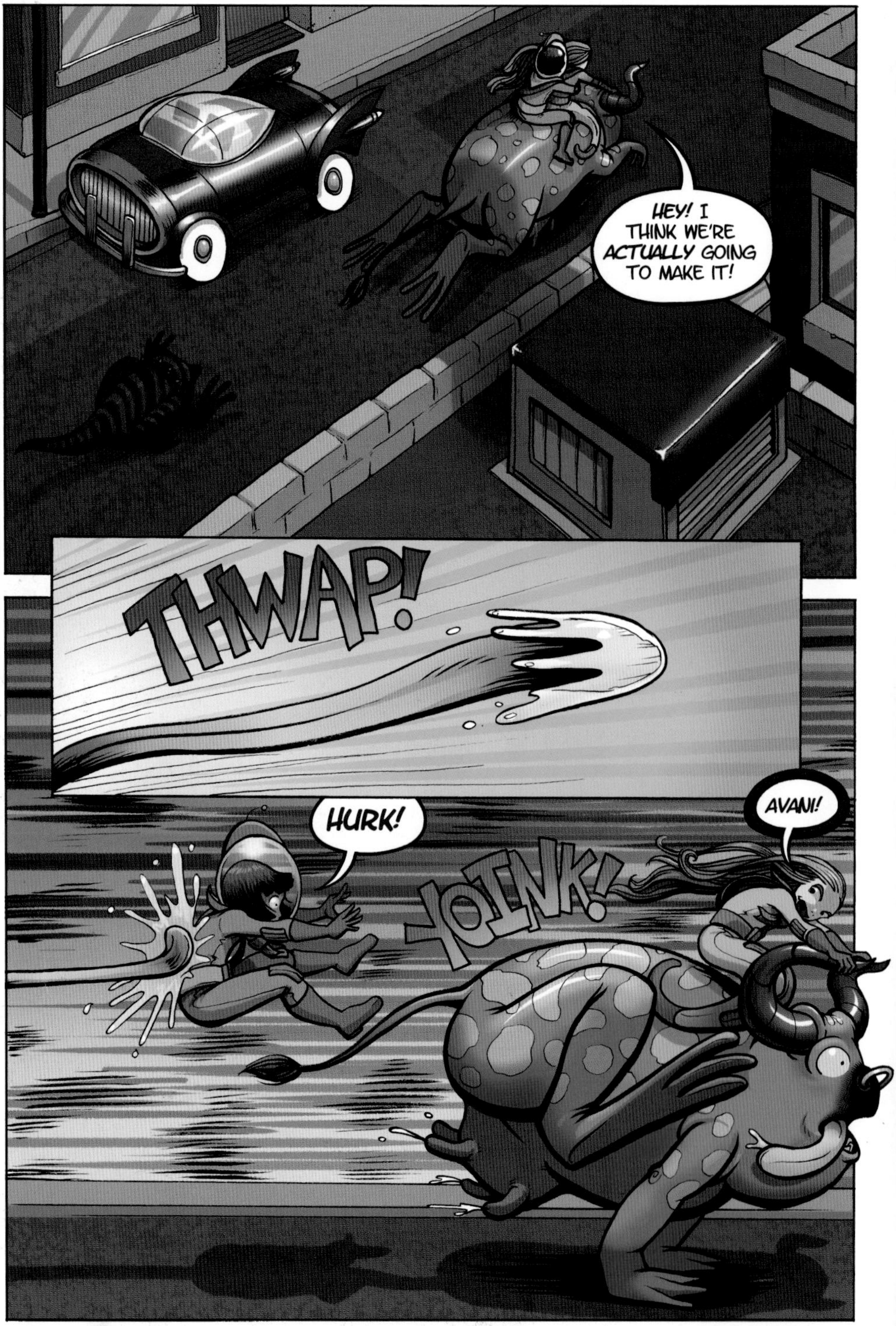

HEY! I THINK WE'RE ACTUALLY GOING TO MAKE IT!
THWAP!
HURK!
YOINK!
AVANI!

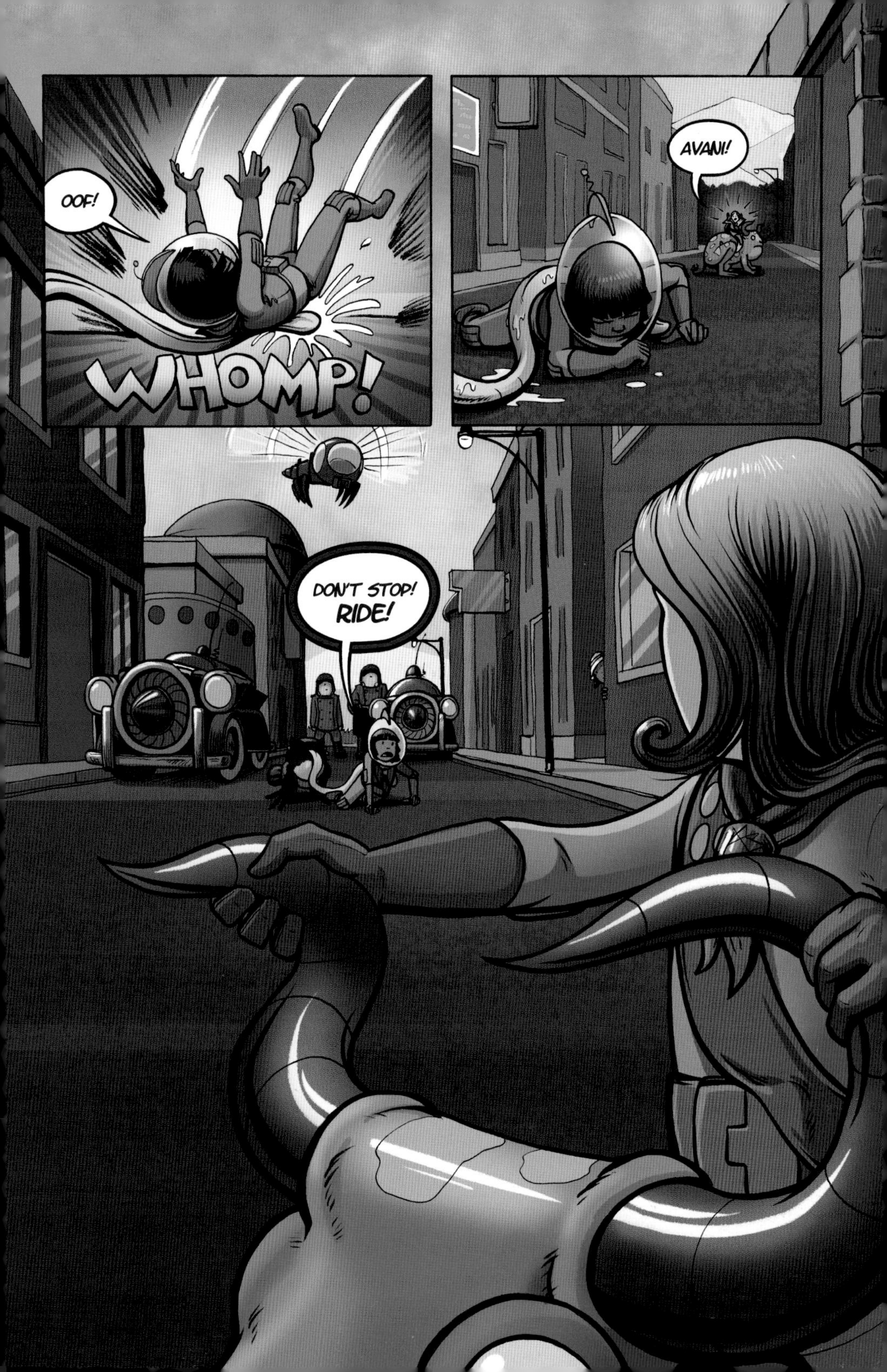
OOF!
WHOMP!
AVANI!
DON'T STOP!
RIDE!

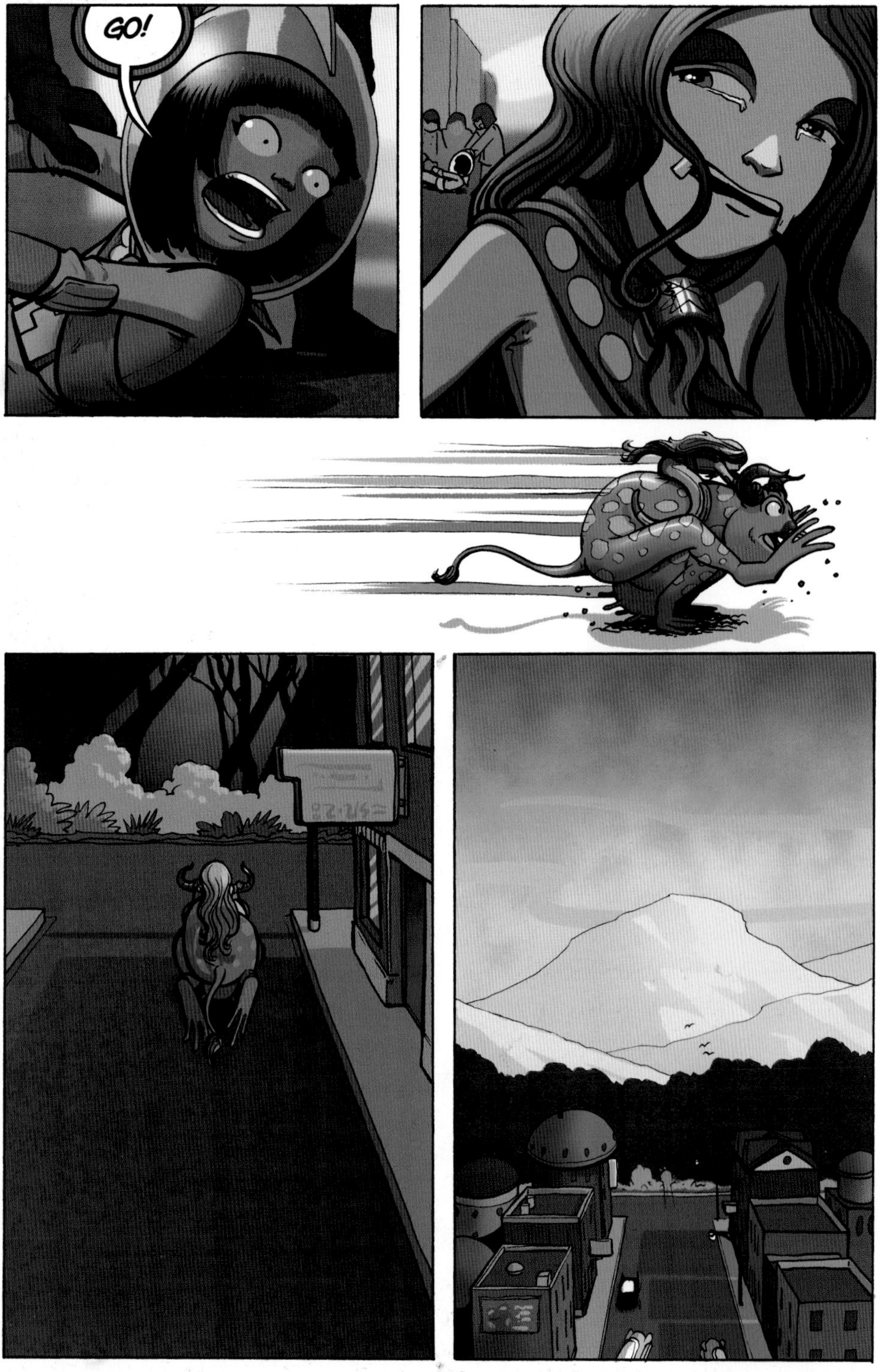
GO!

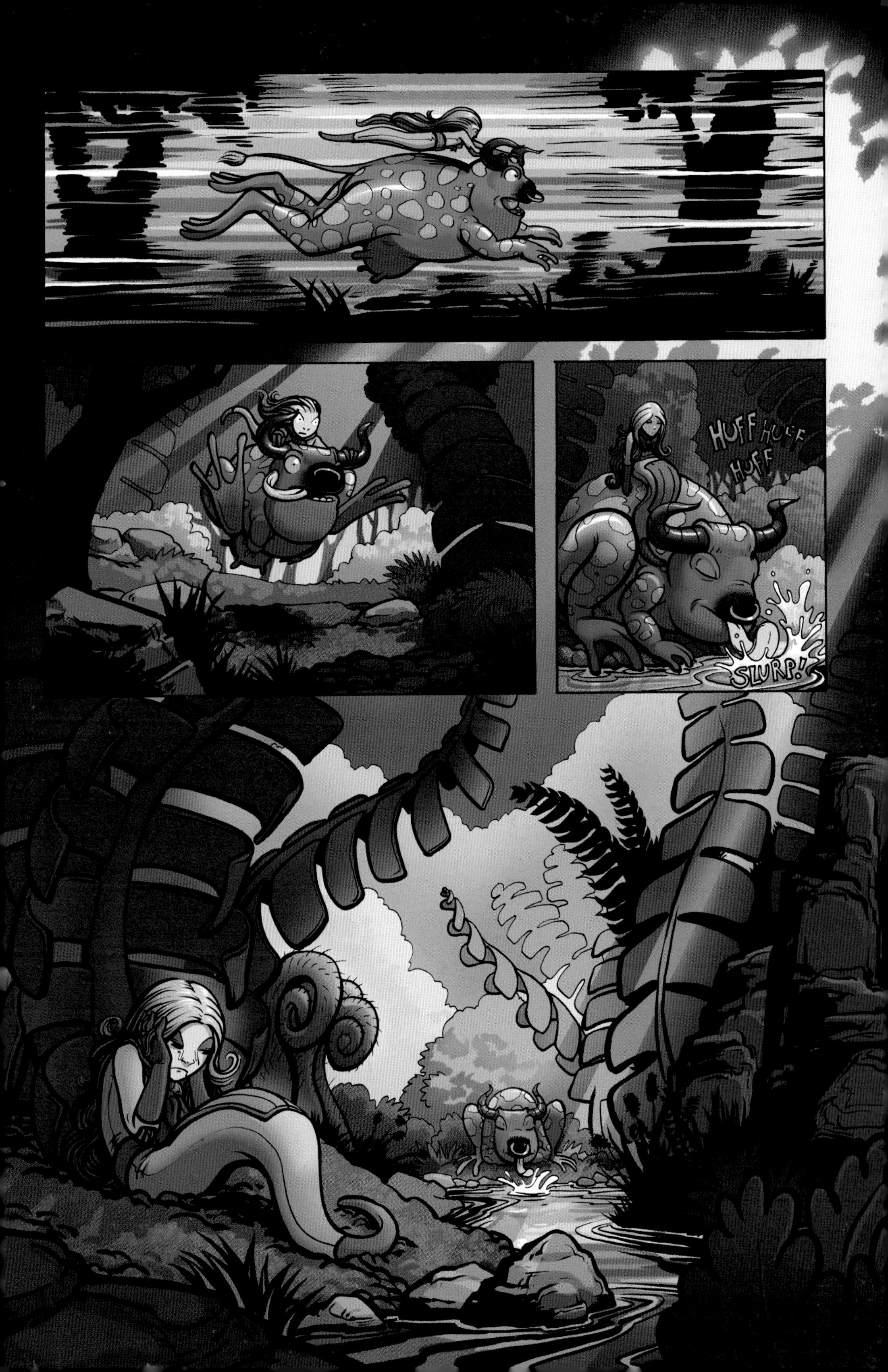
HUFF HUFF
HUFF
SLURP!

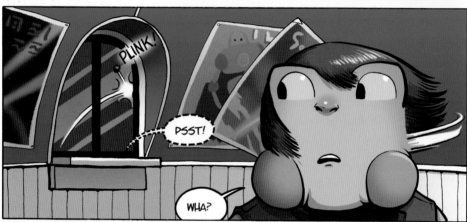

PLINK!

PSST!

WHA?

FRANK! LET
ME IN QUICK!
THERE ARE GUARDS
EVERYWHERE!

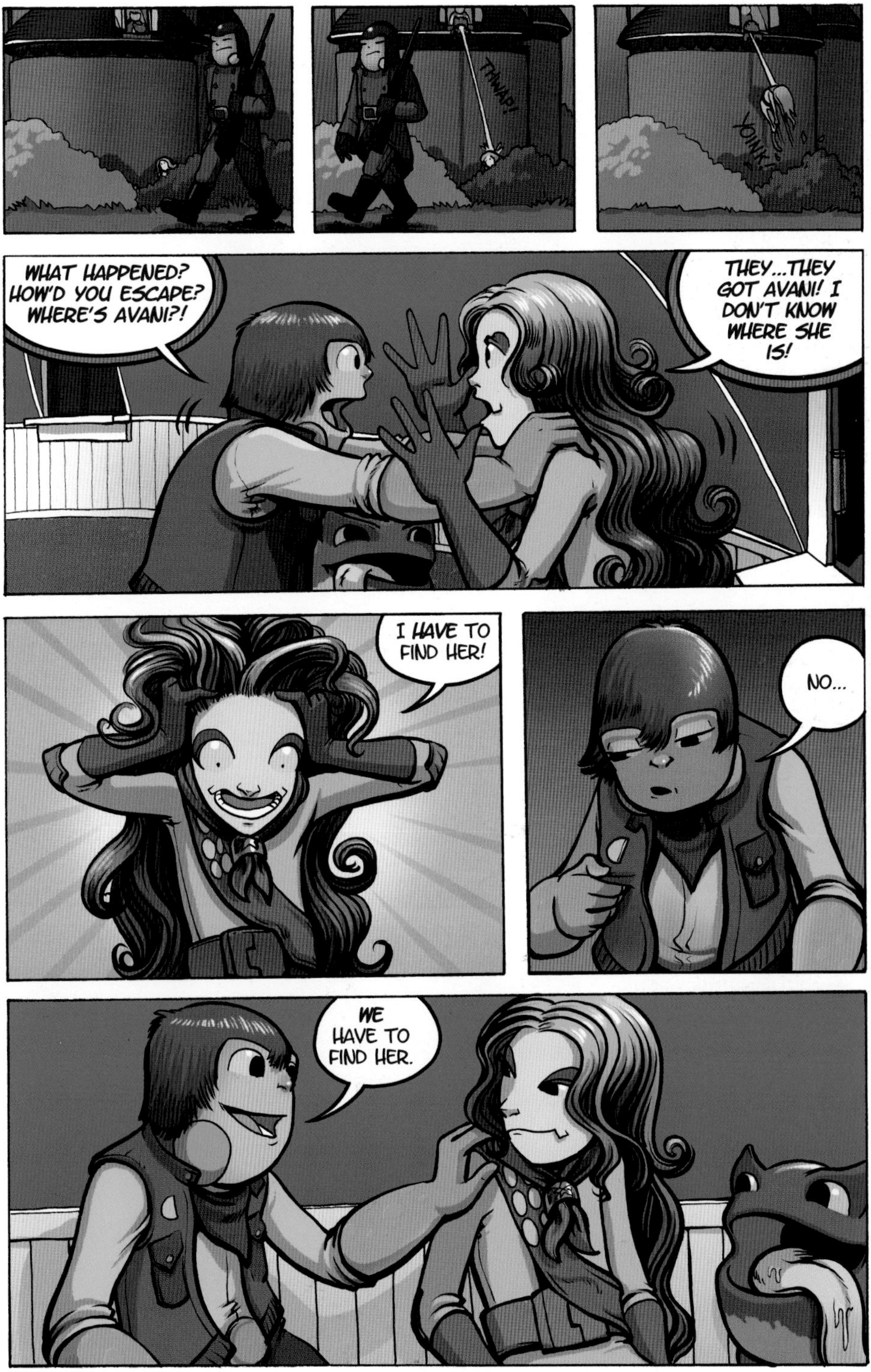
THWAP!
YOINK!
WHAT HAPPENED? HOW'D YOU ESCAPE? WHERE'S AVANI?!
THEY...THEY GOT AVANI! I DON'T KNOW WHERE SHE IS!
I HAVE TO FIND HER!
NO...
WE HAVE TO FIND HER.

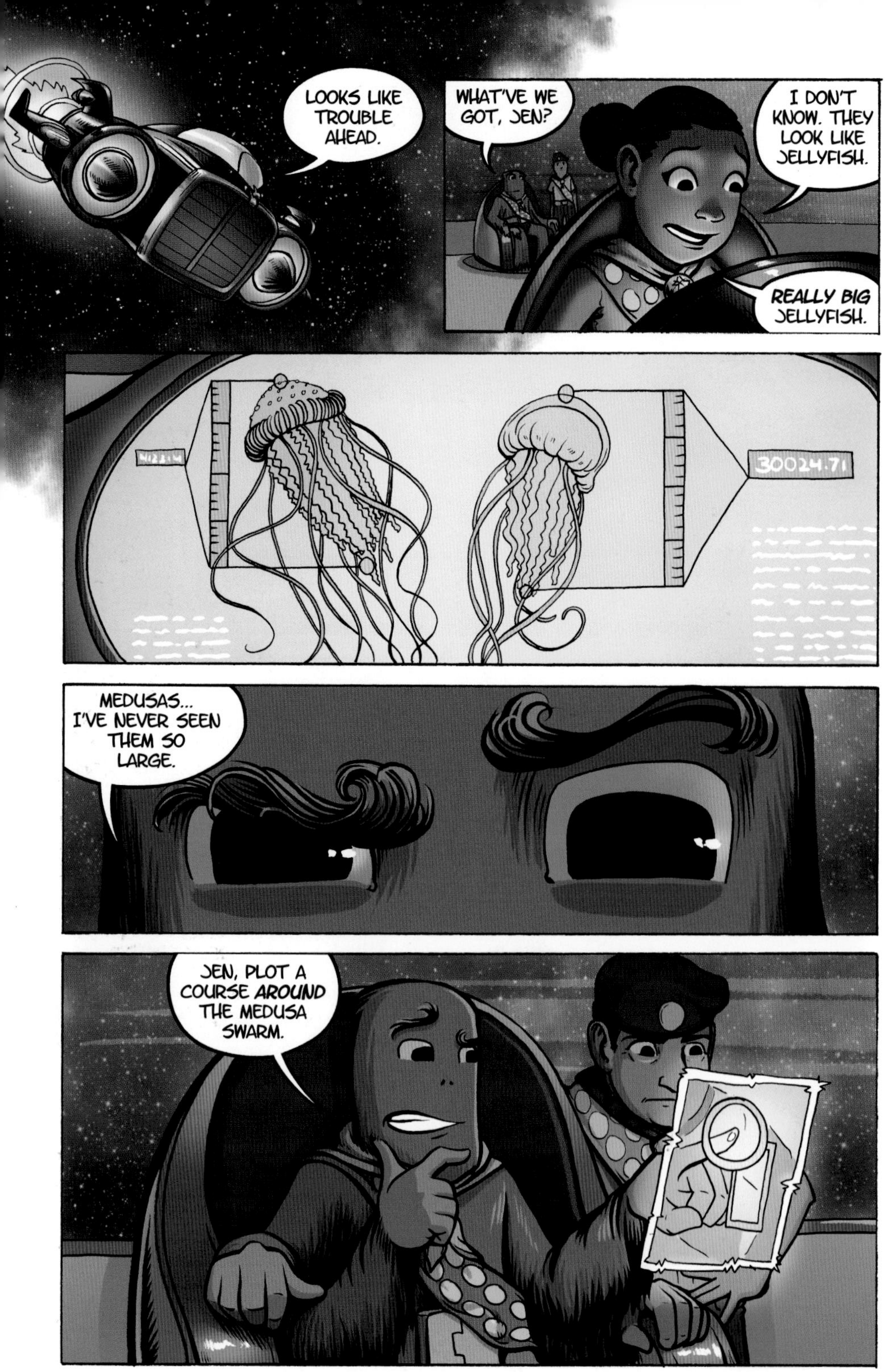
LOOKS LIKE TROUBLE AHEAD.
WHAT'VE WE GOT, JEN?
I DON'T KNOW. THEY LOOK LIKE JELLYFISH.
REALLY BIG JELLYFISH.
30024.71
MEDUSAS... I'VE NEVER SEEN THEM SO LARGE.
JEN, PLOT A COURSE AROUND THE MEDUSA SWARM.

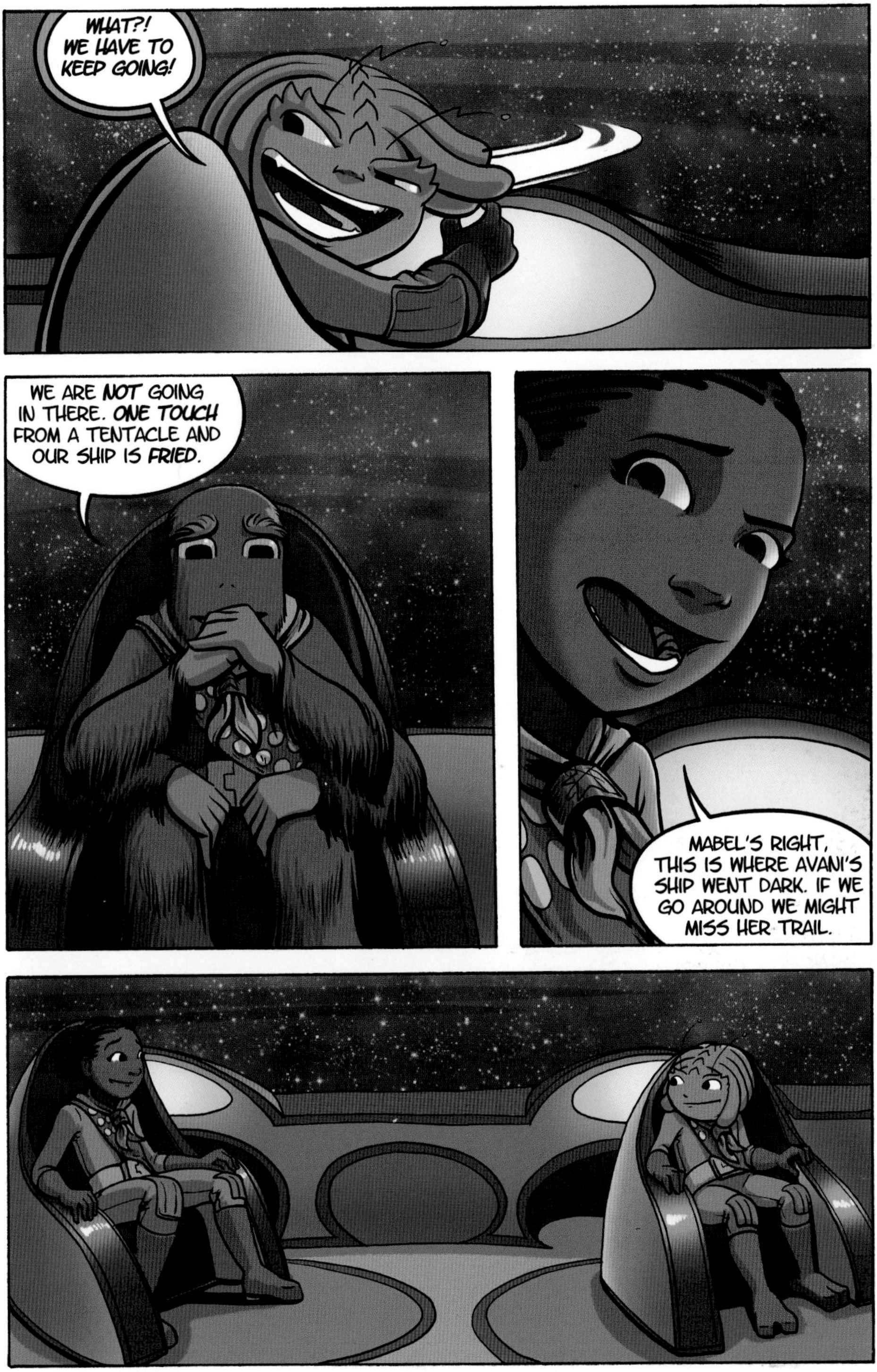
WHAT?! WE HAVE TO KEEP GOING!
WE ARE NOT GOING IN THERE. ONE TOUCH FROM A TENTACLE AND OUR SHIP IS FRIED.
MABEL'S RIGHT, THIS IS WHERE AVANI'S SHIP WENT DARK. IF WE GO AROUND WE MIGHT MISS HER TRAIL.

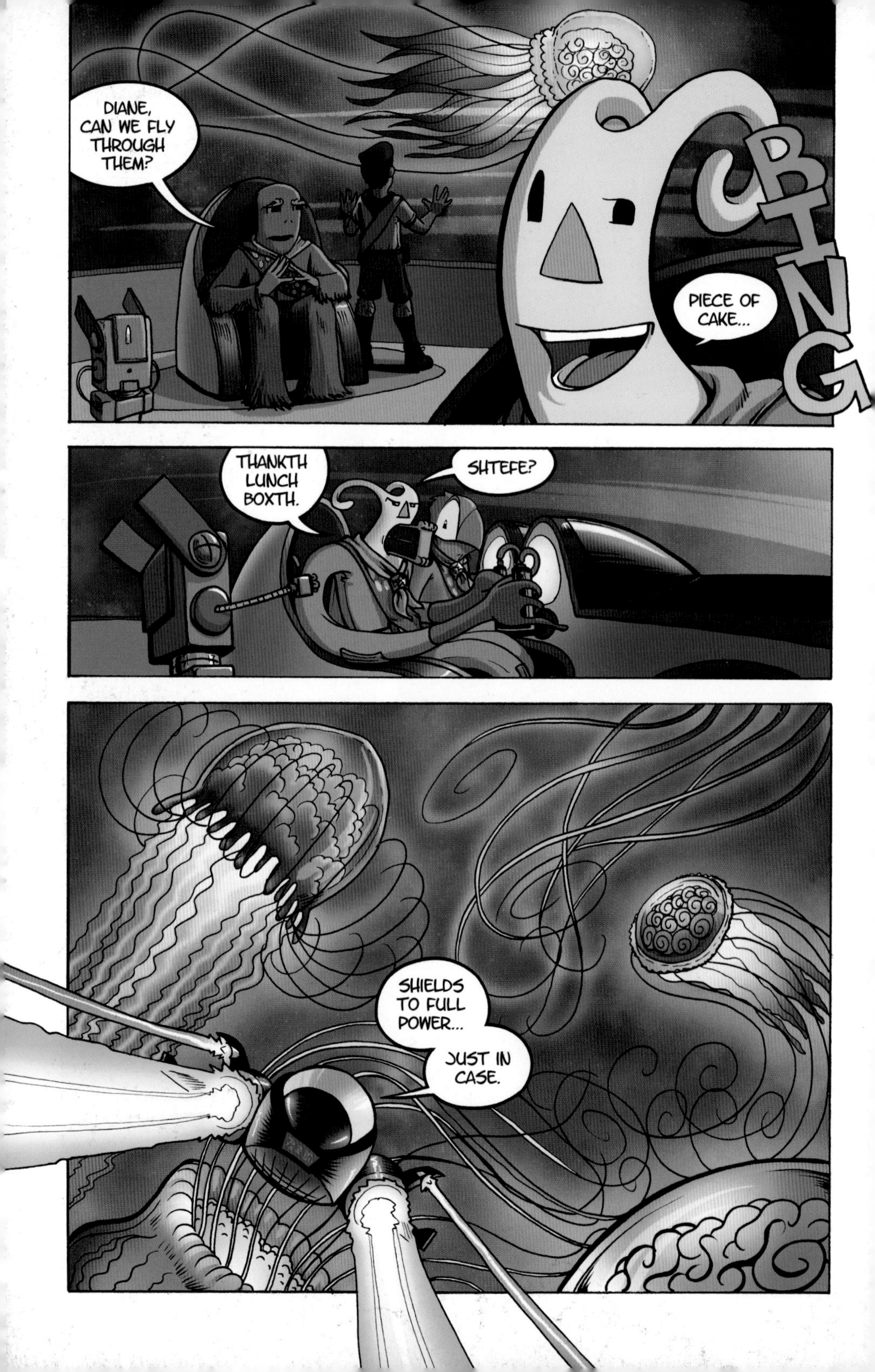

DIANE, CAN WE FLY THROUGH THEM?
BING
PIECE OF CAKE...
THANKTH LUNCH BOXTH.
SHTEFE?
SHIELDS TO FULL POWER...
JUST IN CASE.

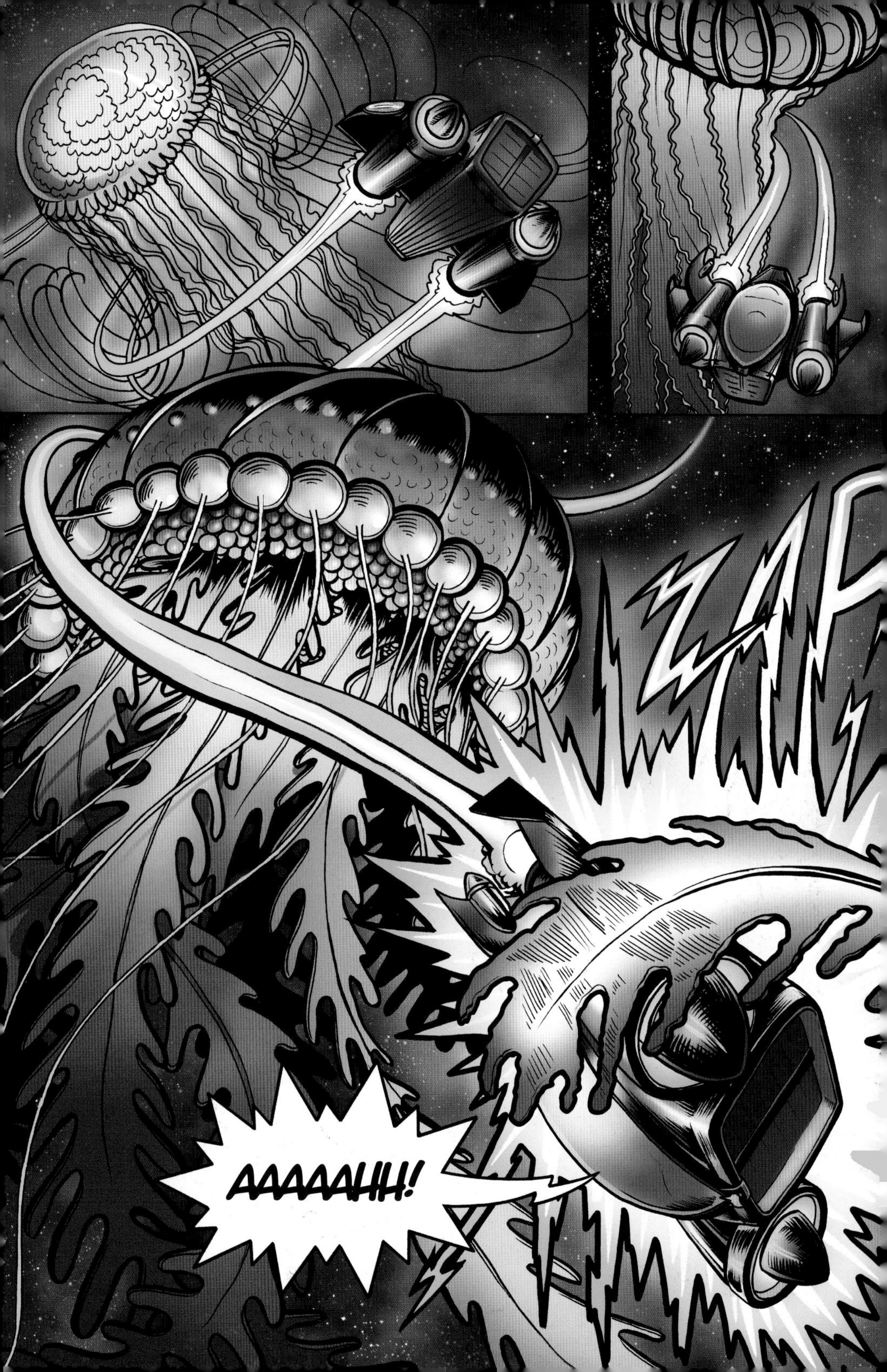
ZAP
AAAAAHH!

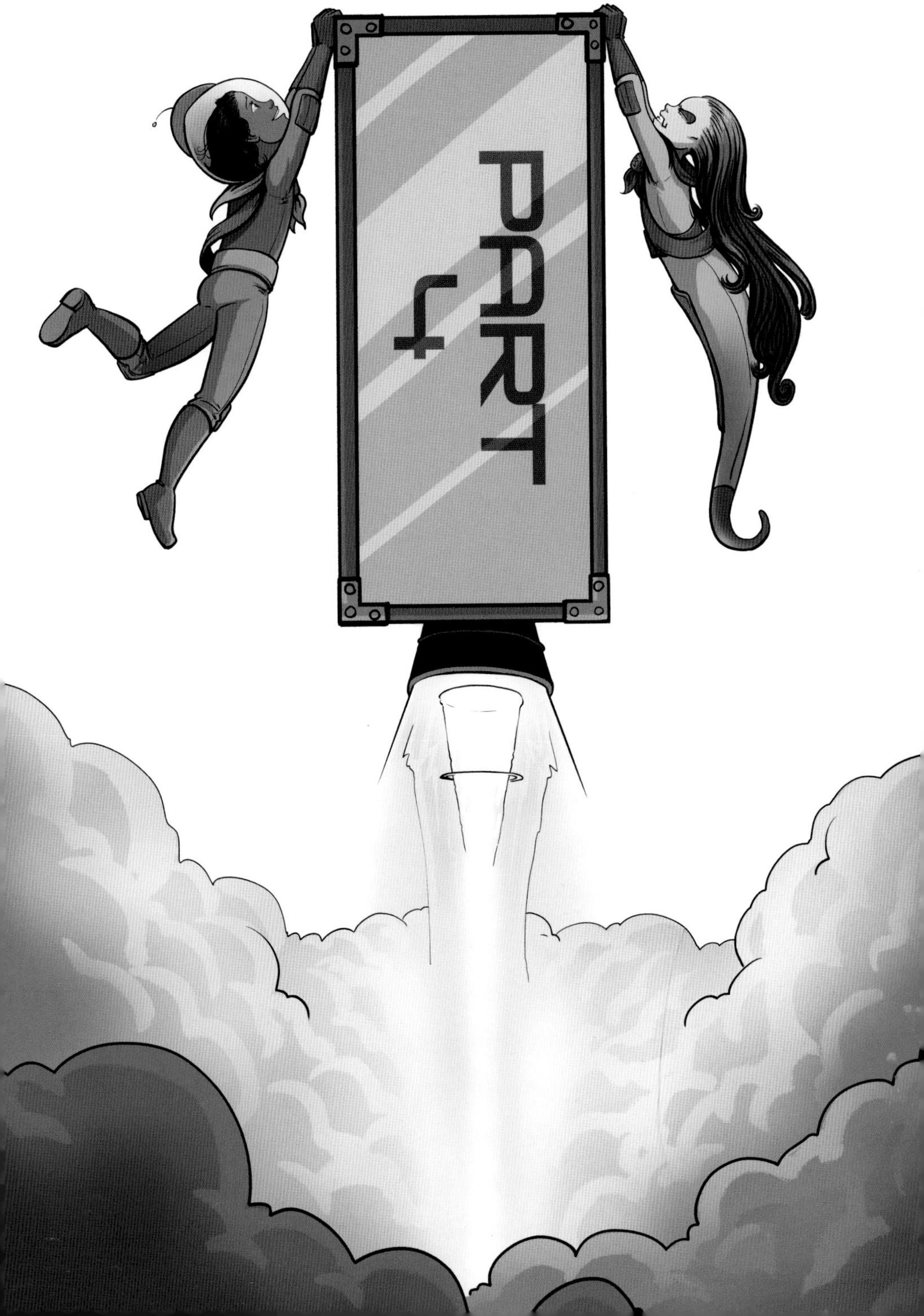
PART 4

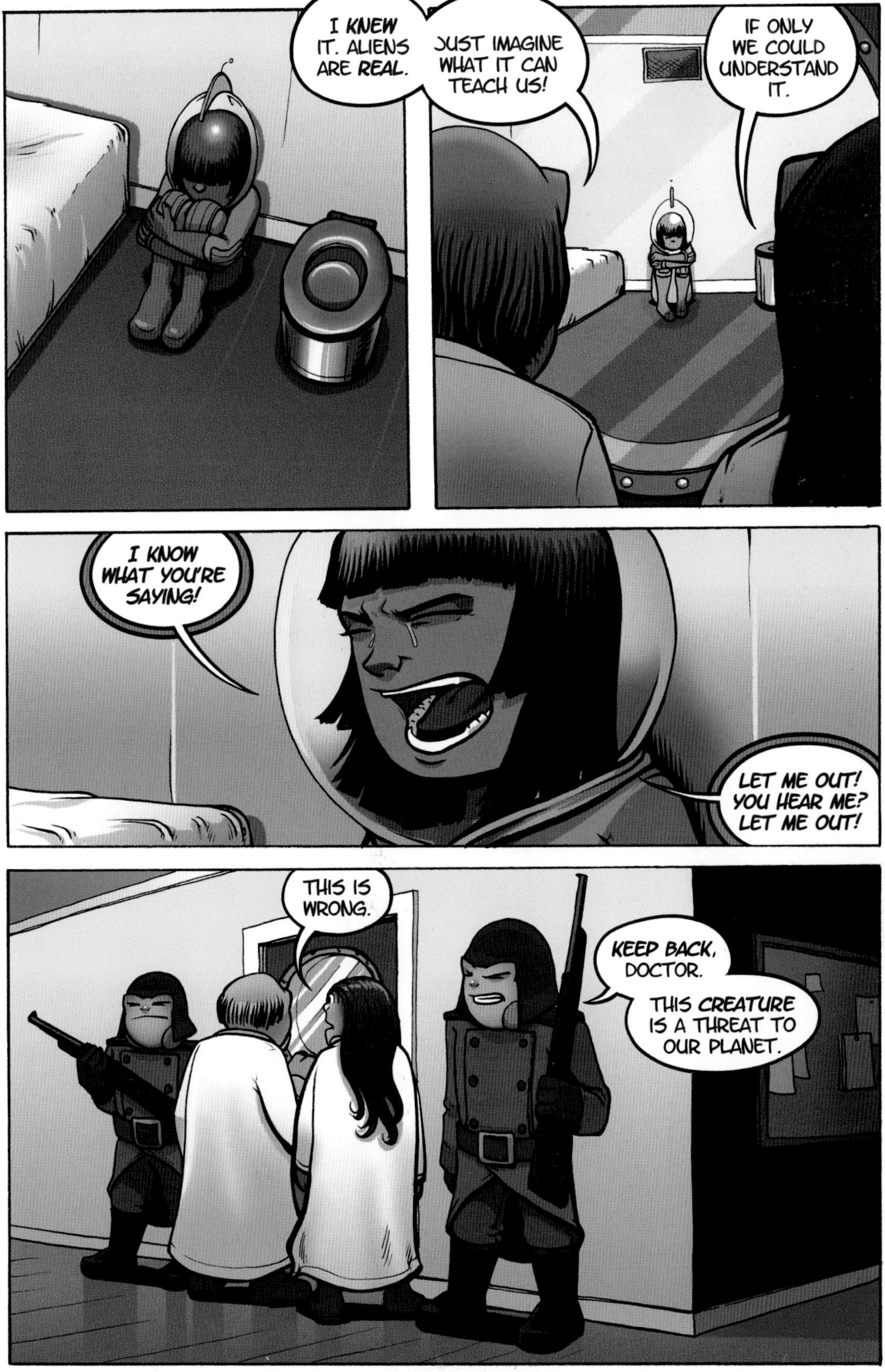
I KNEW IT. ALIENS ARE REAL.
JUST IMAGINE WHAT IT CAN TEACH US!
IF ONLY WE COULD UNDERSTAND IT.
I KNOW WHAT YOU'RE SAYING!
LET ME OUT! YOU HEAR ME? LET ME OUT!
THIS IS WRONG.
KEEP BACK, DOCTOR.
THIS CREATURE IS A THREAT TO OUR PLANET.

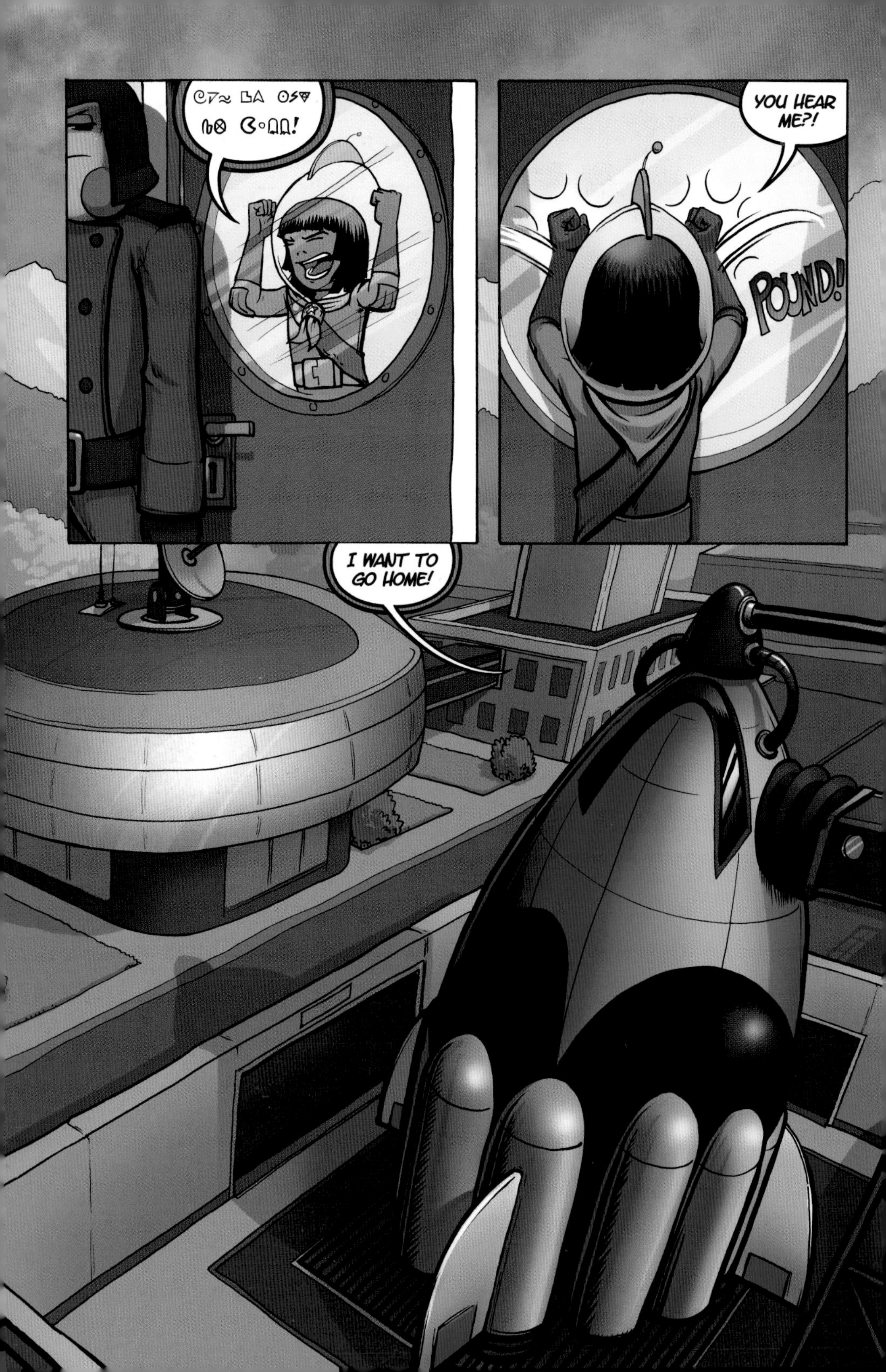
YOU HEAR ME?!
POUND!
I WANT TO GO HOME!

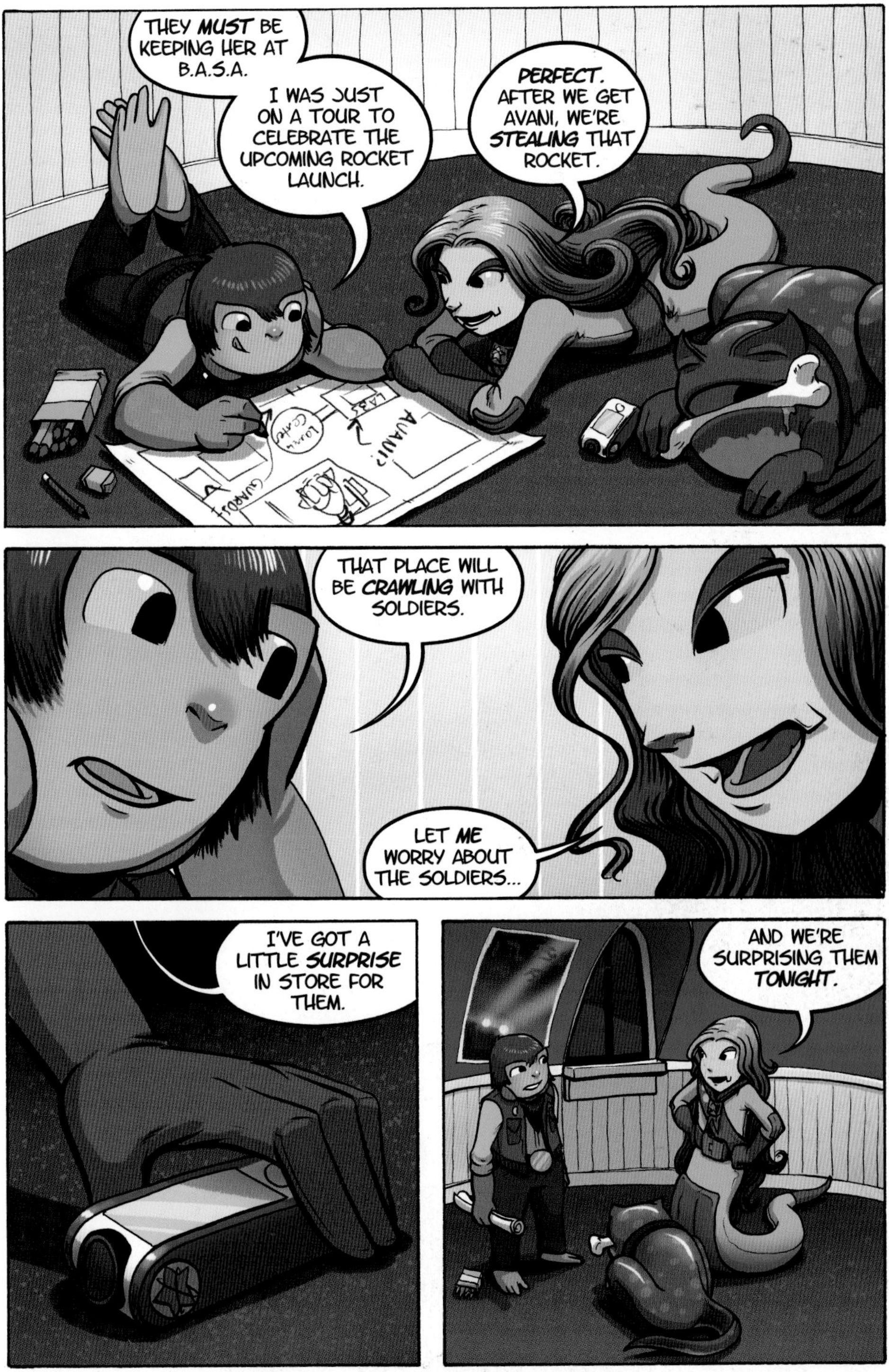
THEY MUST BE KEEPING HER AT B.A.S.A.
I WAS JUST ON A TOUR TO CELEBRATE THE UPCOMING ROCKET LAUNCH.
PERFECT. AFTER WE GET AVANI, WE'RE STEALING THAT ROCKET.
AVANI?
LABS
GUARDS
THAT PLACE WILL BE CRAWLING WITH SOLDIERS.
LET ME WORRY ABOUT THE SOLDIERS...
I'VE GOT A LITTLE SURPRISE IN STORE FOR THEM.
AND WE'RE SURPRISING THEM TONIGHT.

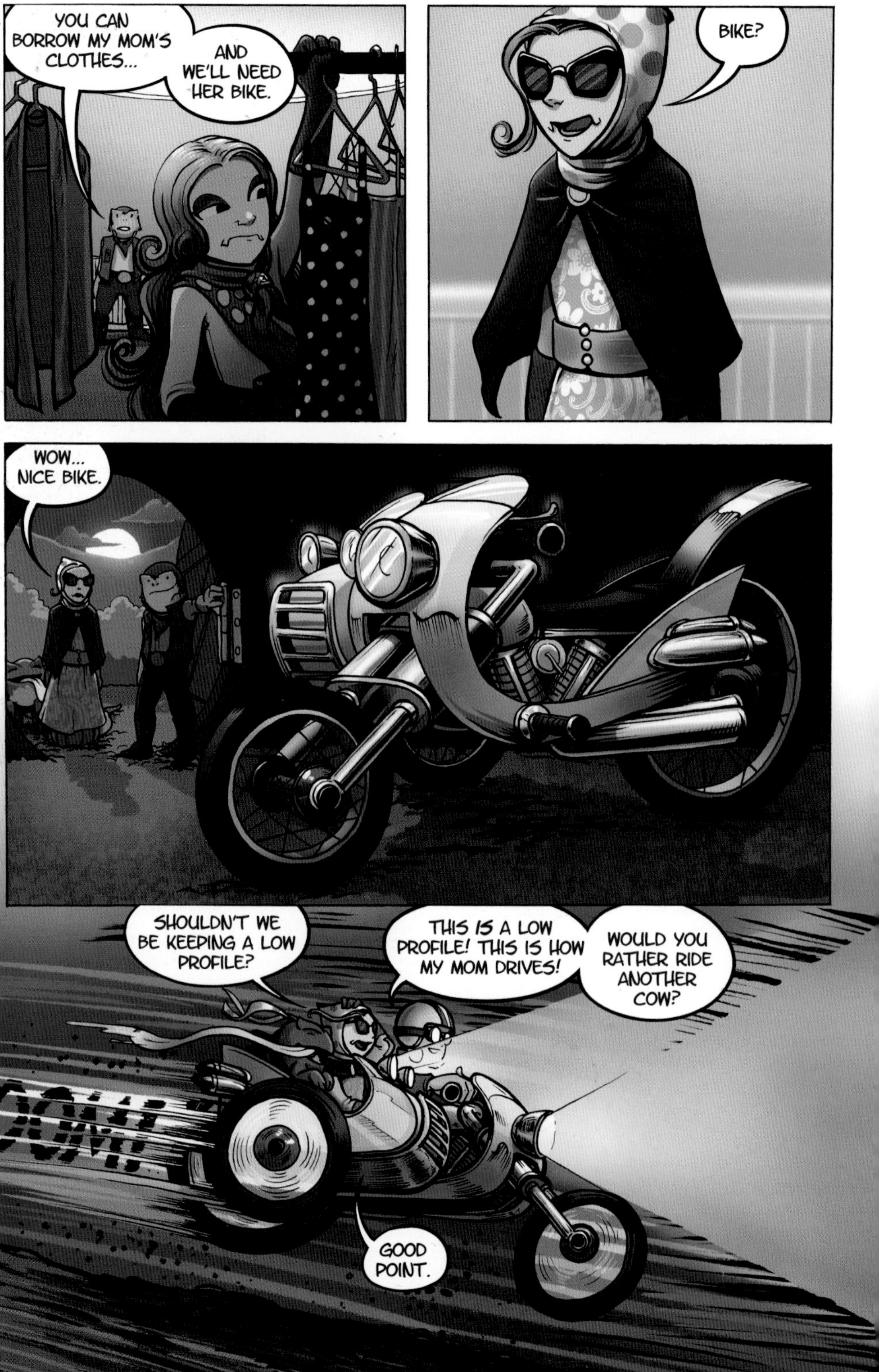
YOU CAN BORROW MY MOM'S CLOTHES...
AND WE'LL NEED HER BIKE.
BIKE?
WOW... NICE BIKE.
SHOULDN'T WE BE KEEPING A LOW PROFILE?
THIS *IS* A LOW PROFILE! THIS IS HOW MY MOM DRIVES!
WOULD YOU RATHER RIDE ANOTHER COW?
GOOD POINT.

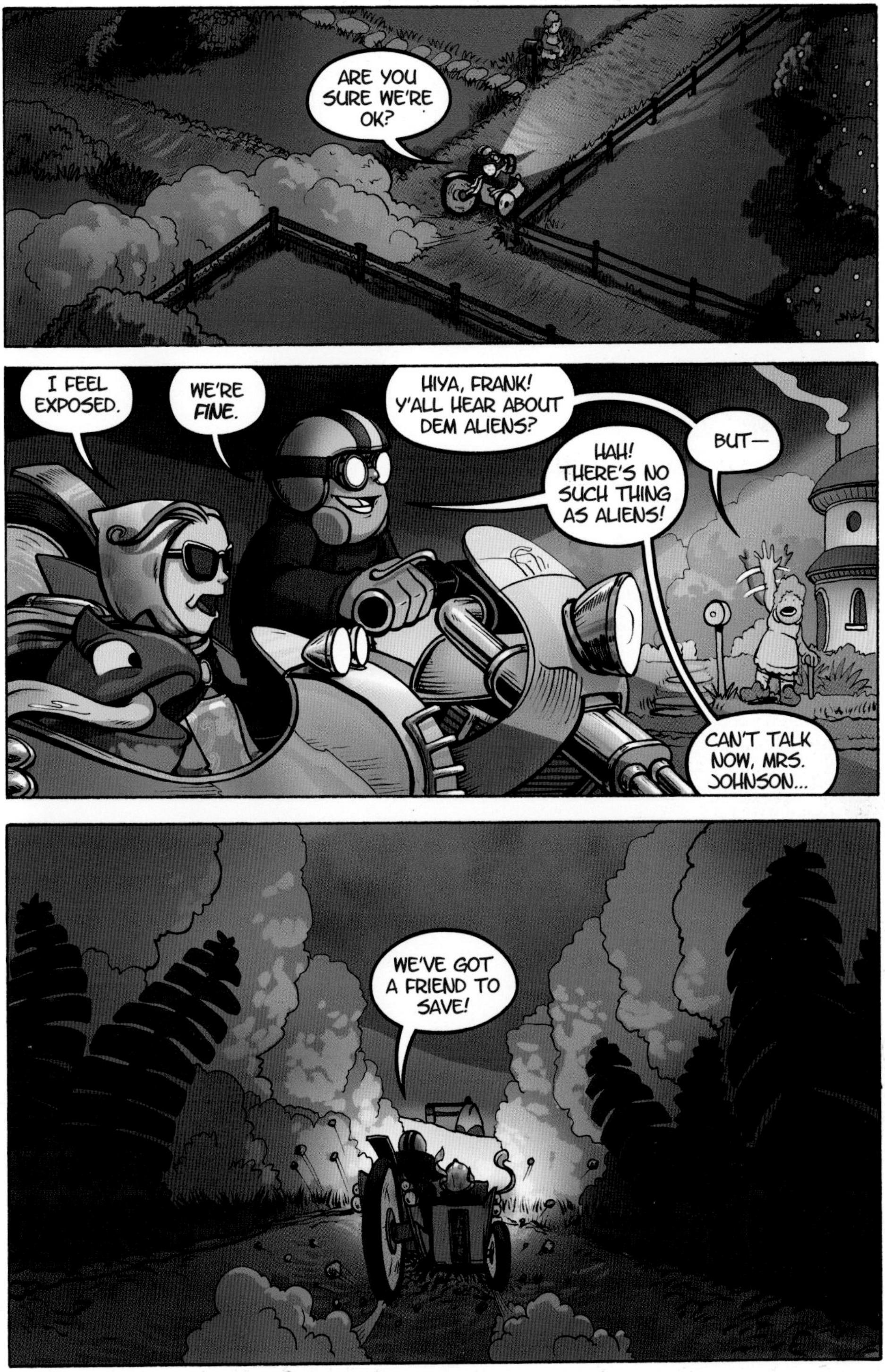
ARE YOU SURE WE'RE OK?
I FEEL EXPOSED.
WE'RE FINE.
HIYA, FRANK! Y'ALL HEAR ABOUT DEM ALIENS?
HAH! THERE'S NO SUCH THING AS ALIENS!
BUT—
CAN'T TALK NOW, MRS. JOHNSON...
WE'VE GOT A FRIEND TO SAVE!

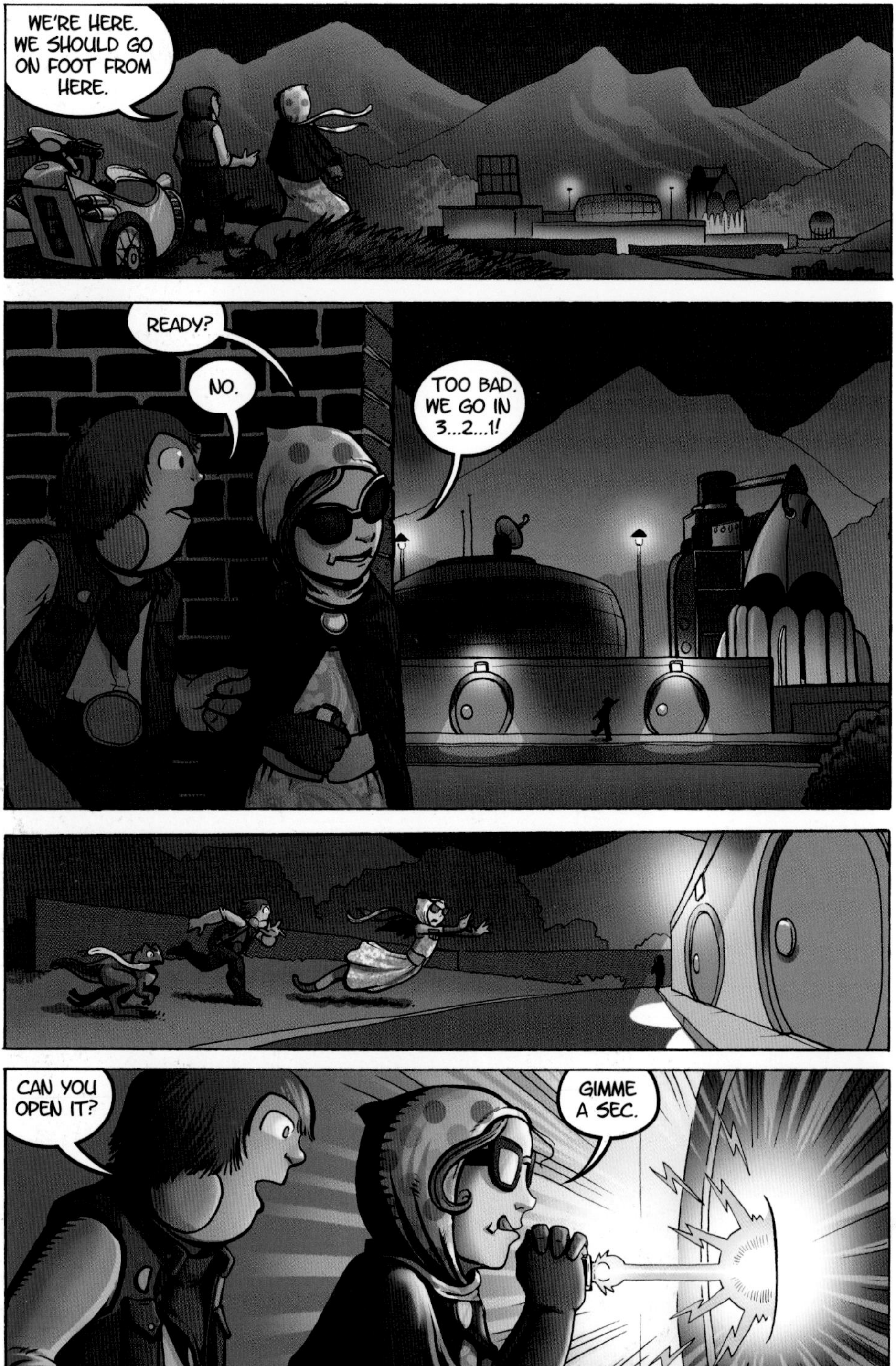
WE'RE HERE. WE SHOULD GO ON FOOT FROM HERE.
READY?
NO.
TOO BAD. WE GO IN 3...2...1!
CAN YOU OPEN IT?
GIMME A SEC.

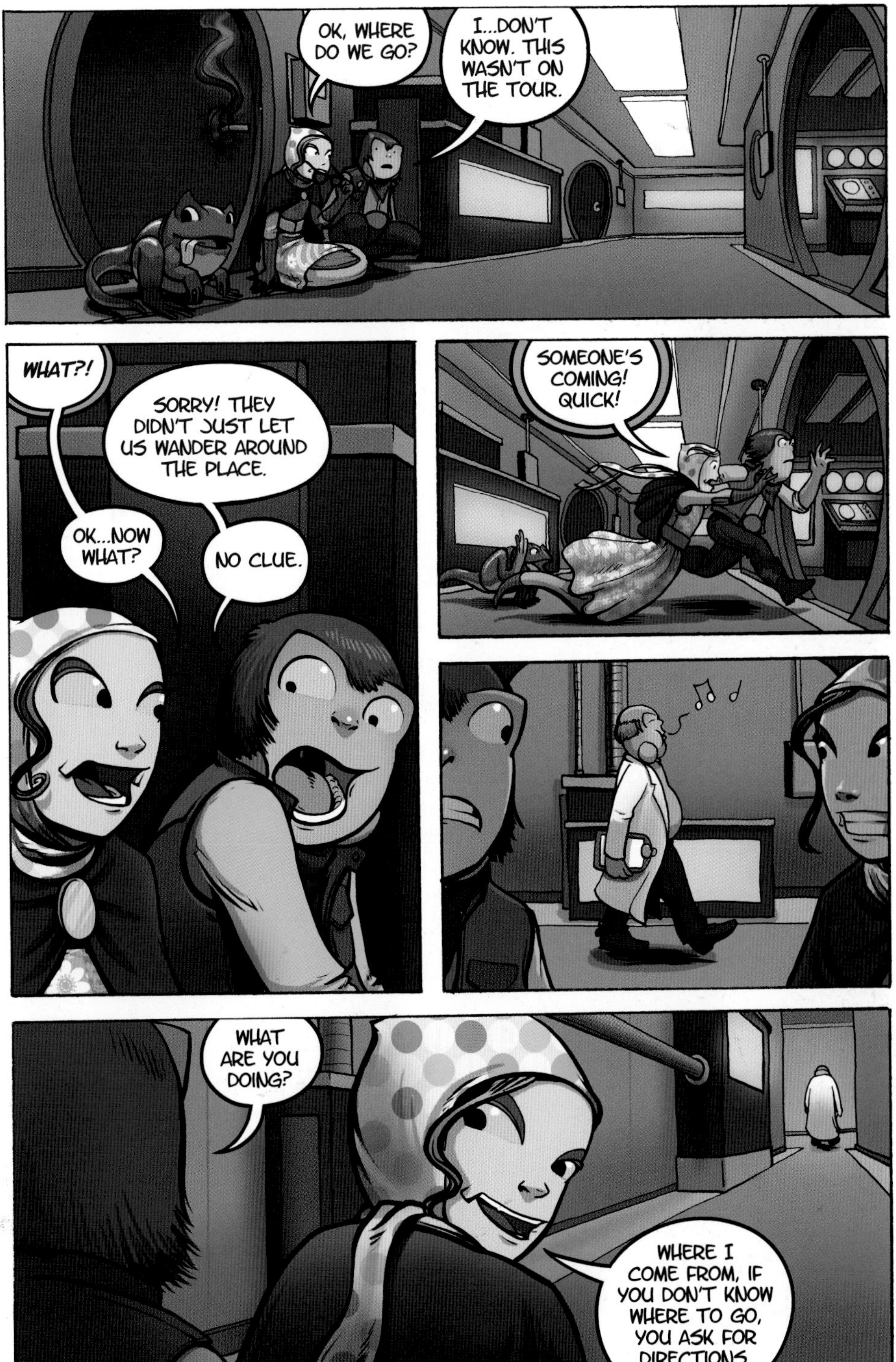
OK, WHERE DO WE GO?
I...DON'T KNOW. THIS WASN'T ON THE TOUR.
WHAT?!
SORRY! THEY DIDN'T JUST LET US WANDER AROUND THE PLACE.
OK...NOW WHAT?
NO CLUE.
SOMEONE'S COMING! QUICK!
WHAT ARE YOU DOING?
WHERE I COME FROM, IF YOU DON'T KNOW WHERE TO GO, YOU ASK FOR DIRECTIONS.

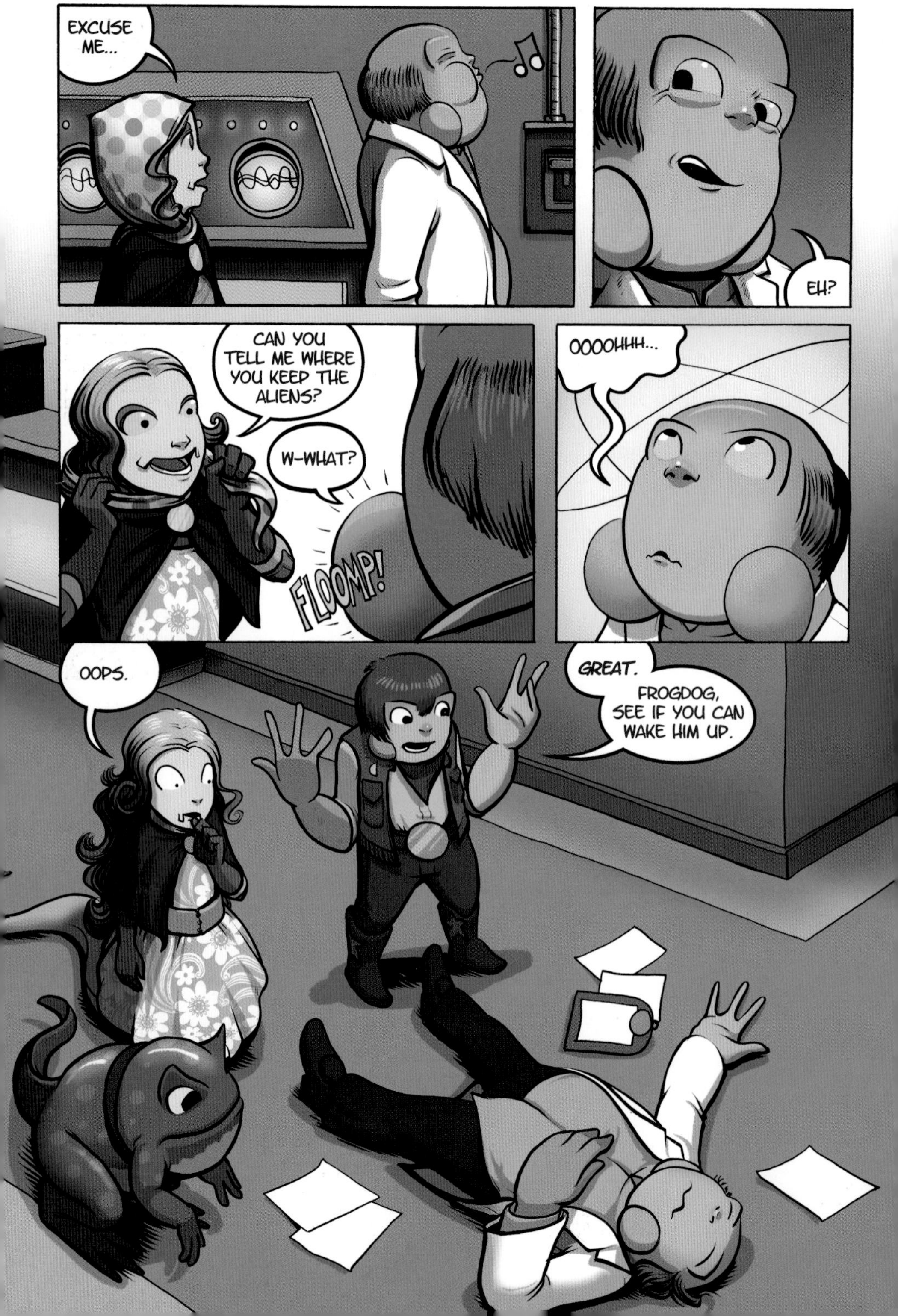
EXCUSE ME...
EH?
CAN YOU TELL ME WHERE YOU KEEP THE ALIENS?
W-WHAT?
FLOOMP!
OOOOHHH...
OOPS.
GREAT.
FROGDOG, SEE IF YOU CAN WAKE HIM UP.

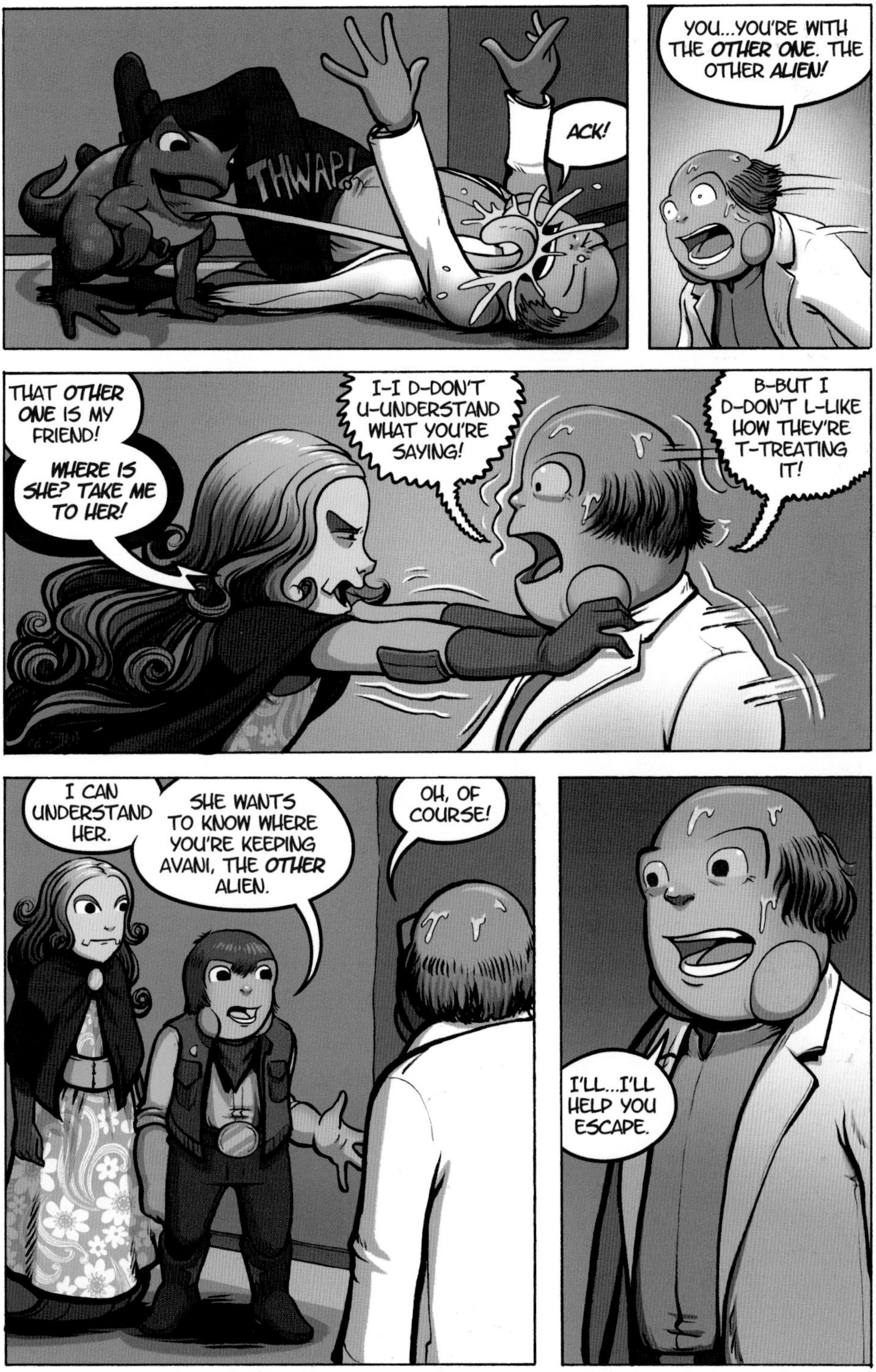
THWAP!
ACK!
YOU...YOU'RE WITH THE OTHER ONE. THE OTHER ALIEN!
THAT OTHER ONE IS MY FRIEND!
WHERE IS SHE? TAKE ME TO HER!
I-I D-DON'T U-UNDERSTAND WHAT YOU'RE SAYING!
B-BUT I D-DON'T L-LIKE HOW THEY'RE T-TREATING IT!
I CAN UNDERSTAND HER.
SHE WANTS TO KNOW WHERE YOU'RE KEEPING AVANI, THE OTHER ALIEN.
OH, OF COURSE!
I'LL...I'LL HELP YOU ESCAPE.

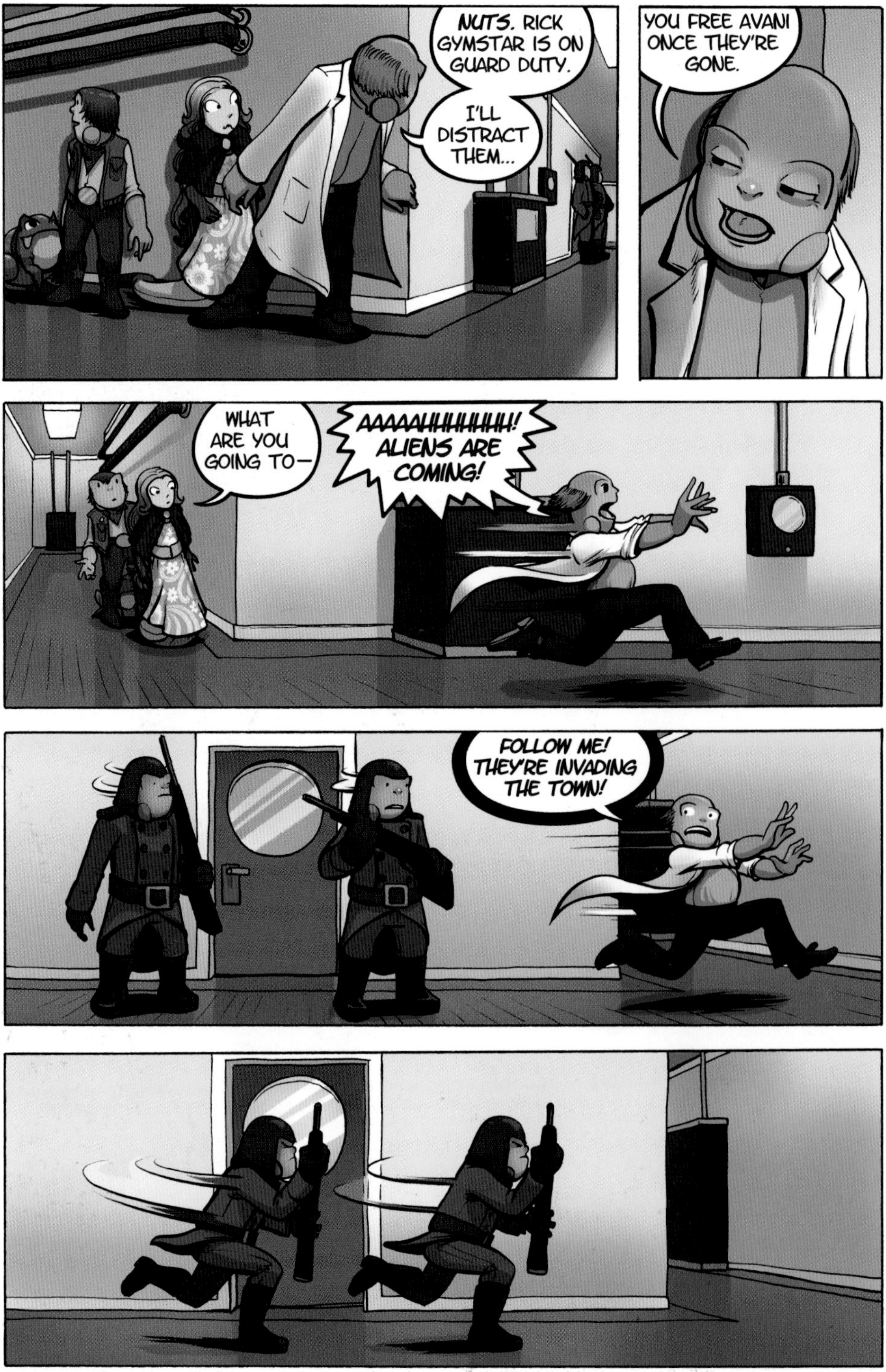
NUTS. RICK GYMSTAR IS ON GUARD DUTY.
I'LL DISTRACT THEM...
YOU FREE AVANI ONCE THEY'RE GONE.
WHAT ARE YOU GOING TO—
AAAAAHHHHHHH! ALIENS ARE COMING!
FOLLOW ME! THEY'RE INVADING THE TOWN!

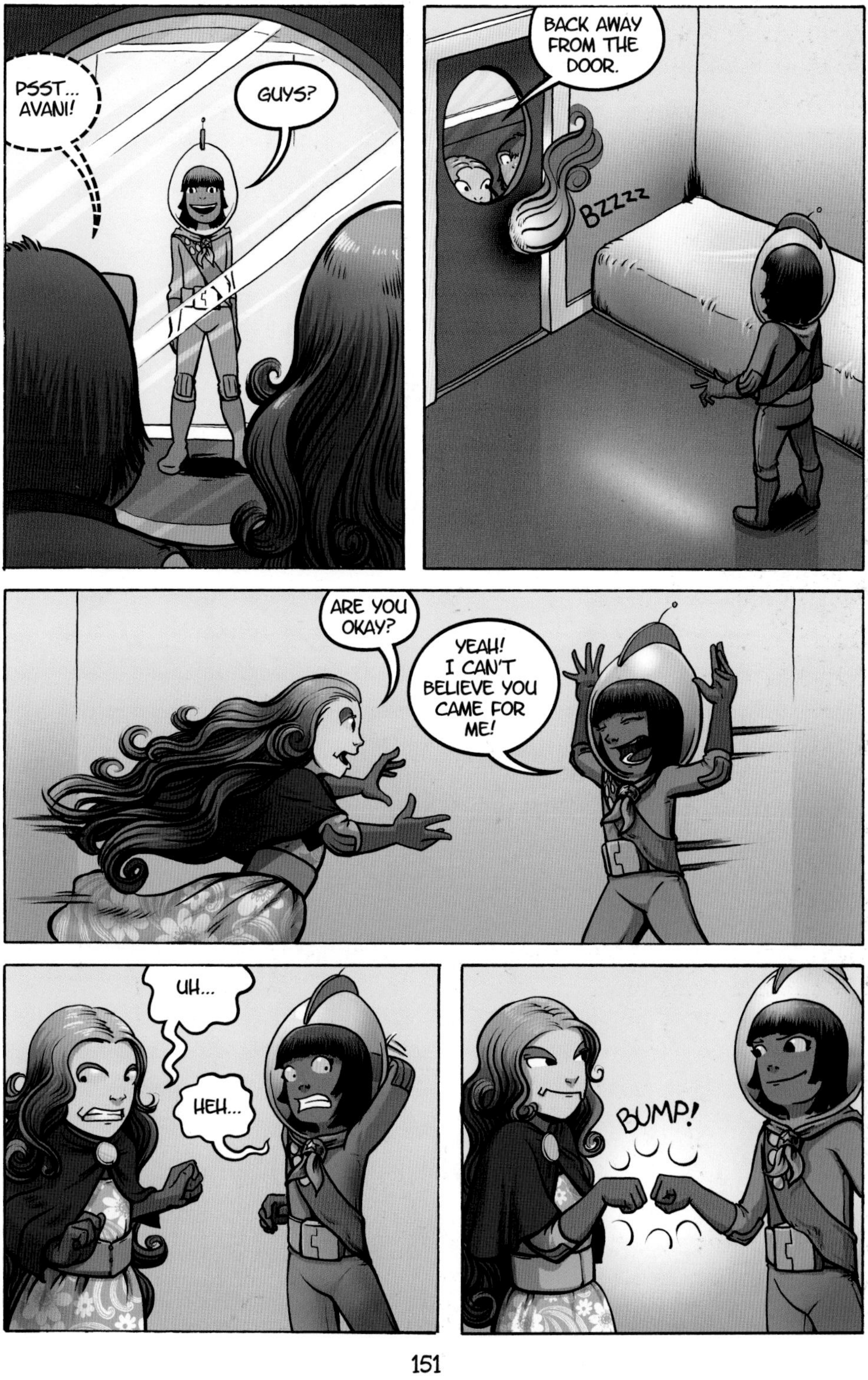
PSST... AVANI!
GUYS?
BACK AWAY FROM THE DOOR.
BZZZZ
ARE YOU OKAY?
YEAH! I CAN'T BELIEVE YOU CAME FOR ME!
UH...
HEH...
BUMP!

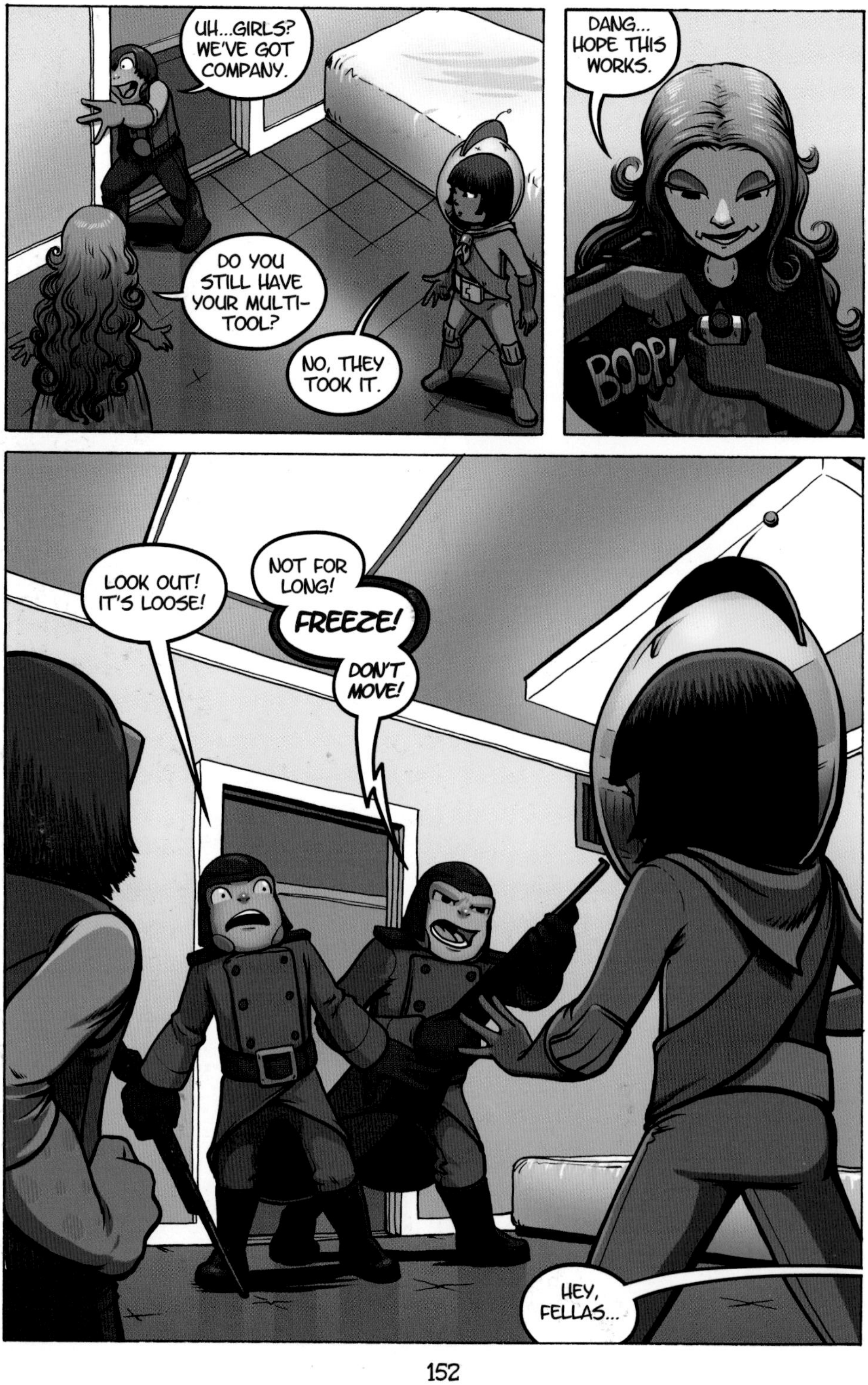
UH...GIRLS? WE'VE GOT COMPANY.
DO YOU STILL HAVE YOUR MULTI-TOOL?
NO, THEY TOOK IT.
DANG... HOPE THIS WORKS.
BOOP!
LOOK OUT! IT'S LOOSE!
NOT FOR LONG!
FREEZE!
DON'T MOVE!
HEY, FELLAS...

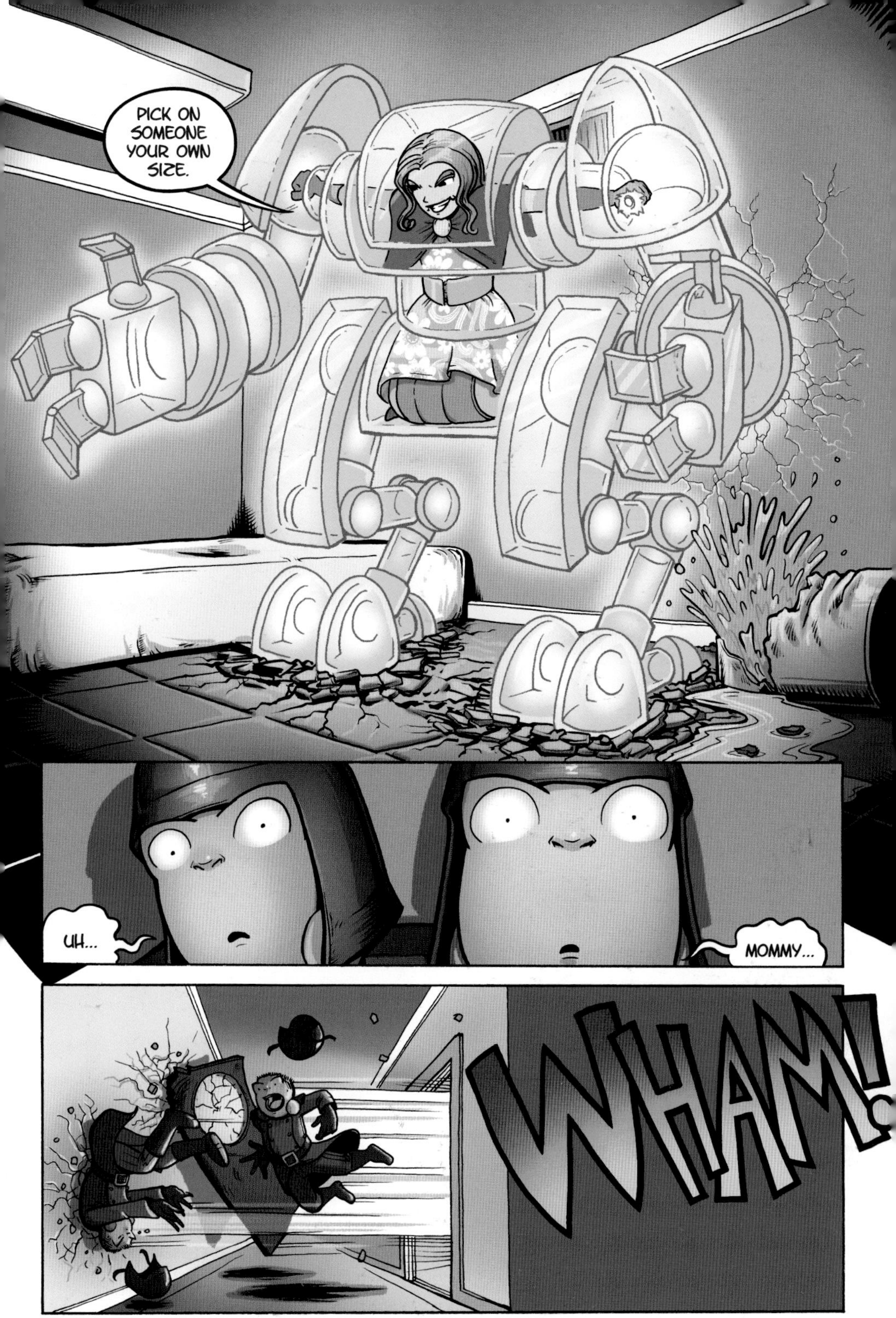
PICK ON SOMEONE YOUR OWN SIZE.
UH...
MOMMY...
WHAM!

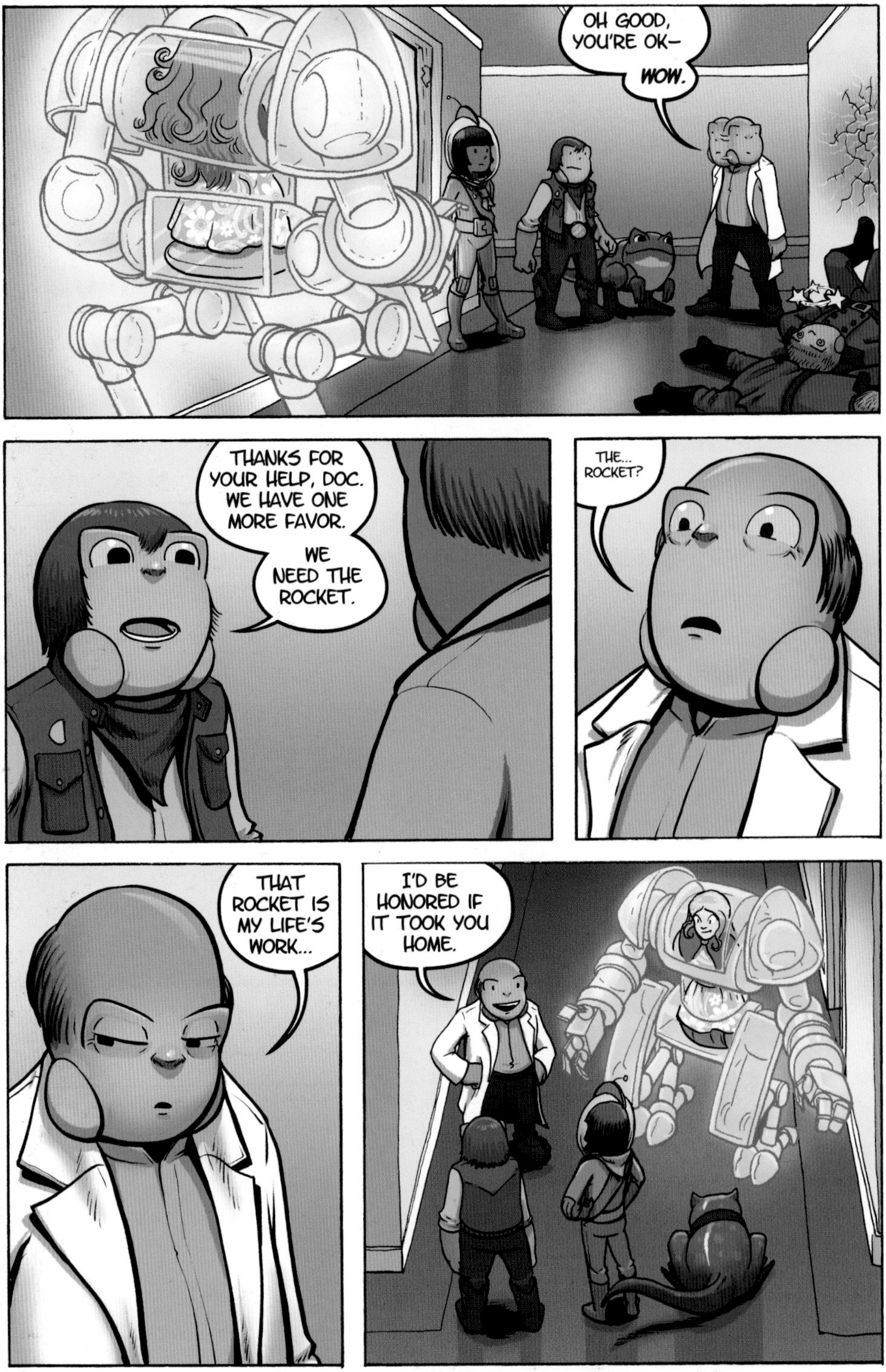
OH GOOD, YOU'RE OK— WOW.
THANKS FOR YOUR HELP, DOC. WE HAVE ONE MORE FAVOR.
WE NEED THE ROCKET.
THE... ROCKET?
THAT ROCKET IS MY LIFE'S WORK...
I'D BE HONORED IF IT TOOK YOU HOME.

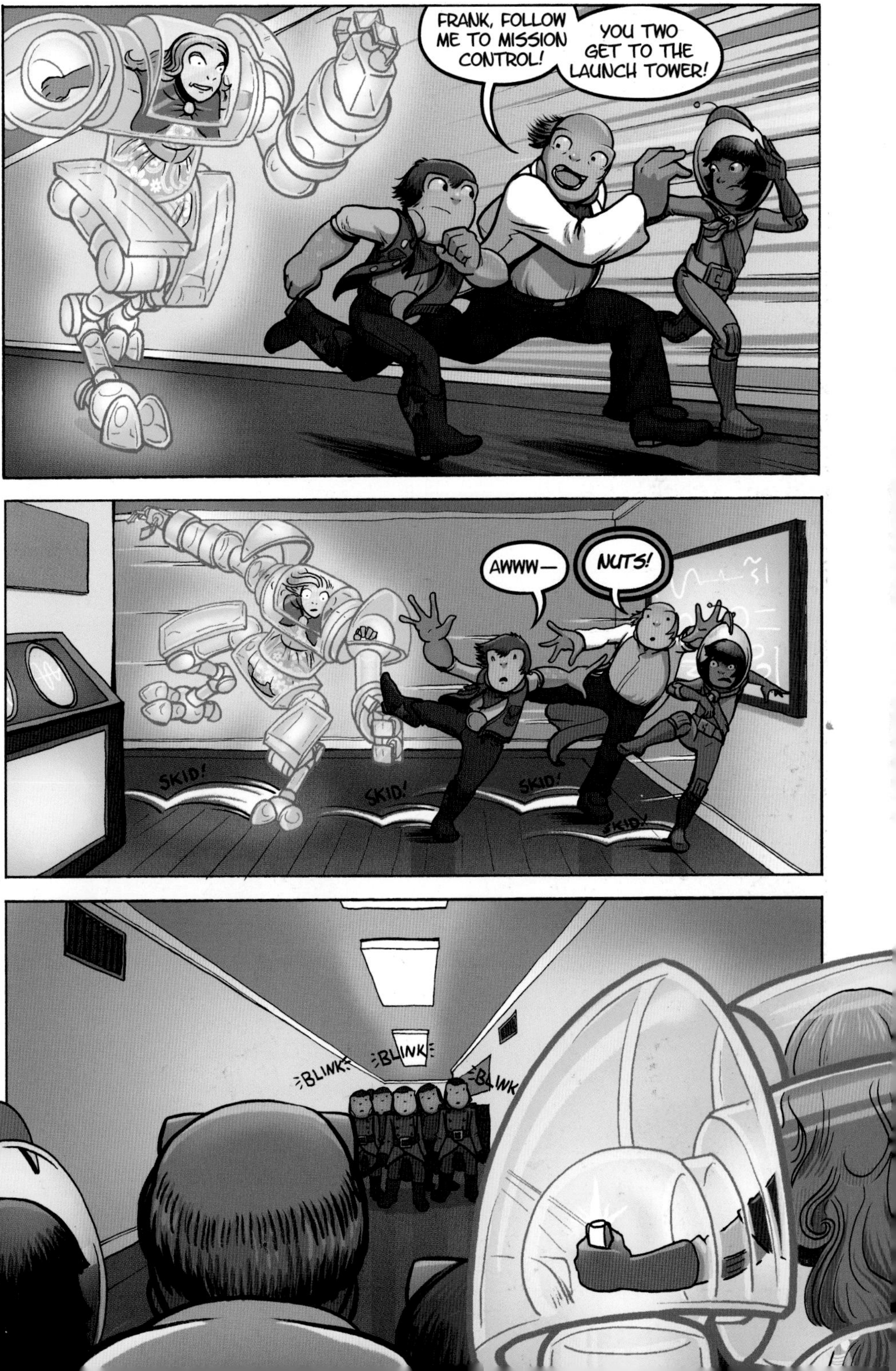
FRANK, FOLLOW ME TO MISSION CONTROL!
YOU TWO GET TO THE LAUNCH TOWER!
AWWW—
NUTS!
SKID!
SKID!
SKID!
SKID!
BLINK
BLINK
BLINK

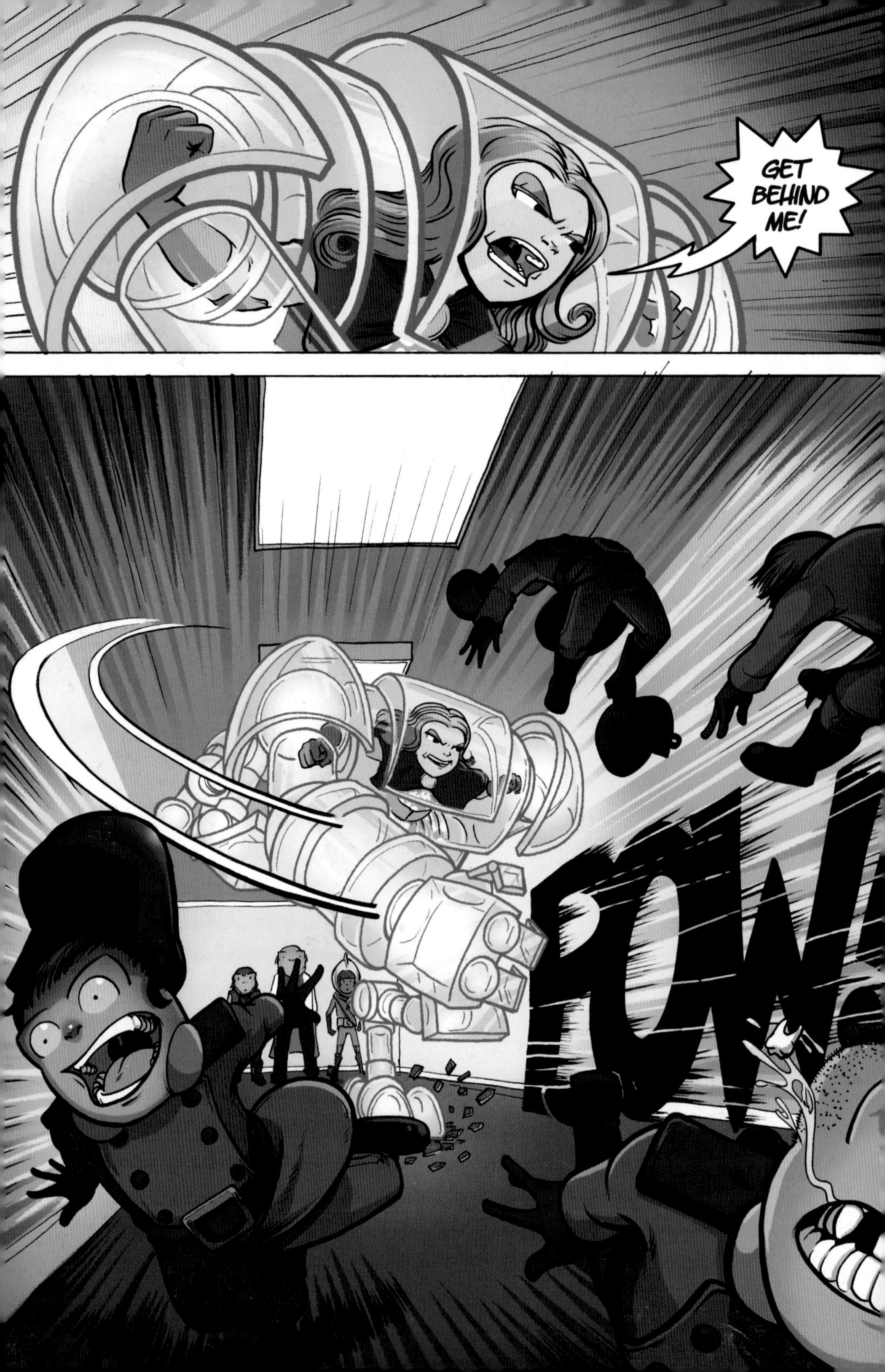
GET BEHIND ME!
POW

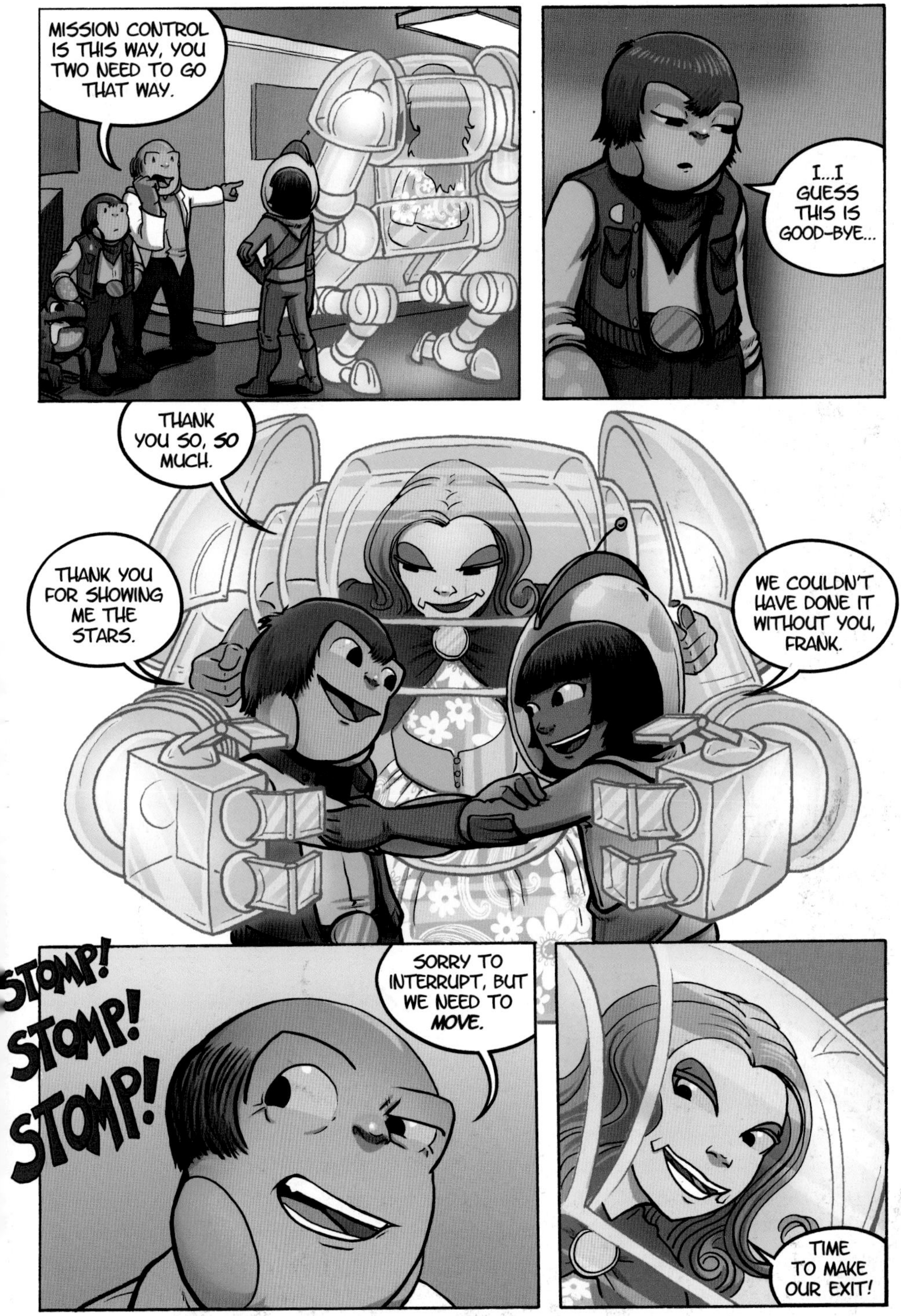
MISSION CONTROL IS THIS WAY, YOU TWO NEED TO GO THAT WAY.
I...I GUESS THIS IS GOOD-BYE...
THANK YOU SO, SO MUCH.
THANK YOU FOR SHOWING ME THE STARS.
WE COULDN'T HAVE DONE IT WITHOUT YOU, FRANK.
STOMP! STOMP! STOMP!
SORRY TO INTERRUPT, BUT WE NEED TO *MOVE.*
TIME TO MAKE OUR EXIT!

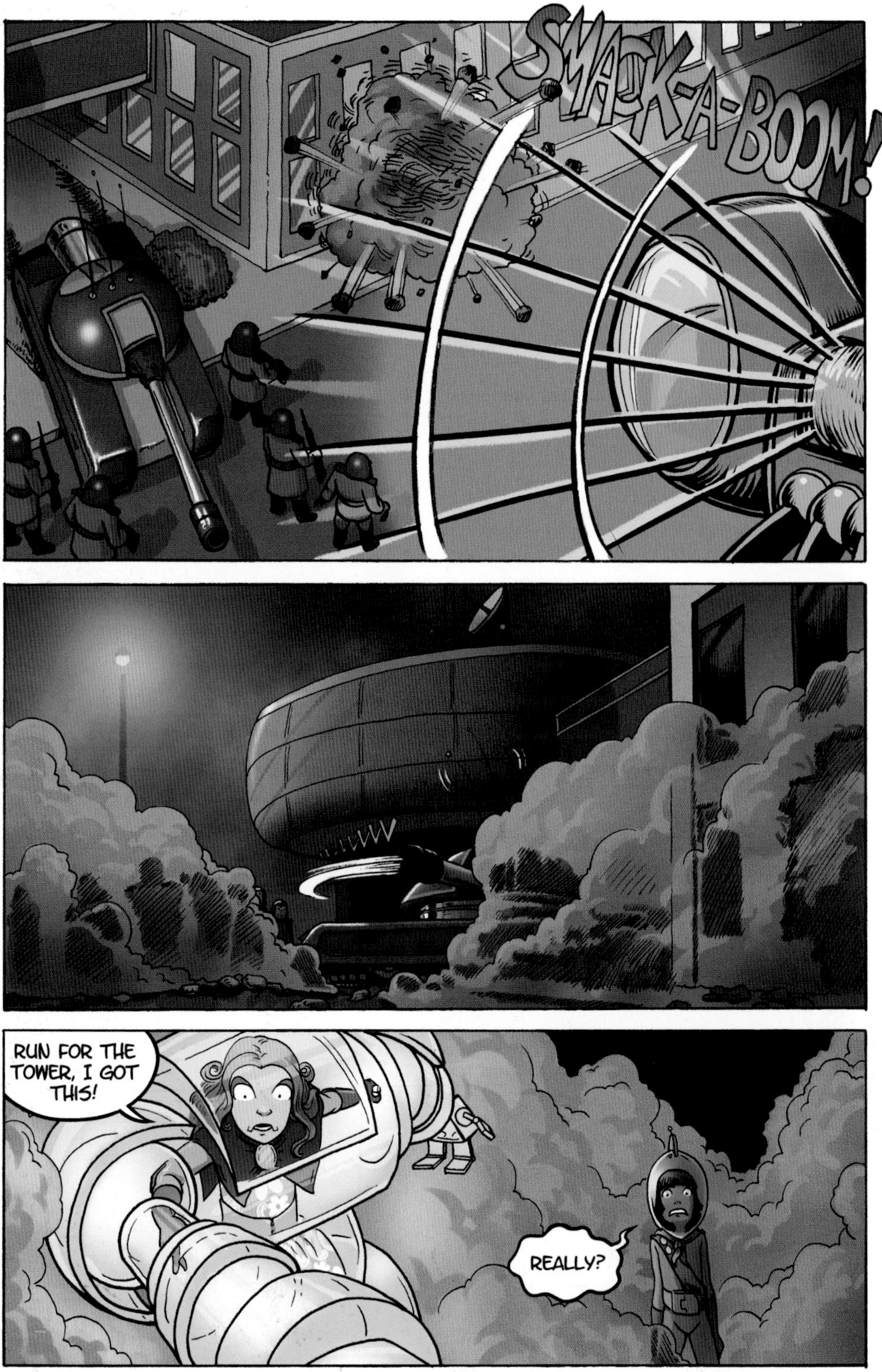
SMACK-A-BOOM!
RUN FOR THE TOWER, I GOT THIS!
REALLY?

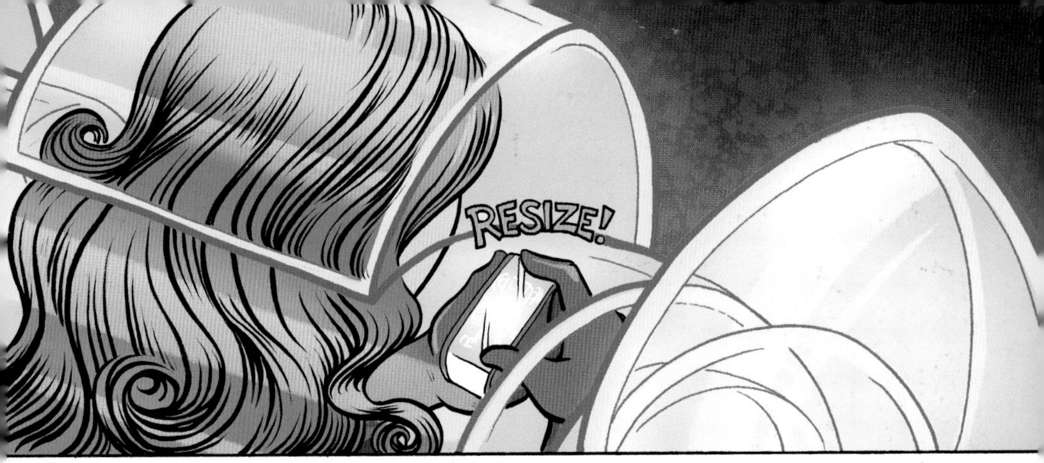
RESIZE!

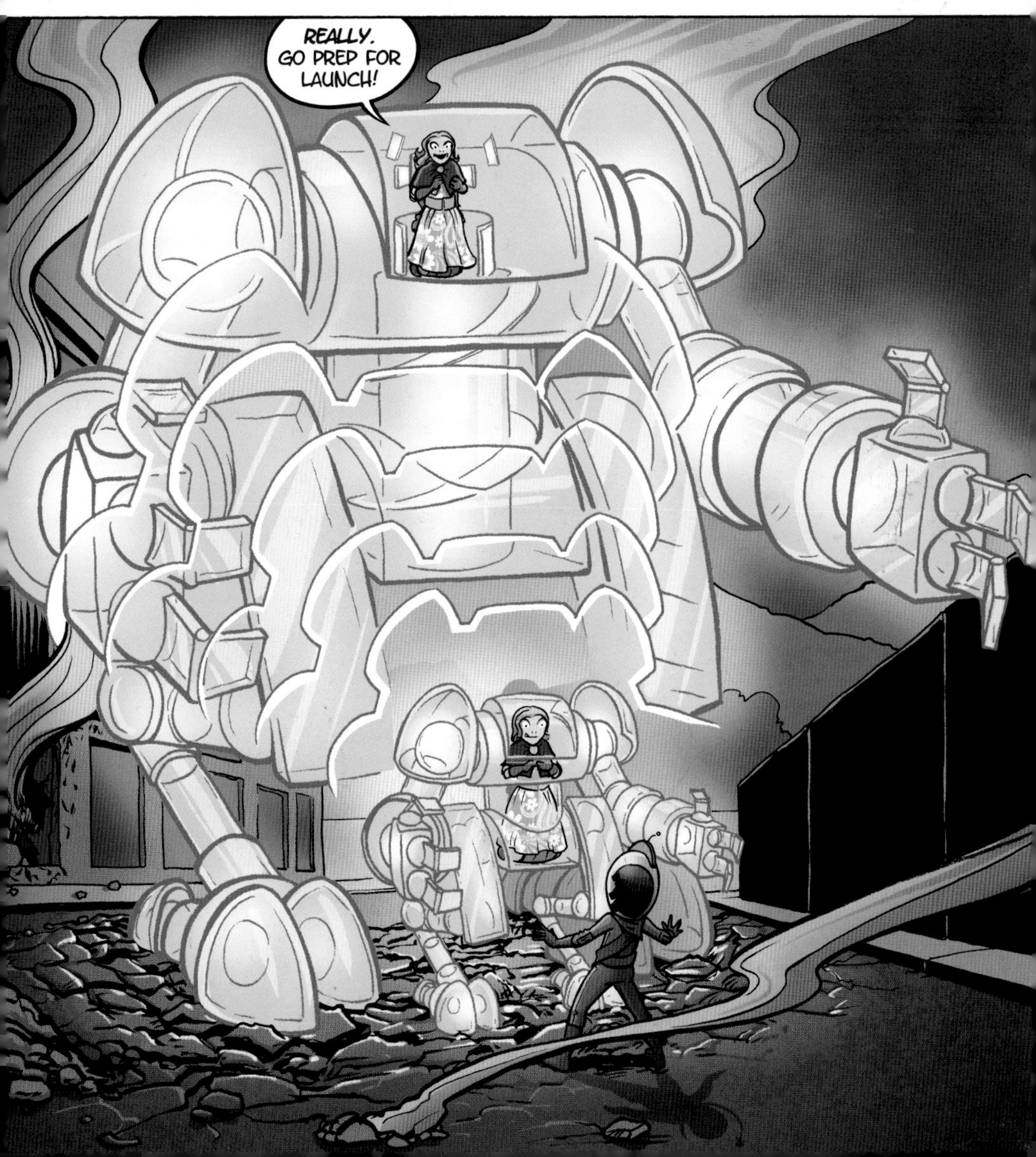
REALLY. GO PREP FOR LAUNCH!

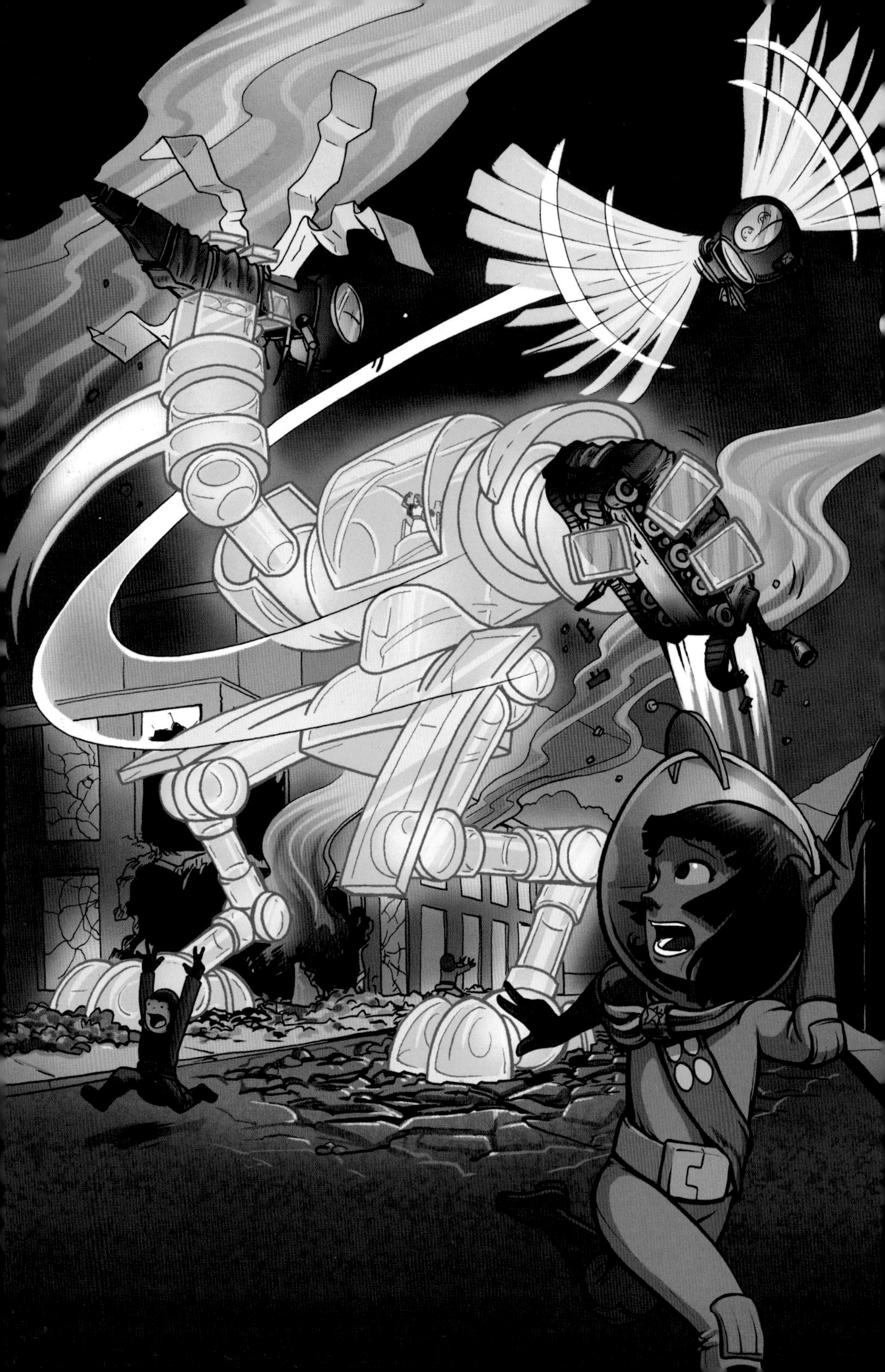

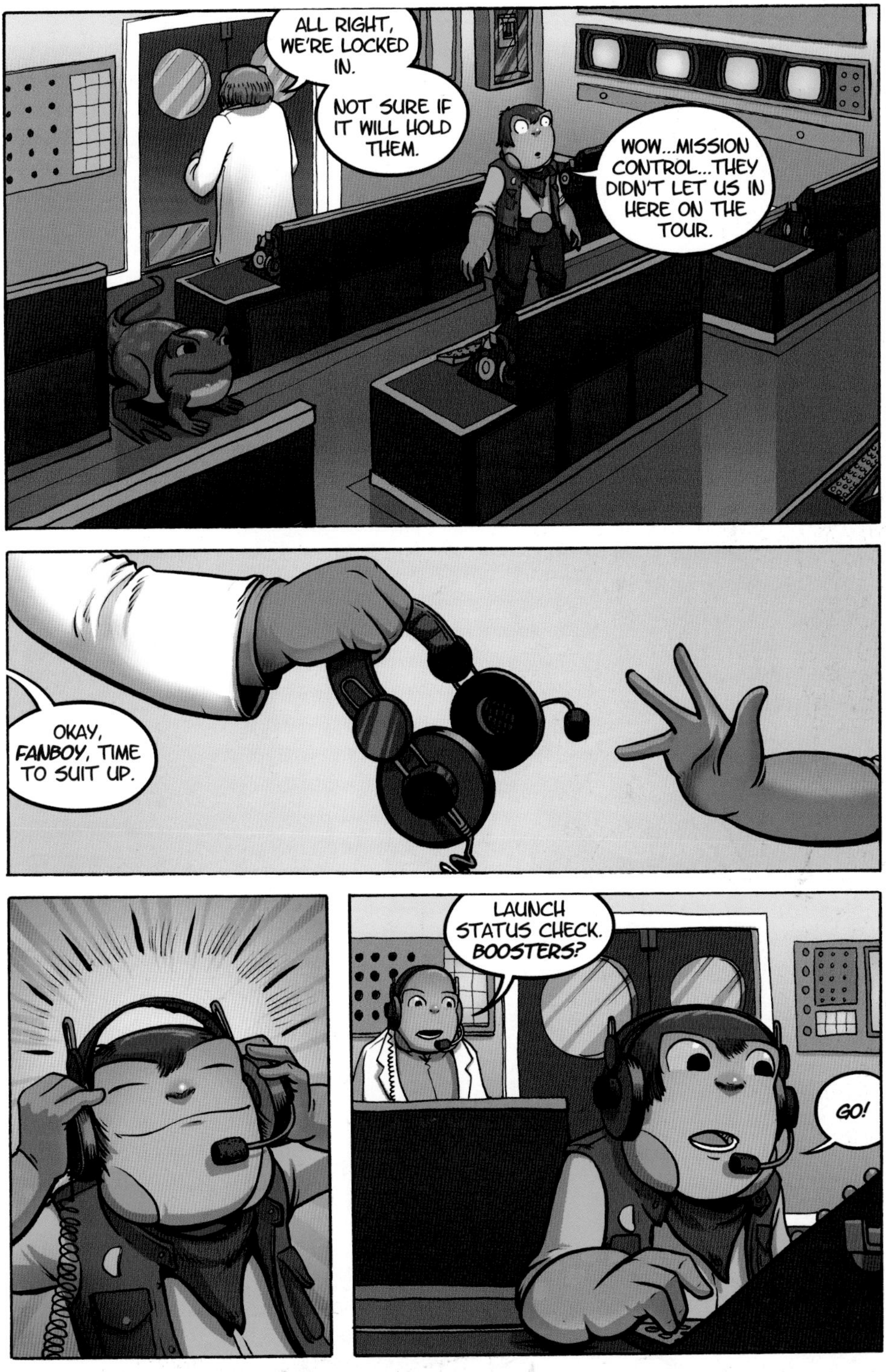
ALL RIGHT, WE'RE LOCKED IN.
NOT SURE IF IT WILL HOLD THEM.
WOW...MISSION CONTROL...THEY DIDN'T LET US IN HERE ON THE TOUR.
OKAY, **FANBOY**, TIME TO SUIT UP.
LAUNCH STATUS CHECK. **BOOSTERS?**
GO!

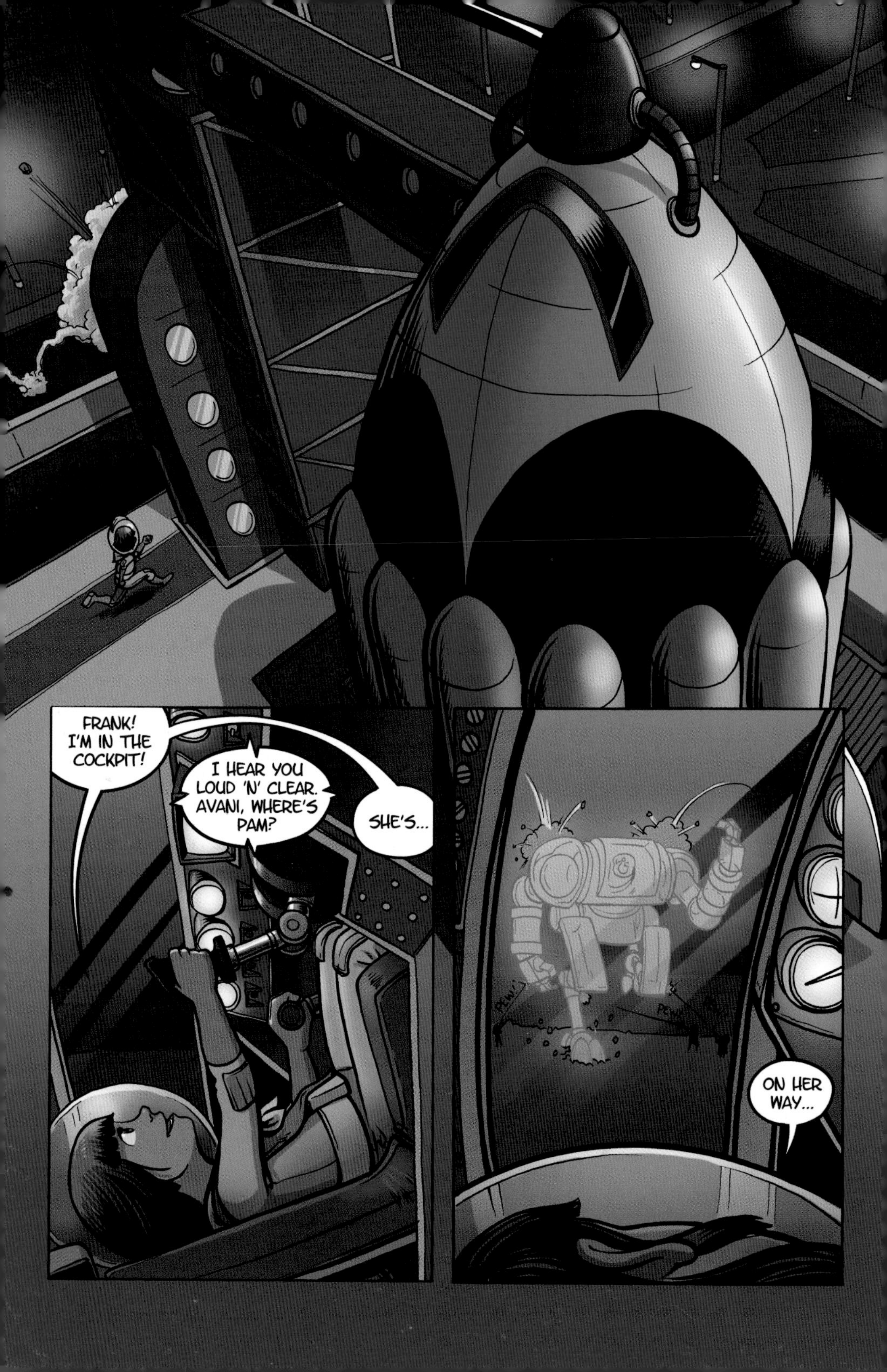
FRANK! I'M IN THE COCKPIT!
I HEAR YOU LOUD 'N' CLEAR. AVANI, WHERE'S PAM?
SHE'S...
ON HER WAY...

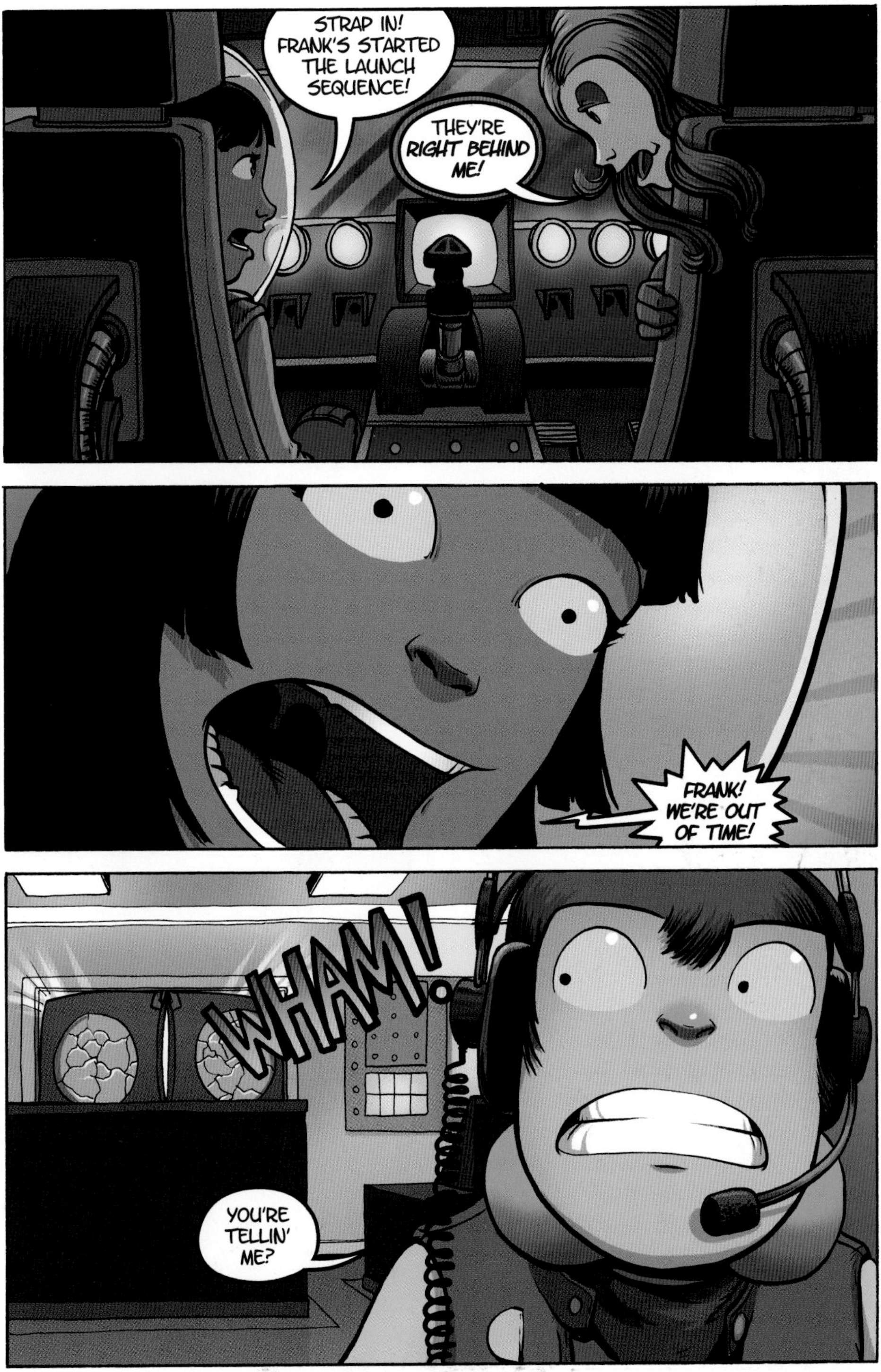
STRAP IN! FRANK'S STARTED THE LAUNCH SEQUENCE!
THEY'RE RIGHT BEHIND ME!
FRANK! WE'RE OUT OF TIME!
WHAM!
YOU'RE TELLIN' ME?

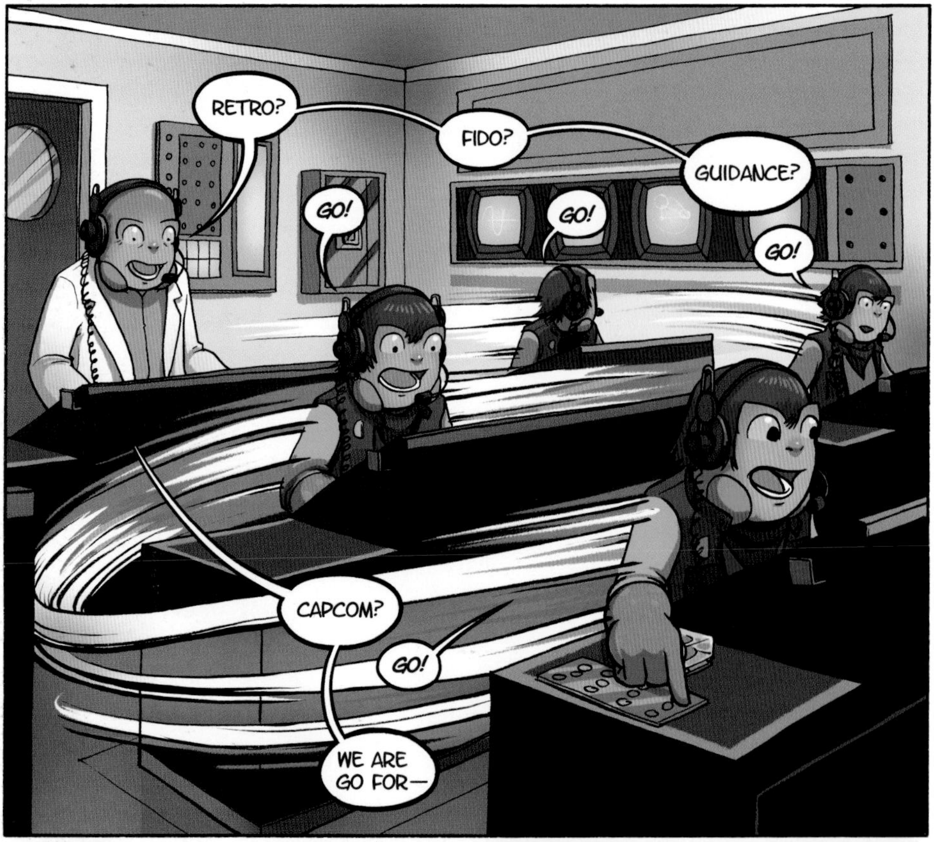
RETRO?
GO!
FIDO?
GO!
GUIDANCE?
GO!
CAPCOM?
GO!
WE ARE GO FOR—

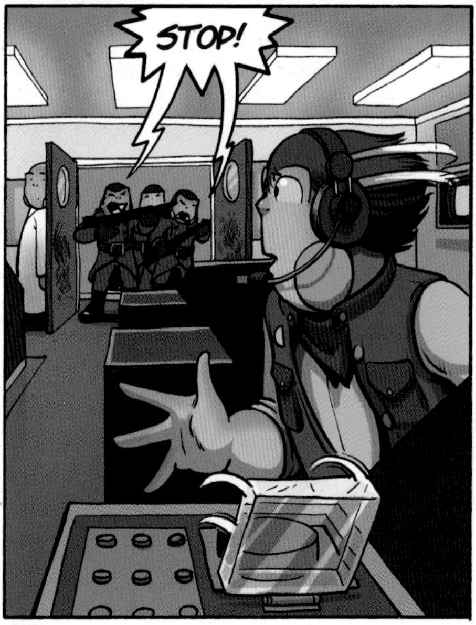
STOP!

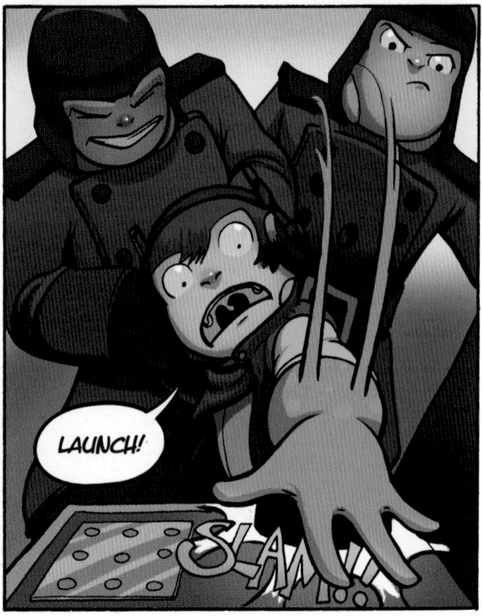
LAUNCH!
SLAM!!

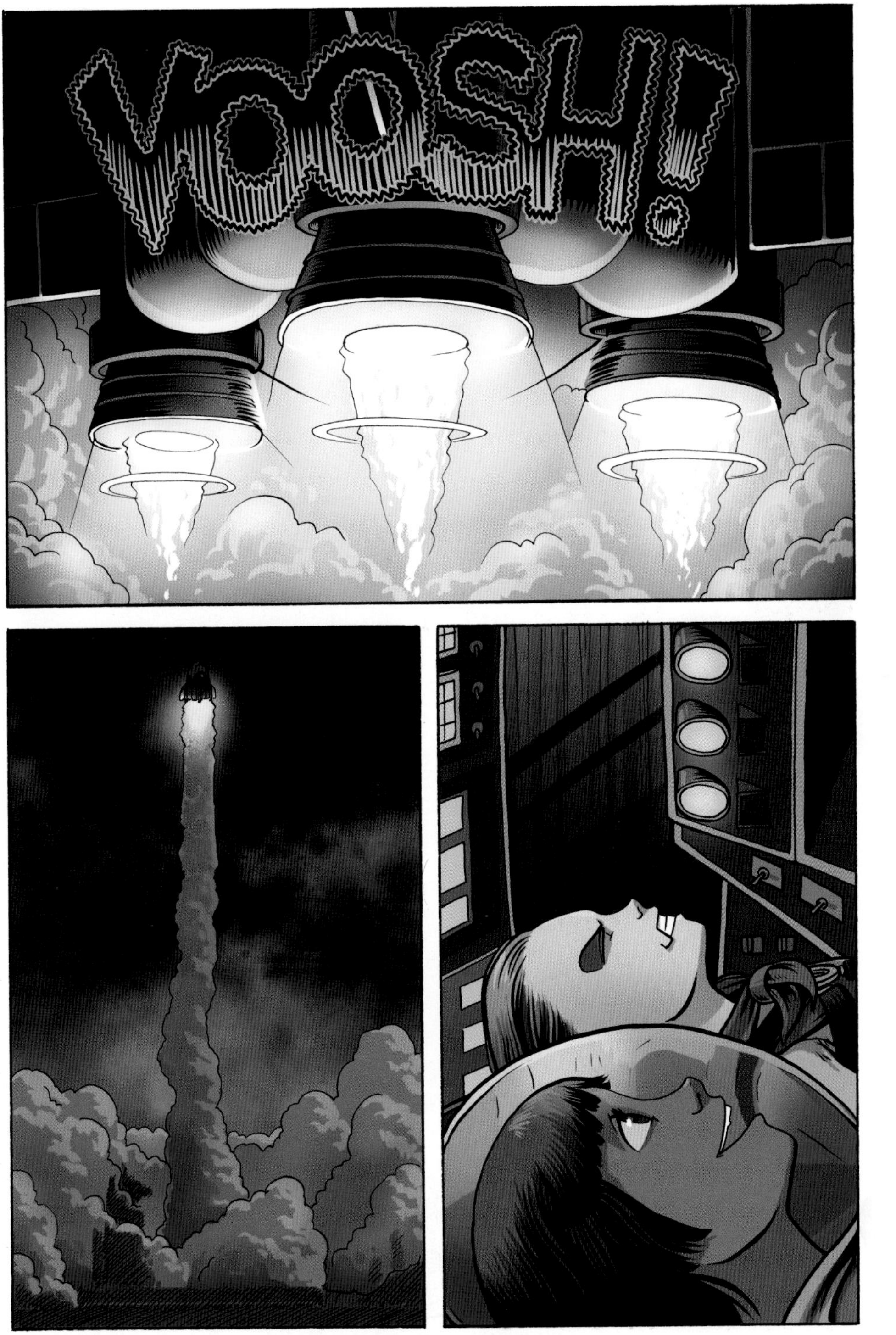
VOOSH!

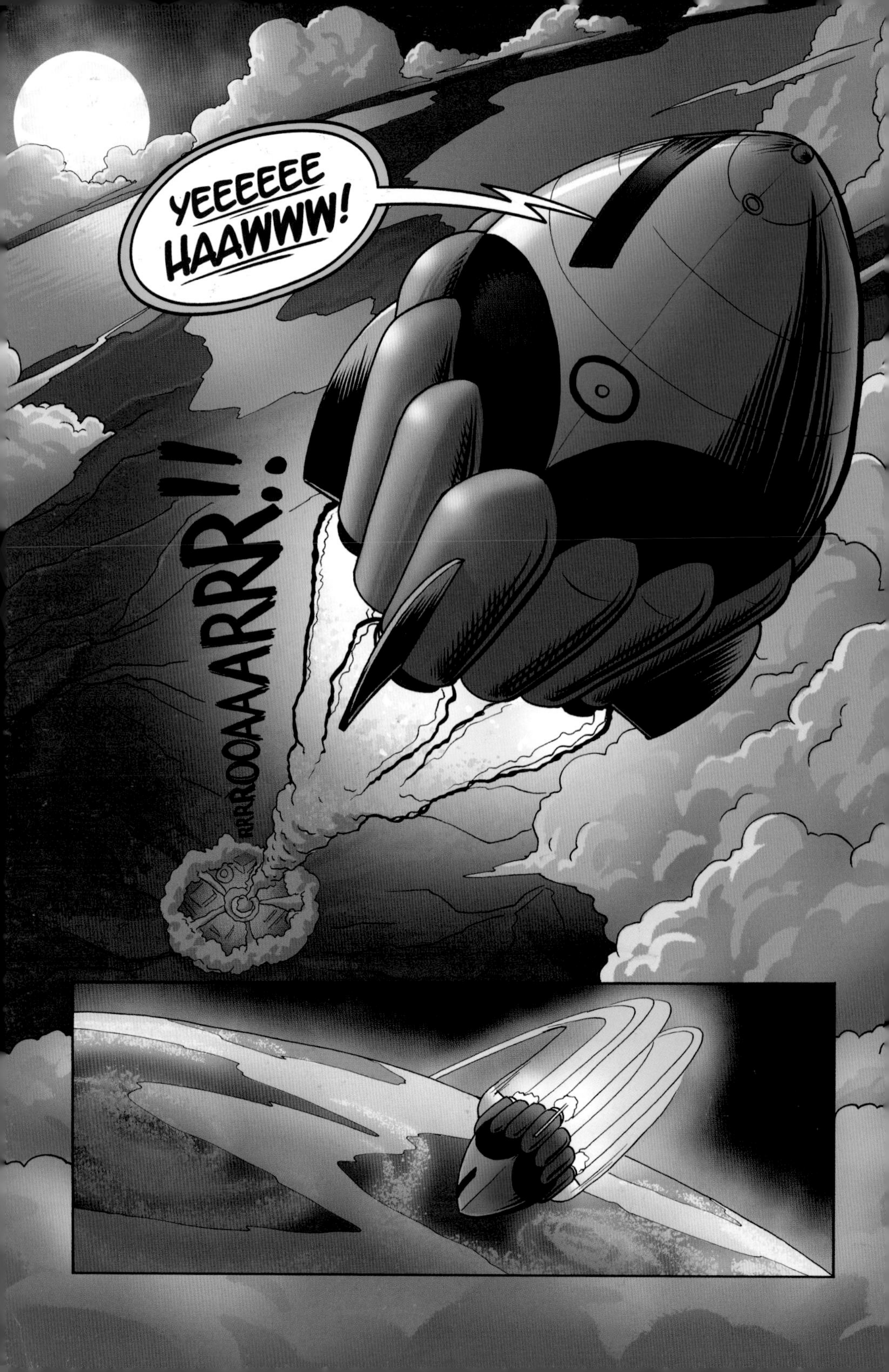
YEEEEEE HAAWWW!
RRRROOOAAAARRRR!!

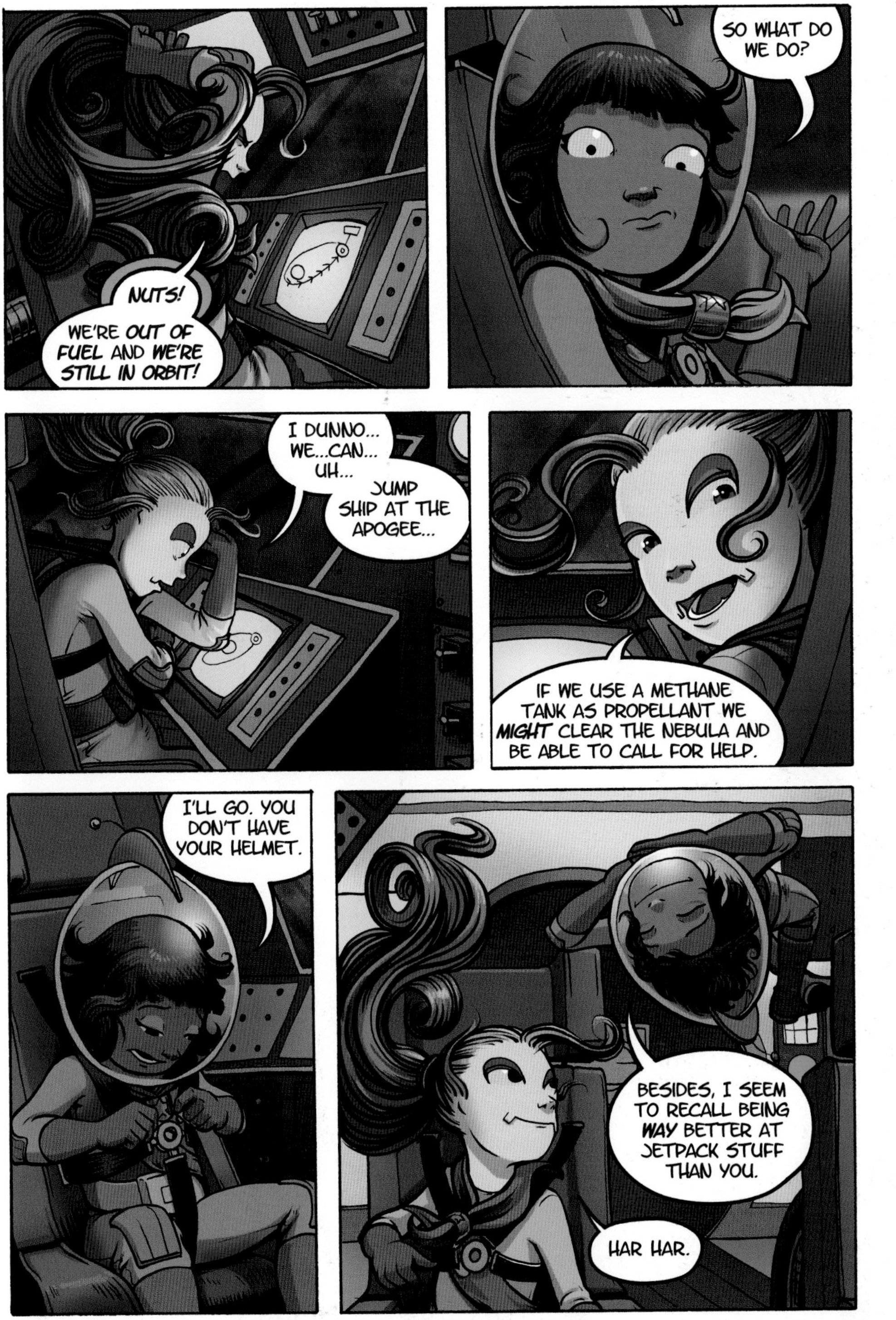
NUTS!
WE'RE OUT OF FUEL AND WE'RE STILL IN ORBIT!
SO WHAT DO WE DO?
I DUNNO... WE...CAN... UH...
JUMP SHIP AT THE APOGEE...
IF WE USE A METHANE TANK AS PROPELLANT WE MIGHT CLEAR THE NEBULA AND BE ABLE TO CALL FOR HELP.
I'LL GO. YOU DON'T HAVE YOUR HELMET.
BESIDES, I SEEM TO RECALL BEING WAY BETTER AT JETPACK STUFF THAN YOU.
HAR HAR.

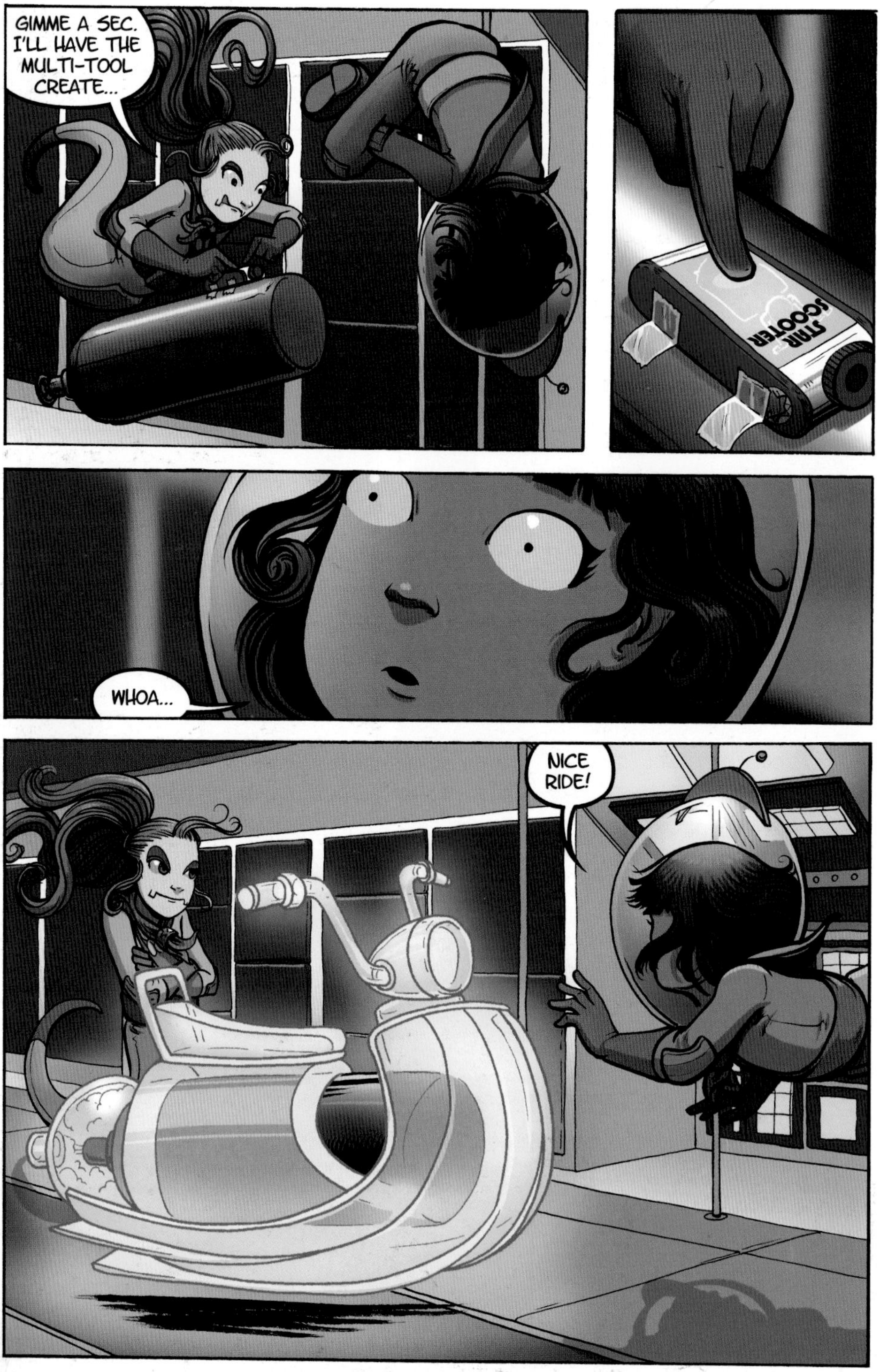
GIMME A SEC. I'LL HAVE THE MULTI-TOOL CREATE...
STAR SCOOTER
WHOA...
NICE RIDE!

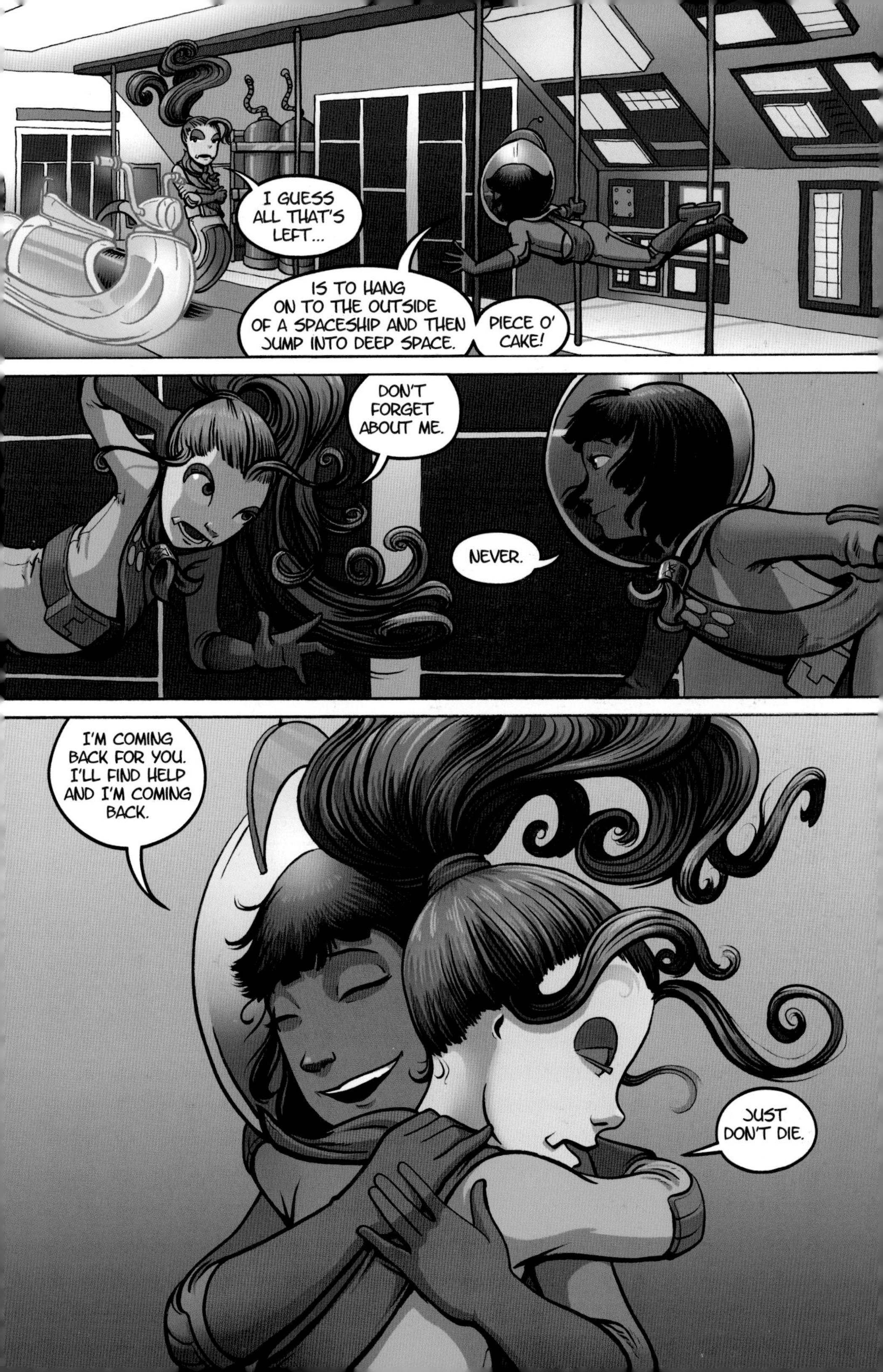
I GUESS ALL THAT'S LEFT...
IS TO HANG ON TO THE OUTSIDE OF A SPACESHIP AND THEN JUMP INTO DEEP SPACE.
PIECE O' CAKE!
DON'T FORGET ABOUT ME.
NEVER.
I'M COMING BACK FOR YOU. I'LL FIND HELP AND I'M COMING BACK.
JUST DON'T DIE.

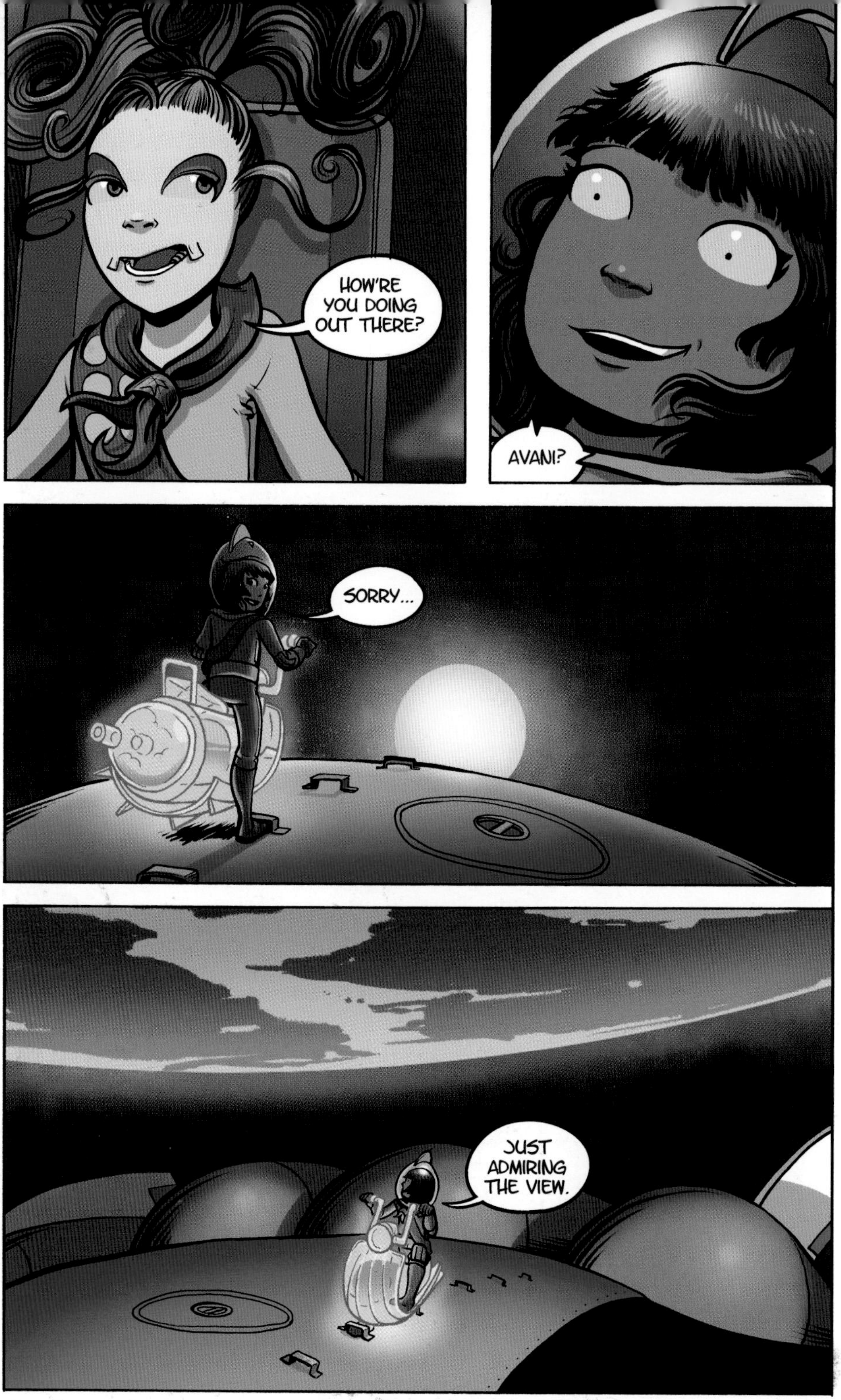
HOW'RE YOU DOING OUT THERE?
AVANI?
SORRY...
JUST ADMIRING THE VIEW.

OKAY, AVANI, GET READY. WE'RE APPROACHING THE APOGEE IN...
THREE...
TWO...
ONE!
PHOOSH!
LEAP!
LEAP!
REMEMBER, COMMS WILL CUT OUT SOON, SO JUST FLY STRAIGHT.
DON'T WORRY, I'LL BE BACK BEFORE YOU CAN SAY "AVANI SAVED MY BUTT AGAIN!"

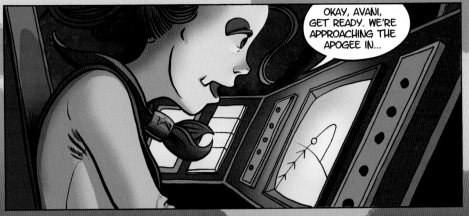

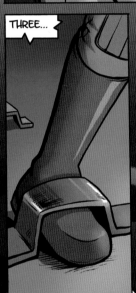

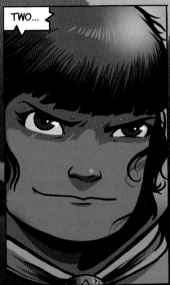

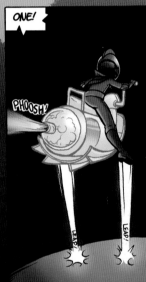

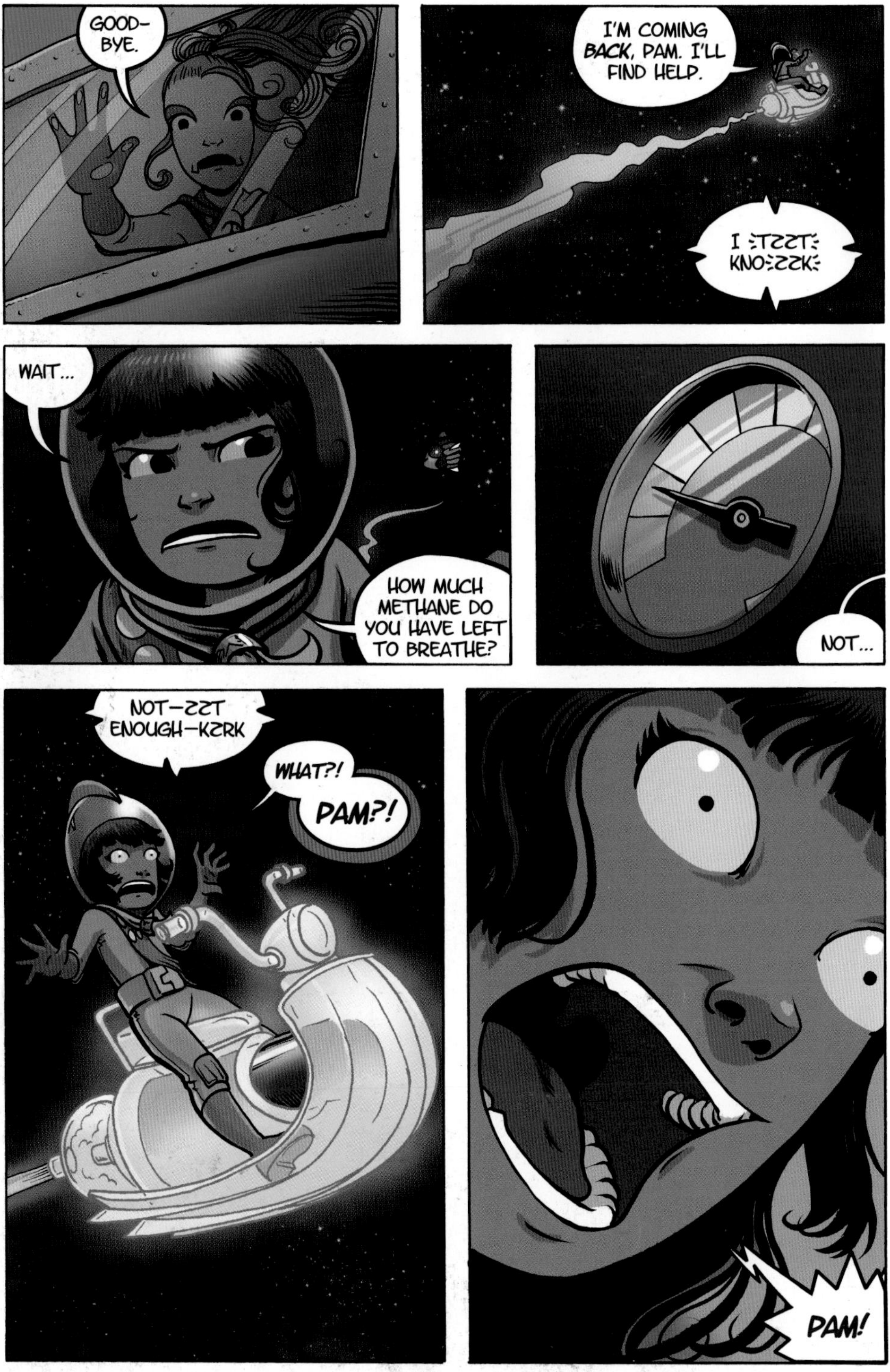
GOOD-BYE.
I'M COMING BACK, PAM. I'LL FIND HELP.
I :TZZT: KNO:ZZK:
WAIT...
HOW MUCH METHANE DO YOU HAVE LEFT TO BREATHE?
NOT...
NOT—ZZT ENOUGH—KZRK
WHAT?!
PAM?!
PAM!

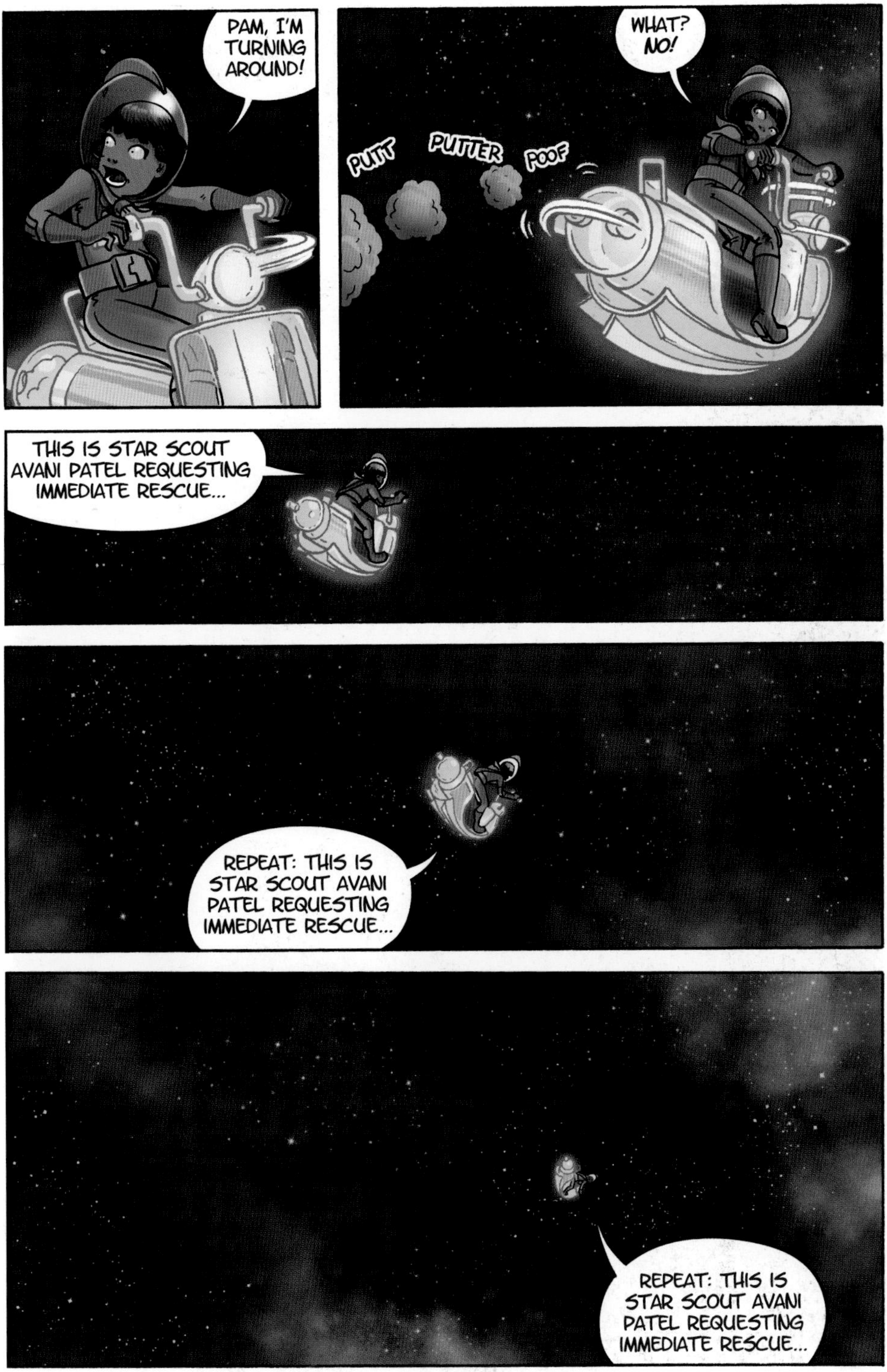
PAM, I'M TURNING AROUND!
WHAT? NO!
PUTT
PUTTER
POOF
THIS IS STAR SCOUT AVANI PATEL REQUESTING IMMEDIATE RESCUE...
REPEAT: THIS IS STAR SCOUT AVANI PATEL REQUESTING IMMEDIATE RESCUE...
REPEAT: THIS IS STAR SCOUT AVANI PATEL REQUESTING IMMEDIATE RESCUE...

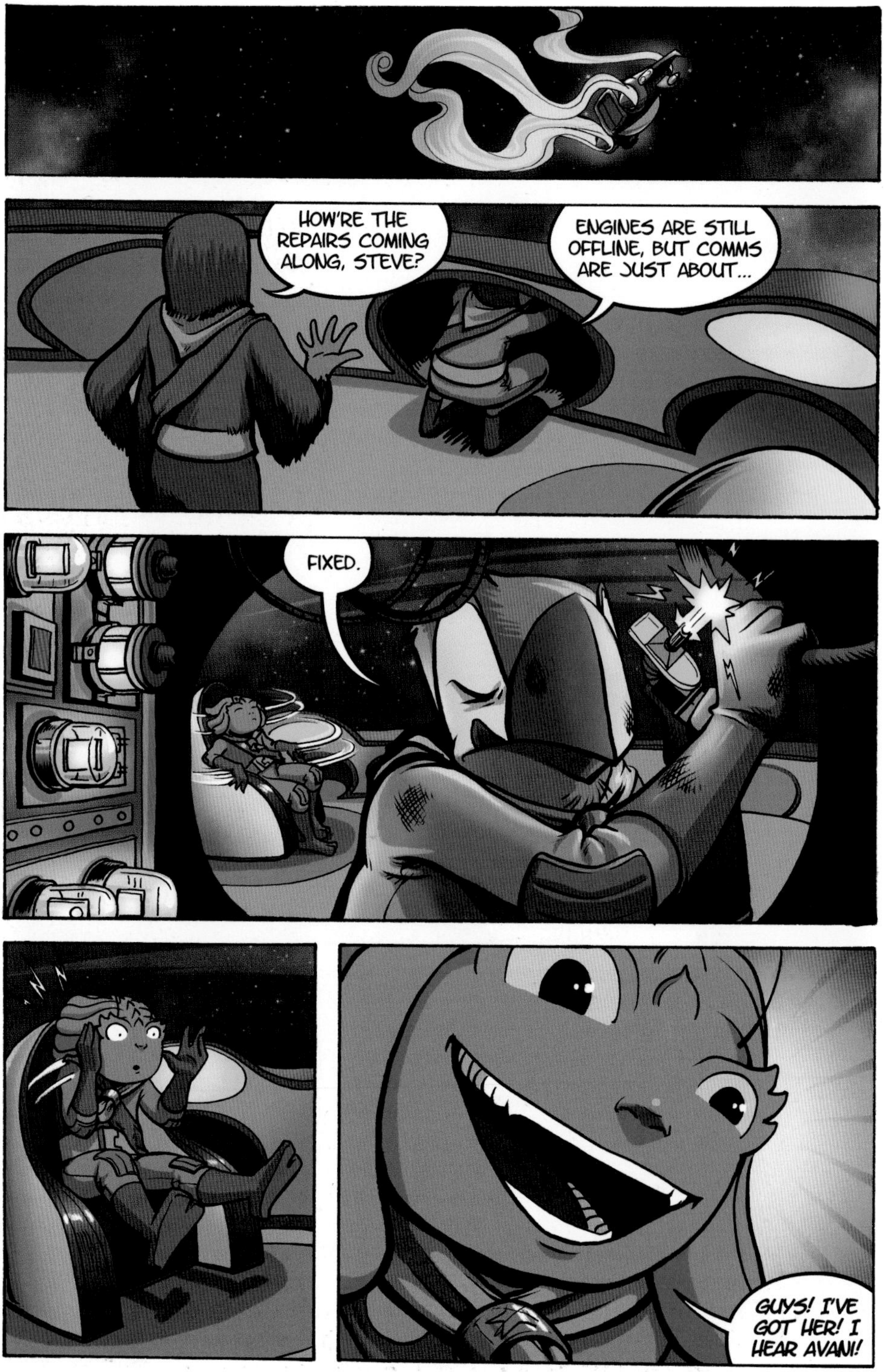
HOW'RE THE REPAIRS COMING ALONG, STEVE?
ENGINES ARE STILL OFFLINE, BUT COMMS ARE JUST ABOUT...
FIXED.
GUYS! I'VE GOT HER! I HEAR AVANI!

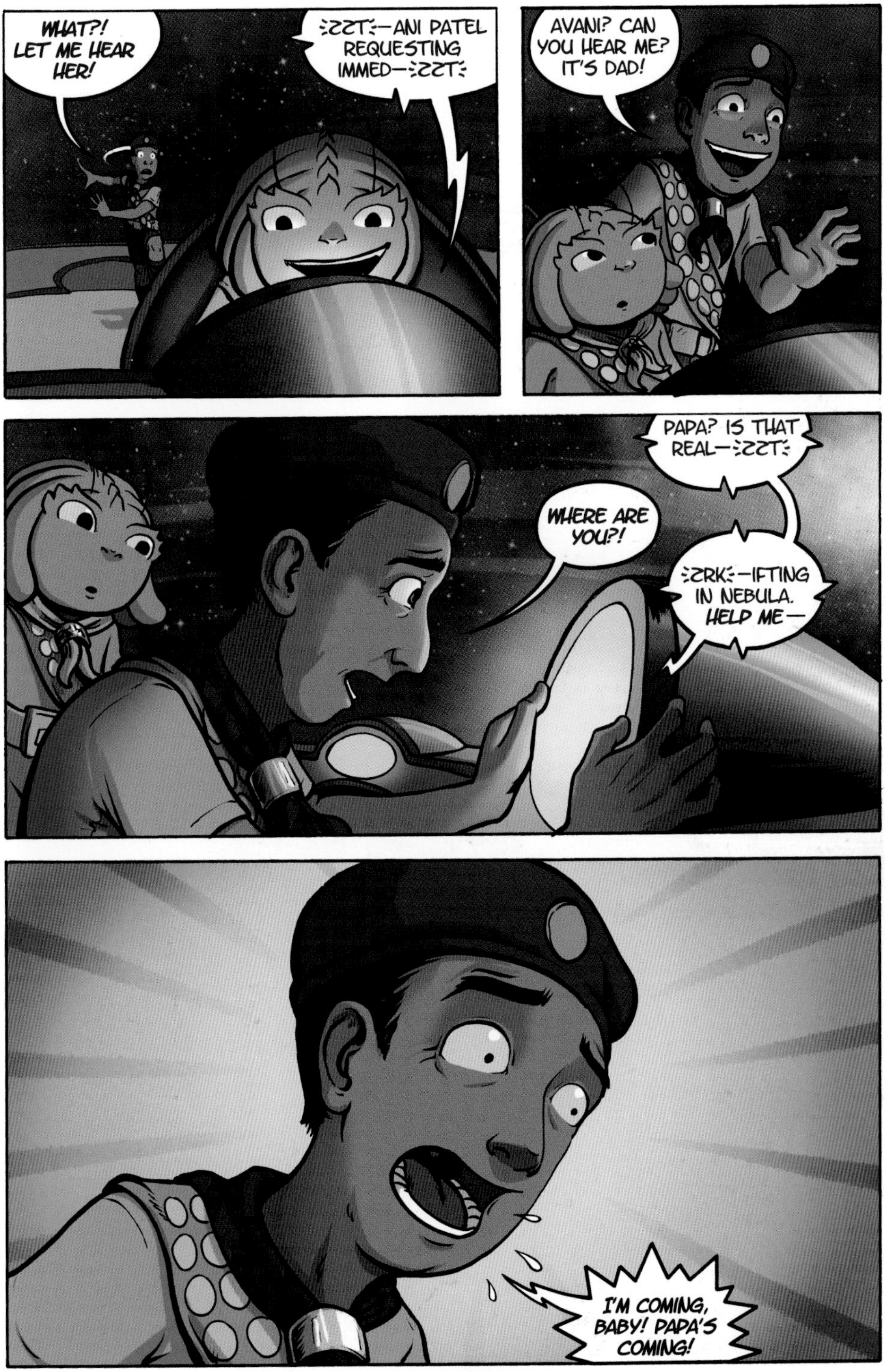
WHAT?! LET ME HEAR HER!
:ZZT:—ANI PATEL REQUESTING IMMED—:ZZT:
AVANI? CAN YOU HEAR ME? IT'S DAD!
PAPA? IS THAT REAL—:ZZT:
WHERE ARE YOU?!
:ZRK:—IFTING IN NEBULA. HELP ME—
I'M COMING, BABY! PAPA'S COMING!

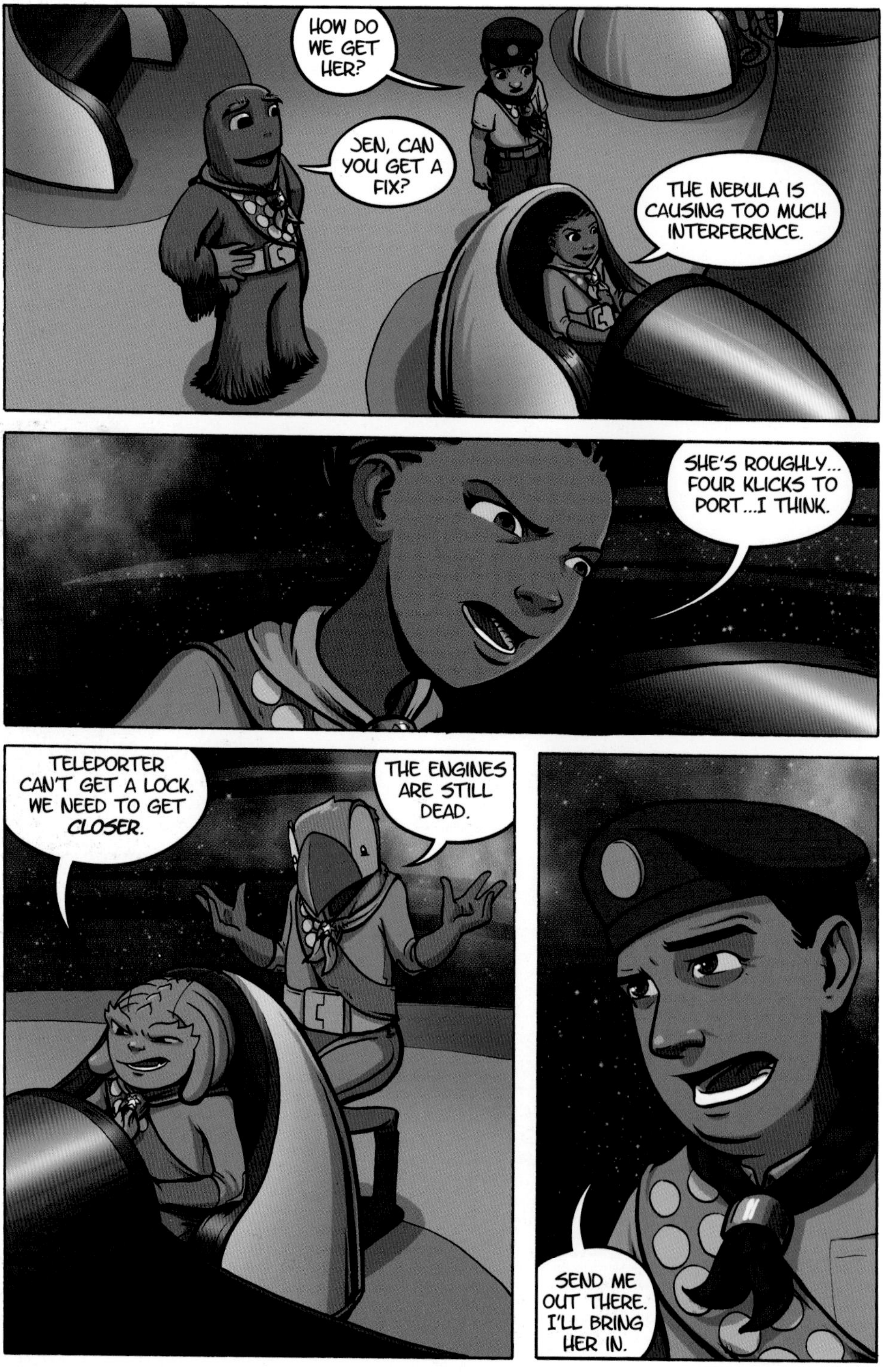
HOW DO WE GET HER?
JEN, CAN YOU GET A FIX?
THE NEBULA IS CAUSING TOO MUCH INTERFERENCE.
SHE'S ROUGHLY... FOUR KLICKS TO PORT...I THINK.
TELEPORTER CAN'T GET A LOCK. WE NEED TO GET CLOSER.
THE ENGINES ARE STILL DEAD.
SEND ME OUT THERE. I'LL BRING HER IN.

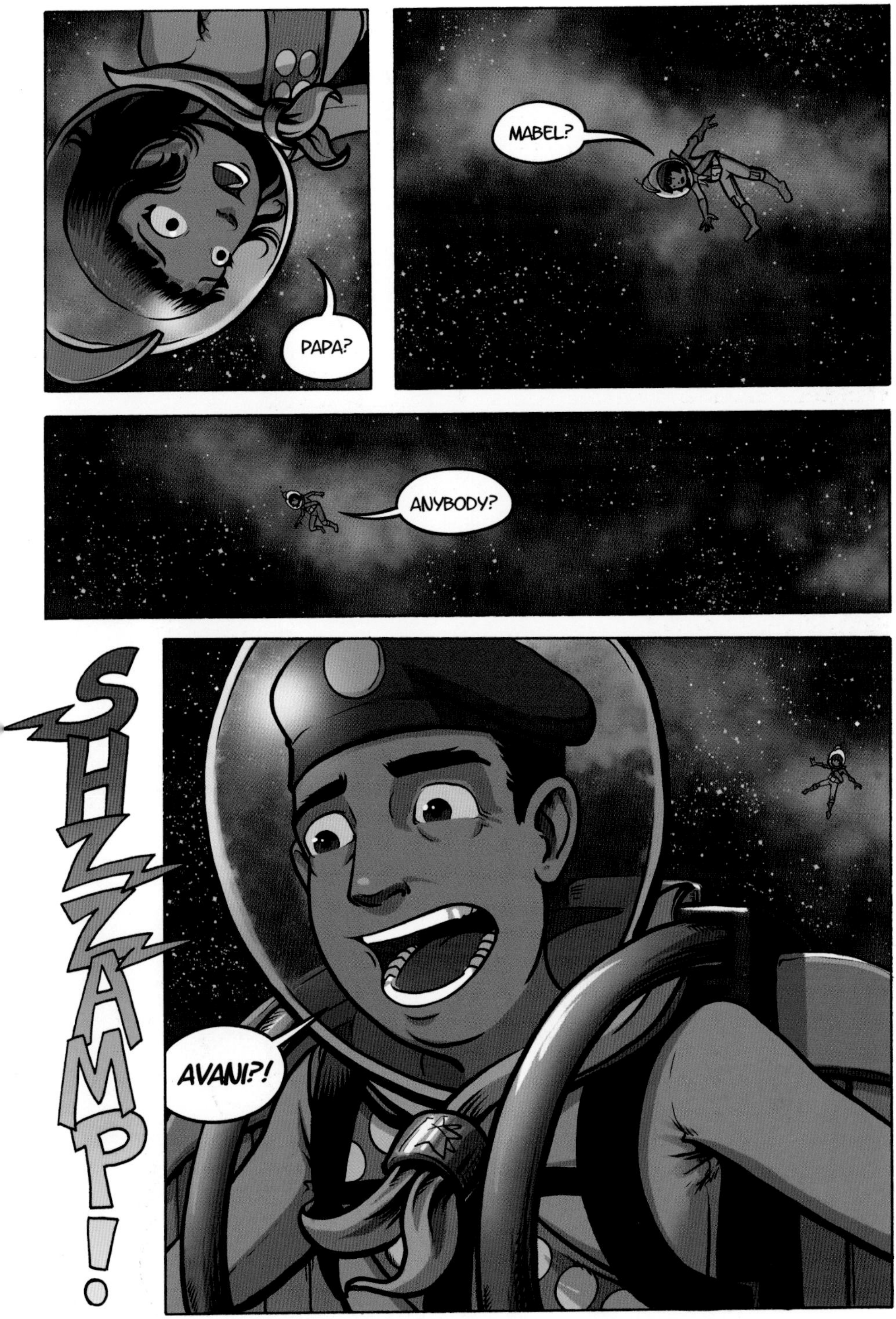
PAPA?
MABEL?
ANYBODY?
SHZZZAMP!
AVANI?!

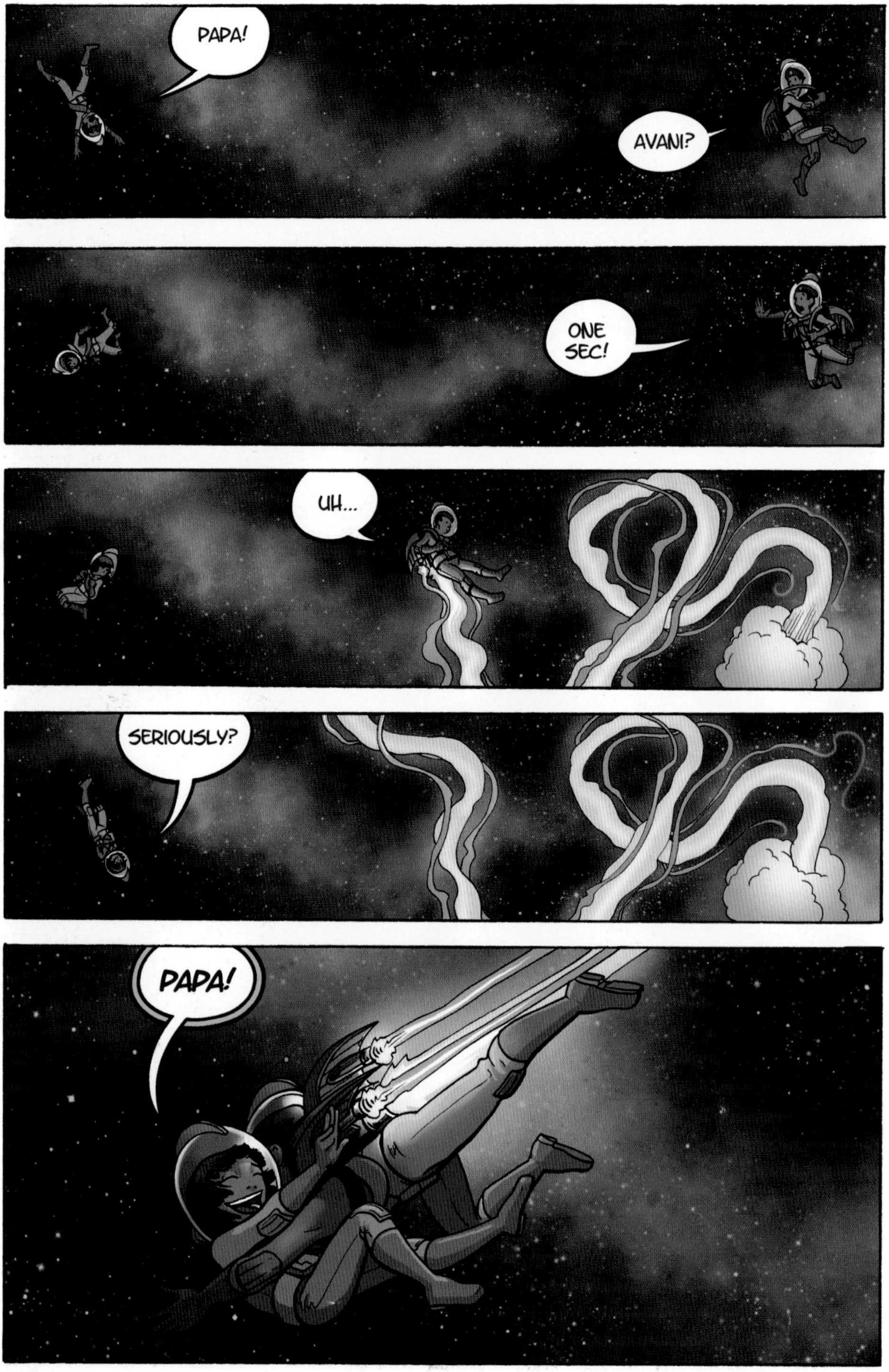
PAPA!
AVANI?
ONE SEC!
UH...
SERIOUSLY?
PAPA!

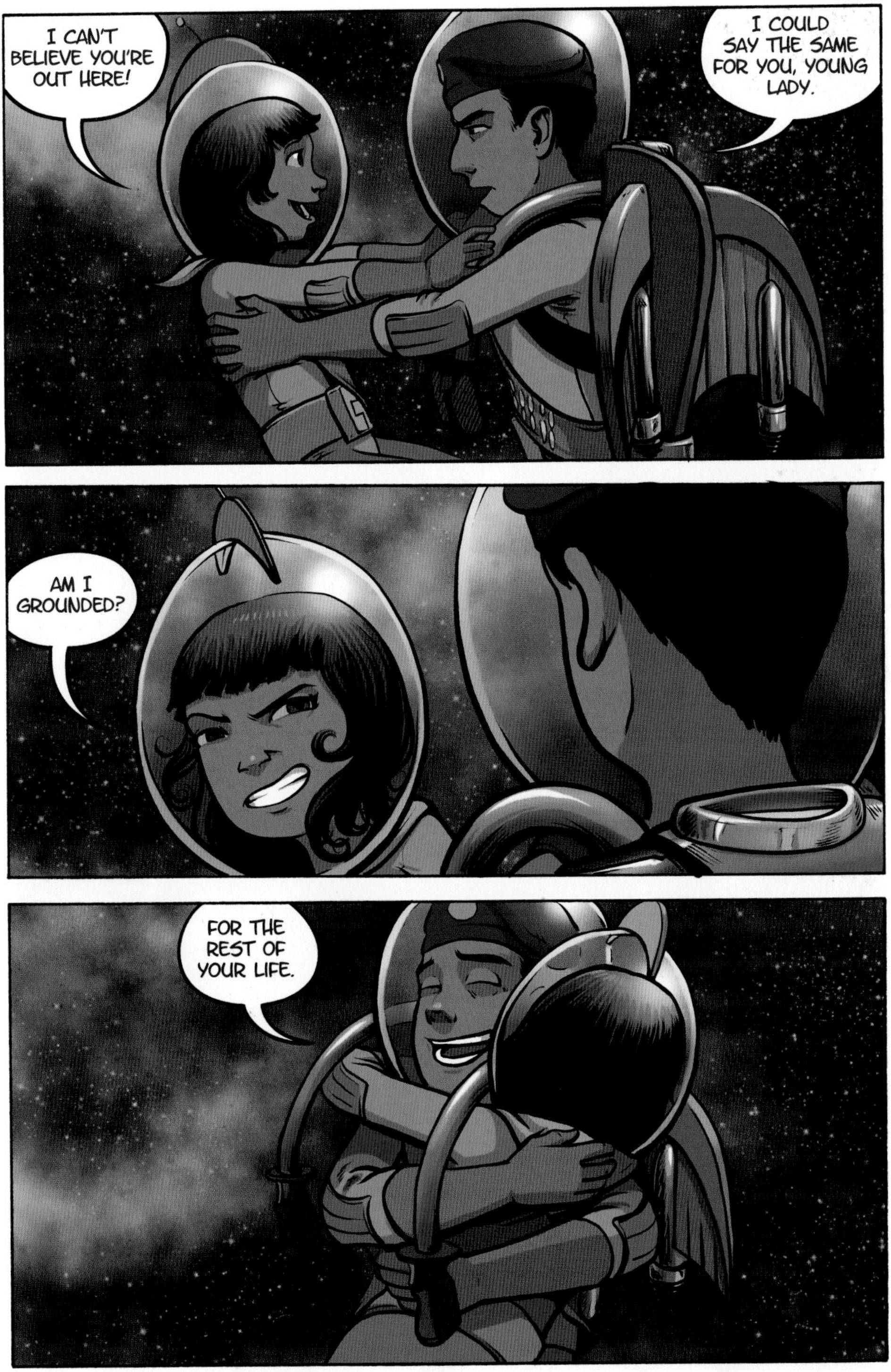
I CAN'T BELIEVE YOU'RE OUT HERE!
I COULD SAY THE SAME FOR YOU, YOUNG LADY.
AM I GROUNDED?
FOR THE REST OF YOUR LIFE.

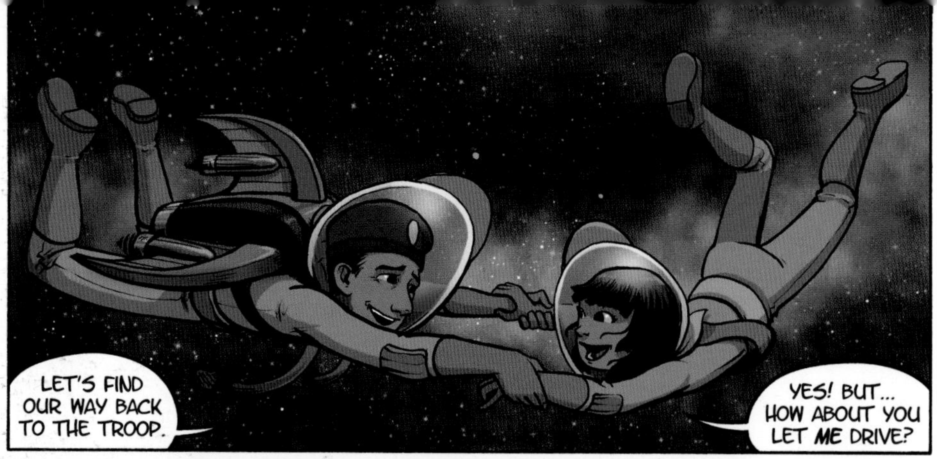
LET'S FIND OUR WAY BACK TO THE TROOP.
YES! BUT... HOW ABOUT YOU LET *ME* DRIVE?

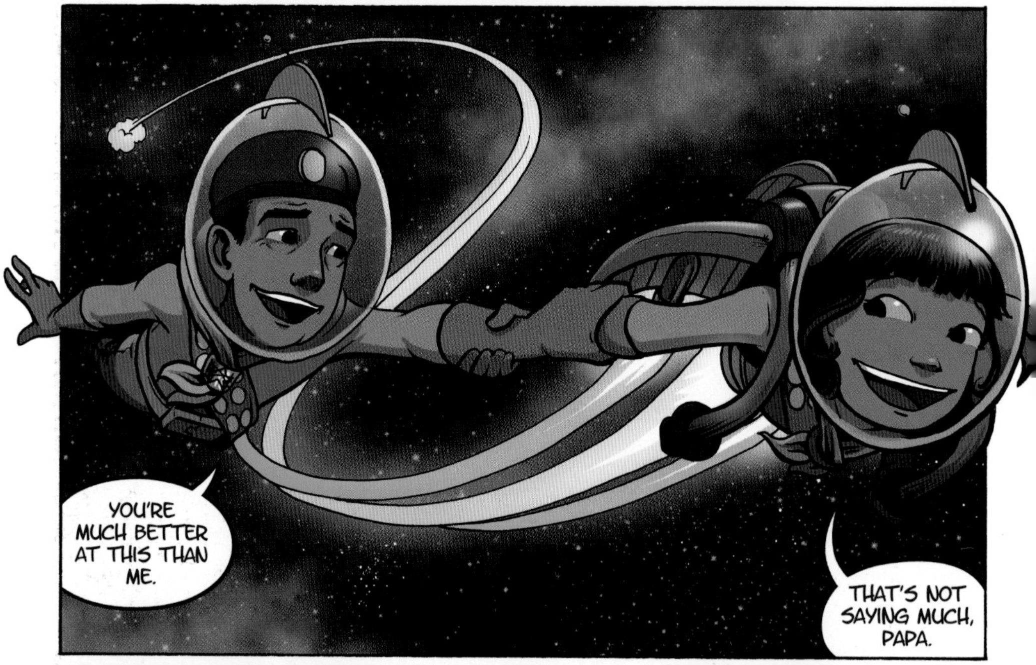
YOU'RE MUCH BETTER AT THIS THAN ME.
THAT'S NOT SAYING MUCH, PAPA.

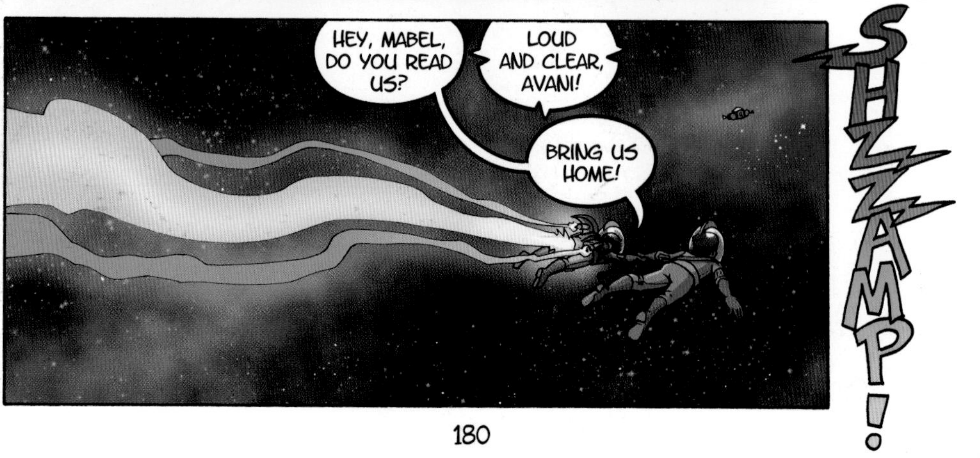
HEY, MABEL, DO YOU READ US?
LOUD AND CLEAR, AVANI!
BRING US HOME!
SHZZAMP!

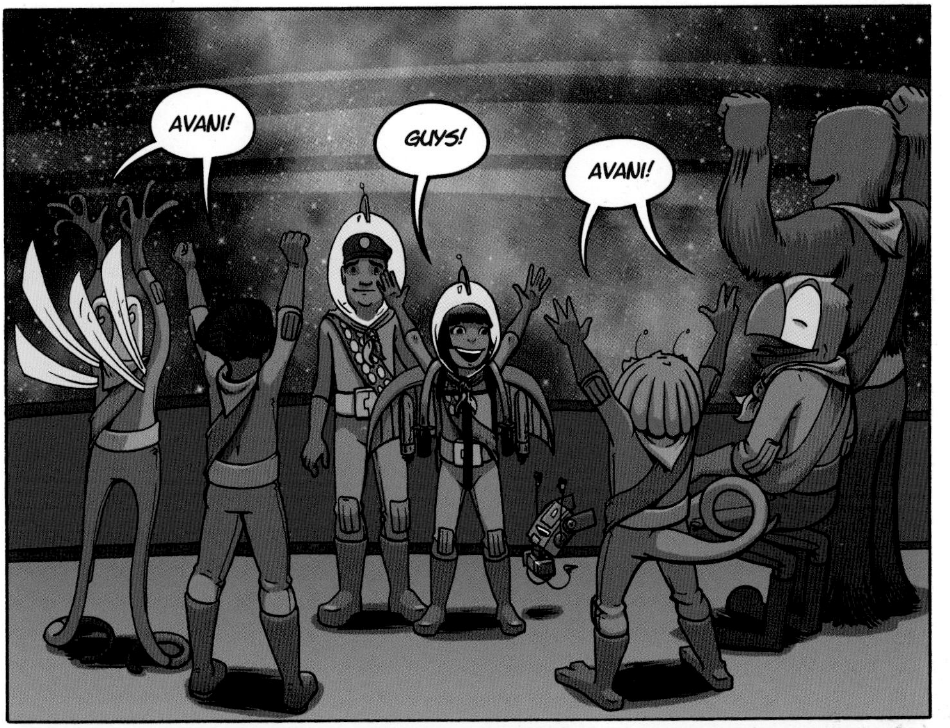
AVANI!
GUYS!
AVANI!

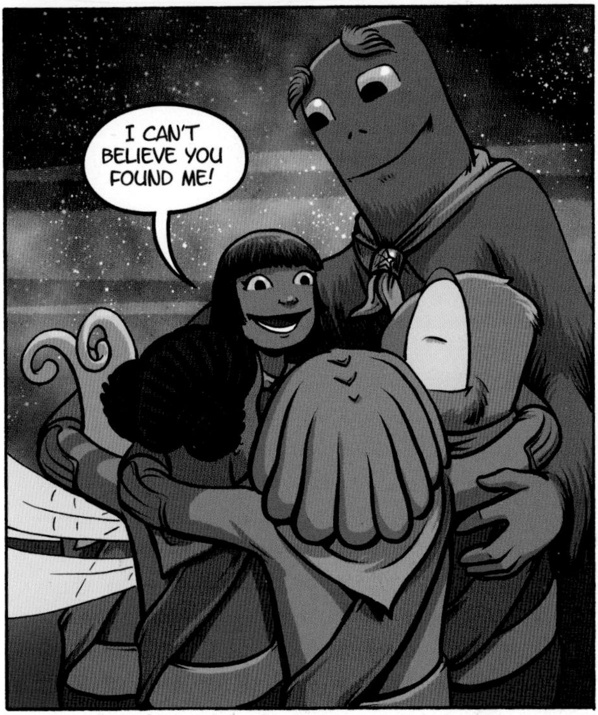
I CAN'T BELIEVE YOU FOUND ME!

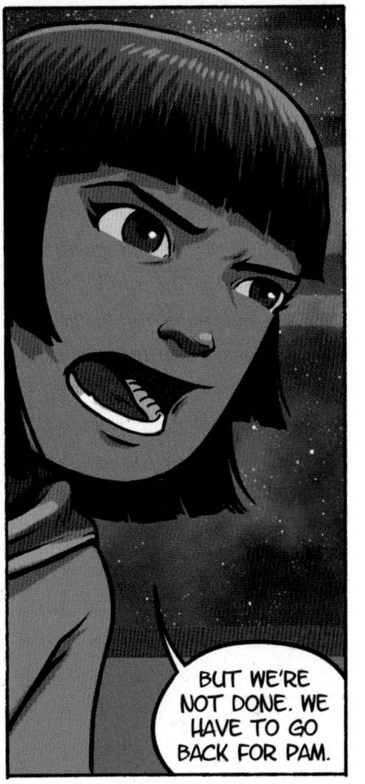
BUT WE'RE NOT DONE. WE HAVE TO GO BACK FOR PAM.

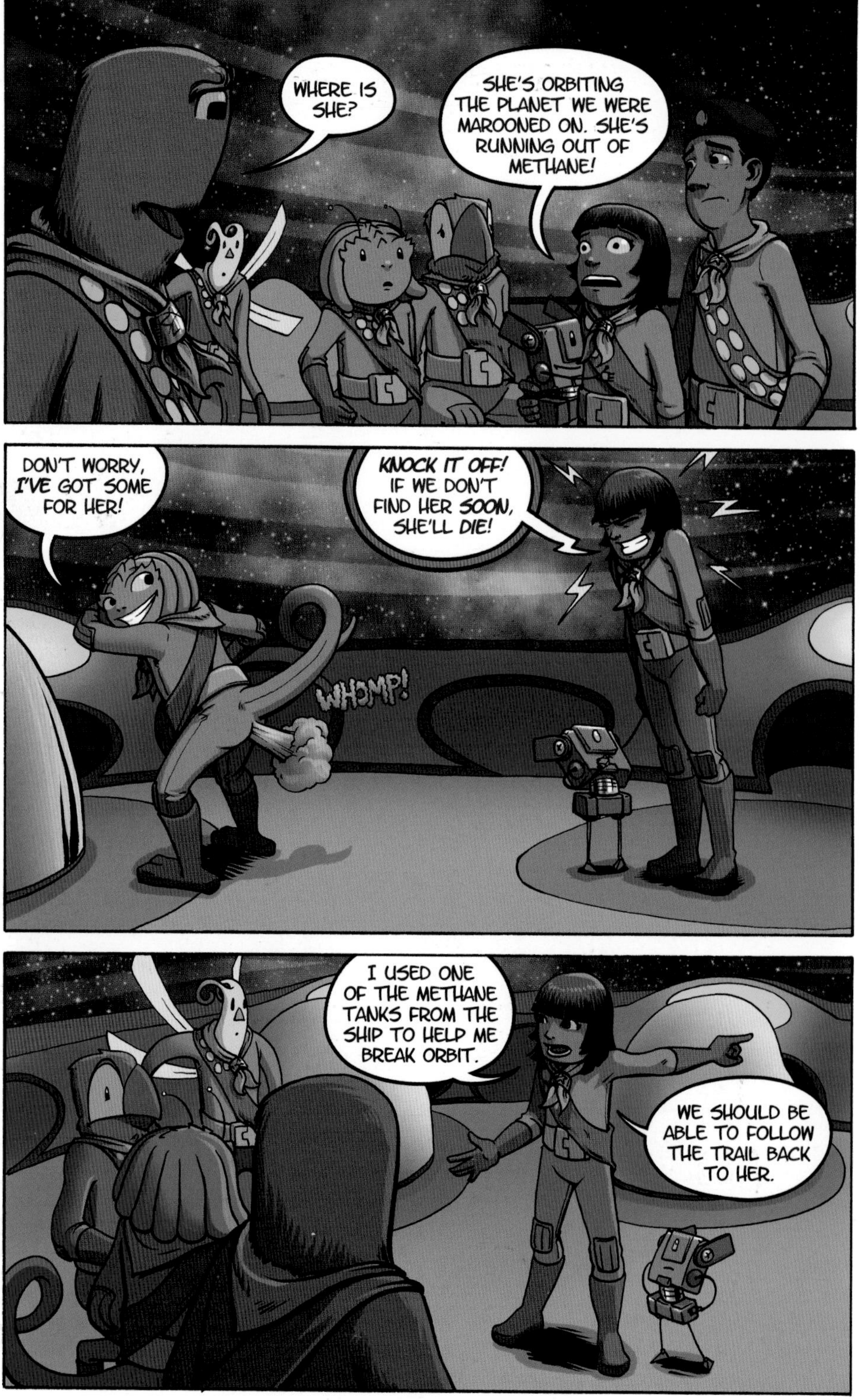
WHERE IS SHE?
SHE'S ORBITING THE PLANET WE WERE MAROONED ON. SHE'S RUNNING OUT OF METHANE!
DON'T WORRY, *I'VE* GOT SOME FOR HER!
WHOMP!
KNOCK IT OFF! IF WE DON'T FIND HER *SOON*, SHE'LL DIE!
I USED ONE OF THE METHANE TANKS FROM THE SHIP TO HELP ME BREAK ORBIT.
WE SHOULD BE ABLE TO FOLLOW THE TRAIL BACK TO HER.

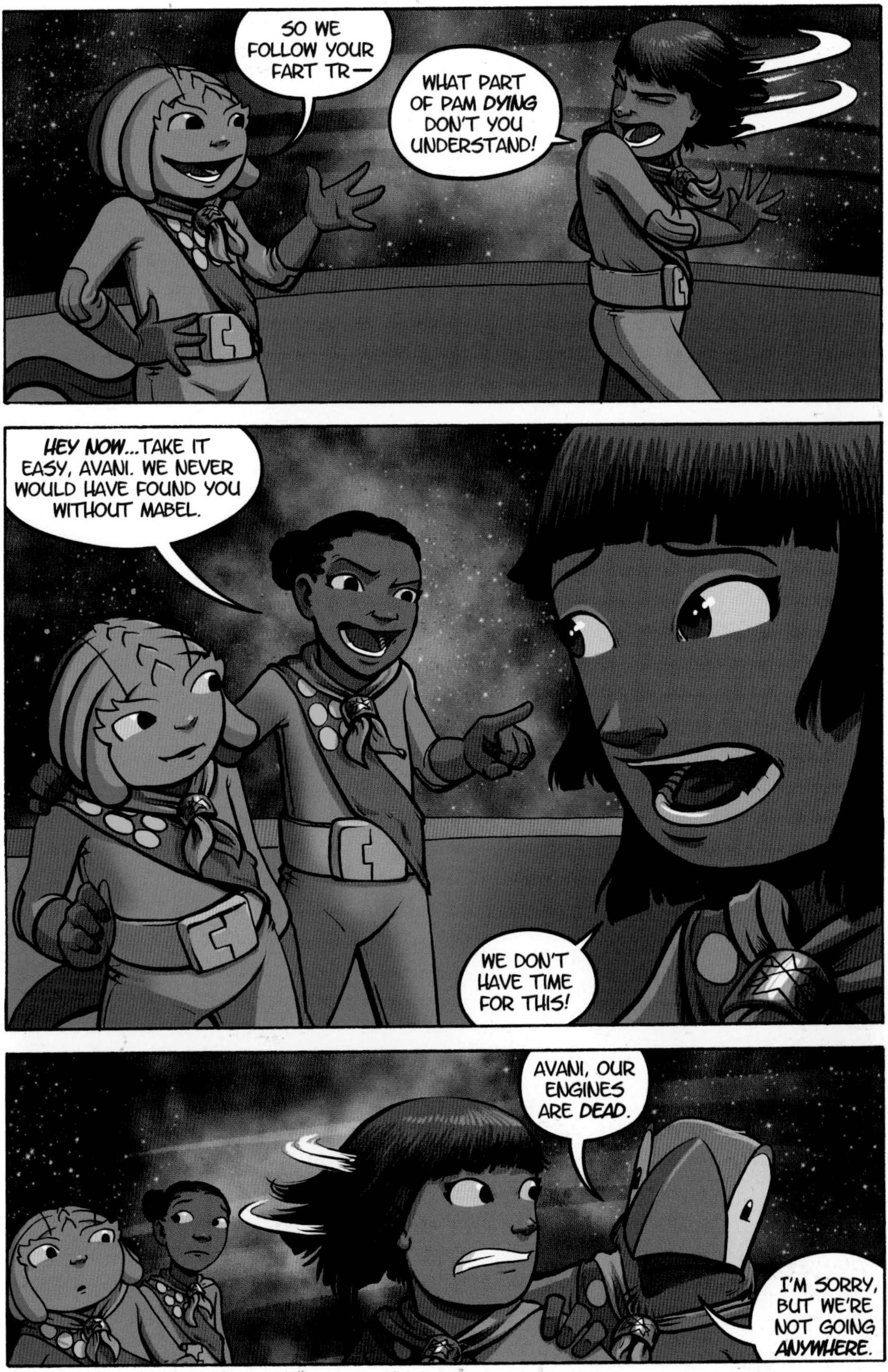
SO WE FOLLOW YOUR FART TR—
WHAT PART OF PAM DYING DON'T YOU UNDERSTAND!
HEY NOW...TAKE IT EASY, AVANI. WE NEVER WOULD HAVE FOUND YOU WITHOUT MABEL.
WE DON'T HAVE TIME FOR THIS!
AVANI, OUR ENGINES ARE DEAD.
I'M SORRY, BUT WE'RE NOT GOING ANYWHERE.

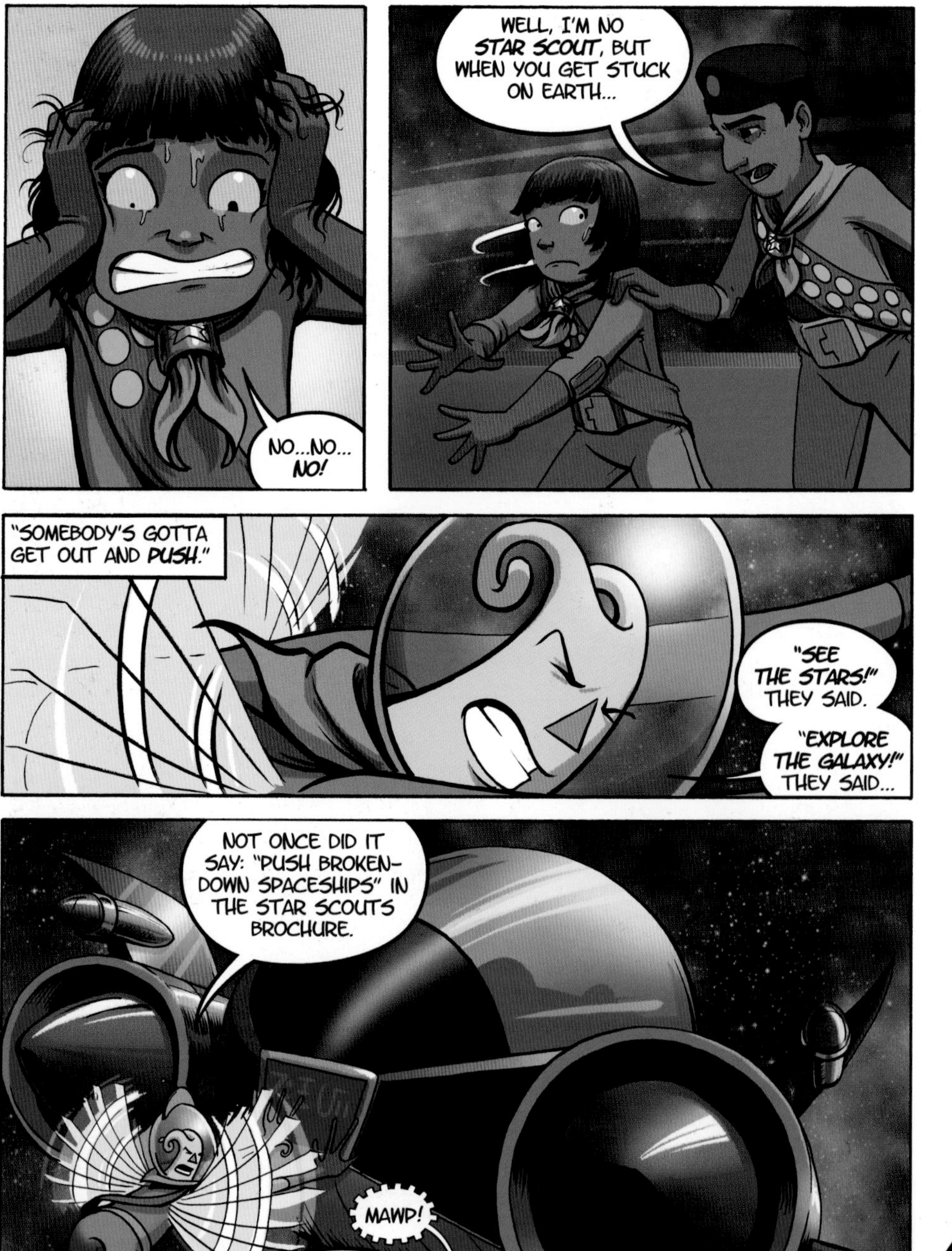
NO...NO...
NO!
WELL, I'M NO STAR SCOUT, BUT WHEN YOU GET STUCK ON EARTH...
"SOMEBODY'S GOTTA GET OUT AND PUSH."
"SEE THE STARS!" THEY SAID.
"EXPLORE THE GALAXY!" THEY SAID...
NOT ONCE DID IT SAY: "PUSH BROKEN-DOWN SPACESHIPS" IN THE STAR SCOUTS BROCHURE.
MAWP!
EXACTLY! YOU KNOW WHERE I'M COMIN' FROM.
MOOP!

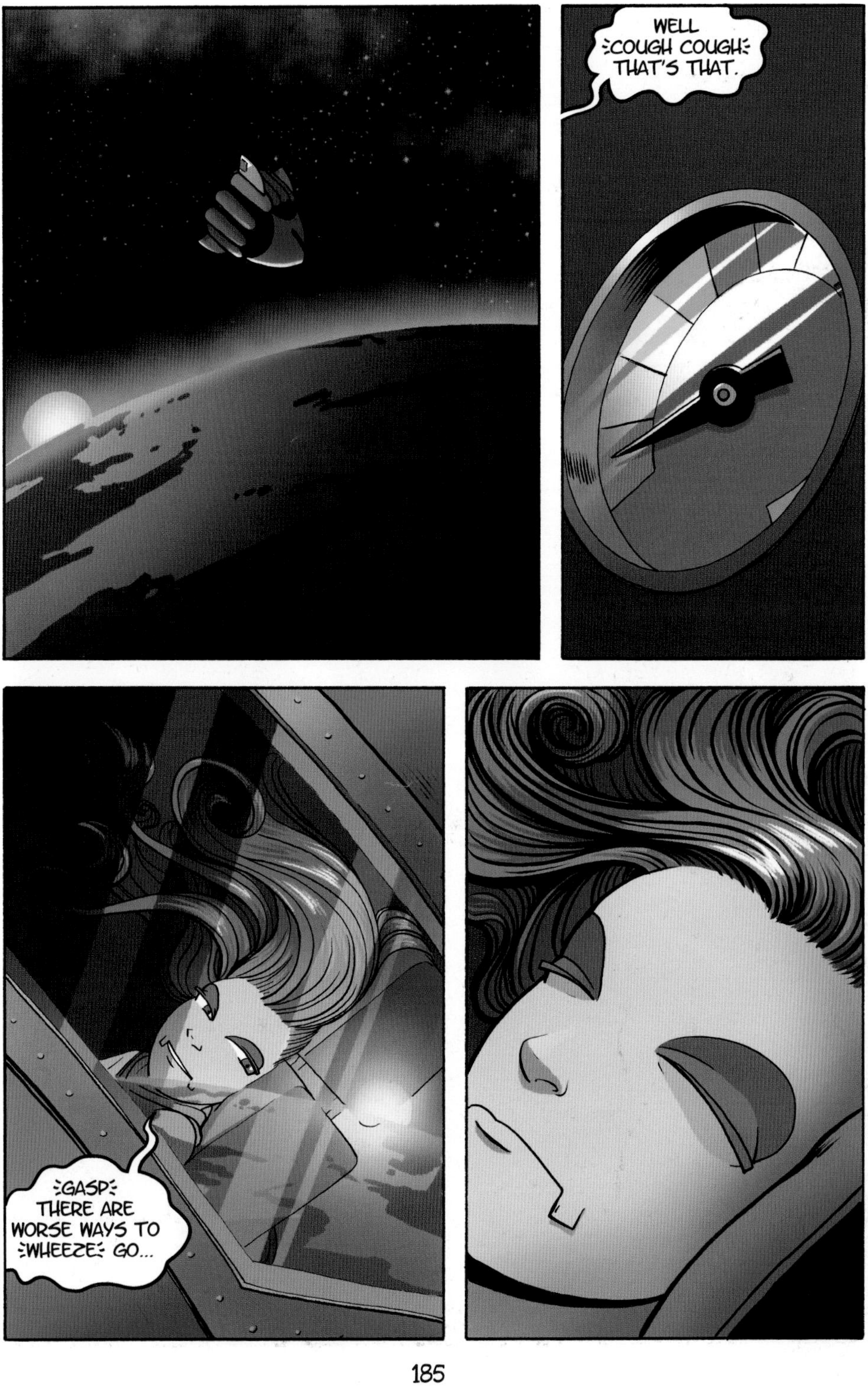
WELL
=COUGH COUGH=
THAT'S THAT.
=GASP=
THERE ARE
WORSE WAYS TO
=WHEEZE= GO...

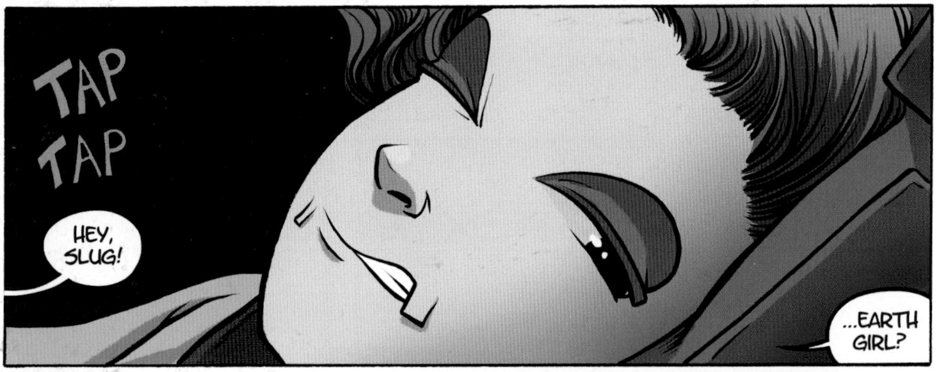
TAP
TAP
HEY, SLUG!
...EARTH GIRL?

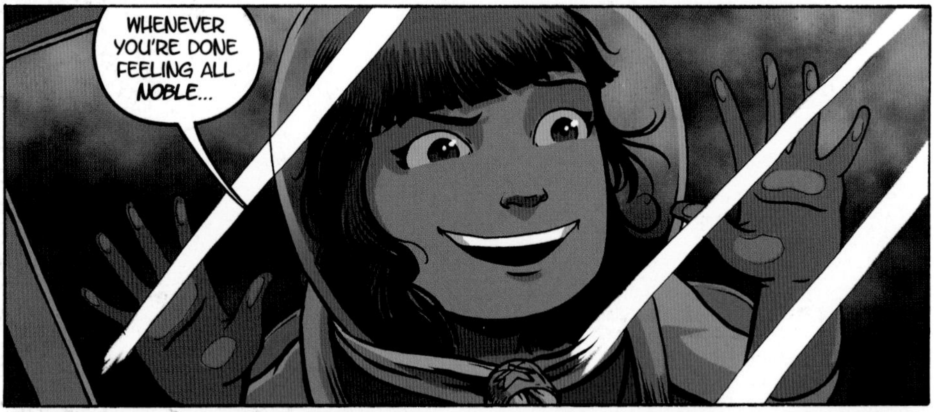
WHENEVER YOU'RE DONE FEELING ALL NOBLE...

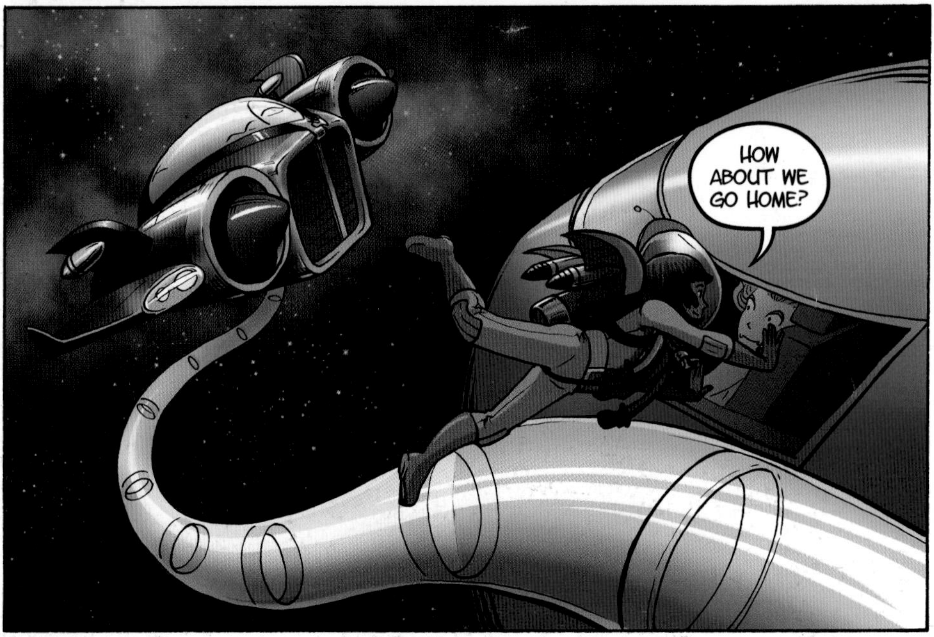
HOW ABOUT WE GO HOME?

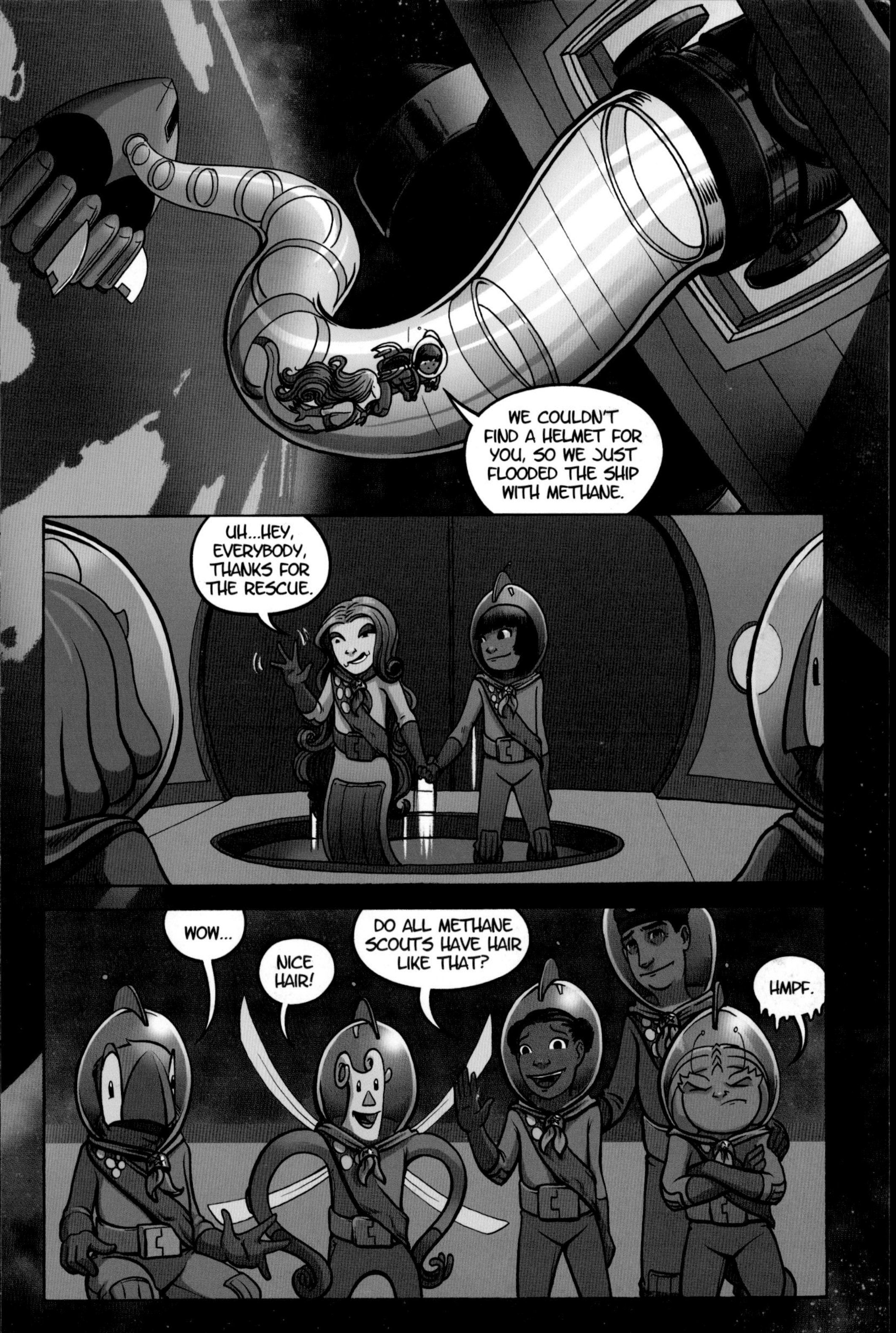
WE COULDN'T FIND A HELMET FOR YOU, SO WE JUST FLOODED THE SHIP WITH METHANE.
UH...HEY, EVERYBODY, THANKS FOR THE RESCUE.
WOW...
NICE HAIR!
DO ALL METHANE SCOUTS HAVE HAIR LIKE THAT?
HMPF.

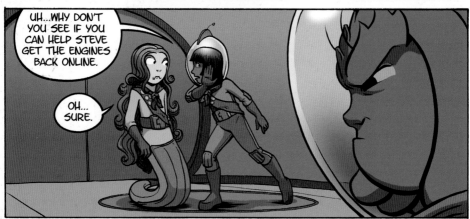

UH...WHY DON'T YOU SEE IF YOU CAN HELP STEVE GET THE ENGINES BACK ONLINE.

OH... SURE.

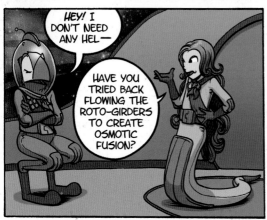

HEY! I DON'T NEED ANY HEL—

HAVE YOU TRIED BACK FLOWING THE ROTO-GIRDERS TO CREATE OSMOTIC FUSION?

ENGINEERING IS THIS WAY.

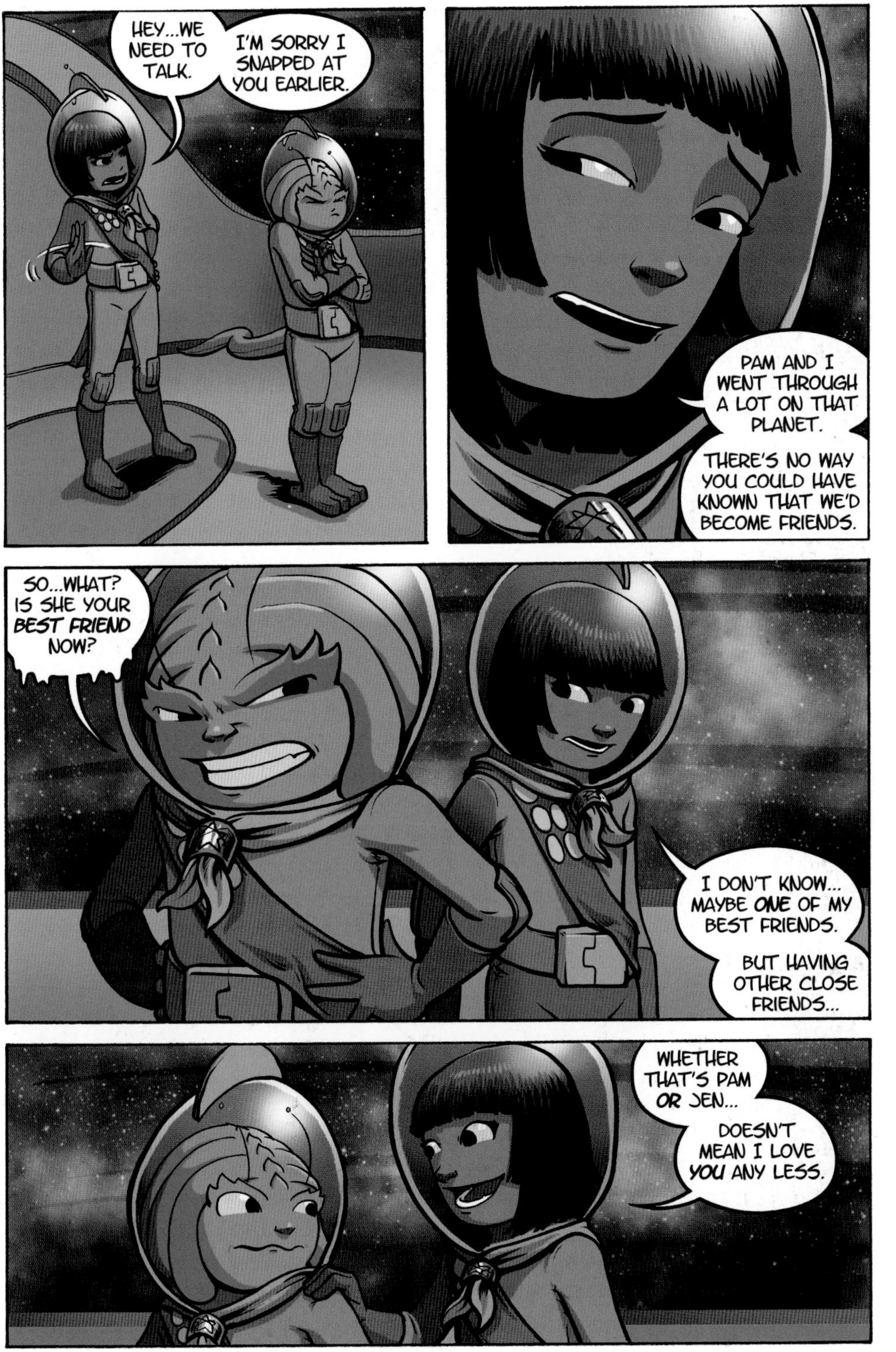

HEY...WE NEED TO TALK.
I'M SORRY I SNAPPED AT YOU EARLIER.
PAM AND I WENT THROUGH A LOT ON THAT PLANET.
THERE'S NO WAY YOU COULD HAVE KNOWN THAT WE'D BECOME FRIENDS.
SO...WHAT? IS SHE YOUR BEST FRIEND NOW?
I DON'T KNOW... MAYBE ONE OF MY BEST FRIENDS.
BUT HAVING OTHER CLOSE FRIENDS...
WHETHER THAT'S PAM OR JEN...
DOESN'T MEAN I LOVE YOU ANY LESS.

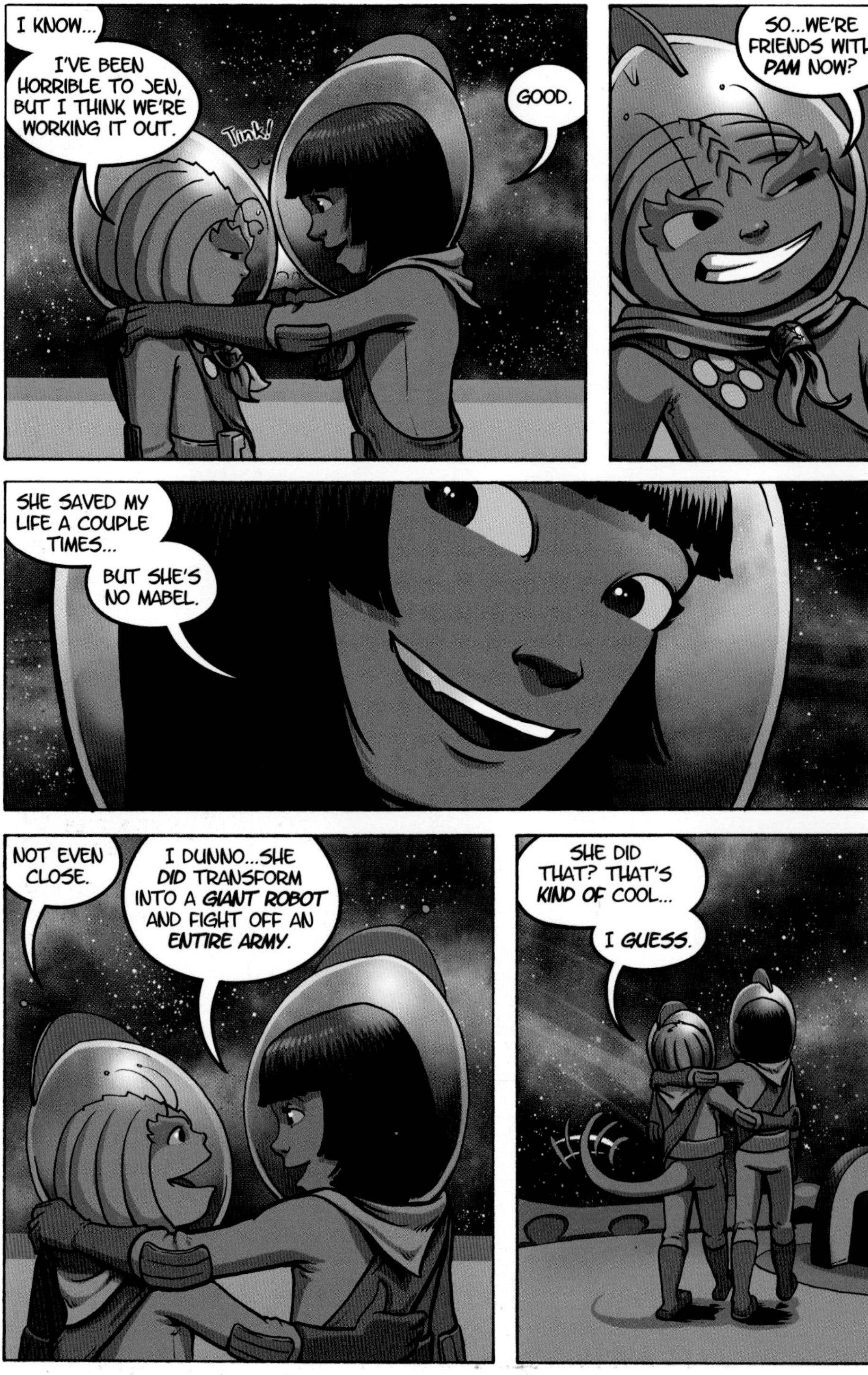
I KNOW...
I'VE BEEN HORRIBLE TO JEN, BUT I THINK WE'RE WORKING IT OUT.
TINK!
GOOD.
SO...WE'RE FRIENDS WITH PAM NOW?
SHE SAVED MY LIFE A COUPLE TIMES...
BUT SHE'S NO MABEL.
NOT EVEN CLOSE.
I DUNNO...SHE DID TRANSFORM INTO A GIANT ROBOT AND FIGHT OFF AN ENTIRE ARMY.
SHE DID THAT? THAT'S KIND OF COOL...
I GUESS.

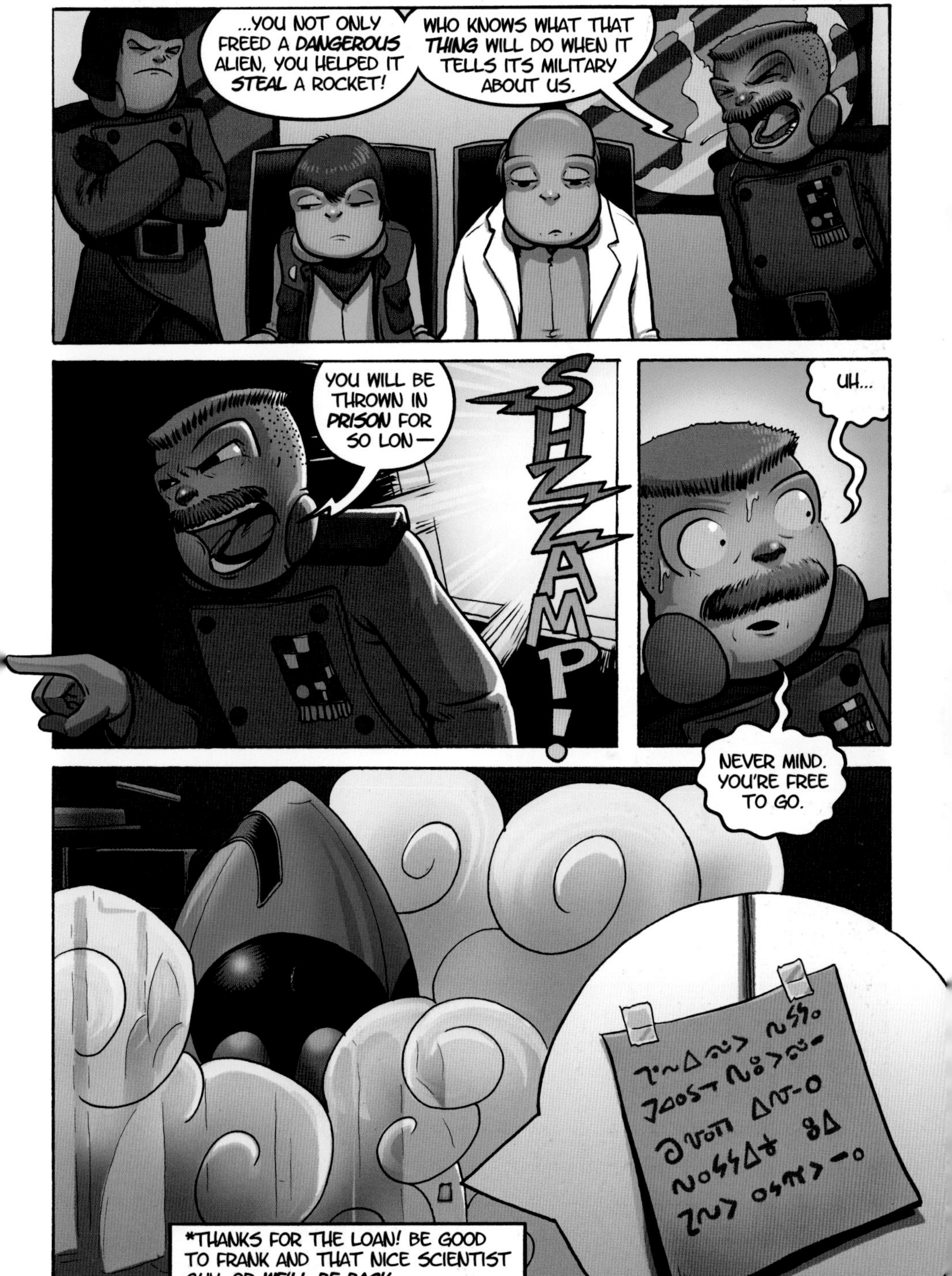

...YOU NOT ONLY FREED A DANGEROUS ALIEN, YOU HELPED IT STEAL A ROCKET!
WHO KNOWS WHAT THAT THING WILL DO WHEN IT TELLS ITS MILITARY ABOUT US.
YOU WILL BE THROWN IN PRISON FOR SO LON—
SHZZZAMP!
UH...
NEVER MIND. YOU'RE FREE TO GO.
*THANKS FOR THE LOAN! BE GOOD TO FRANK AND THAT NICE SCIENTIST GUY, OR WE'LL BE BACK.

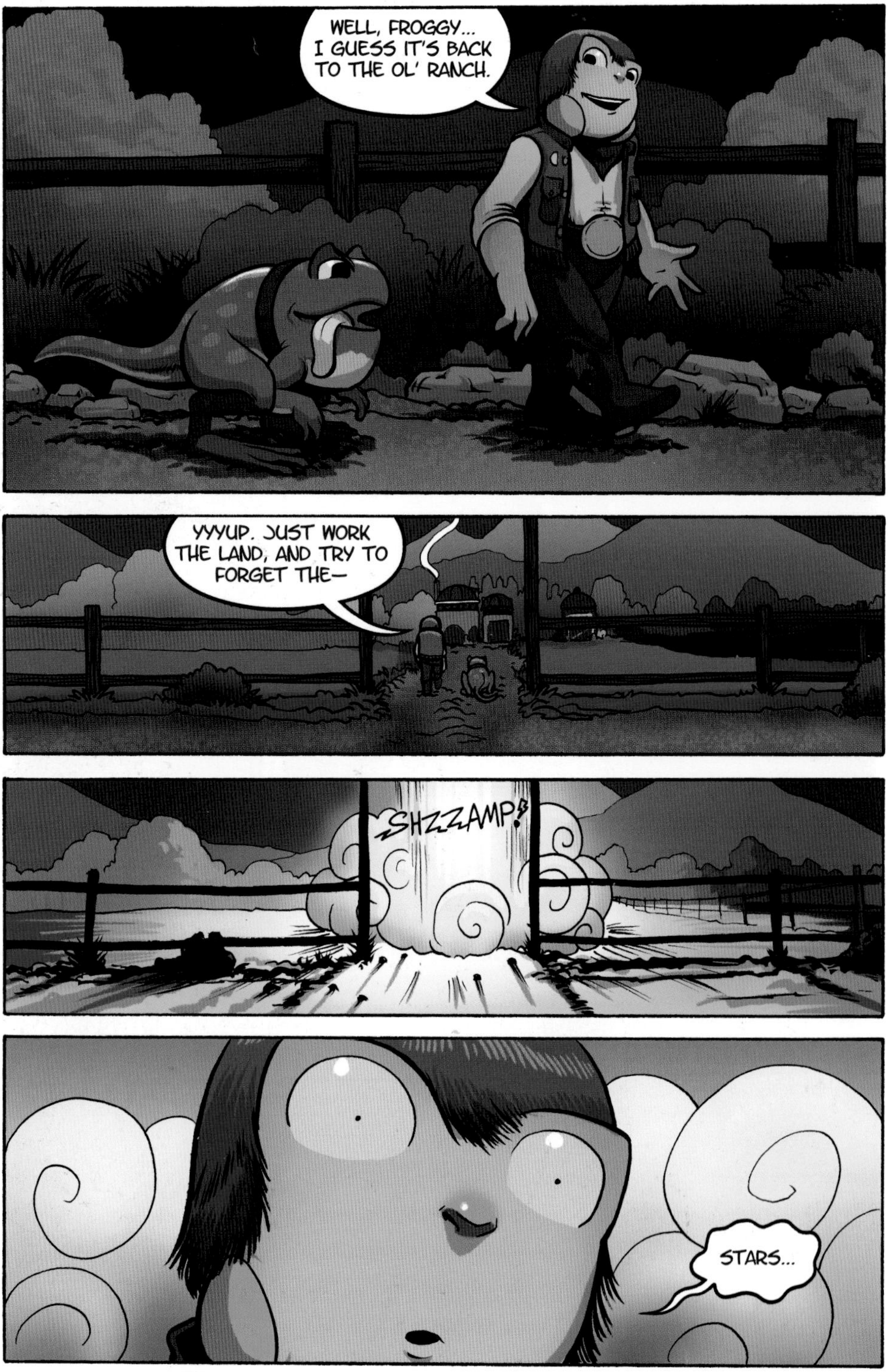
WELL, FROGGY... I GUESS IT'S BACK TO THE OL' RANCH.
YYYUP. JUST WORK THE LAND, AND TRY TO FORGET THE—
SHZZZAMP!
STARS...

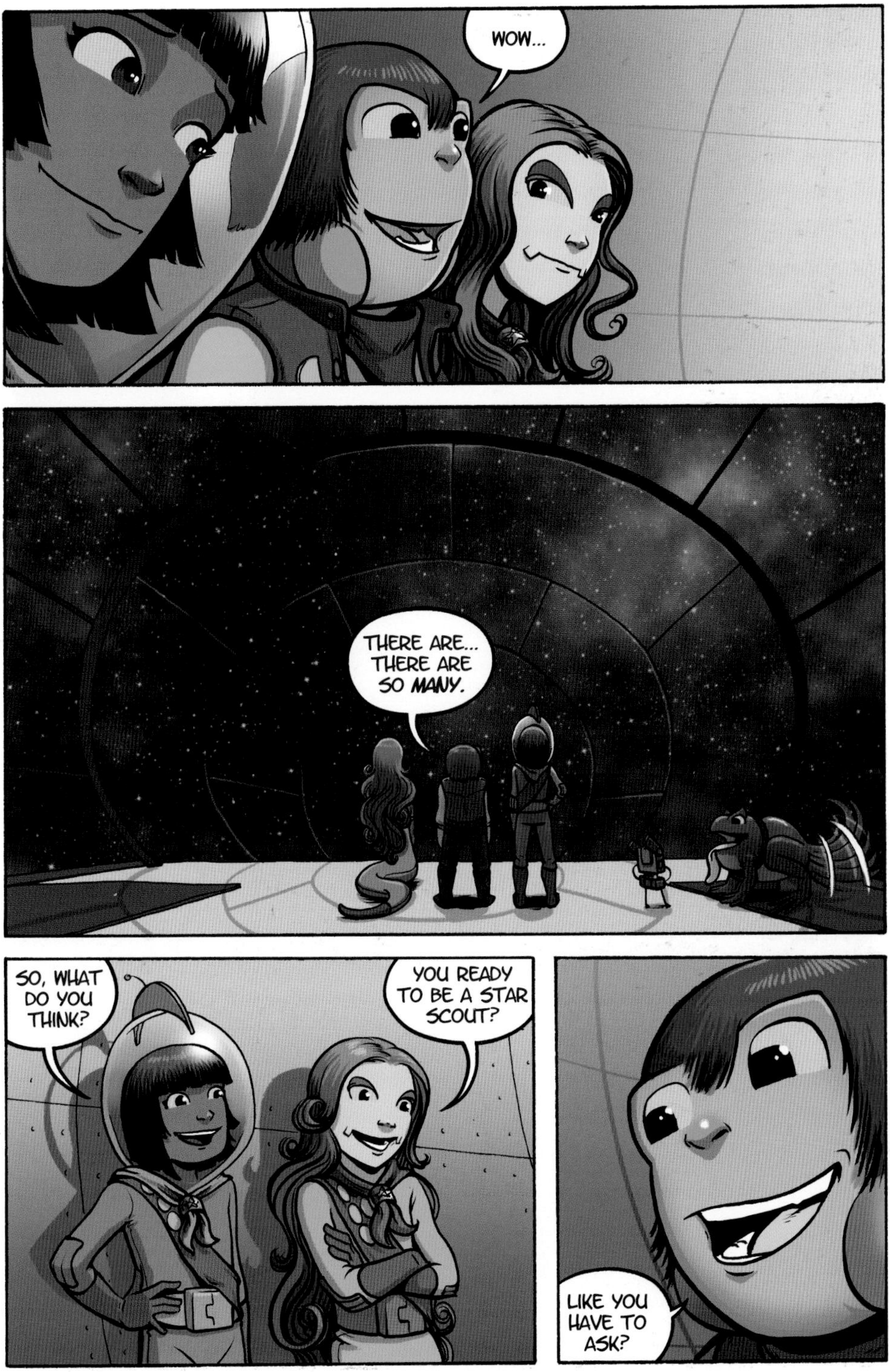
WOW...
THERE ARE... THERE ARE SO *MANY*.
SO, WHAT DO YOU THINK?
YOU READY TO BE A STAR SCOUT?
LIKE YOU HAVE TO ASK?

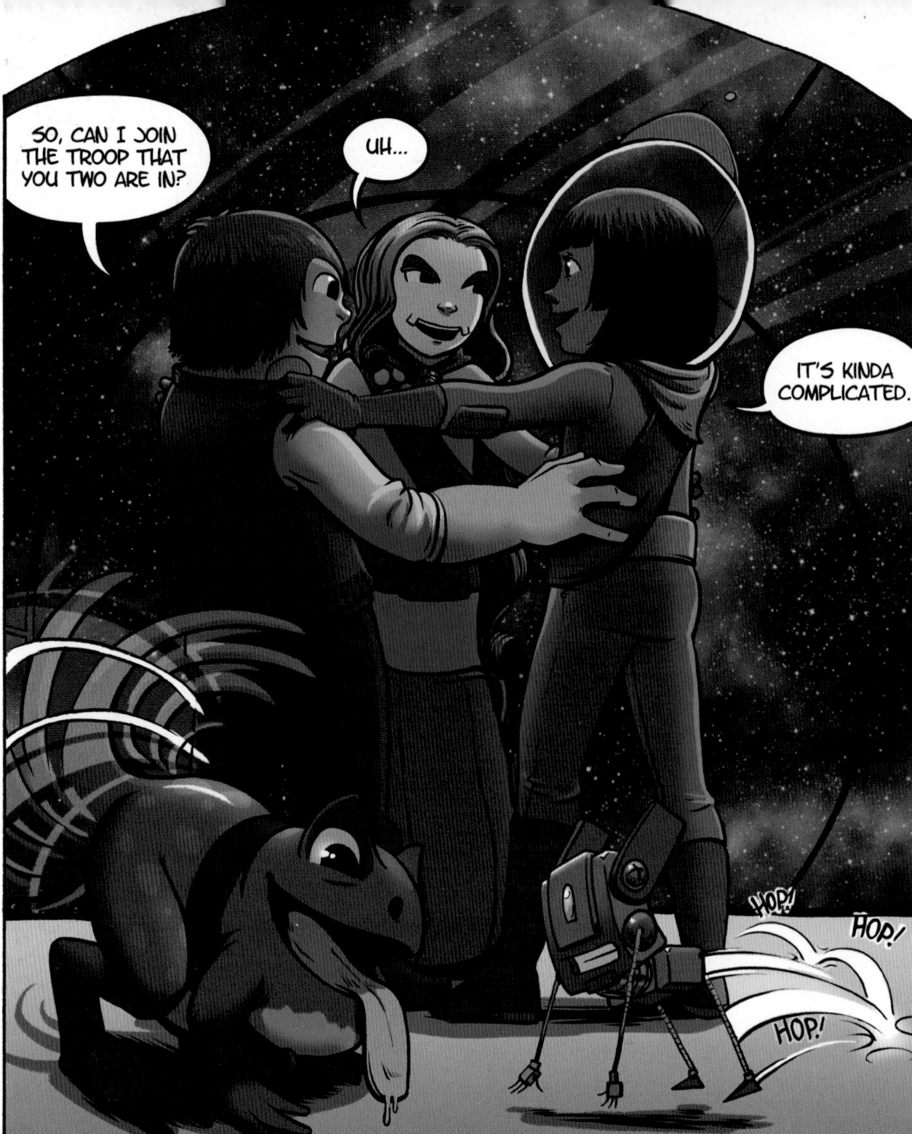
SO, CAN I JOIN THE TROOP THAT YOU TWO ARE IN?
UH...
IT'S KINDA COMPLICATED.
HOP!
HOP!
HOP!

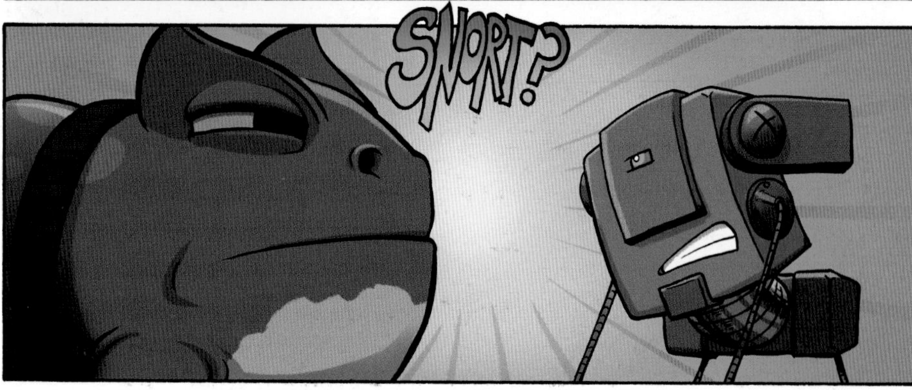
SNORT?

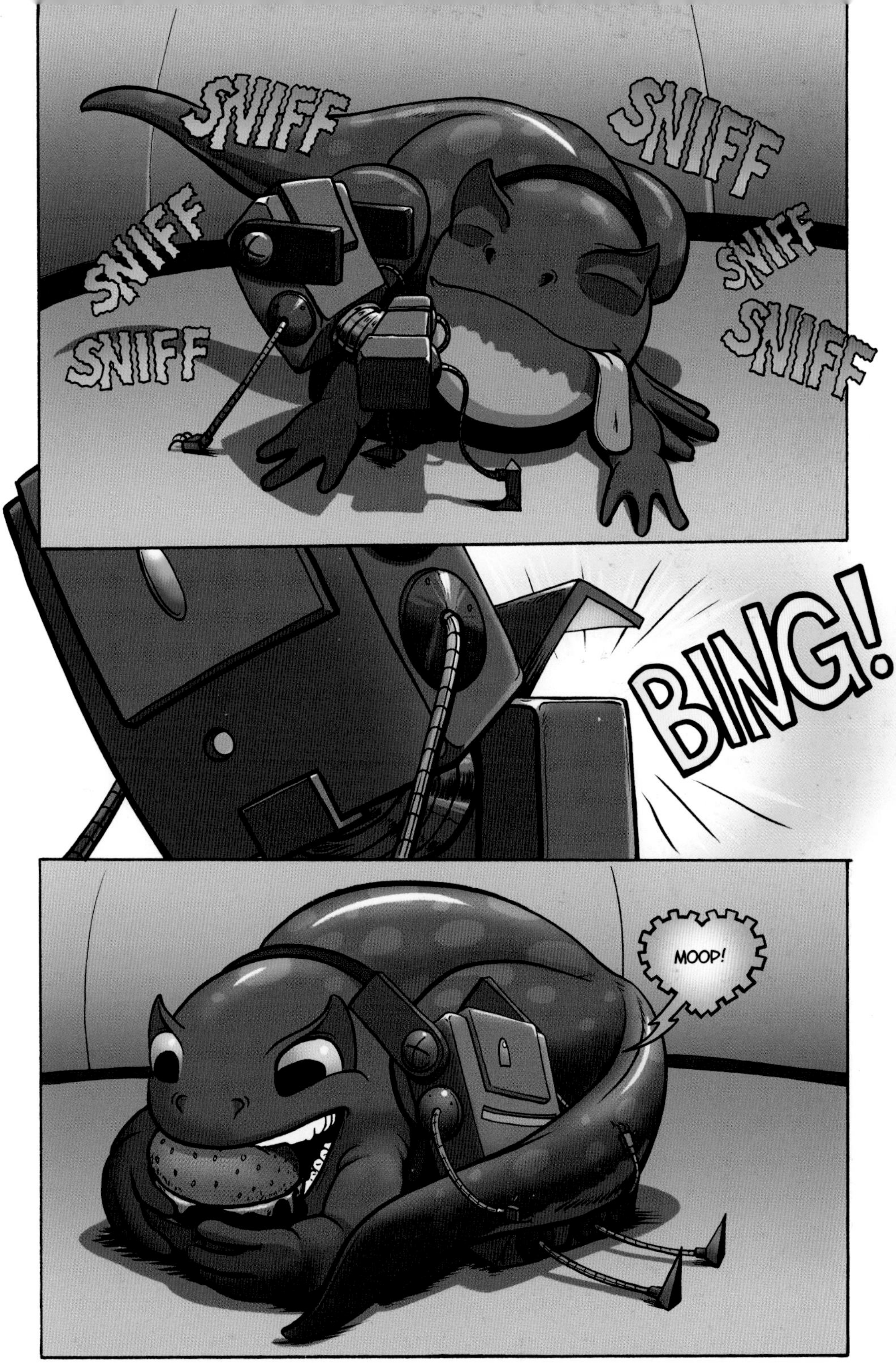
SNIFF
SNIFF
SNIFF
SNIFF
SNIFF
SNIFF
BING!
MOOP!

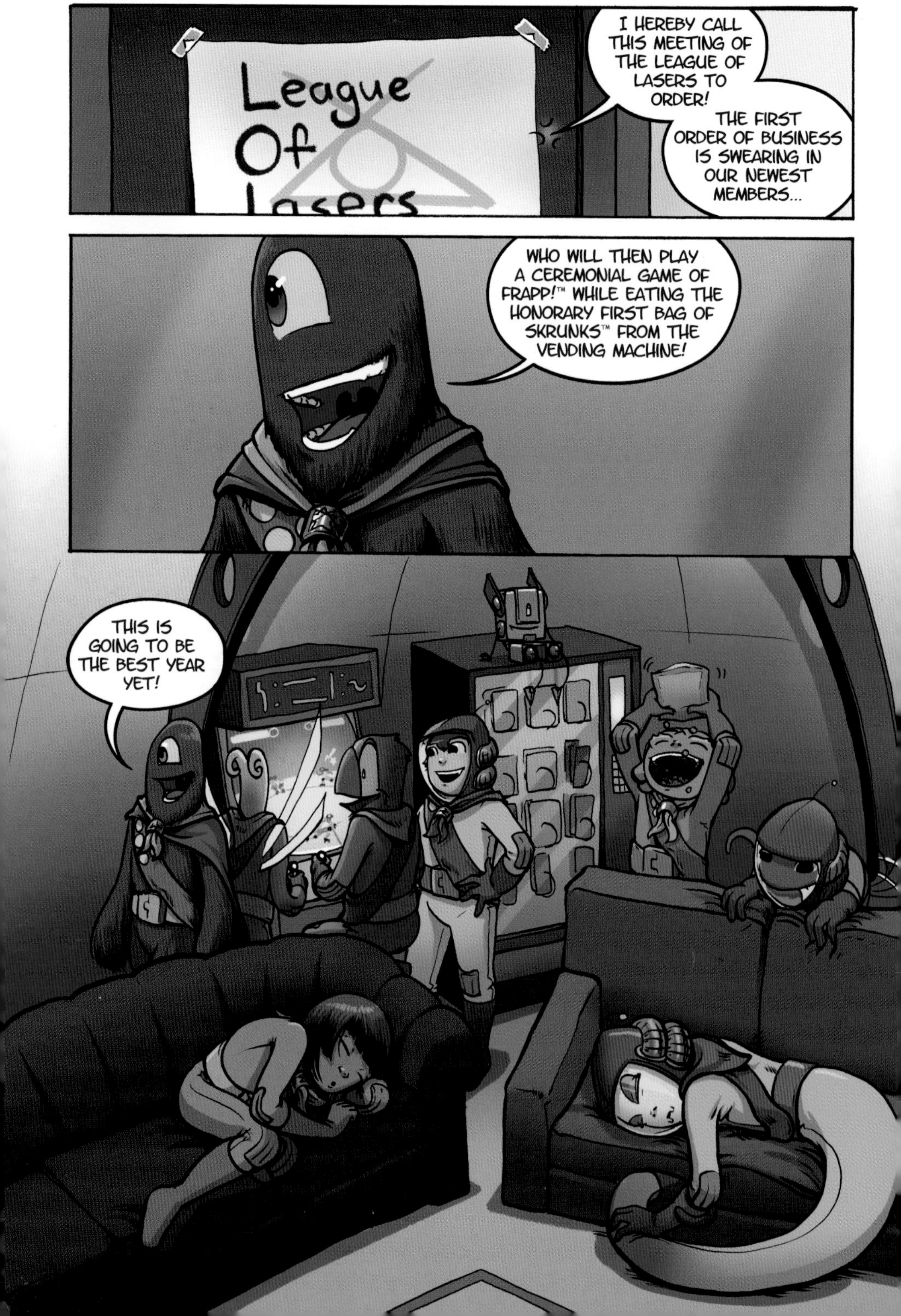
League Of Lasers
I HEREBY CALL THIS MEETING OF THE LEAGUE OF LASERS TO ORDER!
THE FIRST ORDER OF BUSINESS IS SWEARING IN OUR NEWEST MEMBERS...
WHO WILL THEN PLAY A CEREMONIAL GAME OF FRAPP!™ WHILE EATING THE HONORARY FIRST BAG OF SKRUNKS™ FROM THE VENDING MACHINE!
THIS IS GOING TO BE THE BEST YEAR YET!

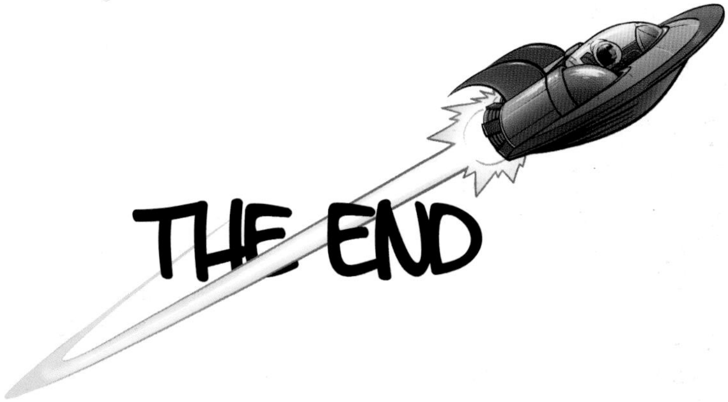
THE END

The Making of Star Scouts: The League of Lasers

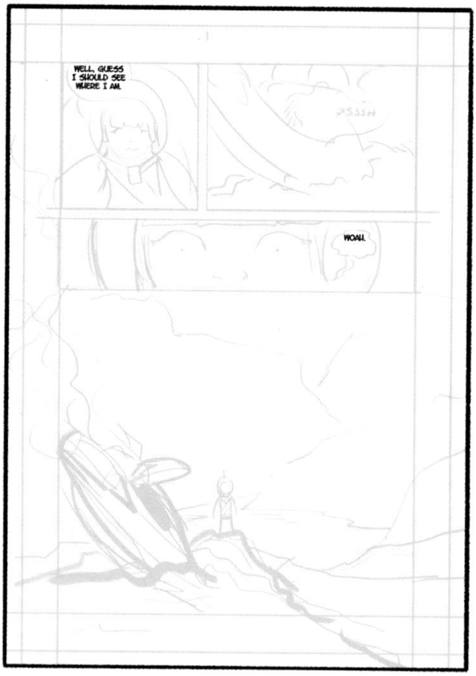
WELL, GUESS I SHOULD SEE WHERE I AM.
WOAH.

LAYOUTS

AS A CARTOONIST, I AM MOST COMFORTABLE WRITING BY DRAWING. I START OUT WITH A LOOSE SYNOPSIS THAT HAS THE BASIC ELEMENTS OF THE STORY MAPPED OUT, AND ONCE MY EDITOR SIGNS OFF ON IT I JUMP RIGHT INTO DRAWING A STICK FIGURE VERSION OF THE BOOK. THIS IS WHEN I FIGURE OUT ALL THE DIALOGUE AND WHAT WILL GO INTO EACH PANEL. I DRAW THESE PAGES ON MY COMPUTER SO THAT IT'S EASY TO EDIT AND SEND TO MY EDITOR FOR APPROVAL.

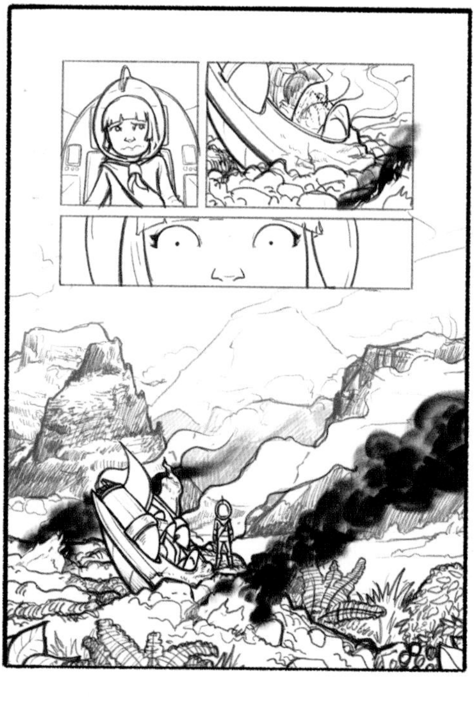

PENCILS

THIS IS MY FAVORITE PART OF MAKING COMICS. I REFINE MY ROUGH LAYOUT INTO A DETAILED DRAWING. THIS IS WHEN I GET TO MAKE MY CHARACTERS "ACT" AND USE REFERENCE PHOTOS TO ADD REALISTIC DETAILS TO MY DRAWINGS. I DO MY PENCILS ON A COMPUTER AS WELL. WORKING ON THE COMPUTER ALLOWS ME TO DRAW FASTER AND MAKE ANY REQUIRED EDITS EASILY.

INKS

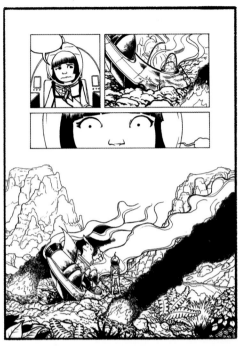

THIS IS WHEN I REFINE MY PENCIL DRAWING INTO CLEAN CRISP LINES SUITABLE FOR PRINT. SINCE I PREFER TO DRAW BY HAND, I PRINT OUT MY COMPUTER PENCILED PAGES AND INK MY PAGES ON BRISTOL BOARD WITH A A PENTEL POCKET BRUSH PEN AND PITT PENS. AS AN ADDED BONUS, IT'S VERY MOTIVATING TO SEE THE STACK OF PAGES I'VE COMPLETED PILE UP.

COLORS

ONCE I'VE INKED A PAGE, I SCAN IT INTO MY COMPUTER AND COLOR THE IMAGE USING PHOTOSHOP. I TRY TO USE COLOR AND SHADING TO ADD MORE DEPTH TO THE DRAWING AND MAKE IT AS IMMERSIVE AS POSSIBLE FOR THE READER. AT THIS POINT, THE PAGE IS DONE, MY PUBLISHER INSERTS THE DIALOG FOR ME BEFORE SENDING IT OFF TO THE PRINTER. IT TAKES ME ABOUT TWO DAYS TO COLOR A PAGE.

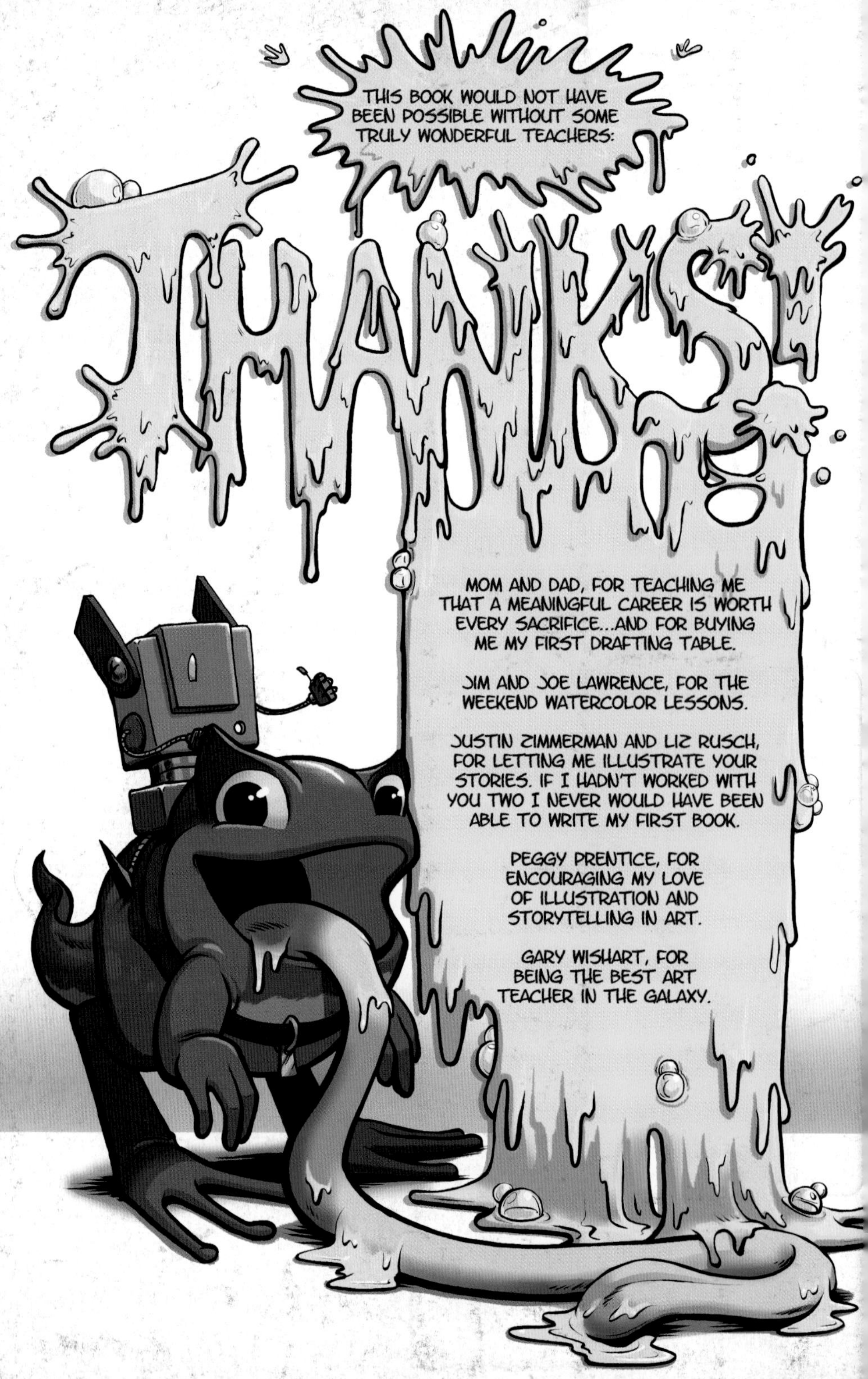
THIS BOOK WOULD NOT HAVE BEEN POSSIBLE WITHOUT SOME TRULY WONDERFUL TEACHERS:
THANKS!
MOM AND DAD, FOR TEACHING ME THAT A MEANINGFUL CAREER IS WORTH EVERY SACRIFICE...AND FOR BUYING ME MY FIRST DRAFTING TABLE.
JIM AND JOE LAWRENCE, FOR THE WEEKEND WATERCOLOR LESSONS.
JUSTIN ZIMMERMAN AND LIZ RUSCH, FOR LETTING ME ILLUSTRATE YOUR STORIES. IF I HADN'T WORKED WITH YOU TWO I NEVER WOULD HAVE BEEN ABLE TO WRITE MY FIRST BOOK.
PEGGY PRENTICE, FOR ENCOURAGING MY LOVE OF ILLUSTRATION AND STORYTELLING IN ART.
GARY WISHART, FOR BEING THE BEST ART TEACHER IN THE GALAXY.

EXPLORE NEW WORLDS WITH :01

First Second
www.firstsecondbooks.com

Foiled
by Jane Yolen and Mike Cavallaro
"An enchanting tale."
—Kirkus Reviews

The Creepy Case Files of Margo Maloo
by Drew Weing
"Smart, spooky mystery."
—Booklist

The Time Museum
by Matthew Loux
"Fresh, fast, and funny."
—Kirkus Reviews ★

Star Scouts
by Mike Lawrence
"Exciting, laugh-a-minute."
—Publishers Weekly ★

The Nameless City
by Faith Erin Hicks
"Breathtaking."
—New York Times

Astronaut Academy
by Dave Roman
"Involved and complex comedy."
—Booklist

Robot Dreams
by Sara Varon
"Tender, funny, and wise."
—Publishers Weekly ★

Giants Beware!
by Jorge Aguirre and Rafael Rosado
"Rollicking fun story."
—New York Times

The Unsinkable Walker Bean
by Aaron Renier
"Rip-roaring adventure."
—Booklist ★

Zita the Spacegirl
by Ben Hatke
"Adventurous, exciting, funny,
and moving."
—ICV2

Battling Boy
by Paul Pope
"Dazzling."
—New York Times

Mighty Jack
by Ben Hatke
"Very mighty indeed."
—Kirkus Reviews ★

Into the Outlands
by Robert Christie and Deborah Lang
"Full of action, humor, and twists."
—School Library Journal

Bera the One-Headed Troll
by Eric Orchard
"Gorgeous."
—Bulletin of the Center for
Children's Books ★

First Second
New York

Copyright © 2018 Mike Lawrence
Published by First Second
First Second is an imprint of Roaring Brook Press,
a division of Holtzbrinck Publishing Holdings Limited Partnership
175 Fifth Avenue, New York, NY 10010

All rights reserved

Library of Congress Control Number: 2017941172

ISBN: 978-1-62672-281-1

Our books may be purchased in bulk for promotional, educational,
or business use. Please contact your local bookseller or the Macmillan
Corporate and Premium Sales Department at (800) 221-7945 ext. 5442
or by email at MacmillanSpecialMarkets@macmillan.com.

First edition 2018
Book design by Danielle Ceccolini
Printed in China by 1010 Printing International Limited, North Point, Hong Kong

10 9 8 7 6 5 4 3 2 1

Drawn digitally in Procreate on an Ipad Pro, inked with a Pentel Pocket Brush and various
Faber-Castell PITT pens on Strathmore 300 series Smooth Bristol. Colored digitally with
Photoshop using Kyle Webster's digital brushes. Lettered with Blambot fonts.